BLACK APRIL

BLACK APRIL

A Novel by

JULIA PETERKIN

Author of *Green Thursday*

INDIANAPOLIS

THE BOBBS-MERRILL COMPANY

PUBLISHERS

To

JULIUS MOOD

CONTENTS

BLACK APRIL

BLACK APRIL

I

APRIL'S FATHER

THE cool spring dusk fell drowsy and soft over Sandy Island, all but blotting out a log cabin that nestled under great moss-hung oaks close to the river's edge. The small drab weather-stained house would scarcely have shown except for the fire that burned inside, sending a bright glow through its wide-open door and showers of sparks up its short stick-and-clay chimney.

A gaunt, elderly black man strode hastily toward it along the path leading up from the river and went inside, but in a few minutes he came to stand in the doorway, his bulk well-nigh filling it as one broad shoulder leaned dejectedly against the lintel. When a moan came from inside, his brawny hands clenched and buckled in a foolish helpless way, and a frown knitted his forehead as he cast a glance at the old black woman who pattered back and forth from the hearth to the bed in the corner with a cupful of root-tea or a bit of hot grease in a spoon or a pinch of salt in the palm of her hand.

Once in a while she called to him that everything was going well. To-morrow this same girl would laugh at all these groans and tears. Birthing a child is tough

work. He must have patience. Long patience. Nobody can hurry a slow-coming child.

The fire crackled and leaped higher, lighting the dirt-daubed cracks of the walls, shining under the bed where it played over the freshly sharpened point of a plow-share. A share ground and filed and put under a bed is the best thing in the world to cut birth-pains, but this one lagged with its work. Its clean edge glittered bright enough, yet as time dragged on the pains lingered and the expected child tarried with its coming.

The moon must be to blame. This new moon was right for planting seed but wrong for birthing. Swift labor comes with a waning moon, not a growing one.

The man heaved a deep sigh and looked out into the gathering twilight. The slender young moon was dropping fast. This birthing ought to get over. When the river's tide turned, life could go out mighty quickly. Ebb tide is a dangerous time for sick people.

Old Granny was too slow. Too easy-going. When this same girl was born sixteen years ago, or was it seventeen, Granny had a long race with Death and lost, yet here she was poking around with her roots and teas, trifling away the time.

"Granny," he stopped to clear the huskiness out of his throat, "better make haste. De tide'll soon turn. Ebb tide ain' to be trusted, you know."

A wry smile shriveled Granny's face. "You's too short-patienced, Breeze. Dis is a long-patienced task. It takes time. You better go cut one more turn o' fat lightwood an' fetch em in. De fire is got to keep up shine to-night."

A pitiful moan from the corner stopped her talk, and, with an echoing grunt, the man stepped down into the yard.

Granny's shaking head bobbed faster as she watched

him hurry to the wood-pile and pick up the ax. Her trembling hands drew her shawl closer around her bent shoulders. Lord, how time does change people, she muttered to herself. Breeze was no mild fellow in his youth. No. He was a wild scamp. But when his own girl got in trouble, he r'ared around and wanted to kill the man that fooled her. As if she wasn't to blame too. A good thing the girl had sense enough to keep her mouth shut. Nobody could make her say who the father of her child was. She was a shut-mouthed creature. But spoiled to death. Rotten spoiled. No wonder. Here she was, disgracing her father's house, after he had raised her nice as could be, but he hadn't a hard word for her. Not one. If he hadn't humored her all her life to everything heart could wish, she'd get to work and finish this birthing before dark, instead of keeping people fretted with worry-ation all day and now, more than likely, half the night. But as long as her soft-hearted old father took her part, Granny was helpless, and her scolding did no good.

The sturdy ax-cuts that rang out gave Granny an idea. That ax was sharp and clean. The plow-share was hampered with rust. Why wouldn't the ax cut the birth-pains far better? Hurrying back to the door she quavered out shrilly, "Bring me dat ax, Breeze! Hurry wid em."

He came with it, but halted at the door. He had ground that ax only this morning. Its edge was awful keen. This was no time to be risking anything. Granny had better be careful.

Granny stretched her old neck forward and her forehead furrowed with a frown as she said sharply that as long as she'd been catching children, if she couldn't rule an ax, she'd better quit right now and go home! She couldn't stand for people to meddle with her when she was doing her best. What did a man know about birthing? Put the ax beside the share. Together they'd fetch the child like a lamb a-jumping!

When steel jangled against steel under the bed, Granny ordered sharply, "Now you git out de door till I call you. You ought to be glad for de pain to suffer dis gal. I'm so shame of how e done, I can' hold my head up. I hope to Gawd you'll lick em till e can' stand up, soon as e gits out dis bed. I never did hear no 'oman make sich a racket! E ought not to much as crack e teeth! I wish e was my gal. I'd show em how to be runnin' round a-gittin' chillen, stead o' gittin' a nice settled man fo' a husband." Granny eyed the girl, then her unhappy old father, severely, but her talk was to no purpose, for old Breeze's eyes were bloodshot with pity, his very soul distressed.

"You's wrong, Granny. I used to t'ink like you, but I know better now. If de gal'll git thu dis safe, I wouldn' hold no hard feelin's 'gainst em. Never in dis world." He leaned over the bed and gave the girl's shoulder a gentle pat, but Granny hurried him away. This was no time for petting and being soft. Some hard work waited to be done. The sooner the girl got at it, the sooner it would be finished.

"Quit you' crazy talk an' go on out de door! Don' come back in dis room, not less I call you."

Granny spoke so sharply, he obeyed humbly, without another word.

The breath of the earth was thick in the air, a good clean smell that went clear to the marrow of the man's bones. God made the first man out of dust, and all men go back to it in the end. The earth had been sleeping, resting through the winter, but now, with the turn of the year, it had roused, and it offered life to all that were fit and strong. The corn crop, planted on the last young moon when the dogwood blooms were the size of squirrel ears, was up to a stand wherever the crows let it alone. Pesky devils! They watched every blade that peeped through the ground and plucked it out with the mother grain, cawing right in the face of the scare-crow that stood up in the field to scare them, although its head, made out of a pot, and its stuffed crocus sack body were ugly enough to scare a man. To-morrow he'd hide and call them. He could fool them close enough to shoot them. It was a pity to waste shells on birds unfit for man or beast to eat and with too little grease on their bones to add a drop to the soap pot, but there'd soon be another mouth to feed here.

To-morrow, he must plant the cotton while the young moon waxed strong. There was much to do. He needed help. Maybe this child being born would be a boy-child, a help for his old age. A sorrowful woman will bear a boy-child, nine times out of ten, and God knows, that girl had been sorrowful. When she helped him plant the corn, she had dropped a tear in mighty nigh every hill along with the seed. No wonder it grew fast.

Soon as the moon waned, the root crops, potatoes, pindars, chufas, turnips, must be planted. Field plants have no sense. If you plant crops that fruit above the ground on a waning moon, they get all mixed up and bear nothing but heavy roots, and root crops planted on a waxing moon will go all to rank tops no matter how you try to stop them. Plants have to be helped along or they waste time and labor, just the same as children you undertake to raise. That poor little girl was started off wrong.

She was born on a moon so wrong that her mammy died in her birthing. He had done his best to raise the little motherless creature right, but he made a bad mistake when he let her go to Blue Brook without him last summer. She went to meet his kin and to attend the revival meeting. She was full of life and raven for pleasure. He couldn't refuse her when she asked to go. But he hadn't made her understand that those Blue Brook men were wicked devils. He knew it. He had been one of them himself. Poor little girl, she knew it now! Now when it was too late for anybody to help her out of her trouble.

Years ago, over thirty of them, he had left Blue Brook and come to Sandy Island on account of a girl. She had named her child April because it was born this very month. Afterward, she had married and forgotten him. Now she was dead, but her child, April, was the finest man on Blue Brook. Barely middle-aged, April was already the plantation foreman, ruling the other farm-hands, telling them what to do, what not to do, and raising the best crops in years. April had made a name for himself. Everybody who came from Blue Brook had something to say about him, either of his kindness or of his meanness, his long patience or his quick temper, his open-handedness or his close-fistedness. On Blue Brook, April was a man among men.

He had seen him, a tall, lean, black, broad-shouldered fellow, so much like himself that it was a wonder everybody didn't know that he was April's daddy. But they didn't. For April's mother had been as close-mouthed as the girl lying yonder on the bed. She never did tell who fooled her and made her have sin. She died without telling.

Some day he'd like to tell April himself. But after all, what was the use? April had taken the name of his mother's lawful husband and he loved the man who had raised him as well as an own father could have done. Why upset them?

Granny's shambling steps inside the cabin took his

thoughts back to the girl there. If the child was born on this rising tide, it would more than likely be a boy-child. April would be a good name for him too. April was a lucky month to be born in; it was a lucky name too. If the child came a girl, Katy, the name of April's mother, would be a good name for it.

The spring air wafted clouds of fragrance from the underwoods bordering the forest. Crab-apple thickets and white haw trees were in full bloom. Yellow jasmine smothered whole tree-tops. Cherokee roses starry with blossoms sprawled over rail fences and rotting stumps, piercing through all other scents with their delicate perfume.

Sandy Island looked just so, smelled just so, on that April night when he came here so many years ago. He thought then that he'd go back some day and fetch Katy here to stay with him. But the years had tricked him, fooled him. They had rolled by so fast he'd lost track of them, and of Katy and her boy, April. Now, he was almost an old man, and Katy was up yonder in Heaven. His own lawful wife and his other boy, his yard son, were up there too. Had Katy told them about April? Or would she stay shut-mouthed for ever and ever?

As he wondered and pondered about the ways of people in Heaven, the river, gorged by a high spring tide, slowly flooded the rice-fields encircling the island. The black water lapped softly as it rippled over the broken dikes and passed through the rotted flood-gates, hiding the new green shoots of the marsh grass and uprooting the tall faded blades, that had stood through the winter on the boggy mud flats.

Frogs chanted. Marsh hens chattered. Wood ducks quacked and splashed. Ganits flew in long lines toward the sunset, squawking hoarsely and flapping the air with blue and white wings. Partridges whistled. Doves

[17]

mourned. Where were the groans from the bed in the corner? Maybe all was over at last.

Granny stood in the door beckoning him to come. Her harshness was all gone. She hobbled down the steps and came tottering to meet him, then laying a bony hand on his shoulder she whispered that the ax was too sharp. It had cut the pains off altogether. They had ceased too soon and she couldn't get them started again. She had tried every tea she knew. Every root. Every ointment. Every charm. She was at her row's end. This moon was all wrong for birthing. A young moon makes things go contrarywise. The child should have waited a week longer to start coming. And two weeks would have been still better.

The girl had dozed off in spite of everything. He must come and try to rouse her up. Girls behave so crazy these days. They do like nobody ever had birthed a child before them. She was fretted half to death the way this girl carried on. He must come and make her behave. If she had been a nice decent girl, all this would never have been.

The girl's eyes opened and looked up at him, and he leaned low over the bed to hear her whispered words. She spoke with worn-out tired breath, begging him to go and get help from somewhere. She hated to die in sin, and leave him, but she couldn't hold out much longer. Death already had her feet cold as ice, it was creeping up to her knees. Couldn't he take the boat and go across the river to Blue Brook? Wasn't somebody there who could come to help her?

He studied. Certainly there was. Maum Hannah, his own first cousin, had a string of charm beads their old grandmother had brought all the way from Africa when she came on a slave ship. They and the charm words that ruled them were left in Maum Hannah's

[18]

hands. Ever since he was a boy, living on Blue Brook, he had heard people say that those beads had never failed to help a woman birth a child safely. No matter how it came, head foremost, foot foremost, or hand foremost, it was all the same when those charm beads got to working.

He'd go fetch Maum Hannah. She'd come. Old as she was, she'd risk the booming river if her beads were needed to help a child come into the world.

His boat was a dug-out and narrow for two people in a river running backward in a flood-tide, but she'd come. He felt sure of it. Barefooted, bareheaded, without a coat, he ran down the steep slope to the black water's edge, and soon the sharp bow of his boat, driven by one short paddle, sliced through the current. Swift wheeling circles of water marked every steady dip it made. Hugging the willow banks, the boat hurried on, then cut straight across the river. Thank God, the high-running tide made the rice-fields a clear sheet of water. The boat could take a bee line to Blue Brook without bothering about how the channel ran beyond the river. The landing aimed for was on a deep, clear blue creek, which gave the plantation its name, Blue Brook. The man's knees were shaking as he stepped out of the boat and dragged it higher up on the bank to wait until he came back with Maum Hannah and the beads. Up the path he trotted, to the Quarters where the long low houses made blurs of darkness under tall black trees. The thick-leaved branches rose against the sky, where the fires of sunset had lately died and the moon had gone to its bed.

Rattly wagons hurried over the roads. Cattle bellowed. Children shouted. Dogs barked. An ax rang sharply and a clear voice sent up a song. "Bye an' bye, when de mawnin' comes!" How trustful it sounded.

He tried to hum the tune, but fear gnawed at his heart and beat drums in his ears and throat and breast.

He was born and reared on Blue Brook. He knew every path and road on it. Every field and ditch and thicket. Every moss-hung oak. He had lived right yonder in the foreman's house with his grandfather, the plantation foreman. The foreman *now* was his son! His blood kin. A proud fellow, that April! Lord, how April strutted and gave himself airs!

The darkness melted everything into one. The whiteness of the Big House was dim.

Fences, cabins, trees, earth were being swallowed up by the night.

Maum Hannah's cabin was the last in those two long rows of houses, and firelight shining out from her wide-open door sent a glow clear across her yard. She was at home. It wouldn't take long to get her and the charm beads into the boat, then back across the river.

Black people were gathered in the doorways, most of them his kin with whom he'd like to stop and talk, but there was no time for one extra word, even with April, the foreman. Dogs ran up to him, sniffed, recognized that he was of the same blood as their masters, and went back to lie down.

II

TAKING Maum Hannah's three steps as one, he called
out a breathless greeting:

"How you do, Cun [Cousin] Hannah?"

She was stirring a pot on the hearth and the long
spoon clattered against the iron sides as she dropped it.
"Who dat call me?" She limped backward a few
halting paces and gazed at him with questioning eyes.

"Dis is me, old man Breeze! Git you birthin' beads
quick an' come go home wid me!"

She stared at him vacantly. "Fo' Gawd's sake, who
is you?" She whispered sharply.

"You don' know me? Is you gone blind, Hannah?"

Her arms dropped weakly as she peered at him,
taking in his bare feet, his patched clothes, his shirt,
open at the neck, showing the swell of his throat, the
panting of his breast. With a sudden burst of laughter
she reached out and took his hand. "Lawd, Breeze, I
thought sho' you was Grampa's sperit come fo' me!
You scared me well-nigh to death, son! Come on een
an' set down! Jedus, I'm glad to see you! But you is
de very spit o' Grampa!"

"I can' set, Hannah. I ain' Grampa's sperit, but I
sho' did come to git you! My li'l' gal is 'bout to die,
Hannah. E can' birth e chile to save life, no matter
how hard e try. Git Gramma's birthin' beads. You
got to go wid me. I couldn' stan' to le' dat li'l' gal die,

[21]

an' don' do all I can to save em. E's so pitiful in e pain.''

Maum Hannah grunted. ''Pain don' kill a 'oman, son. It takes pain to make em work steady till de task is done. I can' stop no pain! No, Jedus! De gal might be well by now anyhow.''

But he was firm. ''Listen to me, Hannah! You got to go home wid me to-night! Now! In a hurry! Make haste, too!''

''It's a mighty black night since de moon is gone down.''

''Bein' black don' matter. I know de way. You come on, Hannah.''

''I declare to Gawd, my cripple knee is so painful I don' know ef I could git in a boat.''

''Den I'll tote you, but you sho' got to come.''

''I'm mighty 'f'aid o' boats an' water in de daytime much less at night.'' She leaned down to fix the sticks on the fire, but he caught her roughly by the arm.

''Don' you tarry, Hannah. You come on right now!''

''What kind o' boat you got?''

''De boat's narrow an' de river's high, but you got strong heart, enty? You'll be as safe wid me in dat boat as ef you was settin' right here by de fire in your rockin' chair. I promised my li'l' gal to fetch you an' you' birthin' beads ef e would hold out till I git back. You better come on! Gramma'll hant you sho' as you fail me to-night!''

Maum Hannah sighed deep. ''I know I got to go, scared as I is. A boat on a floodin' river is a turrible t'ing, but I sho' don' want Gramma's sperit to git no grudge against me. Catchin' chillen is Jedus' business anyhow, an' de river belongs to Jedus, same as me an' you, I reckon. You wait till I git de beads out de trunk. Sometimes I wish Gramma didn' leave me dem beads. It's de truth!''

She groped her way to the shed room and fumbled in a trunk, then called out that she needed a light. He broke a splinter off from a stick of fat lightwood on the hearth and, lighting it, took it to her. The small flame blazed up, sputtering and hissing, and spat black drops of tar on the clean floor, on the quilt covered bed, on the wide white apron she was tying around her waist. The shaking hand that held it was to blame.

''How-come you' hand is a-tremblin' so, Breeze?'' she asked gently. ''You is pure shakin' like a leaf. Trust in Gawd, son. You' gal b'longs to Him, not to you. Jedus ain' gwine fail em now when e have need.''

The light wavered wildly as he raised an arm to draw his shirt-sleeve across his eyes. Big teardrops rolled down his cheeks, and his face twitched dumbly.

''You mus' scuse me, Hannah. I'm so weakened down wid frettin' until de water dreans out my eyes. My mind keeps a runnin' back to de time dis same li'l' gal's own mammy was taken dis same way. When de tide turned, e went out wid em. Dat's how-come I'm hurryin' you so fas'. We mus' git back whilst de tide is risin'.''

He stood, straight and tall, and strong for his years, but the troubled look in his eyes made the old midwife wonder.

Her weight tilted the narrow boat so far to one side that some of the black river water slid over its edge and ran down cold on her feet. ''Jedus hab mussy!'' she groaned. ''If dis boat do go down, I'll sho' git drowned to-night! I can' swim, not a lick.''

''You set still, Hannah. Dis boat knows better'n to turn over to-night. I got em trained. E's got sense like people. E knows e's got to take me an' you safe.''

"I'm mighty glad to hear dat, son, mighty glad."

The boat was already gliding swiftly past the black willows on the Blue Brook's bank and around the bend where the thick trees made shadows and long tresses of gray moss waved overhead. Soon they'd reach the river. When a dark bird flew across the stream Maum Hannah shivered and whispered, "Do, Jedus, hab mussy," but Breeze muttered, "Dat ain' nuttin' but a summer duck."

The whole world lay still, wrapped by the night, quiet, save for the swish of the water against the sides of the boat as the noiseless dips of the steady-plying paddle thrust it on.

As they neared Sandy Island the shrill cry of an owl in the distance caused the boat to falter in its forward going.

"Wha' dat, Breeze?"

"Dat's one o' dem blue-dartin' owls. Dat ain' no sign o' death."

Ripples from the boat broke into glittering sparkles of light laid by the stars on the water. The river murmured. Trees along the bank were full of strange shadowy shapes. Whenever the lightest rustle of wind drifted through the black branches, low smothered sobs fell from them.

A tall sycamore with its white outstretched arms high up toward heaven, reached toward the river waving, beckoning.

The night air was cool, but Maum Hannah took up the edge of her apron and wiped off big drops of sweat that broke out cold as ice on her forehead. "Do, Jedus, hab mussy!" she prayed.

The new moon had gone to bed. Now was the time evil spirits walk and take people's souls out of their bodies. Pines on the island made soft moans. The darkness quivered with whispers. Only the firelight shining out from the cabin on the hill made a clear red star to guide them.

The narrow boat swerved and turned in-shore. A cypress knee, hidden by the water, bumped hard against it, but didn't stop its leap toward the bank. Old Breeze eased himself past Maum Hannah, and hopping out on the wet sand drew the boat up a little higher on the hill.

"Git up, Hannah. Le' me hold all two o' you' hands. Step slow. Hist you' foot. Don' miss an' trip. Now you's on dry land."

"T'ank Gawd! Praise Jedus' name!"

"You got de beads, enty?"

"Sho' I got 'em. Dem beads is all de luck I got in dis world. If dey was to git lost, I'd be ruint fo' true. Pure ruint!"

The steep climb cut her breath and stopped her flow of talk, but Granny who had heard them coming, croaked out:

"Yunnuh better make haste. De chile is done come, but de gal won' wake up an' finish de job. Yunnuh come on."

Maum Hannah lifted the long dark string of beads from around her neck and handed them to old Breeze. "Run wid 'em, son. Put 'em round de gal's neck. Right on e naked skin. If I try to walk fast I might fall down an' broke my leg."

Breath scarcely came and went through the girl's parted lips, and her teeth showed white. Were they clenched? Old Breeze pressed on the round chin to see. Thank God the mouth could open!

Maum Hannah got inside the room at last. The charm words that went with the beads would set things right. Death might as well go on home! Let the girl

[25]

rest. She was tired. Things could wait while she had her nap out.

The big hickory armchair, drawn close to the fire, held a feather pillow on its cowhide seat, and lying in the nest it made was a small black human being Granny laughed as she picked it up and put it into Maum Hannah's hands, saying:

"A boy-chile! An' born wid a caul on e face!"

"Great Gawd, what is dis! You hear dis news, Breeze? Dis chile was born wid a caul on e face!"

The man turned his troubled eyes away from the bed. "Wha' you say, Hannah?"

Laughing with pleasure Maum Hannah and Granny both told him again. His grandson had been blessed with second sight. He had been born on the small of the moon and with a caul over his face. He would have second sight. He'd always be able to see things that stay hidden from other people. Hants and spirits and plat-eyes and ghosts. Things to come and things long gone would all walk clear before him. They couldn't hide from this child's eyes.

"Hotten another pot o' water, Granny. Lemme warm em good, an' make em cry." Maum Hannah cradled the child tenderly in her hands, then held him low so the firelight could shine in his face. With a quick laugh she caught him by one foot and holding him upside down smacked him sharply with three brisk slaps.

"Cry, suh!" she scolded. "Ketch air an' holler! I hate to lick you so hard soon as you git here, but I got to make you fret out loud." A poor weak bleating sounded and she handed the child to Granny.

"You fix em, whilst I finish up wid de mammy."

"Wake up, gal!" she plead, shaking the girl's limp arm. "Wake up!"

The rigid eyelids fluttered open and a faint smile played over the girl's face. She was too weary to draw her breath. The pain had sapped all her strength, every bit.

Maum Hannah stooped and looked under the bed.

"Great Gawd," she grunted. "Who dat put a' ax under dis bed? No wonder de pains quit altogedder. You ought to had chunked dese irons out de door!" She did it forthwith herself.

"Now! All two is gone! Open you' eyes, gal! Ketch a long breat. Dat's de way. Hol' you' two hands togedder. So. Blow in 'em! Hard. Hard as you kin! Make a stiff win' wid you' mouth! Blow you' fingers off. Dat's de way!"

Then something else went wrong. Where was a spider's web? Granny ought to have had one ready. Every good midwife should find one as soon as she takes a case. Maum Hannah's eyes were too dim to see a web on the dark rafters overhead. Somebody must find one and fetch it quickly. Life can leak out fast. Spiderwebs can dam it up better than anything else. But, lord, they are hard to find at night! Where was Breeze?

One was found at last. Then it took careful handling to get it well covered with clean soot from the back of the chimney. Thank God for those beads. The girl would have lost heart and given up except for them and the charm words which Maum Hannah kept saying over and over. With those beads working, things had to come right. Had to. And they could not help working. Couldn't, thank God.

The next morning's sunshine showed plenty of gossamer webs spun with shining wheels. Long threads of frail silk were strung across the yard from bush to bush, traps set by the spiders for gnats and mosquitoes, strong enough to hold a fly once in a while. But it takes a house spider's stout close-woven web to hold soot and do good. For a house spider to make its home under your roof is good luck, for sooner or later the cloth it weaves and spins will save somebody's life.

Old Breeze got up early and cooked the breakfast, fixed himself a bit to eat and a swallow or two of sweetened water to drink and went to the field to work, but the two old women sat by the fire and nodded until the sun waxed warm and its yellow light glowed into the room through the wide-open door. Then their tired old bodies livened and their heads raised up and leaned together while whispered talk crept back and forth between them. Granny held that Breeze was a good kind man to take the girl's trouble as he did. Many a man would have put her out-of-doors. Girls are mighty wild and careless these days. But their parents are to blame for it too. Half the children born on Sandy Island were unfathered. It wasn't right. Yet how can you stop them? Maum Hannah sighed and shook her head. It was a pity. And yet, after all, every child comes into the world by the same old road.

A thousand husbands couldn't make that journey one whit easier. The preachers say God made the birthing pain tough when He got vexed with Eve in the Garden of Eden. He wanted all women to know how heavy His hand can be. Yet Eve had a lawful husband, and did that help her any?

Granny blinked at the fire and studied a while, then with a sly look at the bed she whispered that this same little boy-child was got right yonder at Blue Brook during the protracted meeting last summer. Her wizened face showed she knew more than she cared to tell. Not that it was anything to her whose child it was.

She fidgeted with her tin cup and spoon and peeped

at Maum Hannah out of the corner of her eye, then asked with pretended indifference:

"What's de name o' de gentleman what's de foreman at Blue Brook now?"

"E's name April."

"Enty?" Granny affected surprise. "Is e got a fambly?" she presently ventured in spite of Maum Hannah's shut-mouthed manner.

"Sho', e's got a fambly. E's got a fine wife an' a house full o' chillen too."

"Well, I declare!" Granny mirated pleasantly. "Was any o' dem born wid a caul?"

"No, dey wasn't. I never did hear o' but one or two people bein' born wid a caul. Ol' Uncle Isaac, yonder to Blue Brook is one, and e's de best conjure doctor I ever seen."

"Who was de other one?" Granny inquired so mildly that Maum Hannah stole a look at her hard, dried furrowed face. There was no use to beat about the bush with Granny, so she answered:

"April, de foreman at Blue Brook, was de other one. Dese same ol' hands o' mine caught April when e come into dis world, just like deys caught all o' April's chillen."

"You mean, April's yard chillen, enty?" Granny looked her straight in the eyes like a hawk, but Maum Hannah met the look calmly, without any sign of annoyance.

"I dunno what you's aimin' at, Granny. April's a fine man. Blue Brook never did have no better foreman. An' his mammy, Katy, was one o' de best women ever lived. April was she onliest child. April was born dis same month. Dat's how-come Katy named him April. April's a lucky month an' a lucky name, too. Wha' you gwine name you li'l' boy-chile, daughter?"

[29]

Granny looked toward the bed and listened for the answer.

"I dunno, ma'am," the girl answered weakly, and Granny sweetened her coffee with a few drops more of molasses. She stirred and stirred until Maum Hannah suggested:

"April's a fine name. Whyn't you name em dat? When I git back to Blue Brook, I'll tell de foreman I named a li'l' boy-chile at him. Dat would please em too. E might would send em a present. April's a mighty free-handed man, an' e sho' thinks de world o' me too."

Granny waited to taste the sweetened coffee until she heard what the girl said. The girl didn't make any answer at first, but presently she said with a sorrowful sigh, she'd have to think about the baby's name. She couldn't decide in a hurry. Sometimes a wrong name will even kill a baby. She must go slow and choose a name that was certain to bring her baby health and luck.

She talked it over with her father and named the baby Breeze, for him. No foreman in the world was a finer man, or a kinder, stronger, wiser one. The breeze for which he was named could have been no pleasanter, no sweeter, than the breeze that blew in from the river that very morning.

The old man beamed with pleasure. He was glad to have the child named for him. But since the month was April, why not name him April Breeze? Then he'd have two good-luck names, and two would be better than one.

"We could call em li'l' Breeze, enty?" she asked with a catch in her voice.

"Sho', honey! Sho'! If dat's de name you choose to call dis chile, den e's li'l' Breeze f'om now on. But April is a mighty nice name for a boy-chile."

"It's de Gawd's truth," Maum Hannah declared, and Granny grunted and reached for a coal to light her pipe.

Li'l' Breeze grew and throve and his grandfather prized him above everything, everybody else. He was a boy-child, and, besides, he was born with a caul on his face. Men born so make their mark in this world. Rule their fellows. Plenty of people have no fathers, and many of them are better off. A child that has never looked on his daddy's face can cure sickness better than any medicine. Just with a touch of the hand, too. It was a good thing for Sandy Island to have such a child.

Before Breeze was weaned people began coming to have him stroke the pain out of their knees and backs and shoulders. He could cure thrash in babies' mouths, and even cool fevers.

His mother's disgrace was completely forgotten, when she married a fine-looking, stylish young town man who came to Sandy Island to preach and form a Bury-League. He could read both reading and writing and talk as well as the preacher who read over them out of a book.

Breeze stayed on with his grandfather, helping him farm in the summer and set nets for shad in the spring. When the white people who owned Sandy Island came from somewhere up-North in the winter and crossed over the river on a ferry flat from Blue Brook with their dogs and horses to hunt the deer that swarm so thick on the island that they have beaten paths the same as pigs and rabbits, Breeze went along to help hold the horses and watch the dogs. People said he was Old Breeze's heart-string, and Old Breeze's eyeball. He was, although the mother had other boy-children now, fine ones too.

And instead of the grandfather's getting feeble and tottering with age, he grew younger, and worked harder, so that he and Breeze might have plenty. Every extra cent saved was buried at the foot of a tall pine tree growing on the bank of the river not far from the cabin's front door. When hard times came, they'd have no lack. The money would be there, secretly waiting to be spent.

One spring when the shad fishing was done, Old Breeze got leave from the white folks to cut down some dead pines the beetles had killed. He dragged these to the river with his two old oxen, and made them into a raft which he floated down to the town in the river's mouth, and sold to a big saw-mill there. Breeze stayed with his mother until his grandfather came back home, pleased as could be, with presents for everybody, and a pocket full of money besides. But although he brought the mother a Bible besides many other fine things that made her smile, she shook her head and said, "Dead trees are best left alone. Trees have spirits the same as men. God made them to stand up after they die. Better let them be."

But the grandfather was not afraid of tree spirits, and he cut and cut until no dead tree was left standing and the ground all around the big pine tree was full of hidden money. Then there was nothing to do but fish and hunt, and to hunt in the spring is against the white men's laws. Old Breeze got restless. He gazed in the fire night after night, thinking and thinking.

One morning he got up early and skimmed all the cream and put the clabber in a jug, then he took the brace-and-bit down off the joist where it stayed and walked off to the woods alone. Every morning he did it. There was no more clabber for the pigs or the chickens, but the pine trees began dying so fast that before long enough were ready to cut for a raft to be floated down the river.

The tall pine close to the bank was the biggest tree on Sandy Island. It stretched far above the oaks before it put on even one limb. If that tree ever died, it would make a good part of a raft by itself.

One cold dark dawn, Breeze was roused by the cabin's door creaking on its hinges as it closed behind somebody's muffled steps. Where was Old Breeze going? Easing a window open, he peered out and saw the old man going toward the big pine with the jug and the brace-and-bit.

"Wait on me! I'm a-gwine wid you!" he called.

Old Breeze stopped and stood stiffly erect.

"Who dat call me?"

"Dis me! Breeze!"

The old man broke into a laugh. "Lawd, son, I thought sho' a sperit was a-talkin' to me. How come you's 'wake so soon? Git back in de bed an' sleep!"

But Breeze dressed in a hurry. He wanted to see what would be done with clabber and the brace-and-bit.

Outside in the half-light it was silent except for the rustle of the big tree's needles in the wind. Breeze watched while holes were bored deep in the solid roots and the clabber all poured down them. He promised never to tell a soul. Not a soul. That was a stubborn tree. It swallowed down many a jug of buttermilk and clabber without getting sick at all, but at last the tips of its needles looked pale. The green of them faded into yellow, then brown, and its whole top withered. The old tree gave up. Poor thing.

Its heaviest limbs faced the south, away from the water. That was good. When it fell, the big butt cut, the heaviest one, would be easy to roll into the river, and the next two cuts would not have to be pushed very far. That tree would bring money with its stout, fat heart. A pocket full of money.

[33]

Sunday night came, and Old Breeze wouldn't go to meeting, but went to bed for a long night's sleep. He must get up a high head of strength before sunrise to cut the big tree down.

Day was just breaking through the cracks of the cabin's log sides when Breeze heard it fall. It gave a great cry, and its crash jarred the cabin. The weight of a big tree's falling always leaves a deep stillness behind it, but after the big pine fell the stillness stayed on. Breeze lay quiet and listened. The tree must have dropped wrong, and gone across a clump of bamboo vines. Old Breeze would have to clear them away before his ax could begin to talk.

He'd hear it soon. Lord! Nobody could make an ax speak faster or louder or truer. Nobody. This was Monday morning and he must get the clothes up for the mother to wash. Every Monday he carried them to her and helped her do the washing.

Kingfishers splashed into the river. Once an eagle cried. The day moved on, smooth and bright and yellow, as the sun walked up the sky past the tree-tops, higher and higher until noon stood overhead. But the grandfather's ax had said nothing yet. Not yet. But wait! It would make up for lost time when it started to ring!

Sis, the stepfather's young sister, lived with Breeze's mother and helped her mind the children. Every Monday morning they washed the clothes out in the yard, where the washtubs always sat on a bench in a sunshiny place. The other children, Breeze's half brothers and sisters, roasted sweet potatoes in the ashes under the big black washpot, and kept the fire going.

On that Monday morning, the fire burned blue and kept popping, and every now and then the mother cast her eyes, full of dark thoughts, at the sun. Old Breeze

[34]

always came for dinner with her on Monday. Something must have happened. The big tree must have fallen wrong to keep him so long. But Sis could talk of nothing but the new dress and the ribbon he had promised to buy her with some of the money the big pine brought.

The mother lifted the lids of the little pots that sat all around the big washpot cooking the family's dinner. With a big iron spoon she stirred and tasted, added salt and a pod of red pepper. Pepper is good to help men be strong and warm-hearted. It makes hens lay, too. She filled the bucket with victuals and told Breeze to run, fast as he could, to the big tree, so the dinner would be hot when he got there. Hopping John, peas and rice cooked together, is so much better fresh out of the pot and breathing out steam. When rice cools it gets gummy. The fish stew was made out of eels, and they get raw again as soon as the fire's heat leaves them. Breeze must take his foot in his hand and fly.

Breeze did run, but he soon came running back, for Old Breeze wasn't there. His ax lay almost in the water, with its handle wet, and his throwing-wedge beside it.

The two old oxen were chewing their cuds, but the ground around the tree was all dug up and broken, as if hogs had rooted it up to find worms.

Breeze had called, and called, but nobody answered! When the mother heard that, a shiver went clear through her body. Her hands shook so when she lifted them out of the washtub that all the soap-suds on them trembled.

She said she'd go and call. She knew how to send her voice far away. She could make him hear and answer. Maybe a deer or a fox or a wildcat had come and tricked him away from his work, but her words quivered in her mouth as she said them.

[35]

All the children went trailing after her; Sis went hurrying with baby Sonny in her arms; and they all stood still and listened while the mother's throat sent long thin whoopees away up into the sky. Her breast heaved with hoisting them so far above the trees into the far-away distance. She'd wait for an answer until all the echoes had whooped back, then she'd take a deep breath and cry out again.

An old crow laughed as he passed overhead, an owl who-whooed far in the distance. The wind began moaning and crying in the tops of all the other trees around the fallen pine.

The mother dropped on her knees and laid her forehead down on the earth. Her thin body shook, and her fingers twisted in and out as her hands wrung each other almost to breaking. She prayed and moaned and begged Jesus to call Granddad to come back. To come on in a hurry. She couldn't stand for him not to answer when she called so hard and so long.

All the children began crying with her. Even Sis, who never cried no matter what happened, put Sonny down on the naked ground and with tears running out of her eyes all over her face, reached out and took the mother's shoulders in both arms. She tried to keep them from shaking, but she soon shook with them, for the mother said over and over she had known all the time that something bad was going to happen. She knew it last night when she came home from meeting. Her fine glass lamp shade, the one Granddad brought her from town, with flowers on it, broke right in two in her hand. She hadn't dropped it, or knocked it against anything, but it broke in two in her hand. Her moaning talk changed to a kind of singing as her body rocked from side to side. Her face turned up to the sky, her eyes gazed straight at the sun, and over and over she

wailed the same words until the littlest children all cried
out and screamed them too:

> "Las night I been know
> Somebody gwine dead!
> Yes, Lawd! Somebody gwine dead!
> A sign sesso!
> Yes, Lawd, a sign sesso!
> De hoot-owl ain' talk!
> De wind ain' whine!
> I ain' see a ground-crack needer!
> But I had a sign,
> Jedus gi' me a sign!
> Da lamp-shade!
> F'om de town-sto!
> E come een two
> Een my hand!
> Yes, Lawd!
> E come een two een my hand!
> I ain' drap em. No!
> I ain' knock em against nuttin,
> But e come een two
> Een my hand!
> De lamp-shade know,
> E try fo' talk,
> E broke fo' gi' me a sign.
> My Pa is dead!
> I know, fo' sho'!
> Da lamp-shade broke
> Een my hand!"

Her breath caught in her throat with gasps and her
grieving got hoarse and husky, the steady sing-song
braced by the children's shrill mourning reached the
neighbors who came hurrying to see what was wrong.

At first they tried to cheer up the mother's heart
with big-sounding, bantering talk. Granddad could

outswim an otter. The river could drown him no more than a duck. He had followed a wild turkey, or a hog going to make her bed. It was wrong to trouble trouble before trouble troubles you. Hogs had rooted up the earth around the pine. Nobody had done that. Granny hobbled up, muttering to herself between her toothless jaws. The sun shone right into her eyes and marked how they shifted sly looks from the fallen tree to the earth. Her withered fingers plucked at the dirty greasy charm thread around her wrist. One bony finger pointed at the broken ground.

"Whe' is e, Granny?" the mother asked, and the silence was that of a grave. Granny's palsied head shook harder than ever, and the mother rent the air with her cries. Sis and the children joined in with wails, and the dogs all howled and barked. Granny said Old Breeze was done for! The same as the felled tree. Who was to blame? How could she tell? Had he eaten any strange victuals lately? Had he drunk water out of any strange well? No? Then he must have been tricked by somebody under his roof. Somebody who wished him ill had put an evil eye on him. No strong well man would melt away unless he had been bewitched. Granny peeped sidewise at Breeze. Where was his stepfather? Where? Nobody answered the old woman, but feet shuffled uneasily as she said that the whole of Sandy Island showed signs of bewitchment. When had it rained? The fowls' eggs hatched poorly. The cows lost their cuds. The fish didn't bite. Shooting stars kept the sky bright every night. Black works were the cause! Then everybody chimed in; it must be as Granny said. And the old woman looked straight at Breeze. He was born with second sight. The young moon was here. This was the time when all those who are cheated out of life come back and walk on this earth whenever a young moon shines. If Old Breeze had met with foul death,

[38]

he'd come back that night and walk around that very pine as soon as the first dark came. Young Breeze must watch for him and talk with him and find out what had happened to him. Nobody else on Sandy Island could talk to spirits like that boy. He had been born with a caul over his face, and that strange thing that had veiled his eyes when he came into the world gave them the power to see things other people could never witness. Spirits and hants and ghosts and plat-eyes.

Granny's talk made Breeze's flesh creep cold on his bones. His blood stopped running. Fear tried to put wings on his feet, but he clung to his mother's skirt and wept, for even the shadows began an uncertain flickering and wavering as if they'd reach out and grab him.

"Hogs ain' rooted up de ground. Not no hogs what walks on fo' legs. No. Sperits might 'a' done it—but whe's you' husban', gal? Whe' e is?"

Nobody knew. Nobody ever knew. And Breeze was too coward-hearted to watch for his grandfather's spirit. No matter how Granny scolded him, he couldn't do it.

Days afterward, April, the foreman on Blue Brook Plantation, came to Sandy Island, bringing a pair of blue overalls holding pieces of a man. He had fished them up out of the Blue Brook itself where they had drifted instead of going on down to the river's mouth.

Old Breeze had worn blue overalls that Monday morning. Maybe it was he. More than likely it was he. Granny was certain of it.

The stepfather had disappeared with the money buried at the foot of the old dead pine, but April stayed to help dig a grave and bury the poor thing he had found. The mother shrieked and wailed, but Granny grunted and shook her head. She said Old Breeze's body floated to Blue Brook on purpose so April could find it, for April was Old Breeze's son, and, more than that, April was li'l' Breeze's daddy!

[39]

III

COUSIN BIG SUE

BREEZE had heard about Blue Brook Plantation all his life, but he had never heard about his mother's Cousin Big Sue until one hot October afternoon when he was minding the cow by the spring branch and helping his mother break in the precious nubbins of corn and put them in the log barn. Sis called them to come on home in a hurry! The stepfather had gone to town hunting work. Maybe he had come home. Sis's voice was high and shrill and scared, and Breeze knew something had happened. These hot days the mother always worked in the field until first dark because that was the coolest part of the day, and Sis, who stayed at home and sewed and patched and cooked, never called anybody until after the sun went down.

Breeze forgot that the cow was in reach of the low-ground corn and hurried across the stubby furrows as fast as his skinny legs could carry him, but he stopped short when he saw a big fat black woman with a good-natured smile on her face, standing beside Sis in the cabin's back door. Who was she? Why had she come? Why did Sis look so grieved?

The other children were in the yard, giggling, trying to hide behind one another, but the woman's eyes stayed on Breeze.

"I kin see de likeness!" she laughed. "Lawd, yes! Dat boy is de pure spit o' April! De same tar-black

[40]

skin. De same owl eyes. A mouth blue as blackberry stain.''

Breeze had run so fast he was out of breath and his heart beat against his ribs as he watched his mother kiss the stranger and go inside the cabin with her. Presently Sis called him to come in too.

The mother put an arm around him and drew him up close to her side. Her sleeve was wet with sweat, her body hot and steamy, but her hand was cold and shaking like a leaf. How weak and frail she looked beside the fat outsider, who held out a thick hot hand to shake Breeze's. The gold rings on it matched the gold hoop earrings glittering in her small ears, and they felt hard as they pressed against his fingers.

In the silence that followed Breeze looked at the big woman's sleek smooth face. It was round and tight like her fleshy body but with dimples in its cheeks like baby Sonny's. She took a pair of gold-rimmed spectacles out of her pocket and put them on, then leaned back in her chair and laughed a queer gurgling laugh that widened her flat nostrils and stretched her full lips.

"Lawd, ain't it funny how dat boy favors his pa! Dat's a pity too. A boy-chile ought to favor his ma to be lucky. I hope e ain' gwine be de devil April ever was. April was born wid a caul de same way. Lawd, e's a case too!''

Without giving his mother time to answer she talked on; her son Lijah was like her and her girl, Joy, the image of Silas, her husband. Thank God, Joy didn't have ways like Silas. He was good-looking enough, but God never made a more trifling creature than Silas. He ran off and left her seven years ago and she had raised those two children all by herself. Lijah was in Fluridy now. Or maybe it was Kintucky, she wasn't certain which; but he was the worst man in the town where he lived. Everybody was scared to meddle with Lijah. She laughed and rubbed her fat hands together. Nobody would ever run over her Lijah. He took after her that way. Now Joy was different. Joy was weak and easy. But she was a nice girl. She was in town, going to college, getting educated. Joy wouldn't rest until she got a depluma. When she got it, she'd teach school or marry some fine stylish town man. Joy was a stylish girl herself. Maybe too slim, now, but she'd thicken out. When she was Joy's age, Silas could span her waist with his two hands. Joy would fatten up too when she reached a settled age.

Cousin Big Sue rolled out her talk without stopping to catch one breath, and all the time her small sparkleberry eyes roved from Breeze's face to his mother's, then back to Breeze again.

The mother sat huddled low in her chair, her forehead wrinkled, her shoulders drooped. She reached out and took baby Sonny from Sis, and with fingers that shook she unbuttoned her dirty sweaty dress to feed him. For the first time in his life Breeze noticed her poor ragged underclothes and her bony feet and legs. They looked so lean and skinny beside Cousin Big Sue's tight-filled stockings and wide laced-up shoes.

Two bright tears fell swiftly in baby Sonny's fuzzy wool and shone there, two clear drops. Breeze was about to cry himself for his mother's stooped body looked so pitiful. The corners of her mouth were pinched in and the back of her dress, all darkened with sweat from the hard work she had been doing, was humped out in two places by the bones of her thin shoulder-blades. But baby Sonny bobbed his head in such a funny way as he seized the long thin breast that came flopping out. He crowed and kicked his little feet with joy just as if that ugly flesh was the finest thing in the world. Breeze forgot himself and laughed out loud.

Cousin Big Sue's fat hands stroked each other gently, and the laugh that oozed out of her mouth squeezed her eyes almost shut.

"Dat boy Breeze is got nice teeth, enty? But Lawd, his gums sho' is blue! April's got 'em too. An' April's wife, Leah, is got 'em. Dat's dog eat dog, enty? I wish dis boy didn' had 'em, but I know e won't never bite me. Will you, son?"

Breeze felt so shamefaced he shut his mouth tight and hung his head, and his mother began telling Big Sue about the terrible dry-drought. How it had worked a lot of deviltry since June. The crops had promised to make a fair yield, and she kept stirring the earth to encourage them to hold on to their leaves and blossoms, even if they couldn't grow. But the hot sun wouldn't let a drop of rain fall, no matter how the clouds sailed overhead full of thunder and lightning. The leaves all got limp and dry. Sis said they were hanging their heads to pray, but they stayed limp, then they parched brown and dried up and fell off. The peas-patch didn't make enough hay to stuff a mattress. The corn planted on the hill looked like dried onions. The patch of corn in the rich low-ground, close by the spring branch, had done little better. Mid-summer found every blade with its hands shut up tight, trying to hold on to what little sap the sun left. The grass quit trying to be green and the cow had nothing to eat but the coarse bitter weeds growing alongside the spring branch. She was nearly gone dry. What little milk she gave was skimpy and rank, and turned to clabber soon as it cooled. The cream was ropy, and the curds tough. When the butter was churned it wouldn't gather, but laid down flat like melted lard.

The hens had quit laying and spent the summer panting air in and out of wide open mouths, with their wings away off from their bodies, trying to get cool. The old sow had quit rooting and stayed in the mud-hole wallowing, until the mud baked into squares like an alligator's hide. She had no milk for her pigs, and those that didn't starve turned into runts.

Winter was coming. Not a leaf of collards was growing, the few nubbins of corn left wouldn't make bread to last until Christmas. God only knew how she'd feed the children.

When she leaned down to wipe her eyes on her skirt, baby Sonny raised up his hard little head and jerked it down on her breast with a hungry butt, and Breeze forgot again and snickered out. Not that he would ever make sport of Sonny. Never in the world. He loved every crinkly tuft of wool on the baby's head, every tiny finger and toe. Even if he didn't grow a bit, his lightness made him easy to hold. Breeze loved him better than all the other children put together because he was small and weak.

Big Sue broke into a bright smile. "Son, I'm sho' glad you love to laugh. I love to laugh my own self." Her narrow eyes sparkled through her gold-rimmed spectacles, and her wide loose lips spread across her face. "De people on Blue Brook is almost quit laughin' since de boll-evils come. But boll-evils don' fret me. I cooks at de Big House. An' no matter if de buckra is at Blue Brook or up-North whe' dey stays most o' de time, I has all de victuals an' money I wants. I has more'n I kin use. It's de Gawd's truth. You'll sho' have sin, if you don' give me dat boy to raise. Po' as you is, much mouths as you got to fill, you ought to be glad to git shet o' one. You better listen good at all I say. I'll train em good. I'll fatten em up. I'll learn em to have manners. Dis same boy might git to be foreman at Blue Brook yet. E comes from dat foreman breed. You sho' ought not to stand in his way. No, ma'am."

If she wanted a boy-child to raise why didn't Cousin Big Sue choose one of the others? Maybe she didn't like the way their shirts were unbuttoned, with their naked bodies showing down to their waists. Their ragged breeches were not only dirty but ripped open.

Breeze's heart fluttered like a trapped bird's. Fright had him paralyzed so he couldn't run off and hide. His mother looked shrunken, withered. A few tears fell from her eyes as they stared out of the door.

"I bet you ain't got decent victuals for supper right now. I got plenty, yonder home."

Cousin Big Sue's eyes were riveted on Breeze, as she declared he'd be far better off with her than here with his mother, and a house full of starved-out children, growing up in ignorance and rags. She'd teach him and train him and raise him to be a fine man, to know how to do all kinds of work, to make money and wear shoes and fine clothes like her Lijah.

"April"—she peeped sidewise at the mother when she spoke the name—"April's de foreman at Blue Brook, an' e'll help me raise Breeze. E tol' me so las' night."

The mother listened and looked at Sis. Sis slowly nodded back, yes. Breeze burst out crying. He begged them not to give him away. He didn't want to leave home. He wanted to stay right there and be hungry and ragged. He liked to grow up in ignorance and sin.

The shed-room was open so that Big Sue saw the beds covered with old quilts worn into holes. She said Breeze would have good quilts and a feather-bed at her house. The softest lightest feather-bed in the world. It was stuffed with breast feathers plucked off the wild ducks she'd picked and cooked for the white folks at the Big House. Breeze would think he was sleeping on air. She had dry-picked the ducks so the feathers would be puffy, though scalding would have made picking easier.

She'd buy him a pair of ready-made pants from the store, and two or three shirts. She'd get shirts with tails on them like a grown man's shirt.

After that first outcry Breeze couldn't make a sound with his voice, for a lump rose in his throat and choked him. He'd rather stay at home and do without bread, or bed.

"Please, please——" he wailed. But his words were dumb and his crying did no good.

The day was moving. The shadow cast by the china-berry tree had stretched from the front steps to the four-o'clocks over on the other side. Big Sue said she must go. A long walk was ahead, and her feet were not frisky these days.

Breeze could scarcely take in what had happened. He was given away. When Big Sue closed her warm, wet-feeling hand over his and led him away down the path that followed the deep, wide black river, he wanted to scream out, to yell that he didn't want to go. But he couldn't. He couldn't even stop his feet from stepping side by side with hers, one step after another.

Something about this big fat woman kept his mouth shut. Even when the long sandy path was behind, and he could see the ferry-flat, that would take him across the river, he couldn't speak, and the throat lump had swelled to a great big ache in his breast.

When a sudden patter of feet sounded behind him Breeze looked around expecting to see a fawn go across the road, but instead, there was Sis, with her arms outspread. She ran straight to him, fast as she could, and with a sharp little cry hugged him tight. She pressed her soft cheek, wet with tears, on his and whispered in his ear that he must go like a man, and try to be a good boy. She held him close for a minute, then without another word let him go, and ran. She was soon hidden from his eyes by the bend in the road. He strove for one more glimpse of her, but he could see nothing but trees and shadows.

They had reached the far end of the island and the dim road turned to drop down to the river where the flat waited, floating with one end tied up close to a cypress knee. Nobody was in sight. Big Sue stopped. "Whe' is you, Uncle?" She shouted. Echoes answered and reechoed. "Come on, Uncle! Le's go!" She waited, then grumbled. "Lawd! Uncle's too deef."

A few steps nearer the river showed a little old man, sitting crumpled up with his back against a tree. His head was dropped forward, his old cap awry, showing the milk-white wool on his head. Big Sue broke out laughing and went close enough to him to yell in his ear. At once he jumped awake, jerked his chin up off his breast, sat up straight. His eyes, dazed with sleep, gazed around, groping for the sound. When they found Big Sue hiding, he joined her laughter with a hearty cackle that bared his pink toothless gums set in the midst of the bristling white whiskers that stood out around his jaws and chin, fiercely denying the bright twinkle in his eyes.

"Takin' a li'l' nap, Uncle? I couldn't sleep on Sandy Island, not to save life."

Yes, he admitted, he had dropped off. No use to lie, for he'd been caught. Sleep was a tricky thing. A sly-moving thief. Always stealing time from somebody. He gave a wide-mouthed yawn, stretched his arms to try the sleeves of his long-tailed faded black coat, then strove to get his crooked legs straightened, to unbend his knock-knees, and get his stumbling feet clear of the rough footing made by the great puckered roots around the tree. When he finally reached the clear ground he appeared to see Breeze for the first time.

"Lawd, Big Sue, you had luck fo' true! I too glad! Wha' you' name, son? Come shake hands wid Uncle."

He made a polite bow when he took Breeze's hand, his dry old face shone with a kindly smile, his frock coat opened, showing a flowered waistcoat underneath.

"A good-size boy too. E ought to could plow by next spring. Sho'! How old you is, son?" Uncle stood back on his heels, straight as a ram-rod, his eyes sparkling as he praised Breeze's looks.

"I gwine on twelve, suh," Breeze answered. But Big Sue put her mouth up close to the old man's ear and bawled:

"His mammy say e's gwine on twelve, but e looks mighty small to me. You t'ink e's a runt?"

Uncle's eyes watched her lips.

"No, no, Sue, dis boy ain' no runt. You feed em up. E'll fill out an' grow. Bread an' meat all two is been sca'ce on Sandy Island since de dry-drought hit em las' summer. You keep de boy's belly full, an' dis time nex' year you wouldn' know em."

"I wouldn' live on such po' land!" Big Sue bawled again. "Not me! Dis sand looks white as sugar. T'ank Gawd, us home yonder is on black land what kin hold water!"

"You like de black land, enty? No wonder, black as you is, gal!" Uncle chuckled at his joke.

"Sho'! Gi' me black land eve'y time! You ain't so white you'self, Uncle. "

Uncle missed her last words. He was too busy laughing and talking.

"You like you own color, enty, gal?"

Big Sue nodded and joined in heartily with his hollow clattering guffaws.

"Gi' me de black all de time. White t'ings is too weakly!" she shouted gaily, as Uncle led the way toward

the flat. Big Sue followed, holding Breeze's hand tight.
She picked her way down the short sandy hill with slow
uncertain steps.

"I ain' use to shoes an' dey hinders my feet in dis
sand," she explained loudly, but Uncle was busy starting the flat across the river. Grunting, straining until
veins showed in his forehead, he finally got the water-
logged hulk to moving by means of a rusty cable and a
curious narrow board with notches cut in one side so it
could clutch the cable tight.

The sun fell lower as they slowly crossed. Colors
of the sky on the still water made a band of flame, of
scarlet and purple down the middle of the dark stream,
that spread out into the marshy forest.

The old ferryman paused in his pulling and muttered, as he gazed at the sunset; then with a bright look
at Breeze, and a chuckle, he began pulling hard again.
A flock of crows streaked the sky, going home; a lone
fish-hawk sailed not far behind them; tiny swamp
sparrows twittered and chattered.

Night was coming and the whole world knew it. The
wind dropped into a quiet whispering, waiting for the
tide to turn. Every tree and leaf and bough, even the
water itself, was darkening. Squirrels chittered softly
in their nests, a wildcat yeowled gently. Breeze's
heart, that had been thumping miserably in his breast,
now beat up in his throat and the lump that had risen
when he told his mother good-by swelled bigger and
harder than ever. Tears that had been stinging his eyes
all the way began rolling down his cheeks.

He turned his back, and easing a hand stealthily up
to his face, tried to brush them away. Cousin Big Sue
mustn't see him cry. Sis said he must be a man and try
to be good.

He suddenly forgot his sorrow when swarms of tiny,

almost invisible insects rose from nowhere, and settled in his eyes and ears and nostrils and teeth, with a fierce singing and stinging that was maddening. He took off his ragged hat and tried to fight them away, but they ignored its waving. As fast as he killed what seemed to be handfuls, by crushing them on his face and neck and bare legs, others took their places. Sand-flies and mosquitoes were eating him up. Cousin Big Sue had to fight them too, but Uncle was not troubled at all.

"Is de sand-flies pesterin' yunnuh?" he asked mildly.

"Great Gawd, dey sho' is!"

"Git some sweat out you' armpits an' rub on you' face. Dat'll run 'em!"

"Do, Uncle! Fo' Gawd's sake! I ain' no filthy ol' man like you! I washes myself!"

"Wha' dat you say, daughter?"

Big Sue broke into a laugh. "I ain' say nuttin! Not nuttin!"

Uncle calmly worked on, unconscious of what she said. Sweat trickled over his wrinkled face, but it kept its pleasant smile. More than once Big Sue opened her mouth to speak, but closed it without a word, and her face was as doleful as if, like Breeze, she was lonely and homesick.

Breeze wondered bitterly why he hadn't run away and hidden down in the branch where nobody would ever find him? Baby partridges, or new hatched guineas, will sneak under a leaf and stay there until they die before they'll let a stranger find them. Why didn't he do it? He would rather die by himself in the woods than be here on his way to live with this strange woman whose wind was broken.

The sticky mud on the bank had shown no respect for Big Sue's wide-laced shoes. It clung to their soles and stained their shiny tops. The hem of her stiff starched white apron was streaked with dirt. Everything here was strange and unfriendly. The water and trees, the tangled vines and rank undergrowth were all dark and scary. Snakes and alligators and hog-bears and jack-o'-lanterns lived in such places. More than likely hants and plat-eyes and fever and spirits were thick all around. Suppose he'd see them now, with his second sight! He didn't want to see anything but his home yonder behind him, and it was too far to see even the smoke rising out of its low clay chimney. A thick green dusk had risen up from the earth, cutting off the shore on the other side of the river.

The cable slapped the water as it drew the flat across. The old man kept up his grunting and straining. He was not afraid, although he was so old that the years had dried up the flesh on his crooked bones. Breeze jumped sharply, startled and bewildered, when, without any warning, the old man's laughter cackled out. Looking down where the old bent forefinger pointed, he caught sight of an alligator which settled slowly, noiselessly, under the water until only its two eyes made small dark bumps above the smooth surface.

"De alligator see you, son!" the old man squeaked out gleefully, and Big Sue broke into shouts of laughter.

"Great Gawd," she cried. "Do look how e gaze at you, Breeze. E mus' be hongry! E don' see how you's po' as a snake! You' li'l' bones would pure rattle inside dat big creeter's belly."

Stinging homesickness filled Breeze's heart. Why had he come? Truly, this was out of his world. But there was no way to turn back. None. Shrill piercing bird-cries that rose and fell out of the sky answered something that ached in his heart.

[51]

IV.

JULIA

Overhead the high thin air swished, beaten by the wings of wild ducks that flew swiftly across the sky in an even fan-shaped line. Uncle kept looking up at them. Once when he spoke to them in strange muttered words, Big Sue observed:

"Lawd, do listen at Uncle! A-talkin' to dem ducks same as if dey was speerits!"

The trees leaned dreamily over the water which trembled as the sun turned it to dark blood. Uncle's pulling slackened. The flat touched the firm earth at last.

With amazing nimbleness the old man hopped out and tied it fast to a tree, his crooked fingers fumbling stubbornly with the frayed rope until he was satisfied it would hold; then he followed Big Sue and Breeze up a short sandy climb where the road made a swift bend and ran underneath great trees whose thick branches lapped overhead, shutting out all but small white pieces of the sky.

A bony gray mule hitched to a two-wheeled cart stood tethered to a limb. Uncle hobbled to the beast's head: "Wake up, Julia! Open you' eyes, gal! You too love to nod! Dat's de biggest fault I got to find wid you! Lula was a wakeful mule! Lawd, yes!"

Big Sue was panting and climbing in over the cart's wheel, using the hub for a step. She sat on a board laid across the body. Breeze got in and sat on the floor.

Uncle crawled over the dashboard, and jerking the rope lines urged Julia to move on.

"Mind, Julia! Don' git me vexed! I ain' used to no triflin' ways! Lula was pearter'n dis!" Uncle sat up very straight and his tone was terribly threatening.

Julia shook the gnats out of her ears, then snorted them out of her nose, but not until Uncle got to his feet and, raising a long dry stick high as his arm could reach, brought it down on her hip with a powerful whack did she move out of her tracks.

"Git up, Julia!" He gave her another lick, and she turned slowly about and got into the sandy road.

Big Sue heaved a weary sigh.

"Julia is de laziest mule I ever seen in my life, Uncle! Whilst you was a-buyin' one, whyn't you git a spry one?"

"Julia ain' lazy. E's just careful. Julia knows dis cart ain' so strong."

"I hear-say Julia kicks awful bad sometimes!"

"Who? Julia? No, ma'am! Julia's kind as kin be!"

"E looks awful old, Uncle."

"Julia ain' no more'n ten."

"How come e front knees is so bent over if e ain' old?"

"Bent over? Julia's got to bend e knees to walk, enty?"

"Well do, fo' Gawd's sake, lick em an' make em walk a li'l' faster. We wouldn't git home befo' to-morrow if you don't. Lawd, I'm sorry Lula's dead."

"Me too, Big Sue. Now Lula was a mule fo' true. Lula was de finest mule ever was on Blue Brook. Julia ain' got no time wid em. Lula had sense like people. I miss em too bad. I ruther de boll-evils had eat up all de cotton on de plantation dan to 'a' had Lula pizened.

I told April to don' fetch dat pizen to de place. I knowed somet'ing bad was gwine happen soon as he done it. But April is a headstrong man. Nobody can' change him when he gits his mind made up.''

"April tries to be big doins' like de buckra, enty?''

"No, gal, not like de buckra. April's done passed by de buckra! April aims to do like Gawd now!''

"Shut you' mouth, Uncle! You's a case!'' Big Sue roared with laughter.

"April better quit pizenin' all dem bugs Gawd put in de cotton!'' Uncle contended.

Big Sue pondered over this, but presently she grinned and slipped a look at Uncle.

"When Lula died, whyn't you bought a awtymobile, Uncle? I hear say you got plenty o' money buried all round you' house.''

"Who? Me? Great Gawd! I ain' got fi' cents buried! But if I had a t'ousand dollars I wouldn' buy a awtymobile! Not me!''

"How come so?''

"Lawd, dey smells too bad! An' I seen how dey treats de buckra. Dey goes sound to sleep on de road any time dey gits ready. Soon's dey gits in deep sand whe' de pullin' is tight, dey squats right down an' dozes off. You can' lick 'em wid no stick like I licks Julia to wake 'em up. No, ma'am. You have to set an' wait on 'em till dey nap is out. Dey kin dead easy too. I wouldn' trust to buy one. No, Jedus. Dey breath is stink as a pole-cat too.''

"Lawd, Uncle, you is a case in dis world! A heavy case!''

Uncle's eyes twinkled. "You ax me so much a questions, now le' me ax you one. How come you' wind is so short, daughter? You been puffin' like a steamboat ever since you come up dat li'l' small hill.''

Big Sue's hands caught at each other anxiously. "I dunno, Uncle. My wind is short fo' true. E's been short since last Sunday was a week. I eat a piece o' possum what was kinder spoilt fo' my supper last night, an' I ain' been hardly able to travel all day. Spoilt victuals never did set right in my stomach, somehow. I don' know how come so."

As Uncle studied, his eyes snapped. "Sp'ilt possum meat wouldn' hurt nobody. You looks to me like you's conjured. You' eyes looks strainin'. You must 'a' crossed somebody dat Sunday."

Big Sue's fat face looked ready to cry. "I ain' never done nobody a harm t'ing in my life, Uncle. I stays home all de time. I goes to church on Sunday, den I comes straight back home. I don' hardly go to meetin' on Wednesday night. I went all de way to Sandy Island to git dis boy, by I was so lonesome yonder home by myself. Who you reckon would conjure me, Uncle?"

Uncle shook his head gravely. That was hard to tell. Some people get mighty mean if you cross them.

"I don' cross nobody, Uncle." Big Sue was whimpering. "Not nobody! I ever was peaceable."

"Is you an' Leah friendly dese days? Leah is a mighty jealous 'oman, Big Sue." Uncle's eyes sparkled as they sought Big Sue's, but she met them boldly.

"I ain' got April to study 'bout, Uncle."

A smile twitched Uncle's dry wrinkled face. "How 'bout de new town preacher, daughter? I hear-say you an' Leah all two is raven 'bout em. Better mind. De next t'ing you know dat same preacher'll make you have sin."

Big Sue laughed with relief. "No, Uncle. You's on de wrong trail now. A preacher couldn't make me have sin, anyhow."

"How come so?"

"De preacher's a Christian man, enty? An' I is a Christian, enty? One clean sheet can' soil another, Uncle.'"

"Shut you' fool-mouth, Big Sue. You, neither dat preacher, neither Leah, ain' no cleaner'n nobody else. You kin have sin de same as me. Sho' you kin!"

Uncle brought his stick down with a whack on Julia's back.

V

BLUE BROOK

LITTLE by little the cart creaked along, leaving the grove of live-oaks at the landing behind, then crossing the pasture where the rich land lay unplowed, unsown, but covered with lush grass and sprinkled with flowers. Some of them bloomed so close to the ruts that their heads were caught in the cart wheels and shattered.

The fields came next, ripe corn-fields, hay-fields ready to be harvested, brown cotton-fields, dripping with white locks of cotton. Whirls of yellow butterflies played along the road. Flocks of bull-bats darted about overhead in the sky, twittering joyfully as they caught gnats and mosquitoes for their supper. White cranes flew toward sunset, field larks sang out, killdees rose and sailed off crying. The whole earth was full of sound.

Beyond the field near the river a group of low houses, "the Quarters," crouched in a grove of tall trees. Smoke from the chimneys settled in long bands of still blue haze. Breeze could smell its oak flavor. Human voices called out to one another, children shouting, laughing, playing, all of them strangers to him. It set his limbs to quivering, his heart to fluttering. He had nobody here. Nobody!

On a path that skirted the cotton-field a skinny little black girl swinging on the end of a rope was being jerked along by a large red cow that stubbornly refused to follow the narrow path threading across the field.

[57]

The beast had run out between the rows of cotton stalks, and with a deft tongue was licking, right and left, swallowing lock after lock of white staple. Uncle got to his feet.

"Git a stick, Emma! Lick em! April'll kill you, an' de cow too, if you knock out da cotton! Lawd, de field's white! We sho' made a crop dis year!"

The girl's quick eyes glanced back, her small mouth gave a grin. Taking one end of the rope for a whip she fell to beating on the sides and back of the cow with such zeal that it left off its eating, and with a long mournful low, turned into the path that crossed the field and led toward the Quarters. The child tugged at the rope and strove to master the beast, whose dragging steps raised a cloud of dust that shone as it floated low through the evening's bright afterglow.

The dusk crept out across the fields wiping out the day's light. Fires in the cabins made every doorway shine. Long blue streams of smoke rose up from the chimneys and trailed in the sky. Tiny birds flitted and cheeped in the thickets. Sheep bleated. Shouts and snatches of song mingled with wagons rattling.

"Emma's a funny li'l' creeter!" Big Sue remarked. "E look like a witch to me."

But Uncle hadn't heard her, for he was busy jerking the rope lines, trying to hurry Julia's slow steps. When a closed iron gate finally embarred them, Julia stopped short and Uncle gave a sigh. "T'ank Gawd, we's home at last."

At each side of the gate was a house: one a small church, with a steep roof and pointed windows; the other a cabin with a fire blazing high in its wide chimney.

Big Sue yelled out at the top of her voice, "Do, Uncle! Please, suh! Go all de way wid us."

But the old man pretended not to hear her, and said to Breeze, "Son, I knowed you' grampa good, when e wa'n't as high as you. You' grampa was my own sister's chillen."

Then he got out of the cart, went into the cabin and came out bringing a big iron key. He unlocked the gate and opened it wide enough for them to pass through.

Big Sue shouted in a coaxing tone, "Do, Uncle, let Julia take us all de way. I so scared o' de boggy place yonder in de middle o' de avenue. If I was to git in em Gawd knows how deep I'd sink down."

At the thought of such a dreadful thing Uncle joined in Big Sue's gales of laughter, chattering in between his cackles. "Great Gawd, daughter! Sho! You right! I better go long wid you! Da bog can' fool me. I know em too good. I'll go long an' show you de way."

"You ought to try an' git em drained befo' de buckra comes home dis winter. Dat bog likened to swallowed up a big awtymobile las' year."

Breeze was sure Uncle Isaac heard her, but instead of answering, the old man gave a powerful grunt and said the weather would be casting up for rain soon. The misery in his crippled knee had been jumping up and down all day long.

Big Sue told Breeze "de buckra" were white people who owned the plantation. They didn't stay here much, but they would come from up-North as soon as frost killed out the fever here and wild ducks got thick in the rice-fields.

The wabbly cart creaked slowly on. The weird loneliness and strangeness of the twilit avenue made Breeze feel very lonely and sorrowful. The mule's feet were heavy and made unwilling logy steps as they slowly carried Breeze farther and farther from all the paths and places he'd ever known.

Uncle Isaac jumped out of the wagon, and putting the rope lines in Big Sue's hands, began poking and feeling with his stick in the still black water that covered the two ruts in the driveway. Julia must keep to the right of the road. The middle looked safe, but it was tricky. It didn't show how deep and miry the mud in it was. It couldn't fool Lula, but Julia was strange to it. With his stick and queer words he told Julia exactly where to walk until the bad boggy place that Big Sue feared was behind them. He'd walk the rest of the way. Julia would move faster if he went ahead.

The long avenue was bordered with enormous live-oak trees, whose great low branches, almost hidden by drooping gray moss, completely shut the road in, making it a long damp dimly-lighted shadow. Uncle pegged along steadily in front, his stick stepping as importantly as either crooked leg. Once in a while he turned around and spilled out broken stammering words, his cheerful grins showing his empty gums.

The avenue of those gloomy moss-hung oaks began to seem endless, for the road was soft and wet and the mule would not hurry, but at last a white fence made of slender pickets stood in front. Julia stopped short and Uncle Isaac sighed. "You an' de li'l' boy may as well git out now. You kin go de rest o' de way by you'se'f."

He suggested that they'd better go through the front yard. Nobody was at home so it wouldn't matter. The path around the side was weedy. Snakes were walking fast now and he'd hate for Breeze to be bitten as soon as he set foot on Blue Brook.

Taking off his ragged cap, he bowed a low good night. He was glad a boy blessed with second-sight had come to live on the plantation. April was wise to get him here.

Big Sue thanked him, and, taking Breeze by the

[60]

hand, led him through the gate and along the driveway that curved between box-borders around a large bed of shrubbery that Big Sue said was shaped like a heart.

If the white folks were home they couldn't come this way, but since they weren't she was glad for Breeze to see the Big House. It was the finest and largest one ever built on the Neck, and that was saying a lot, for in the old days, before most of the houses were burned or left to rot down, the Neck was a vast rich country.

In the fading light the great white house had an old gray look like everything else here, from Julia and the wool on Uncle Isaac's head, to the moss swinging down from the huge age-twisted limbs of the giant oaks. Breeze counted the six white columns rising from the brick-paved porch, a step above the ground, to the corniced roof. Every door, every green window shutter was closed. No sign of smoke rose from the tall red brick chimneys. The background of shrubs and flowers was deadly still and so full of deep darkness, Breeze held his breath.

Big Sue sniffed. "Lawd, ain't de flowers sweet? Jedus, have mercy! Dey pure cuts at my heart strings! Watch whe' you step, son. Seems to me like I smell a snake too."

"No'm, dat's a watermelon."

"Enty? Dey smell a good deal alike, rattlesnakes an' watermelons. It's easy to take one fo' de other, specially when de watermelons is kind o' green."

They crossed the back yard, which was clean-swept and white with sand, then passed by the kitchen where Big Sue cooked the white folks' victuals. It was a long low white-washed building with plenty of room inside, but Big Sue said when the duck shooting and deer hunting started that kitchen could hardly hold all the game. Not only ducks and deer, but partridges and wild

[61]

turkeys and squirrels and oysters and turtles. As soon as a killing frost made the place safe from fever they'd be coming. Lots of ducks were already here. Lord, how she had to turn! Those white folks were heavy eaters.

Breeze could make himself mighty useful helping her, bringing in stove wood, running fast with the hot waffles, so they'd get to the dining-room before they got cold. Cold waffles are not fit to eat, and the kitchen was so far off it took quick moving feet to get anything into the house crisp and hot. But it's dangerous to have a kitchen on to a house. Some of the best houses on the Neck caught fire and burned down as soon as kitchens were built up close to them.

A short straight clear path ran from the kitchen to the door of Big Sue's home, a squatty cabin of white-washed boards with the floor of its tiny front porch only one step up.

Big Sue pulled up her top skirt and her fat hand fumbled for the pocket of her petticoat, her hussy, she called it, where she carried her house key tied to a small flat piece of wood. She unlocked the padlock fastening the rusty chain that held the door tight shut, and went into the dark front room.

A few coals blinked with red eyes from out of a mound of ashes in the big fireplace. Big Sue well-nigh jarred them out when she threw a heavy knot of fat lightwood on them.

"Git down on de hearth an' blow up de fire, Breeze. I got to git off dese shoes. My toes is pure got de cramp wid dem."

While Breeze placed the fat knot carefully on the live coals, and blew on them with well-aimed puffs of his breath until a bright yellow flame sent smoke and sparks flying up the chimney, Big Sue groaned with trying to bend low enough to reach the strings in her shoes. She gave it up saying:

"Do unlace dese strings, son. My wind is too short fo' me to strain a-tryin' to bend down low."

As his nimble fingers quickly undid the hard knots and the wide flat shoes were slipped off her fat feet, the firelight flamed past him and lit up the room. The walls were covered with newspapers, the floor was scoured almost white, and the wooden bed in the corner puffed up high with its feather mattress and many-colored quilt.

Taking her shoes off made Big Sue a different person. From being heavy and slow she became light on her feet and quick. She took a black iron spider off the hearth and put it over the clear hot blaze, then dropped slices of white bacon on it to cook. While the bacon hissed and curled up with frying, Big Sue pulled sweet potatoes out from under the pile of hot ashes in one corner. Those that a squeeze from her fingers showed soft and well done she put in a pan to be eaten, the others were put back in the ashes to cook longer. She stirred a pot full of white cornmeal mush; collard greens, cooked with chunks of bacon, half filled another. The smell of food went all through the cabin every time a pot-lid was lifted.

Big Sue gave Breeze a tin pan and a spoon, while she took another; but just as she leaned down to dip up the food she glanced toward the bed. Breeze had put his hat on it. She stopped still and glared at him.

"Great Gawd, boy! You put bad luck on my Joy's bed. I got a good mind to lick you. Take dis pin. Go stick em in da hat. Don' never put a hat on no bed. You ain' had much raisin', or you'd know better."

Breeze took the pin and stuck it, as she said, in the hat's crown. It must stay there until morning, then he must hang the hat on a nail in the newspapered wall.

"Lawd," she sighed as she leaned over the pot again, "dat hat sho' scared me. S'pose I didn' had a pin! Come fill you' pan now. Eat a plenty. I want you to grow fast so you'll git big enough to help me work. Put some pot liquor off de greens on you' mush. Mush an' pot liquor is good fo' you. It'll stick to you' ribs. Sweet potatoes an' fat meat'll fatten you too. You's too small. You' ma says you's gwine on twelve, but you can' be dat old! I hope to Gawd you ain' a runt!"

Breeze was ready to cry, and she changed her tone and told him that April had a goat for him to break and ride and drive, if he'd be a good boy and mind all she said. April would get a goat harness and a goat wagon, too. Breeze must get the goat tame before the little white boy who lived in the Big House came home. White people are so subject to fever, they can't risk even one night on the river before killing frost. When the nights get warm, in the spring, they have to go away. White people have some mighty weak sickly ways.

Breeze had eaten too much. He was packed so full he felt tight and uneasy. He wanted to go home to his mother, but Big Sue kept talking fast to keep his mind from dwelling on his troubles. Over and over she said he was a lucky boy to be here with her at Blue Brook. While he washed his pan and spoon, she got a tin basin off the water-shelf by the door and poured it half full of hot water out of the big black kettle simmering on the hearth. She gave it to Breeze with a big new bar of turpentine soap. "Wash you' feet good and get ready for bed, son."

But he had no night-clothes, no day clothes either, except the few he brought tied up in a white cloth. He couldn't sleep between her clean white sheets in those dirty breeches and that filthy shirt! No! His tears poured out when she got a great big garment out of the trunk in the corner, and putting it over his head drew the great sleeves up over his arms. As she buttoned it up at the neck, her laughing broke into such funny snorts Breeze had to stop crying to look at her. Her wind must be broken fo' true!

He had to sleep in the big bed in the corner, Joy's bed, to-night, to take off the bad luck his hat had put on it. To-morrow night he'd take the bed she fixed for him in the shed-room where Lijah used to sleep when he was a little boy.

When Breeze crawled into Joy's fine bed, the soft feathers rose up gently, kindly, around his tired body, and Big Sue leaned over and gave him several light pats.

"Sleep good, son. Dream a nice dream." She fixed the big pillow under his head, and drew up the quilts close over his shoulders. "All you dream to-night'll come true, so don't git on you' back an' dream a bad dream. Sleep on you' side. So."

VI

BREEZE roused from a doze when a man's deep booming voice called from the outside, "How you feelin'
to-night, Miss Big Sue?"

And Big Sue called back heartily:

"Come in, Uncle Bill. I too glad fo' see you! I'm
lonesome as kin be."

Cracking his eyes Breeze peeped at the tall raw-
boned man who shambled in, bringing a tin bucket
which he put on the shelf, saying he'd brought some
sweet milk for the little boy and a few sticks of wood.
Reaching up stiffly he pushed his hat farther back, then
he scratched his head awkwardly, while his deep voice
rolled out, "You sho' looks fine, Miss Big Sue! I declare
to Gawd, you could pass fo' a flowers garden!"

"Do shut you' mouth," Big Sue returned playfully.
"You talk too much sweet-mouth talk, Uncle Bill. Some
day you gwine miss an bite you' tongue in two. Better
mind! You couldn't preach no mo'."

He declared he was not to blame. How could his
mouth fail to talk sweet when he saw her? It was a
wonder the bees didn't eat her. He dropped the handful
of sticks on the hearth, saying they were a few pieces of
driftwood he'd brought to put on her fire for luck to-
night while the old moon was in her bed.

"You must be feelin' mighty peart to go all de way
to de beach to pick up driftwood, Uncle Bill."

"Sho', I feel good. Like a lamb a-jumpin'. I could

[66]

start now and travel till to-morrow's sun shine, an' I wouldn't feel noways weary.''

"Lawd, you have luck," Big Sue sighed. "But do lend me de loan o' you' pipe befo' you fix de fire. I'm pure weak I want to smoke so bad. I'm scared to smoke my own. I believe it's conjured. It ain' smoked right since I lent em to Leah last Sunday a week gone, right yonder at Heaven's Gate Church." Her breath had been cut off shorter than ever to-day. She ate a 'possum leg last night for her supper and it was kinder spoiled from being kept too long. She hadn't felt exactly well since. Spoiled food ever did make her sick. She didn't know why.

"It's because you's such a delicate lady!" Uncle Bill declared. "You ought to learn to drink milk. Nice sweet milk. And eat honey. De angels lives on 'em. So de Book says."

"I dunno," Big Sue answered doubtfully. "I never could stand nothin' 'bout a cow. Not de milk or de meat or de ways. Gi' me a hog all de time."

Uncle Bill got his pipe out of his side coat pocket, twisted its rough wooden stem tight into its bowl and handed it to her, his lean face brightening with a smile.

"E ain' gwine smoke good by its new. I went to de fig trees no longer'n yestiddy an' cut dis stem, by my old stem was wore out altogether. E's gwine bite you' tongue. I'm too sorry. I wanted you to talk some sweet talk to me to-night!"

"Lawd, Uncle Bill, you ought to know my tongue better'n dat. I got a strong tongue in my mouth. E's trained. I done got em used to tastin' all kinds o' red pepper an' seasonin'. E kin make friends wid any pipe stem ever was. But you go look at my li'l' boy."

Breeze shut his eyes tight as Uncle Bill leaned down to look at his face.

"E's a good-size boy, but you'd be better off wid a husband, Miss Big Sue. You see dese sticks? I went all de way to de beach to git em. Dey's driftwood, an' I'm gwine burn 'em on you' fire to-night, an' make a wish whilst dey's green."

"Wha' dat you gwine to wish to-night?"

"I'm gwine wish fo' you to marry me."

"Great Gawd, Uncle Bill!" Laughter almost choked her. "I can' marry you! I got a livin' husband right now! You must be forgot Silas ain' dead!"

"Silas is been gone seven years, Miss Big Sue. Gawd don' expect no lady to live single longer'n seven years. No, ma'am. You kin marry me if you want to."

"I dunno," Big Sue tittered. "Sometimes my mind do tell me to marry again. But didn't you promise Aun' Katy you wouldn' marry nobody? What 'ud she say?"

Uncle Bill heaved a deep sigh. "I can' help dat. I miss Katy so bad, I mighty nigh goes crazy yonder to my house by himself. If you would marry me Katy wouldn't mind. Not a bit. Katy had sense like a man. Lawd, how I miss dat 'oman! I done made up my mind to marry again an' I'm gwine wish a weddin' dress on you whilst I burn dese same sticks on you' fire to-night."

He spoke solemnly, and kneeling on the hearth he laid the driftwood sticks carefully crossed on the coals. Then he blew deep breaths until a slow green flame curled up. "Fo' Gawd's sake, Uncle Bill! Quit you' crazy doin's! You might miss an' conjure me fo' true." Big Sue giggled until her fat sides shook.

"Hush you' laughin' till I makes my wish, Miss Big Sue! You got me all eye-sighted!"

"Mind how you wish in de face o' dat fire!"

A woman's voice flung the drawled words into the room so unexpectedly that Big Sue jumped to her feet,

calling, "Who dat?" and Uncle Bill gave such a start
that his wish was knocked clean out of his head.

"Don' git scared. I ain' nobody but Zeda. How
yunnuh do dis evenin'?"

"Lawd, Zeda, you ought not to slip up on people dat
way!" Big Sue scolded, but Zeda broke into a laugh.
She stood in the door where the white cloth on her head
made a clear spot against the darkness, but her face and
hands were one with the night.

"Don' le' me stop you' wishin', Uncle Bill. Go on. I
might give you luck." Zeda's teeth flashed as she saun-
tered in with noiseless barefoot steps. She couldn't sit
down; she was on her way to Bina's birth-night supper
at the Quarters. She just came by to see the boy-child
Big Sue had brought from Sandy Island.

"E's sleep right yonder in Joy's bed."

"Lawd, you got a sizable boy, enty? E looks mighty
long. Long as Leah's Brudge to me. I wouldn' gi'
way a boy big as dat. E's done raised."

Again Breeze shut his eyes and pretended to sleep
while Zeda leaned so low over him searching his face
that he could feel her breath on his cheek.

"Don' gaze at de child so hard, Zeda. You'll wake
em up."

Big Sue was plainly out of temper, her tone was
sour, pettish.

"I ain' gwine wake em. I just want to see who e
looks like. Leah says his mammy had em for April, but
e don' favor April to me."

"Do, for Gawd's sake, shut you' mouth, Zeda! To
hear Leah tell it, half de chillen on Blue Brook belongs
to April, well as dem on Sandy Island. Leah don' count
nobody when e gits to talkin' 'bout April."

Zeda laughed. "I dunno, Big Sue. I told April
to-day, if he don' mind, he's gwine catch up wid Uncle

Isaac. De people say Uncle Isaac has fifty-two chillen livin' right now.''

Breeze peeped up in time to see the grin that lit her face as she turned on her heel, saying she must go, and let Uncle Bill finish his wishing. But he'd wish a long time before he got a wife as good as Aunt Katy.

Uncle Bill sat up straight in his chair. "Now you talkin' what Gawd loves, Zeda; de truth. Katy was one in a t'ousand. I miss em so bad, I can' stan' it no longer by myself. If Miss Big Sue would marry me, I'd treat em white. I sho' would.''

Zeda took her pipe out of her apron pocket and leaned for a coal to light it. After one or two stout pulls she let the smoke trail slowly out between her smiling lips. ''I hear-say Big Sue an' Leah all two is a seekin' de second blessin' since de new Bury League preacher was here last Sunday was a week gone. Is dat so, Big Sue?''

"I know I ain' seekin' em. I don' know nothin' 'bout Leah, an' I don' want to know nothin' 'bout em.'' She snapped the words out fiercely; but Zeda set her arms akimbo and puffed at the pipe between her teeth, her eyes flashing bright in the firelight that flared past her to the framed pictures of faces looking down from the walls.

Big Sue sat grum, silent, until Uncle Bill heaved a great sigh and said he was mighty sorry for Leah. She'd been sick three days. Salivated. Her mouth was raw. Her teeth were loose, ready to drop out. Leah was in a bad way.

Big Sue's fat body straightened up. She was full of interest. How did Leah get salivated?

Uncle Bill shook his head. He didn't know what had done it. Leah hadn't been well since this moon came in. He couldn't say if seeking a second blessing had made her sick or if some medicine she'd bought from the store had done it. He caught her wallowing on the ground and praying and crying off in the woods by herself one day last week. Now she was salivated. Zeda looked at Uncle Bill's sorrowful face and her own became serious.

"Dat's what Leah gits fo' prankin' wid white folks' medicine. I told em so too."

"I bet Leah's conjured," Big Sue put in cheerfully.

"Who in Gawd's world would bother to conjure Leah?" Zeda asked. "Any 'oman dat wants April bad enough kin git em. April's weak as water over anyt'ing wid a dress on."

"You ought to know," Big Sue snapped out tartly.

A smile curled Zeda's lips. "I does know. If anybody knows April, I ought to. April's de same as a bee at blossoms. You wait. You'll see. Leah's a fool to fret 'bout April. I done been to see em an' told em so. No man livin' is worth one drop o' water dat dreans out a 'oman's eye. It's de Gawd's truth. If April buys em rations an' clothes, Leah ought to be sati'fy, 'stead o' frettin' an' cryin'."

Zeda's bright hoop ear-rings glittered, her teeth flashed, then she turned and spat in the fire. "Leah ought to be used to April's ways by now. E ought to learn how to meet trouble better. Trouble comes to everybody. If e ain' salivation or sin or men, e's somet'ing." Zeda stretched her arms, then her body to its full height. She must go. She'd promised Bina to help cook the birth-night supper.

Big Sue didn't turn her head to say good night, but Uncle Bill got up and went to the door and bowed low as she stepped out into the still black night, which came right up to the open door.

In the silence that followed, the muffled roar of the

sea rose and fell. Big Sue said Zeda had ruined many a man. She was a bold sinful woman.

"Zeda's a fine field-hand, dough, an' de clothes Zeda washes is white as snow," Uncle Bill defended warmly.

"It's a wonder some 'oman ain' cut Zeda wide open befo' now," Big Sue came back sharply.

"But if anybody is sick or in trouble, nobody is better to em dan Zeda. If Zeda had been my Katy's own sister, e couldn' 'a' been better to em whilst e was down sick. Gawd ain' gwine be too hard on Zeda. You'll see it too."

"Shucks! Zeda kin grin at you, an' you fo'git all dat deviltry Zeda's done; but Gawd's got it wrote down in a book. Zeda kin fool de breeches off o' you, but 'e can' fool Gawd. Zeda's got ten head o' livin' chillen an' no two is got de same daddy. You b'lieve Gawd is gwine ex-cuse Zeda? You must be crazy. Zeda's as sho' fo' hell as a martin fo' his gourd. You'll see, too. Gawd ain' gwine let people off light as you t'ink. No, suh. Zeda don' like to see no other 'oman hab no man. Zeda wants 'em all. All!"

VII

A BIRTH-NIGHT SUPPER

THE birth-night supper had begun, and the big drum, answering licks that somebody laid on its head, called the people to come on. Louder and louder it boomed until the air itself was humming. Now and then when a rackety thump sounded in an unlooked for place Big Sue laughed. When the measure shortened beat by beat her fat toes made pats on the floor.

"Lawd, de drum's got de people steppin' light tonight. Is dey marchin' or dancin'?"

"Marchin'. Dat's Sherry a-beatin' de drum, now. When de dancin' starts Uncle Isaac beats de drum an' Sherry squeezes de accordion."

Big Sue got up and went to the door to hear better, and her thick stumpy body rocked softly from side to side. "Po' ol' Uncle! Most ready fo' de grave an' de biggest sinner roun' here." But the thought of Uncle's sin made her laugh, as she swayed this way and that. "I feel light as a feather, Uncle Bill. Ain' Sherry got dat drum talkin' funny talk! E don' sound noways sinful to me. You t'ink marchin' is a sin?"

"No. It ain' sinful to march. How 'bout walkin' out an' lookin' at 'em a while."

Breeze sat up. "Please lemme go too, Cousin Big Sue. I ain' sleep. I too scared to stay by myself." The corners of the room were full of darkness, the shed-room at the back was black, and the sea's roar unsmothered by the drum-beats.

"How come you had you' eyes shut, so? You been playin' possum, enty? I caught you. I don' like dat. No. Don' you never make like you sleep if you ain' sleep. No. But git up an' dress. Me an' Uncle Bill would walk on. You dress fast an' catch up wid us."

When Breeze overtook them, Uncle Bill, who walked in front, called back, "How you do, stranger? I glad to see you. Come shake han's wid me." Then he added, "A cowardly heart makes swift-runnin' feet, enty?"

When Breeze answered promptly, "Yessuh," Uncle Bill chuckled.

"You's got manners, boy! Nice manners! I'm glad to see dat."

"Sho' e is!" Big Sue agreed. "All dat breed is mannersable people. Dat's how come I took so much pains to git em."

"Dat is nice," Uncle Bill approved. "I ever did like people to hab manners."

"Me too! I can' stan' no-manners people, specially a no-manners boy-chile. I'm all de time tellin' Leah, Brudge'll git hung if e lives. Brudge is too no-manners. I'd skin em if e was my own."

The noise from the birth-night supper grew thicker and stronger as they got nearer the Quarters. Every beat of the drum throbbed unbroken by the laughter and singing and loud-ringing talk. Breeze's feet stepped with the time it marked, and so did Uncle Bill's and Big Sue's.

The Quarter houses were all solid darkness but one, and its doorway was choked with people pushing in and out; its front yard hidden by a great ring of march-ing couples, that wheeled slowly around a high-reaching fire. These were holding hands, laughing into one another's faces, their feet plumping down with flat-footed steps that raised the dust, or cutting little extra fancy hops besides the steady tramping bidden by the drum.

Two big iron washpots sat side by side with the fire leaping high between them. Zeda stirred one with a long wooden paddle, and a short thick-set woman stirred the other. They added seasoning, stirred, tasted, added more seasoning, until a tall fellow, black as the night, and strong-looking as one of the oaks around them, broke through the ring and stepped up to the pots, and put his hand on Zeda's shoulder. What he said was lost in the noise, but his teeth and eyes flashed in the red light as Zeda put a hand on each of his broad shoulders and quickly pushed him outside the ring again. The short woman took the steaming paddle out of the pot and shook it gaily at him, shouting to him to get a partner and march until the victuals were done and ready to sell instead of setting such a bad example for the young people.

The marchers laughed, and the drummer, a long-legged young man, dropped his sticks and yelled out, "How long befo' supper, Ma! I'm done perished. I'm pure weak, I'm so hongry!"

Zeda stopped short in her tracks and yelled back to him, "Shut you' mouth, Sherry! You ain' perished, nothin'! You beat dat drum or Bina'll put all two feets on you' neck!"

The other woman pointed her paddle at him threateningly, shouting as she did it, "You' ma is sho' right, son! I wouldn' pay you, not one cent to-night, if you don' beat dat drum sweet as you kin! Keep de people marchin' a while yet. I got a whole hog an' a bushel o' rice a-cookin'! Right in dese pots. I wouldn' sell half if you don' git ev'ybody good an' hongry! Rattle dem sticks, Sherry! Rattle 'em like you was beatin' a tune fo' Joy to step by!"

This brought a shower of laughter and funny sayings and jokes as the crowd bantered Sherry about the way he beat the drum when Joy was here to march. But instead of answering a word, Sherry rolled the sticks softly on the drum's head, making a low sobbing sound that held on and on, swelling, mounting until a battering roar made the air throb and hum, then he stopped off short with a sudden sharp drub.

For a second there was a dead silence, then somebody cried out, "Lawd, if you much as call Joy's name, Sherry kin make dat drum talk some pitiful talk! Joy ought to heared em to-night!"

"I got goose bumps big as hickory nuts all over me!"

"Me too. I'm pure shakin' like a chill! Beat, Sherry! I got to march to warm up now!"

Everybody laughed and the clatter of voices made a merry confusion.

Zeda laughed with the crowd. Then she added a handful of salt to her washpot, tasted it, smacked her lips and added several pods of red pepper.

"Yunnuh got to dance nice if you want to eat dis rice an' hash! I ain' mixin' no cool Christian stew!"

Bina laughed and chimed in, "Dat's de Gawd's truth, Zeda! Not wid all dat pepper."

But Big Sue sucked her teeth. "Zeda don' know one kind o' seasoning f'om anudder. Pepper an' salt; dat's all Zeda knows. E never could cook no decent rations."

A short fat man, with a well-greased face and a good-natured smile, who stood waiting for Bina to say the word, began bawling with all his might, "De victuals is ready, peoples! Come on up, men! Treat de ladies! We's got t'ings seasoned fit to make you miss an' chaw you' finger! Liver-hash an' rice! Chitterlings an' pig feet! Spare-ribs an' back-bone! All kind o' hog-meat."

He trailed off into a sing-song chant, while the crowd pressed close around the pots.

Uncle Bill treated Breeze and Big Sue to heaped-up panfuls of food and tin cups of molasses-sweetened water to wash it down. "Dis is sweetened wid store-bought molasses. It ain't fittin' fo' nobody to drink." Big Sue made an ugly face and threw the sweetened water on the ground. "I wouldn' have de face to sell sich slops to people an' call it sweetened water. Bina ever was a triflin' 'oman. Gittin' money is Bina's Gawd!"

"How 'bout a little nip o' toddy?" a deep voice spoke out of the darkness and Big Sue turned quickly around to face it, then she laughed out with pleasure. "No, t'ank you, April. I wouldn't fool wid dat whisky. You don' know if it'll kill you o' not."

"Come off, Big Sue," the voice chided, "when did you get so scared o' whisky?"

"I ain' scared o' good whisky," Big Sue gurgled as he walked up near and took her hand. "Dat last one you fetched me is sho' fine. But I sho' don' trust de whisky Jake makes! Lawd!" She broke into a loud laugh. "I'm pure shame' to say it but somebody told me when Jake gits in a big hurry fo' de whisky he don' stop wid puttin' lye in de mash! Dat scoundrel goes straight to de horse stable an' gits de yeast to make em work! My stomach tries to retch if I much as t'ink on de way Jake makes whisky! Jake's a case in dis world!"

April and Uncle Bill both laughed with her, and Jake's voice called out cheerfully from the fire-brightened doorway, "Git you' partners ready fo' de square dance! Git you' nickels ready too! Fi' cents a set! All you chu'ch-members better git on home befo' Sherry squeezes dat 'cordion. I'd hate to see anybody hab sin to-night! Sherry's gwine mash out tunes dat would tickle a preacher's toe! A deacon's ear would git eetchy! Git you' partners, boys! Don' be wastin' time!"

"How you like de boy's looks?" Big Sue mumbled, casting a smiling look up at April.

"I ain' had a chance to look at em, not yet," he answered low.

Sherry squeezed a long chord out of the accordion and the crowd shouted with laughter. Uncle Isaac battered the drum, and swarms of them trooped inside the cabin, falling into step with the accordion's frolicsome measure, but instead of Uncle Bill's leading the way straight home, he took a stand outside the cabin by an open window to watch. The tall strange man leaned over and said to Breeze, "You's too low to see, son. Le' me hold you up." And he lifted him as if he were no heavier than a feather.

The light was dim. Two glass kerosene lamps burned on the high mantel-shelf, doing their best to help the fire light up the room. Music and drum-beats and lively chatter swung into time with dance steps. The confusion flowed into clean-cut swing.

Every man had his hat on. Some were tilted back, some balanced on the side, some pulled to the front; few were right and straight. Many of the dancers wore shoes, and the loose boards on the floor rose and clattered to the regular beat of their feet.

"Did you ever seen people dance before?" April murmured in Breeze's ear.

Breeze's bashful "No, suh" was lost in noise, for Jake, who took up the nickels at the door, was yelling briskly, his words guiding the dancers into figures. "Hands 'round, all!" shifted the couples into a wide circle that had to crumple in spots because the room was too small. As it turned around every heel bumped the floor until the stamping tramp shook the cabin from pillars to roof. Once in a while Breeze could feel the big chest pressed against him shaking with laughter.

"Ladies to de center! Gentlemens surround dem!" Jake yelled it, and the ring split and went double ply. "Make a basket!" he howled. Feet shuffled and scraped the floor, as the men made a cord of long arms and tight clasped hands that slipped over the ladies' heads. The swaying bodies were tied together tight. Sweat shone on every face. Eyes gleamed. Teeth flashed.

"How you like dat, son?" April asked, and Breeze answered, "I like em nice."

"Wheel de basket!" Jake bawled, and the solid ring turned, slowly, evenly at first, then faster and faster until its wild whirling threw the dancers into knots of dizzy cavorters. Hot breath poured through the windows. The rank smell of over-heated sweaty bodies ran high. The house shook and creaked. Breeze could feel the strong throb of the heart in the man's breast beating against him. Gradually the long black face leaned forward nearer to his.

"Right hand to you' partner!" Jake cried, and hands trembling with excitement squeezed each other and held fast.

"Do de gran' right an' left!"

Jake dashed the sweat out of his eyes with a bare hand, as the dancers fell into two lines. A thread of ladies wound in and out between the gentlemen, whose feet kept up a frisky jumping and jigging and jerking, like drumsticks gone crazy and trying to hammer in the floor.

"Ain' dey done dat nice!" Big Sue exclaimed.

"Dey done it mighty well," the big man approved, his mouth close to Breeze's ear

When the ladies had gone clear 'round and come to their partners again, "Swing you' own true love!" set every skirt to spinning in a giddy ring that twirled until "Sasshay, all! Croquette! Salute de lady on de right!" unwound them, let them fall limp.

Shrieks of laughter followed smacking kisses. Sherry's accordion blared out. Then something went wrong. The joyful clamor died into a frightened hush as a long arm shot up. A razor flashed. A muttered curse was followed by a slap on a cheek. Everybody stood still for the length of a heart-beat. The muscles of the arms holding Breeze hardened. A long low hiss of sucked-in breath made him shiver with terror as the tall man leaned forward and said coolly:

"If yunnuh don' quit dat doins' it wouldn' take me two minutes to come in dere an' butt you' brains out o' you' skull! We ain' gwine hab no cuttin' scrape here, not to-night, boys. Outen de lamps, Sherry. Outen de fire, too. Dis dance is done broke up!"

"No, Cun April," Jake began pleading. "Nobody ain' fightin' now. Dem boys was just a-playin'. Dey ain' gwine be rough no mo'. You wouldn' broke up a dance not for a li'l' prankin', would you?"

The two fighters were held apart, one with his bullet head crouched forward, his fists clenched; the other with his razorless fingers reaching out to grab and strangle. April looked at them with a half smile.

"Put dem boys out de door, den, Jake. Dey ain' fit to be wid ladies. Let 'em go wallow wid de hogs an' cuss all dey please, so long as dey don' cut wid no razor."

But Uncle Bill spoke out, "Dey is too no-manners to wallow wid de hogs. Yes, suh. My hogs yonder to de barnyard is too nice to 'sociate wid any such mens. Cussin' befo' ladies! Dey makes me feel pure blush."

Big Sue wanted to go home, but April and Uncle Bill said there'd be no more trouble, and as the accordion sang out with a low sad whine, another dance set was made up. Pairs of feet were already cutting happy capers patting flat-footed and with heel and toe.

They were going to black bottle, and that was a dance that beat the four-horse altogether. The cabin room, packed with a seething mass, rocked with the reeling and rolling inside it. The accordion's mournful crying timed to the beat of the drum sounded faint above the confusion, but its pitiful wailing went clear through to Breeze's very backbone.

Gusts of hot breath poured out through the window. The smoky lamps sputtered low. The yellow light grew dim. Little sharp outcries mixed with mad stormy thundering steps. Big Sue called out shrilly that she wanted to go! People get drunk if they listen to music too long. Sherry was squeezing out a mighty wicked tune. First thing they knew somebody would kick both those lamps off the mantelpiece and when the crowd started jumping out of the windows, they'd get trampled to death. She hadn't forgotten how the last birth-night supper broke up in a terrible fight. April could hold those boys down a while, but when that music got to working in their blood, the devil himself couldn't stop them.

She could feel that music going straight to her head, and she was a good quiet Christian woman. April laughed and put Breeze down and bowed low and said good night. Big Sue invited him to walk home with them and when he declined, saying he was tired and ready to go home to bed, she insisted, but he declared that he hadn't the heart to get in Uncle Bill's way. He'd see them to-morrow or some time soon.

On the way home Big Sue asked Uncle Bill why it

was so sinful to dance, yet not sinful at all to march by the drum. She never could exactly understand. Uncle Bill said that crossing your feet is the sinful thing. The people in the Bible used to march. Of course it was wrong to march by reel tunes. Christians ought to march by hymns.

Breeze fell into a sound sleep and left Big Sue talking, but he woke up in the night with his throat tight and dry sore, and a hoarse cough that barked. Everything was dark and Big Sue's heavy snoring was the only sound to be heard. What must he do? Suppose he choked to death! Nobody would ever know it. His mother was way off yonder on Sandy Island, and Big Sue sound asleep. He'd wake her. He couldn't die here in this dark by himself.

Crawling out of bed and guiding his way toward the sound of the snortles that were all but strangling her, Breeze went to Big Sue's bed in the shed-room, felt for her shoulder and coughed as loud as he could in her ear.

"Great Gawd, who dat?" she cried out. "Who dat, I say!" Big Sue was on the other side of the bed!

"Dis is me," Breeze whispered.

"How come you's up a-walkin' round, boy? Git on back to bed. You' ma didn' told me you was a sleep-walker. Great Gawd a'mighty! I can' stan' a sleep-walker."

"I ain' 'sleep," Breeze whispered again, but she didn't hear him, so he gave a loud cough that all but split his throat in two.

"Who dat cough? You, Breeze?"

"Yes'm."

"Jedus, hab mussy! I ain' never hear such a cough. You' palate must be fell down. Git on back in de bed. If you keep coughin' I'll gi' you a spoonful o' kerosene.

[82]

If you' palate is down Maum Hannah must tie up you' palate lock. Go on back to bed. I sho' am sorry you' palate is fell, but don' you ever walk in on me a-sleepin', not no mo'!''

The threat of the kerosene made Breeze struggle to hold in his coughs, and whenever one tried to burst out he covered up his head, although it seemed to him somebody was laughing in the shed-room with Big Sue.

VIII

Breeze slept late next morning. When he woke Big Sue stood by his bed, looking straight into his eyes. A bar of sunlight fallen through a crack in the wooden window blind laid a dazzling band on her face.

"Looka de sun shinin' on you, son. You is gwine be lucky. Git up now, I'm got to off a piece. But you' breakfast is settin' on de hearth. I bet you had a bad dream last night. Don't tell it befo' breakfast. Dat'll make it come true."

But Breeze couldn't remember any dream at all, and, slipping out of Big Sue's night-gown and into his own clothes, he took his pan of breakfast and went to sit on the front step in the sunshine while he ate. He swallowed down the grits and bacon grease in a hurry, keeping the sweet potato for the last. A lean spotted hound trotted up and sniffed at his feet and legs, then turned to the empty pan on the step and licked it clean. When he looked beseechingly at the potato, Breeze gave him a taste and patted his head and stroked his long silky ears and together they went to look around the premises.

Big Sue had told Breeze that Blue Brook was the finest plantation on the whole Neck, and the Big House the largest dwelling, but those chimneys, towering high as the tree-tops, and the tall closed windows and doors had a cold unfriendly look. The yard was empty except for a few chickens and a flock of geese. The old gander looked at Breeze and flapped his wings and screamed out, and Breeze turned back, frightened by his threats.

Behind Big Sue's cabin were a tiny fowl-house and a pig-pen with a big hog lying down inside. When Breeze looked over the fence the creature grunted and struggled to get to his feet. Fat had it weighted down, yet its snout made hungry snuffles at the empty trough, and the small bright eyes watched through the cracks to see if Breeze had brought any food. The hound stopped to smell a fresh mole-hill, then walked leisurely on, and Breeze left the hog to follow him and see what the premises held.

Weeds narrowed the path. Once a lizard barely got out of his way. He must watch out for snakes. The morning was sunlit, sweet with fragrance that the sun, already high up in the glittering sky, wrung out of the shrubbery; but everything was so silent.

As Breeze went toward the still shadowy garden, with its boxwood borders and bird pool and old gray sun-dial, Big Sue, unexpectedly, came out of the side door in the Big House and behind her came April, who had held him last night. Without a word April strode off in a different direction, but Big Sue called to Breeze that she'd walk with him. Going in front she led him past flowers of every color, bushes of all leaves, telling him about them as she went. Years ago the garden had been stiff and trimmed, and the shrubbery had grown in close-cut bushes between straight box hedges. But time had changed everything. Uncle Isaac was old and deaf, and instead of staying home at night and resting so he could work at the roses and keep them from running wild and getting all tangled up with vines, he ran around to birth-night suppers and cut up like a boy. She pointed out boughs that reached across the path.

Clumps of paper-white narcissus, not waiting for spring, bloomed in the wrong places. White patches of sweet alyssum crept right up to the edge of the box-wood borders, the delicate perfume making the air honey-sweet. But it was out of place, and ought to be cut away. Uncle Isaac was too trifling to be the gardener now.

Tall tangled heads of grass were in some of the beds, and a bold vine whose topmost branch was gay with orange-scarlet bells swayed from the tip of a magnolia tree. The bright bunch of blossoms nodded at Breeze with a slow persistence, sunlight filled each flower cup, and its hot scent streamed out in the soft wind. There was something queer in its steady silent bowing. A light sound hissed through the stiff magnolia leaves whenever the mild wind freshened, but the magnolia tree held every crisp, brown-lined leaf still. Unmoved. The light stir of the morning's breeze could not move that tall dark tree, which was splashed here and there with over-ripe blossoms.

"Son, is you see de way dat trumpet vine is a-wavin' at you? Better bow back at em!"

Breeze did bow the best he knew how, but Big Sue laughed.

"When you bow, you must pull you' foot." She showed him how to do it.

She reached up and broke off a half-open bud, and tearing its creamy petals apart showed Breeze how they closed over a core of gold. She showed him the sun-dial marking the time of day. A spattering of water called them to see the birds enjoying a bird bath; a flock of pigeons dropped with a slanting flight, then hurried off. A tinkling of sheep bells told that a flock browsed peacefully not far away. When a blue-jay perched overhead with a screech, Big Sue shook a fat

fist at him. "Git off," she scolded. "You don't know
to-day's Friday. Is you forgot you is due to tote a stick
o' wood to Satan? Git on to torment, lessen you done
been dere a'ready dis mornin'!" A streak of scarlet
flashed where a cardinal darted across a bright path of
sunlight as a hammer banged down on a nail. Old deaf
Uncle Isaac was mending a broken place in the fence,
and talking to himself. His deaf ears had not heard
Big Sue and Breeze, and his murmured talk droned on
out of his stammering lips.

"Po' old Uncle Isaac!" Big Sue sighed. "When e
can' talk to de livin' e talks to de dead. His eyes is so
full up wid speerits right now, he don' see we. You
kin see speerits, too, son, enty? You' ma said so."

Before Breeze had time to deny it, all of a sudden
she turned on him and gave a sharp cry. "Looka here,
boy! You been a-steppin' in my tracks! I know it!
A' awful pain is come right on de top o' my head!
You done it! You needn' shake you' head. I was
feelin' good when I come in dis flowers yard. Git a
stick! Now broke em in two an' cross 'em! Put
em in one o' you' tracks! Git me shet o' dis pain! I
declare to Gawd, dat's a provokin' t'ing you done! I
was feelin' so good too. If you try to conjure me, I'll
kill you!"

Breeze denied it humbly. He had not meant to step
in her tracks. He didn't even know it would work her
harm. When he had placed the broken sticks as she
bade him, she spoke more kindly, and warned him to be
careful never to step in anybody's tracks.

Once she missed and stepped in Uncle Isaac's tracks
and it gave him a terrible tooth-ache. She had to cross
twenty sticks before she got him rid of it. Poor Uncle!
They'd better not go near him. He was on the side of
the garden where spirits stayed. Let him talk to them.

"My head is done better now, t'ank Gawd," she sighed, adding that she'd ask Uncle Isaac to supper to-night. He could tell so many funny stories. He could explain, exactly, why the grass is green and the sky is blue. Why the sun shines in the daytime and the moon and stars shine at night. He knew what the thunder said when it spoke. He could whistle the first tune the wind ever whistled. One time, the night was a great big black giant that ran round the sun, trying and trying to catch the day. Uncle Isaac said so and he knew more about the first men and women who ever lived than Adam and Eve ever dreamed of. He got it all at first-hand, by word of mouth, from Africa, where the world itself was born and a terrible black God made all men black. Big Sue's narrow black eyes softened, her voice grew mild, her fat fingers toyed with a rose. She said Uncle Isaac knew a strange tale about the high tide and the evening star, and another about why the morning clouds eclipse the moon. They were pretty tales, all about love, but Breeze was too small to hear them.

IX

SATURDAY AFTERNOON

SOON after the noon bell rang on Saturday, Big Sue gave Breeze a panful of dinner, cooked on the hearth where a sleepy fire nodded and dozed over a few chunks of hard oak wood.

"Hurry an' eat, son, I want you to go wid me to de sto'. I got a lot to buy, an' I'm scared to come home by myself after dark. To-morrow's Sunday. I got to buy a kerosene an' some rations. I'm gwine to git you some clothes, too."

As he followed Big Sue down the long avenue Breeze was careful not to step in her tracks. Outside the gate, the road ran through a gloomy forest, where tall pines and live-oaks stood among magnolias and cedars and fragrant myrtle thickets. Big Sue talked about the country as they walked on.

The old road, now dwindled to this narrow dim way, was once a fine highway. Important gentlemen and lovely ladies used to drive over it in fine carriages drawn by fiery horses. The gold and silver on the harness used to blind people's eyes the same as summer lightning. Men who had run the whole country had gone along here many a time, right where the trees sprung tall in the old dead ruts. Thorny yupon branches reached out and scratched Breeze on the arm, trying to tear the holes in his shirt bigger than they were. Big Sue called out greetings, for numbers of black people were walking the same way. Some in groups. Some walking by twos and threes. All dressed in their Sunday best, going to the Landing.

The boat stopped on its way up and down the river twice a week, bringing supplies and mail from the town in the river's mouth to the shabby little stores that squatted along the water's edge. This row of dilapidated houses was strung close together, and scrawny, mule-bitten hackberry trees, some with hollows clear through their bodies, stood in front of the wide-open doors, making hitching-posts for the restless beasts that had to be tethered. Many of the mules and oxen stood free to go if they liked, but they waited, dozing, switching flies, the oxen chewing cuds.

Flashy colors of hats and ribbons, gay headkerchiefs and curiously fashioned dresses wove in and out as crowds of black girls and women tramped up and down the path that ran from one shop to another. Sunday shoes, dulled with gray dust, made a cheerful squeaking as they blotted out tracks made in the soft dirt by bare feet.

Some of the men were tall, with bold strong faces. Brawny muscles of powerful arms and legs could be seen bulging under faded patched shirts and overalls.

Droll shapes of merry laughter mixed with greeting voices. There were graceful bows and handshakes and kindly inquiries. Old men, who might have had great-grandchildren, tottered about importantly on uncertain legs, bantering the girls with words that belied the white hairs bristling from their withered ears. White wool peeped through their tattered wool hats. Rheumatism spitefully twinged their joints and put a hitch in every gay step. But lively spirits cheered their shriveled flesh and lightened clouded eyes. Laughter deepened the creases in old wrinkled faces, and swelled the tendons in ropy wilted throats.

[90]

Uncle Isaac and Uncle Bill sat, side by side, on a box outside the post-office, chewing tobacco and spitting with calm delight. After each bit of close talk, Uncle Isaac broke into sudden fits of high cracked laughter, and pounded Uncle Bill gleefully on the back. He was old and deaf, yet he took a full part in the pattern of Saturday's joy. Breeze wished he could hear one of the stories that made him laugh so, but he knew by Uncle Bill's bashful look that those stories should never have been told at all.

"How's you' rheumatism?" Uncle Bill shouted, to change the subject.

"E's better. A lot better dan e been. I been totin' a' oak-gall in my pocket 'stead o' dem buckeyes. I b'lieve de oak-gall is stronger. Seems to me like I kin git 'roun' more better since I made de change."

Uncle Bill looked doubtful and his head shook a little, but he spat thoughtfully, then yelled, "I made me a li'l' pokeberry wine, an' I tell you, suh, it's a fine t'ing! A fine t'ing! I ain' hardly been bothered wid any kind o' misery since I been drinkin' em."

Uncle Isaac's mild old eyes watched every word, for they had to help his deaf ears understand. "You say elderberry wine?" he queried.

"No! Pokeberry! You know pokeberry, enty? Elderberry wine wouldn' do rheumatism no good. My Gawd, no," Uncle Bill answered, laughing at such a mistake. "You ain' turned to no lady, is yuh?"

"No, t'ank Gawd!" Uncle Isaac screeched. "If it wan't fo' my crippled knee, I wouldn' feel no more'n forty years old. No, suh. Not a bit more'n forty. April's gwine git a rattlesnake to make me some snake tea. Dat's a good medicine."

"E might be fo' true," Uncle Bill agreed. "I ever did hear say so. But my stomach is too weak to stand sich a strongness. Rattlesnake tea be de same as con'trated lye! Better mind how you projec' wid em, Uncle!''

"Sho'! Sho'! I'm old enough to know medicine ain' somet'ing fo' play wid. I ain' no chillen, son. I been in dis world a good while.''

The mail was not open yet, and Big Sue waited for it all to be given out so the storekeeper, who was postmaster too, could let her have what she wanted. Breeze stood close beside her, watching the black people who loitered and laughed and talked, as they crowded into the dirty crank-sided store. Each man invariably paid her a compliment, such as, "I declare to Gawd, Miss Big Sue, you look sweet," or, "It do my eyes good to see you." Uncle Bill said, "I'm gwine buy you a treat soon as de mail is finished."

The men took off their hats and pulled a forelock and drew one foot back to make their bows. The women made easy graceful curtsies. Big Sue whispered to Breeze that he must pull his foot and bow too. Look at Uncle Bill and Uncle Isaac. He must learn manners. But Breeze hadn't the heart to try here where so many would see him.

Outside, near the road, Brudge, a black boy as ragged as Breeze, but apparently happy, parched peanuts in a round, black, fire-heated oven. Over and over he patiently turned the sooty cylinder with a black iron handle, all the time chattering and grinning, as from time to time he dished out paper sacks-full, not only for the children, but for grown men and women who bought them to eat right then. The smell of the peanuts was delicious, but it was almost smothered by the scent of fried fish, which came from a shack near by.

Big Sue said it was a restaurant, and Breeze was craning his neck to see inside when April took him by the hand and led him in, while Big Sue, laughing as she came, walked behind them. The afternoon light, aided by a large kerosene lamp, whose glass shade was dim with smoke, shone on the white oil-cloth that covered several small tables. Big Sue said, "Set down, Breeze," and he dropped into a chair by a table. He ate big thick slices of store-bought baker's bread that the boat had brought from town and squares of fried fish that Big Sue said were caught in the sea by regular fishermen.

April had a powerful look. He was very tall, his forehead high, his mouth straight and wide, his bony chin and cheek-bones set forward. He left most of his good bread broken all up but uneaten on the greasy tin plate.

"Whyn't you eat you' victuals, April?" Big Sue asked him.

"I ain' so hongry, not dis evenin'," he answered, smiling and with his glowing eyes on Breeze.

Reaching a long hand down in his pants pocket, he took out a piece of paper money and gave it to her. "Buy de boy some clothes, Big Sue. Feed em good, too. I want em to grow."

Big Sue took it and told Breeze to go outside and watch the people until she came.

Some of the women and girls were fat and funny-looking, but others were slender, with well-formed bodies. All of them looked at Breeze searchingly, some slyly, but most of them with brazen eyes. Many of the older women were smoking small clay pipes, and when they laughed their teeth showed brown, stained with tobacco.

Young men strutted past them, with hats cocked on one side of their heads. Some caught the girls' hands and held them and offered to treat them. Bottles of coca-cola and bags of candy rivaled peanuts and the

[93]

small sweet-cakes, just come on the boat from town in a big wooden box that opened like a trunk. As Breeze gazed, his mouth watered at the sight of so many good things to eat.

Big Sue kept talking to April, who stood strong as an oak, his eyes riveted on her face. She looked uneasily at the door when he took her hand. As she drew it away he laughed, then spat far outside and left her.

Pulling up her skirt, Big Sue got a handkerchief out of her underneath pocket, and untying the knot in its corner, added the piece of paper money to what it already held. She gave Breeze two pennies. "Go buy you a cake, son," she bade him. Then she halted him with, "Wait, gi' me back dem pennies. Here's a nickel. Git t'ree. I want one o' dem cakes myself."

Forgetting his fear in his eagerness for the sweet-cake, Breeze ran into the store next door. Every man and woman who had come to do serious purchasing carried a crocus sack into which the things were crammed: groceries, cloth, shoes, were all crowded in on one another. Those who bought kerosene had it in quart glass bottles tied with strings around the necks.

Breeze had never seen so many red sweaters in his life. They were in all shapes and sizes and conditions. Some quite new. Some patched and faded. Some with rolled collars. Some with frayed elbows. They were worn with blue overalls and khaki breeches, white aprons and full skirts and short skimpy dresses. Old and young wore them jauntily, as a sort of badge of Saturday's joy.

The doorway was hidden as the happy people pressed in and out of the store. The sidewalk, thick flaked with bits of white oyster shell, became trashy with empty peanut hulls, and scraps of tissue-paper torn from candy kisses.

Everybody looked happy and light-hearted. Breeze envied them their easy friendly ways, their gaiety. As he stood apart, looking on, listening to them, he felt more homesick than ever. Even the sweet-cake, that dropped rich crumbs on the floor with every bite he took, couldn't make him forget that he was a stranger here.

The postmaster called out Big Sue's name, and there was a dead silence, then much laughter. "Who? Big Sue Goodwine? My Gawd! Who dat wrote she a letter?" Breeze was sent in a hurry to call her to come get it. There was much chaffing. "It's de sheriff, Big Sue. Dat's who." And, "You got so much beaux you can' member who is home an' who's gone off."

When Big Sue stumbled in half out of breath, they called out to her, "Hurry up an' read em. Le' we hear de news!"

But Big Sue sucked her teeth and said, "I don' tell ev'ybody my business. Not me!" She took the letter and put it deep down in her apron pocket where not a soul could even see it.

The mail was all given out at last, and the buying was done. The threads of color unraveled as the negroes left the stores and walked away down the road, some young couples hand in hand. Big Sue was among the last to start buying, for she had spent the time talking with her friends. She waited until the store was almost empty, then she chose a pair of pants and two shirts for Breeze, holding the garments up to his body to get the right size. She gave him the package to hold, saying, "Walk roun' an' look at de store. I want to git my letter read."

The store was almost clear of people, but its air was still thick with the acrid smell of hot sweaty bodies. Breeze knew few of the things offered for sale, for the

[95]

rickety shelves were crammed with much besides cloth and shoes. He recognized the gay paper-covered tin cans of salmon, but the little bottles of cologne labeled "Hoyt's German" were strangers to him. He couldn't read, so he couldn't tell that paper covers on a big batch of china jars claimed in emphatic black words that they held a cure for the darkness of dusky skins, or that the few bottles left on a shelf that was lately full would straighten the kinks out of crinkly hair.

Heavy sacks of green coffee berries were piled high between paunchy barrels of moist brown sugar, and smaller, neater barrels of pure white flour. Bolts of scarlet flannel waited to make garments that would keep the cold from old painful knees and shoulders. Rolls of gay outing and checked homespun for dresses were out on the counter. Piles of strong brogans were only a few steps away from boxes of Sunday shoes. Kits of chewing tobacco stood near a lot of little cloth bags full of Bull Durham. Cakes with pink and white icing, and red-striped sticks of candy were under a glass case along with black and white ball thread and needles and fish-hooks.

The big kerosene lamp, tied with a wire to a rafter overhead, filled the room with a pale yellow flare of light that showed the floor, whitened with corn-meal, and spattered with stains of greasy salt that fell on it whenever fat chunks of cured hog meat were taken out of the barrels and passed over the counter to the customers.

When at last nobody else was in the store, Big Sue reached down in her pocket and got out her letter. "Please, suh, read em fo' me. I'm ravin' to know who's wrote me a letter," she asked. The storekeeper was a kind-looking white man with blue eyes and red skin, and a mouth stained at both corners with tobacco. He wiped his hand on his trousers, then took the letter and tore it open and took out a single sheet covered with pencil writing.

"It's from Silas Locust. He's your own husband, isn't he?"

"Great Gawd!" Big Sue fairly panted. She put the fat hand up to her breast and held it there for a minute before she could get breath enough to say, "Do hurry, suh. Tell me wha' dat nigger is writin' to me 'bout."

The letter said Silas was in Wilmington, North Carolina. He was a preacher now, and married to a big fine-looking yellow woman, who had three nice children for him. But lately his mind kept turning back to Big Sue and Blue Brook Plantation. He wanted to see them. He was coming home, in short. Big Sue repeated the words "in short" two or three times. She seemed to have no feeling against Silas at all, or against the fine-looking yellow woman he had married.

When the storekeeper handed the letter back to her, saying, "You may as well get married, too, now that Silas has a wife," she gave a shamefaced giggle at the idea and said she couldn't marry, not with a living husband. The storekeeper said she needn't laugh, she'd do it yet, and she owned that she had thought about it a little.

The last time she went on an excursion to town, a man who had a nice restaurant took her to ride in a painted hack, and said he'd buy her an organ if she'd marry him. They could run the restaurant together. (She giggled again.) But now she was glad she hadn't done it, since Silas was a preacher, and he'd be a-coming to see her, in short. Her sides shook, and her round eyes rolled, until a serious thought came to her mind, and she inquired, soberly, "Did Silas say if he's Runnin'

Water Baptist, or a Stale Water?" The storekeeper said Silas hadn't mentioned either one, and Big Sue pondered over it until the white man asked her if Silas came back what she'd do with all her other beaux. Jake and Uncle Bill and Uncle Isaac, too, and what about the foreman, April?

"Great Gawd! Do hush!" Big Sue shouted with clamorous laughter, as each name was mentioned. "You make me too shame. I don' care nothin' 'bout none o' dem old mens! Not me! An' April just got me to fetch dis li'l' boy here to Blue Brook. E's April's own, by a 'oman on Sandy Island."

But the storekeeper was in earnest, and he said, "If I were you, whether Silas ever comes home or not, I'd leave April alone. Leah will get you if you don't. You've forgotten her gums are blue, haven't you? She'll bite you some day, and what will happen then? You'll die, and those white folks will have to hunt another cook when they come to Blue Brook to shoot ducks. Better be careful. Blue gums are worse than a rattlesnake bite. Leah's not going to stand outside that restaurant and see you eating bread and fish with her husband inside, without doing something about it. I heard her say so a while ago."

Big Sue tossed her head. "Humph! I ain' scared o' Leah. Fat as e is, I could squeeze em to deat' in one hand." She opened and clenched her powerful fists. Years of kneading dough had given strength to her thick wrists and round fingers, for all the soft cushion of flesh that covered them.

It was late and Big Sue and Breeze took a short-cut by a path that ran through the woods, then by a smooth planted field where new oats sprouted green tips and covered the earth. They looked tender against the dark even green of the trees. The evening light was thin and

[98]

misty. Shadows and colors and forms all melted into a cool pale dusk.

Big Sue warned, "Watch out for snakes, son. I can' smell good. A fresh cold is got my nose kinder stop up. A cold ever did hinder my smellin'. I must go stand round de stables a while to-morrow. Dat'll broke up a cold quicker'n anyt'ing else."

X

THE BARNYARD

EARLY Sunday morning Uncle Isaac came to ask Big Sue for an old worn-out sieve. Uncle Bill was having a bad time. Hags rode all the horses at the barnyard every night God sent. Every morning the manes and tails were so tangled up it took Uncle Bill hours to get them greased and smoothed out again.

Red sunsets promised a killing frost and the white folks would be likely to come any time after that. Bill had the horses' coats all rubbed down like satin, every fetlock trimmed, the bridles and saddles in good order, but the hags were deviling him to death. Big Sue said she had already given Uncle Bill a string of red pepper pods and a straw broom too, to hang up on the stable door. If they didn't stop the hags, what good could a sieve do?

Uncle explained to her how hags are fools about counting things. They won't go inside a door until they count the boards on the door-facing, and the nails, then they'd count all the pepper pods and the straws in the broom, and have time enough left before day to ride the horses, and plait their manes and tails. But a sieve would stop them, for by the time all the holes in the sieve were counted, those hags would be weary and ready to go home and rest.

Big Sue gave him the sieve and he invited Breeze to walk with him to the barnyard where Uncle Bill had a nice little milking goat to give him. Breeze could break

Uncle Bill had tried to teach the chickens to sleep in a fowl-house, but the younger ones would slip out here and roost in these fig trees. Uncle Isaac pointed to a handful of white bloody feathers that lay scattered over the grass. An owl caught the best white pullet last night. She would roost in the top of the fig tree, no matter how often she was shooed out. Foolish chicken. But Bill would get that owl. Sooner or later he'd get him. Bill was a dangerous man to cross. Uncle Isaac was emphatic.

Putting a kind hand on Breeze's shoulder, he said, "You ax Bill to le' you go wid him an' l'arn how to call a owl. Bill kin call crows and wild turkeys an' alligators too. E'll larn you all dat, son, if you speak a good word for him to you' Cun Big Sue. Bill is raven 'bout dat lady. Pure raven."

"Do hush you' fool talk, Uncle!" Big Sue chided, with a pleased laugh. "I ain' got Uncle Bill to study 'bout."

The great square barns were filled with corn and hay. A long narrow building cut into many stalls made a shelter for the mules and horses. As they opened the wide heavy gate, Uncle Bill came out of the barn door with a pitchfork full of hay on his shoulder. He was lining out two lines of a hymn to sing, but broke off in a laugh of delight when he spied them.

"Why, Miss Big Sue! Great Gawd! I too glad fo' see you! Lawd! Look a' de li'l' boy." He laughed again with pleasure.

"I got de sieve fo' de hags, Bill, an' I bring Breeze an' Big Sue to hear you talk to de animals an' de chickens. All two is got a fresh cold. Take 'em inside de stables first."

Uncle Bill invited them to come look inside the stables. "I got 'em all clean, an' full o' de nicest pine

[103]

straw beddin' ever was. I'm too sorry. Dey wouldn' help you' cold, not a bit, but come look at 'em, anyhow.''

"Whe's de run-at cow?" Big Sue asked.

Uncle Bill laughed at her fear. The run-at cow was in the pasture—she needn't be scared. He wouldn't let anything hurt her.

In the long row of stables, bars of sunlight shining through the cracks were blurred with dust raised by hens, roosters and little chickens, scratching vigorously in the crisp dry straw. The cocks were saying brave things, the hens sang contentedly as they looked for the grains of corn and oats hidden under wisps of fodder and hay and straw.

"Scratch, chillen, scratch," Uncle Bill encouraged them. "De mules will come in to dinner befo' long, den you-all 'll have to go home."

"Make dem go home now," Big Sue requested. "I wan' see how you rules dem, so I kin rule Breeze."

He hesitated. "It ain' quite time yet. De mules don' come in till noon."

"We won' be here den," she persisted.

"How come you sends de chickens home when de mules come?" Breeze asked.

"So dey won't git trompled under foot, son. De hens is greedy, an' a mule's foot is blind. Whilst de mules is chawin' an' droppin' grains, dey feet'll step on a hen same as on pine straw."

"Send de chickens home now," Big Sue asked again with such a warm smile that he put down his fork full of hay and, standing in the stable door, waved his big arms and shouted:

"Shoo outa here, chickens! Git on home! Be quick as you kin! I hate to git a stick atter you to-day! Dis is Sunday! Git on out an' go home!"

The chickens became terribly excited. Some of them

huddled in the straw, trying to hide, others cackled and ran. The hens with little chickens clucked briskly and hurried away, for Uncle Bill's face was hard until every feather was out of sight.

The straw lay still. The dust whirling in the sunlight took its time and dawdled. Stable flies, with shiny wings and short fat bodies, strutted out in buzzing circles. Uncle Bill's practised eyes spied a scarlet comb away under a trough, far back in a corner.

"Who dat hidin'?" he demanded sternly, and a shamefaced young cockerel cackled out in terror.

"Didn' I told you to go home?" Uncle Bill asked him. "You ain' know yet you got to mind me? I ain' got time to be foolin' wid such as you. No, suh! I'm too busy."

The poor frightened creature made a few weak gaggles and tried his best to hide.

"You' head will be chop off to-morrow. I'd do it now if it wa'n't Sunday. Dem I can' rule, I kills. I don' mean to mistreat nothin', Miss Big Sue, but I got to be strict."

He sighed as he came out and closed the door behind him. "Dat's a fine young rooster. I was gwine to keep him for seed. I sho' hates to kill him."

"I wouldn' kill him. Not dat nice rooster. You got to scuse a chicken sometimes."

"I done already scused em. Dat's how come e's so spoilt. E's ruint. If I let him live now e'd keep me worried all de time," Uncle Bill contended.

"Fetch em to me an' I'll fry em nice fo' you!" Big Sue offered so kindly that Uncle Bill declared, "Now, dat makes me feel a lot better."

"Show us you' hogs." Big Sue smiled sweetly. "I wan' to see if you got one as fine as my Jeems."

"I got fine ones, but deys all out in de pasture."

"You kin call dem in, enty?" she persisted, and Uncle Bill gave in with a happy laugh.

First he went by the open door and got a few ears of corn, then on to the edge of the short slope, down by the water, where he drew a deep breath that filled his great lungs. He gave a loud mellow call: "Melia! Oh, Melia!" Before the echoes had died away, to the right and the left was a hurried swishing of water, an eager grunting, the sucking sound of quick feet lifted out of mud.

"Dey's a-comin'!" he laughed, then he called again, "Come on, Melia! Make haste, gal!"

His old face softened as they came in sight, crowds of them. The little pigs squealed with delight as they hurried to get to him. The older ones moved more slowly, for their bodies were heavy, but all the time they grunted encouragement to their children. Uncle Bill's big hand let a few white grains of corn trickle through his fingers and fall near his feet. Their quick eyes saw, and running forward they snapped up the bits greedily, pushing one another, crowding, sniffing at Uncle Bill's dusty brogan shoes, hunting for more.

Uncle Bill lifted the wide sagging gate and opened it wide. "Come on een!" he said, and the gluttonous crowd trooped inside. When every one had passed he threw them whole ears on the ground. As they scrunched the grains and smacked over them, he reached down and patted one on the head, scratched another's back with a cob, said some kind thing to another. It was plain he loved them.

"Dese is my chillen," he said to Breeze, with a kind smile filling his soft black eyes.

"Dey is fine chillen, too," Big Sue praised them. "Uncle Bill's hogs is de finest in dis whole country. I was dat proud when he brought me Jeems, yonder in my pen, home. Uncle Bill raises fine hogs an' nobody can' cure hams, or make sausages to taste like de ones he fixes. Nobody."

"Well, I tries my best."

It was a wonderful sight to Breeze. The shade between the fence and the water held hogs of every shape and size. Huge and black, with soft silky hair, they lolled, resting, panting, feeding their young.

"Git up, Ellen, an' come here," Uncle Bill called out to one of them. "Le' Miss Big Sue see you an' you' chillen good." The words were hardly out of his mouth before a great beast roused and lazily got to her feet and walked toward him, followed by her children. Uncle Bill took an ear of corn from his pocket, shelled a few grains and tossed them over the ground, which made the pigs come faster.

"Po' Ellen! E's blind. I had to stick e eyes out. Lawd! I did hate to do it!"

"How come so?" Big Sue asked him.

"Ellen would catch de chickens an' eat em. A deer couldn' beat Ellen runnin'. A hen couldn' git away f'om em nohow. Ellen would swallow down a mother an' whole brood o' biddies quicker'n I could swallow a pint o' raw oysters. It's de Gawd's truth. E'd eat de mammy an' all. I had to hinder em somehow. I didn' wan' to kill a fine hog like Ellen, so I hottened a wire till it was red an' jobbed it in all two o' e eyes. Ellen can' see how to run chickens down, not no mo'. Po' ol' gal!"

"How come some pigs is different f'om de rest?" Breeze asked. "How come some is red an' dey ma is black?"

Uncle Bill and Big Sue exchanged smiles. "May as well say, Uncle Bill. Boy-chillen has to know sich t'ings."

The old man smiled behind his rough hand and said, "De ma's name is Melia, son."

Uncle Isaac drew nearer to hear, and Uncle Bill told how Melia had been the apple of his eye since the day she was born. He planned to have her raise the finest litters ever born on this plantation. But Melia was a head-strong person. She had a mind of her own.

Uncle Isaac chuckled and murmured, "Dat's de Gawd's truth!"

Jack, the boar heading the herd, would take a prize anywhere. He had tremendous size, yet he was so well-bred that in spite of his bulk his skin was smooth, his hair soft and fine. He had every mark of a perfect Poland-China.

Uncle Isaac agreed emphatically. "Yes, e sho' is. Sho'! Sho'!"

But when Melia grew up she would have nothing to do with Jack. She didn't like him. Uncle Bill tried to encourage her to do her duty, but Jack wasn't to her taste, and that's all there was to it. No amount of coaxing could make her change.

Last spring Uncle Bill made up his mind Melia would have to be killed. He hated to do it. The very thought cut at his heart-strings. But there was no use to keep Melia unless she had children. He'd have killed her then, but she was too large to be killed in hot weather. Her ham couldn't be cured properly, and so she was left to be made into meat this winter.

Uncle Isaac broke out laughing. Lord, Bill was a doleful soul when he fixed on Melia's death. Uncle Bill nodded:

"It's de Gawd's truth! I pure had to go off an' pray, I was so fretted over Melia! My prayers was answered, too. Dey sho' was!" He said soon after his sorrowful decision, he went to the pasture one morning and found a strange sight: the pasture fence had been broken down, and a low-down, ornery, red razor-back hog was inside. He was dirty and lean and ugly. His red hair was stiff and coarse and caked up with mud. He was a sneaky, no-mannered beast. But Melia liked him.

Before many moons Melia had a fine litter of pigs. Red pigs, that took their color from the father Melia chose for them, a scrubby, ugly no-account hog that came from God knows where.

"Dey's fine pigs, dough. Dey's out-growin' all de rest. Melia's a case. A heavy case." His proud chuckle ended with a sigh. "I reckon I'm too easy on Melia. She played a bad trick on me. I know I ought not to let em do so. But I'm gittin' old an' soft-hearted, an' Melia knows it. Melia's got too much sense. God ought not to 'a' made Melia a hog. No. Dat was a mistake. Ought I to 'a' killed Melia, Uncle?"

"No. No," Uncle Isaac said gently. "You couldn' be hard, not on Melia. Melia had a right to choose her man. Ev'y 'oman ought to could do dat, enty?"

Big Sue laughed and curtsied good-by, after thanking Uncle Bill for showing Breeze the barnyard creatures, and Uncle Bill and Uncle Isaac both pulled back a foot and bowed and touched their bald foreheads, where forelocks should have been.

With a happy heart Breeze followed Big Sue on the path that swung along the edge of an open field, close to tall pines whose dark plumy tops lifted high above the red ripened leaves fluttering on bushes at their feet. The dogwood was crimson; haws and wild plum thickets gay scarlet. Partridges whistled. Across a reaped field larks rose and called out plaintively to one another from the stubble. High vines of black muskadines perfumed the air. Persimmon trees bent with fruit waiting for frost to make it mellow and sweet. The sun beat down hot, but summer had given way to fall.

The road to the Quarters, strewn with fallen leaves that almost hid its ruts and holes, ran past sugar-cane patches where green blades rustled noisily over purple stalks. Sweet potatoes cracked the earth under vines shading the long rows. Pindars were blooming. Okra bushes were full of creamy red-hearted blossoms and pointed green pods. Butter-bean vines clambered over the hand-split clapboard garden fences that kept pigs and chickens out of small enclosures, where wide-leaved collards waited for frost to make them crisp, and scarlet tomatoes spotted straggly broken-down bushes.

Birds chirruped everywhere. The fields murmured in the soft wind. The Quarters, although made up of houses that tottered and leaned crank-sided, seethed with noise and life.

A large wagon, drawn by two mules, and with new planks laid across its high body for seats, rolled by, filled with church-goers. A flutter of hand-waves and a chorus of "good mawnin's" greeted Big Sue as she stopped to let it pass.

"How come you ain' gwine to church to-day, Big Sue?" somebody called out.

"I ain' ne Still-water Baptist, gal! I wouldn' go to hear no Still-water preacher. No, ma'am!" she answered. "Jedus was baptized in de River Jurdan, an' dat's runnin' water. Still water gits stale an' scummy too quick. It can' wash away sin! No! Sin needs runnin' water."

The Quarters' houses, long, low, shabby buildings, had two front doors apiece. Each house sheltered two families, a huge chimney in the middle marking the division. Moss adorned the gray shingles of the sagging roofs. Steps were worn thin. Rust reddened the old hand-wrought hinges of the leaning doors and gave a creak to wry window shutters.

Maum Hannah lived in the house where she and her mother and her grandmother were born. As they approached it a miscellany of goats and chickens and pigs and dogs and half-clothed little children scampered away from the door-step. The door was ajar, but a chorus of voices called out:

"Maum Hannah ain' home. E's yonder down de street!"

"Come look inside de door at Maum Hannah's nice house," Big Sue pushed the door wider open with a stick, so Breeze could see. The huge chimney had big strong black andirons, where heavy logs of wood were slowly being charred in two by a sleepy fire. All kinds of pots sat around on the clean white sand of the hearth. One pot on a pot-hook that reached out from the chimney's back had steam spurting from under its cover, filling the room with a savory smell. Big Sue sniffed. "Dat goat-meat stew is seasoned mighty high," she said. "De floor was scoured wid mighty strong lye soap, too."

The thing that took Breeze's eye was the tiny black child that sat on the hearth warming its bare feet on the naked sooty pots. He knew it was Emma, but if he had not seen her before he could never have told if she were a girl or a boy, her small features were so sharp and her clothes so shapeless.

"Looka, Emma!" Big Sue called out with a laugh, and the child's small head perched on one side, one round black eye narrowed and a broad grin showed her two rows of milk-white teeth.

"You's Maum Hannah's heart-string, enty, Emma?"
But Emma didn't answer a word.
Big Sue said Emma's mother was dead and she had
[111]

no daddy, but she was worth a lot, for she had power to cure sickness and sorrow by the touch of her hand. That was because she had never looked on her daddy's face. Somebody stepped over her when she was a baby; that was why she had never grown much. She'd never grow, although she sat there on the hearth roasting potatoes and eating them all day long.

All children loved to come here and sit inside Maum Hannah's chimney on the end of a log. Big Sue used to sit there and watch Maum Hannah put ash-cake in the ashes to cook, and sweet potatoes to roast. The fire never went out in Maum Hannah's fireplace. It's bad luck for a fire to die in a house and this fire had never gone out altogether since it was first started by Maum Hannah's great-grandpa, who was brought from across the sea to be a slave. The first houses ever built here were sheds to keep the fires from the rain and wind, for nobody had any matches in those days. The fires that burned in all the Quarter houses came from that same first fire that had burned for years and years. It was a lot older than anybody on the plantation. Big Sue's fire was a piece of it. It burned hotter than match fire. Steadier too. It's unlucky to start a new fire with a match. Breeze must learn how to bank the live coals with ashes every night, so the next morning they can be uncovered and started into a blaze. If the fire goes out, borrow a start from Maum Hannah, or one of the neighbors who have the old fire.

Maum Hannah's cabin was very clean. Newspapers were pasted all over the walls, the dark naked rafters almost hidden by fringed papers that swung from the barrel hoops on which they were tied. A few split hickory chairs sat near the small pine table, a water-shelf beside the door held a wooden bucket and a long-handled gourd. The wide boards of the floor were scrubbed until they were almost white, and a string of egg shells by the chimney dangled in the draught. They'd been hung there to make the hens lay.

Between the two rows of dingy old houses that squatted low under the great oak trees the hot sunshine brought rank scents up out of the earth. Odors of pig-pens and cow-stalls and fowl-houses and goats, mixed with Hoyt's German cologne and the smell of human beings.

Children were playing around almost every door-step. Plump. Bright-eyed. Boys with loose-hanging, ripped-open trousers, their black bodies showing where shirt-fronts lay wide open. Girls with short, ragged skirts flapping around slim prancing legs. Babies cried. Tethered goats bleated. Penned pigs squealed. Men, women, some in every-day clothes, others in their Sunday best, sat on the door-steps, leaned out of windows, lolled on the bare earth, where there was sunshine. Talking. Parading. Laughing. Some of them combing and wrapping hair, others putting shoe-strings in shoes, or smoking and idling.

As Big Sue passed, she bowed or curtsied, and called out hearty good mornings that fell limpid on the lazy hum of voices.

"Whe's Maum Hannah?" Big Sue asked, and everybody pointed to the last house where an old woman sat in a chair in the yard in front of a doorway, near a group of black children playing in the dirt.

A large clean white cloth, folded into three corners, lay across her head and shaded her eyes from the sun. Her arms were crossed, and each narrow flat bare foot rested on a brick. Side by side they slept, almost hidden by the wide white apron that fell stiffly from her lap in starched folds, with corners that reached the ground.

"Maum Hannah don' trust de ground. E won't as much as let her feet sleep on it. I bet e's been awake all night, an' e's makin' up for lost time now."

Maum Hannah's face bore a strong resemblance to Uncle Isaac's. It was smoother and had smaller features, but the same rich brown tone was on the black skin. The wool that edged out from under her black headkerchief was snow-white too, but her face was almost unlined, except for the wrinkles that smiles had marked around her mouth.

The little black children stared and giggled as Big Sue went tripping forward and put both her fat hands over Maum Hannah's eyes:

"Guess who, Mauma!"

"Oh, I know you good," Maum Hannah answered. "Dis is my Big Sue. I went to sleep a-thinkin' 'bout you, gal. My mind must 'a' called you till you come."

"I declare!" Big Sue mirated. "I knowed it! I called you' name, too, in de night. Dis is de boy-chile I fetched f'om Sandy Island. I want you to tie up his palate lock. E coughs so bad at night I can' sleep."

Maum Hannah gave Breeze a warm kindly smile, and her keen black eyes, deep-set underneath her bony brow, scanned him swiftly from his head to his heels. "Lawd, son, I too glad to see you. De last time we met, you wasn' no bigger'n my hand. How come you' palate is down? I too sorry. Did you know I had to gi' you de first spankin' you ever had? Lawd, I had to pop you hard to make you holler! I hope you is hard to make cry, yet."

The little black children playing in the dirt around her forgot all about their games, so engrossed were they in Breeze, and what Maum Hannah said. They forgot their manners, too, until she prompted them.

"Yunnuh speak to you' Cousin Big Sue. Git up!

[114]

Stan' up straight an' pull you' foot an' bow nice! Dis li'l' boy is yunnuh cousin, too. E come f'om over de river. Tell him good mawnin'. Gawd bless him!''

There was great scrambling and giggling, and many shy ''good mawnin's.'' The sleek bodies were half-clad, but the whiteness of teeth, and brightness of eyes made up for lack of garments.

Maum Hannah's own teeth were strong and sound, and set in deep blue gums which stressed their yellow tinge. The cane stem of a rank-smelling pipe showed above the top of her apron pocket.

''Lawd, you' pipe do smell pleasant!'' Big Sue sighed. ''But looka my li'l' boy. Who does e favor?''

Maum Hannah's warm wrinkled hand gently lifted Breeze's chin so the sun could shine full on his face. ''Dis boy is de very spit o' April. Gawd bless em, all two!''

Breeze felt that her wise old eyes took account of everything he was. No secret could be hidden from them.

''I glad you got a li'l' boy-chile fo' raise. I too love boy-chillen myself, even if dey does bring most of de trouble what's een dis world. My old mammy used to say ev'y boy-chile ought to be killed soon as it's born.''

''I ruther have boy-chillen dan gal-chillen,'' Big Sue said. ''But I know good and well boy-chillen does bring most o' de misery dat's een dis world.''

Maum Hannah nodded sorrowfully, as if she weighed Big Sue's words, then she spoke slowly:

''I dunno how come mek so.

''Gawd mus' be makes boy-chillen and trouble, all two, one time.

''Eby 'oman hab joy when e buth one.

''Eby gal hab joy when e love one.

''Dey ain' see misery hide behime joy.

[115]

"Till de misery grow.

"Grow big till e choke de joy!

"Till e bust de 'oman heart open.

"Boy-chillen brings most o' de misery dat's een dis worl'.

"Boy-chillen!"

"Dat's de Gawd's truth, Maum Hannah! I know so. I was so crazy 'bout my Lijah, yonder to Fluridy, an' e run off an' left me when e wasn't much higher'n dis same boy-chile."

"How's Lijah when you heard las'?" Maum Hannah inquired.

"Fine! Fine as kin be. E sent me a' answer to say e's de baddest man at de town whe' e stay."

"Dat's nice. I glad to hear good news f'om Lijah. But e better not be too rash. No. When you write em back tell em I say don' git so bad e can' rule hisself."

Big Sue laughed.

"I'll sho' do it. I'm gwine git a letter wrote to him as soon as Uncle Bill has time to come by my house an' do em."

Maum Hannah raised her eyes to Big Sue's face and laughed. "Git de letter wrote to you' boy, but don' tarry too long wid de writin'. Gi' Uncle Bill time to court some, too."

Big Sue laughed too, until Maum Hannah added, "Better keep out de Big House, honey. You'll hab sin if you don' mind!"

"How come so, Maum Hannah?" Big Sue appeared to be surprised.

"You know how come good as me. Better'n me, too. But dat's you' business. Not my own. My business is workin' for Him up yonder." Maum Hannah held up her arms to the sky and lifted her face as if she were praying, but her gaze became so fixed that they all looked up. There, away above them in the sky like a tiny bird, sailed something so high that its buzz was hardly more than the hum of the wind.

Maum Hannah got to her feet, and quickly untying her white apron, held it up and waved it overhead as she called out loud as she could:

"Pray, chillen, pray! Talk wid Jedus! I too sorry to see you dis mawnin'!" She shook her old head, and shouted again. "Gawd don' like mens to go up in de elements! Dis is His day, too! Pray, chillen, pray! Do, Jedus, hab mussy on dem. I hope dey ain' none o' we white folks."

"I hope not," Big Sue joined in. "But most white folks is sinners, Maum Hannah."

"I dunno, gal. I can' see inside nobody's heart, an' I tries to love de sinners same as de rest."

"You love sinners, Maum Hannah?" Big Sue was amazed.

"Sho', honey, I loves de sinners, an' hates de sin."

"Dat's right, Mauma. Right." She gave the old shoulder an affectionate pat. "Dat's how come you has such good luck catchin' chillen. Gawd blesses you. How much did you catch last night?"

Both old hands went up with a gesture of importance. Two!

She'd caught two children last night. Two angels since first dark. The spring love-making was bearing fruit early this fall.

"When's de white folks comin' home?" she asked with a sudden change of expression.

Big Sue didn't know for certain, but she thought soon as white frost came to kill the fever.

"How come you want to know?" Big Sue was curious.

Maum Hannah hoped they would hurry and come

[117]

while she was well and able to talk with them. Something was on her mind, worrying her, and she wanted to get it settled. She was fretted about the graveyard. It was too full. Every grave dug lately uncovered old bones. There was no more room, and a new graveyard ought to be started.

"Do, Jedus!" Big Sue exclaimed. "I sho' would hate to be be first one buried in a new graveyard. Dey say you wouldn' never rest, not till Judgment Day, if you gits buried first, off by you' lonesome self."

"Not if you trust Gawd, honey."

"I trust Gawd, Maum Hannah, but I ever did hear dat de first one to be bury in a new graveyard is bound to be unrestless."

A gentle smile shone on Maum Hannah's face. "I know, honey. I ever did hear so too. Gawd knows if it's so or not. But I done made up my mind to dis: I'm willin' to be de first one. I'm gwine ask de white folks to set off a piece o' new ground an' when my time is come to let me be de first one to be buried in em."

"Great Gawd!" Big Sue panted. "You's got a strong heart, fo' true, Mauma. I couldn't do dat to save life."

"I know, chile. My heart gits weak as branch water too when I t'ink on death. But I'm done old. I got to go soon. I may's well put my trust in Jedus. E knows I done de best I could. I talk wid Him every night. I talk wid em 'bout de graveyard in de new ground. I'm gwine to hab faith dat E'll help me to rise up on Judgment Day an' fly straight to glory, same as if I was a-layin' yonder longside my mammy an' all dem what's gone befo' me."

Big Sue pondered and shook her head. She couldn't stand to let her mind run on death. She couldn't sleep at night if she did.

"Dat's 'cause you's healthy. If you was weakened down wid a sickness you'd as soon go as stay."

"Not me! No, Jedus! I hope I kin stay till I'm old and dry as Aun' Trecia!"

"I hope you kin if you craves dat. But I know my time is most out. I'm willin' to sleep in new ground when my work is done."

"Nobody else'll mind a new graveyard if you sleeps dere ahead of dem, Mauma."

"I can' do nobody no good if dey dies in sin. You must git right befo' you' time comes. Do, honey, git right. Right wid Jedus!"

Big Sue answered she *was* right. And she wanted to stay right. But she was worried half to death now, because she had broken a looking-glass.

"Now, dat is a pity! I too sorry you broke a lookin'-glass. But you go see Emma. Emma kin help you git shet o' dat back luck. Po' chile, e had ear-ache e'se'f las' night. Dat cow make em run an' fret e'se'f so bad. Emma pure cuss de cow!" Maum Hannah burst into a laugh. "Emma's bad! Bad! I haffa all de time lick em! Po' li'l' creeter! Emma will cuss dat cow!"

"Emma is too small to lick fast, enty, Mauma? Looks like lickin' would stunt em worser."

Maum Hannah laughed again, and all the children laughed too.

"Lickin' don' stunt chillen! No. Lickin' loosens up dey hide, an' makes 'em grow. Now, Emma's small, but e hab sense. Since de nights is cool e sets by de fire an' warms e feet on de pots. Dem same smutty pots I cooks de victuals in. I tell em to don' do so! But Emma keeps right on. Dat smut leaves de pots to stick on Emma's feets, den when Emma goes to bed de smut leaves e feets to stick on my clean sheets an' quilts. It takes tight scrubbin' to make 'em git off. Smut too loves cloth! Dat's how come I lick Emma so much. I try fo' make em hate smut same ez I hate sin. But Emma's feets is so black e can' see de smut on 'em."

"Why you don' git Emma some shoes, Mauma? Dey'll keep her feets warm, better dan de pots."

"No, honey. I ain' got de heart to make po' li'l' Emma wear shoes. E too love to jump round an' dance an' shout. Shoes would hinder em. I'll dis keep on lickin' em till e knows better. I'll break em f'om de pots soon ez I git time. I been too busy lately. All de chillen needs so much doctorin'. De womens run round too much, a-pleasurin' deyselves, to hab good chillen dese days. Times is changed, honey. Womens ain' quiet an' steady like dey used to be. No."

She sighed and pointed to the head of a little girl where a bit of wool was tied so tight right over the middle of her forehead that the poor child could hardly blink her eyes.

"I had to tie up Tingie's palate-lock dis mawnin'." Tingie's big eyes looked up solemnly, and Tingie's sore throat gulped with a great effort to swallow. "Tingie hab de so' t'roat, bad."

"I's feelin' better now," Tingie declared huskily.

"You'll soon be well, honey," Maum Hannah told her with a kind smile, and the child smiled back, sure that Maum Hannah knew.

"I needs some buzzard-claw mighty bad, Big Sue. I wish you'd tell Uncle Bill so. De babies is teethin' so bad dis fall. I tried puttin' a hog-teeth on a string roun' dey neck, but hog-teeth is too weak to do any good. Do tell Uncle Bill to shoot me a few buzzards. De gal-chillen is teethin' 'most hard as boy-chillen dis year. But boy-chillen is mighty scarce. De womens pleasure deyself too much to hab boy-chillen. Boy-chillen picks sober womens fo' dey mammy. Dese gals buy so much

trash out de sto' to eat, dey breast-milk is weak as water.
I tell 'em so, but dey don' listen at me. No.''

"My Lijah was plagued wid de grow-fast. You
'member, Mauma?''

Maum Hannah nodded. ''I 'member, but grow-fast
is a easy complaint to cure. I had to work on one yeste'day.'' She told how she and the mother had taken
the child into the room where it was born, and stood in
opposite corners to throw it back and forth to each
other, singing the grow-fast song as they did. A sure
cure for grow-fast. ''When de room is big, it's stiff
treatment. My arms mighty near broke yeste'day.''

Instead of going home the way they came, Big Sue
followed a path through the woods, and crossed a clear
brown stream that flowed without a single ripple to
break its smooth dark surface, or coat it with foam.
The water's breath smelt warm as it rose into the cooler
shadows.

In a small hollow, near its banks, washtubs were
turned upside down on wooden benches, and a big black
washpot sat over dead embers. Waiting for Friday, the
plantation wash-day. All the first days of the week are
field-days. On Friday the women gather and wash
their clothes and gossip. It is a great day for them. A
sort of holiday. Full of things to talk about. Every
bit of the sunshine between the trees is strung with
clothes-lines, heavy weighted with clothes, the old trees
stand around silent and dolesome, with black shadows
cooling their feet.

By Saturday noon the ironing is done, the week's
work over, then the fun begins. Crap games and
parties and dances for the sinners; prayer-meetings and
church for the Christians. Something goes on all the
time until Monday morning. Everything that matters

happens between Saturday night and Monday morning. A week's earnings can be lost, or a wife, or a sweetheart.

Even one's soul!

When they passed a smooth clean piece of ground with a pile of charred blackened sticks on it, Big Sue laughed and said, "Do look! De crap-shooters been here last night. See where dey had a fire? Firelight makes de bones rattle better, so dey say. An' naked ground brings luck to de players."

"Is you a sinner or a Christian, Cun Big Sue?" Breeze blurted out before he knew it.

"Who? Me? Great Gawd! I been a Christian ever since I was twelve years old." After a minute she added, "I did got turned out o' de church one time. I stayed out mighty nigh a year. Silas was de cause of my havin' sin. E deviled me too bad befo' e left me. But de earthquake come dat summer, an' I got so scared it didn' take me long to seek and find peace. I joined de church an' I been in it ever since. You's mighty nigh twelve, enty? When you's twelve Gawd'll hold you responsible fo' you' sins."

Near the creek stood the schoolhouse for the black children on the plantation. A log house with a doorway cut in one end, and fitted with a rude door made of clapboards swung on iron hinges. The big chimney at the other end was overspread with clay mortar. This cabin occupied a lovely spot, overshadowed with a great oak tree from whose roots a small spring trickled and ran to join the larger stream behind it.

Big Sue said there were too many children to get inside the schoolhouse at one time. Half of them had recess while the other half recited lessons. The teacher taught with a long keen whip in her hand, and she made every child learn the lessons. One word missed brought a sharp cut across the palm of the offender's hand. Two words brought four cuts that would not soon be forgotten. Big Sue said she had never bothered to learn to read and write. She didn't have any use for either. Sometimes she'd like to read a new receipt. Still, she could cook better out of her head than most people could cook out of a book.

The old people didn't believe in book learning. They thought learning signs and charms more important, and they discouraged having a school. But Zeda's girl, raised right on the plantation, was the teacher, and she worked wonders with the children. Lijah had never liked books. Playing and riding and shooting and swimming interested him more. He'd have made a good conjure doctor. Once he put some of his own hair in a hole in a tree, and it cured his sprained ankle. He cut an elder stick for Maum Hannah's asthma, and tied it by the neck and hung it up in the loft, and it cured her, too. For a while, before he ran away, he saved all his toe-nails and finger-nails to put in his coffin, but that was so much trouble he quit after he got one little bottle full. It takes a lot of learning to be a good conjure doctor, for there's black magic as well as white. Magic can save as well as kill. Breeze ought either to pray now or start learning magic. He was almost twelve.

The path ran close to a group of trees surrounded by an old rusty iron fence, where tombstones gleamed white. Deep shadows rippled whenever a breeze made its way through the thick, moss-hung woods. Enormous live-oaks stood at regular intervals, all of them festooned with trailing moss that made a weird roof overhead.

Cicadas chanted shrilly in a tangle of rose vines and honeysuckles. White oleanders and japonicas crowded one another, the fragrance of the blossoms mingling with the stench of decaying leaves and wood. Raising the rusted creaking latch of the iron gate, Big Sue

tipped inside the enclosure where gnarled roots of the
old trees crawled across the paths and slipped under
pink-plumed tamarisk bushes. They disappeared, but
they tilted the heavy tombstones, and crumbled the brick
foundations from under marble slabs thick with words.

Some of the graves were smooth and clean, others
were smothered with vines stretched across sunken hollows. Plantation masters and mistresses had been
crumbled, melted, to feed blind groping roots.

Big Sue went toward a corner where a massive gray
stone marked a grave. "Old Cap'n lays here. Gawd!
Dat was a man! Not scared o' anyt'ing or anybody!
Mean! Jedus, he was mean!"

Big Sue sighed. How times change! That same
man lying in his grave had lorded it over this whole
Neck, once. Not only over the black people who worked
his fields after freedom the same as in slavery days, but
over the white people too. Most white people hereabout
now were trash. Poor buckra. Gray-necks. Children
and grandchildren of overseers. When the war to free
the slaves was going on they stayed home and sold
whisky. They ran under the bed and hid if anybody
started a racket. They made money and saved their
skins. Some of them owned plantations now, and lived
in houses whose front doors had been shut to their
grandfathers!

Times had changed. The man who had ridden over
this country with the loosest rein and the sharpest spur,
was down under the ground feeding tree roots and
worms to-day. One little boy, one lone grandson, was
all that was left of his seed, and he was being raised
up-North, among Yankees. The child's own ma was
dead and his stepma had taught him the strange ugly
speech of the Yankees. Enough to make his grandpa
turn over in his grave! Wouldn't the old man curse!

This land must be too rich, too rank for white people to thrive on it. Their skins were too thin, their blood too weak to bear the summer heat, and the fevers and sickness that hid in the marsh in the daytime, then came out to do their devilment after dark.

Black people ruled sickness with magic, but white people got sick and died. White people leave money to their children, but black people leave signs. Give her signs every time! Uncle Isaac was getting old. He might die soon. Breeze had better start learning all he could right now, before Uncle Isaac's mind failed. She'd see Uncle Isaac and tell him.

As she spoke a faint rustle of wind went through the trees and a lizard, carefully colored to match the soil, scurried across the path, rattling dead leaves as it slid under the solid gravestone. Big Sue leaned over the grave and stirred the earth, selecting bits of the coarser sand.

"I want seven li'l' rocks now. One fo' ev'y night in de week. I gwine keep 'em tie up in my pocket-hankcher, so I would stop havin' so much bad dreams all de time."

Breeze shivered. If spirits of the dead ever haunt the paths of the living, they lurked in the deep gloom of the shade made by the overgrown shrubbery, by those coiling, writhing twisted vines. The swift wings of a cardinal spun a scarlet thread before them. Clear notes were flung in a spray of song from the top of the tallest tree. Big Sue called up at him: "It's twelve o'clock, enty? I hear you sayin' dis is de brightest time o' de day!" She tried to make her lips smile bright enough to fit her words, but Breeze could see that the graveyard had made her afraid too. "Le's go, son. Le's git out o' here," she said.

She trampled on a wild rose, full of frail blossoms.

[125]

As Breeze stepped aside to keep from crushing another, a soft wind seized the delicate petals and scattered them over leaves that were already dead.

The road went through the woods past a cleared place, then brought them to the negro graveyard. Every grave held something valued by the dead. A white china pitcher and basin. Old bottles, still holding medicine. Small colored glass vases. Cups and saucers. A few plates. Some of the graves were decorated with clusters of wooden sticks, skilfully carved to make heads of wheat. Breeze wanted to take one, but Big Sue objected. To take one off a grave would be bad luck. Uncle Isaac would be glad to make him one if he'd ask him.

Bright and early Monday morning, Big Sue began fitting together small, carefully cut scraps of cloth, sewing them into squares with strong ball thread. Breeze sat on the step in the pleasant sunshine threading her big-eyed needle as fast as it worked up arm-lengths of thread into firm-holding stitches, while she sat in a low chair on the porch.

Squirrels chased one another across the yard, and up into the live-oak trees. Showers of ripe acorns jarred down by their playing spattered over the ground. Those acorns were sweet as chinquapins, and the squirrels were fat with eating so many. But Big Sue would not let Breeze kill even one for dinner. His fine new sling-shot, made out of a dogwood prong, could hit almost as hard as a gun, but Big Sue said the white folks who lived in the Big House wanted the squirrels left. Even if they ate up all the pecans in the fall, and all the peaches in the summer, not one was to be killed. White people have foolish notions, but it is better not to cross them if you can help it.

She was working hard to get her quilts quilted before the white folks came down for the duck-shooting this winter. They didn't stay long these last years. They had another home up-North, so li'l' "Young Cap'n" could go to a fine school there. Poor little boy! He liked this home a lot better, but his Yankee stepma ruled him and his pa too.

Each day got shorter now. She must sew fast. Get all her squares patched and ready. She'd scarcely have time to draw a long breath for the turn of cooking to be done after they came. Nobody else on the plantation could season victuals to suit them. Zeda helped sometimes, but Zeda didn't know when ducks were done to a turn and not too done. Zeda was apt to get venison as dry as a chip, and if she as much as looked at a waffle it fell flat.

Uncle Isaac's wife was the cook before Big Sue. She used to be the finest cook on the whole Neck. Nobody knew how she made things taste so good. She wouldn't tell. One day she dropped dead. Right in the kitchen. Some people thought she was conjured, but too much rich eating may have done it. After that Uncle Isaac tried to train two or three people to fix the food, for he knew a lot of his wife's secrets from watching her. Big Sue was a girl then, but she was a natural-born cook. When Uncle Isaac found that out, he let her have her own way. She could beat everybody now. Lord! When she had the right kind of victuals, people gnawed their fingers and bit their tongues just to smell the steam when she lifted the pot lids.

The next moon might bring cold weather. She must hurry and get these quilts pieced and have a quilting. She had quilts enough for herself. These were for Joy. She'd ask all the plantation women to Maum Hannah's house, where the big room stayed ready for meeting on Wednesday nights, and for quiltings any

day in the week. If it turned cold, Sherry would kill
enough wild ducks for her to cook for the women to eat
with the rice. Wild ducks and rice are fine. If it
stayed warm, she'd cook chickens and rice, instead.
Make a purleau, with plenty of hard-boiled eggs. Uncle
Bill would give her the chickens.

Sherry loved Joy so much he'd get anything she
wanted for this quilting! The women could easily quilt
ten quilts a day. If they came early and worked fast
they could do fifteen, but she'd be satisfied with six,
for she wanted hers quilted right. With fine stitches,
run in rows close together. Then the cotton batting
could never slip, no matter how many times the quilts
were washed.

She was piecing a "Monkey wrench" quilt now. She
had a "Log-cabin" finished, and a "Primrose" and a
"Star of Bethlehem" and a "Wild-goose Chase" and a
"Pine-burr." She had begun a "State-house Steps,"
but that was a hard one to do. It couldn't be worked
out in a hurry and look right. She'd wait and finish it
next year. Joy could wait for that one.

Some women don't care how their quilts look. They
piece the squares together any sort of way, but she
couldn't stand careless sewing. She wanted her quilts,
and Joy's, made right. Quilts stay a long time after
people are gone from this world, and witness about them
for good or bad. She wanted people to see, when she
was gone, that she'd never been a shiftless or don't-care
woman.

XI

HUNTING 'POSSUMS AND TURKEYS

BREEZE learned something new almost every day. He grew taller each week. His skinny muscles were filling out, his arms and legs growing longer and tougher. Big Sue said he'd be useful if he kept on. He fetched all the water they used from the spring, three full buckets at a time, one bucket on his head, one in each hand. He cut all the wood they burned, without fatigue, since Sherry had taught him the trick of swaying his body forward from the hips as he brought the ax down on the wood. Sherry made a game of wood-cutting, and could cut a thick oak log in two with nineteen whacks. Breeze took two or three times as many, but he did it with one or two less each day.

He made up both beds every morning and swept the floor so clean that Big Sue couldn't find a speck of dust anywhere. He knew how to crack hickory-nuts and walnuts so the goodies came out whole for Big Sue to put in sweetened bread. He had helped make soap with ashes, pot-grease and the fat of a lot of spoiled hog meat April gave Big Sue. He took a sack of corn on his shoulder to mill every Saturday morning, and brought it back, ground fine, and hot from the grinding rocks. He milked the cow, churned the cream, fed the chickens, and the hog in the pen. He could even patch his own clothes.

The regular field-hands drew rations on Saturday,

one peck of corn, three pounds of cured hog-meat. The women who had no man living with them, paid rent for their cabins with one day's work a week. April saw to it that every one paid. He was close and careful. Everybody had to come right up to the notch since he was foreman, but the house of Big Sue was rent free, since she was the cook. Breeze drew rations like a regular field-hand, and by hunting and fishing with Sherry and Uncle Bill he provided many a good potful of meat. With a line tied to the end of a long swamp cane, and a slick wriggly earthworm for bait, he caught strings of perches that made rich morsels when dipped in cornmeal and fried.

Sherry's coon dog, Zip, had a faithful nose, and when Sherry and Breeze took him out at night they seldom came home without coons, or 'possums, enough to satisfy both Big Sue and Zeda.

They came in earlier than usual one night with nine 'possums and found April sitting by the fire with Big Sue. Breeze saw Sherry's frown and the two men hardly spoke to each other, until April eyed the 'possums with a sneering smile and said:

"Yunnuh's got a lot o' 'possums to-night. I heared Jake's calf got in a bog. E must 'a' died."

April poked the fire until sparks flew into the room.

"Wha' you doin', April? Is you crazy?" Big Sue cried sharply.

April spat contemptuously far back into the live embers. "I'd as soon eat a buzzard as one o' dem 'possums!"

"How come?" Breeze, Big Sue, Sherry, all darted astonished looks at him.

"Dey's full up wid carrion. A 'possum ain' decent as a buzzard. Dey's so coward-hearted, dey durstn' come out in de day-time to eat. No. Dem sleek-tailed devils wait till night, den goes creepin' to carcasses and stuffs on all what de buzzards scorns.''

"Shut you' dirty mout', April! I declare to Gawd, you's a-turning my stomach! Torectly, I couldn' eenjoy eatin' dese possums at all!'' Big Sue laid stress on every word.

"When did you git so awful delicate, Big Sue?'' April asked with a grin.

"I ever did have a delicate stomach. I don' hardly have no appetite at all lately.''

Sherry gave a loud guffaw and April frowned in sudden ill-temper. "Wha' dat tickle you so turrible, now, Sherry?''

April's irritation showed in the jerky shifting of his hands and feet, and Big Sue's eyes stretched open and rolled toward Sherry, who answered sourly:

"Oh, I ain' so awful tickled. No. I just had to laugh when I thought on how it takes a thief to catch a thief. Night-walkers meets night-walkers, enty?''

"I do'in' un'erstan' wha' dat you's a-drivin' at.'' April stroked his mustache and eyed Sherry coldly.

"Me neither,'' Big Sue chimed. "Whyn' you talk plain talk, Sherry? It's mighty no-manners to stand up an' laugh a horse laugh in somebody's face.''

"Do ex-cuse me, Cun Big Sue. Ev'y now an' den, I forget an' speak out o' turn. I was just talkin' fool talk. I ain' laughin' at nobody. Come on, Breeze. Le's divide de 'possums. You take four, I take five. We sho' had good luck to-night. Good night, ev'ybody!''

Sherry flung himself out of the door and April sat silent, vexed, upset; but his anger lasted only a short time. When he spoke, his tone was pleasant enough. He ought not to have joked with Sherry. The boy was too easy to get plagued. Zeda had spoiled him all his life, instead of breaking him of his sassy ways. Such a pity to ruin a nice boy. April got to his feet and stood stiffly erect.

Big Sue's gimlet eyes watched his face, then leaning to knock her pipe on the hearth she said sadly: "Lawd, I wish dem 'possums was somet'ing fit to eat. A wild turkey or somet'ing. If dey was a wild turkey, I could stuff dem wid oysters an' roast dem. Jedus, wouldn' dey taste good! Whyn' you kill a turkey, April? Looks like nobody else can shoot one but you? Ain' you got a blind baited?"

She smiled up at him so sweetly, April smiled back. "Whyn' you take Breeze an' go in de mawin'?" she pressed. "We could eat turkey to-morrow night." She smacked her lips.

April turned her words over in his mind, thinking, calculating. Presently he asked, "How 'bout gwine turkey huntin' wid me in de mawnin', boy?"

Breeze was rapt with pure joy. April's smile made him tingle all over. Instead of being bashful and afraid, he looked straight into April's eyes and nodded.

"Lawdy! Lawdy!" He murmured low, and his heart went pit-a-pat. He was going turkey-hunting with April, the foreman, who had scarcely ever noticed him before!

"Git on to bed, son!" Big Sue said so gently, so kindly, Breeze was at a loss to know why. He walked slowly back to the shed-room, the blood beating clear up in his cheeks, but Big Sue sat down in her chair by the fire to smoke another pipeful. "Set down, April," she said. "De night is young, yet."

She woke Breeze before daylight when the black sky held only a narrow moon, without any sign of sunrise. A thin gray mist hung over the earth and all was quiet except a few crickets and the occasional bark of a dog. Breeze had slept little, but he felt wide awake, breathless, as he followed April's slow ponderous steps. April spoke seldom. He seemed to be brooding over something. Breeze pitied him. A foreman has so much to think about, so many people to rule, so much land to manage. Sherry was wrong to be impudent last night.

They turned off from the road into a path which Breeze could barely see although his eyes worked well in the dark. April led the way, and Breeze hung close at his heels for the silence in the forest was full of strange sounds and shapes.

The turkey blind was a great bush heap, with one small opening in its side, looking straight out on a narrow trench. The bottom of the trench was strewn with white shelled corn, so when April called the turkeys, and they got to eating, their heads would be down in a bee line. One shot might blow two or three heads off. Wild turkeys fly too fast for any gun to have a good second chance at them.

Breeze sat perfectly still inside the blind, while April yelped and yelped. Once a hen yelped back, but she came no nearer. Breeze's feet went to sleep. Both his legs got cramp. His back ached. The cold morning air chilled his very bones, but he dared not move so much as one muscle. April had warned him not even to whisper. The silence made him drowsy, but when April sniffed and Breeze drew in a long breath of air, then his body's discomfort fled! Cold fear took its place, for a rattlesnake was near.

"Le's go, Cun April!"

"I'm gwine git dat snake first, son. You set still till I call you."

Day was coming. Tree branches overhead talked softly to one another. Leaves brought down by the wind fell rustling. Birds chirped and twittered. Squirrels barked. Breeze's blood drummed in his temples.

[133]

The forest around them was old and great, most of
the trees gums or poplars, with an occasional pine
appearing. The undergrowth crowded close together,
twining and tangling with limbs and branches so dense
the light could scarcely reach the ground.

April found a dogwood tree and cut a long forked
stick, then he moved slowly, stealthily, in the direction
of the smell. Breeze thought his heart would stop beating altogether, so great was his terror. If that snake
struck April and killed him, how'd he ever get home
himself? He didn't know the way. His hands thrust
deeper into his pockets and one felt his knife. Uncle's
directions for helping a snake-bitten person came to him.
Cut the wound wide open and suck out the poison.
Could he do it? Could he cut April's flesh and suck his
blood? He'd have to, if it came to the worst.

April thrashed about in the undergrowth with his
long forked stick, calling out as he did so, "Whe' is you,
snake? Hurry up an' rattle! I wan' git you!"

When a clear dry rattle sang out, he laughed. "Now
we'll see who's de best man, me or you! Breeze, git
you' pocket knife! Cut a shell open! Have it ready so
if I miss an' git bit you kin pour de powder in de bite
an' set em afire. I got a box o' matches here in my
pocket. You better take 'em. You understand, enty?
Burnin' de pizen out is better'n suckin' it out. Fire kin
fight em stronger'n you' mouth."

The thick-bodied, large-headed snake was coiled,
ready to strike. The rattles on the end of its tail raised
and shook angrily. But instead of dread, April showed
a fierce pleasure in the dry ear-splitting whir. Breeze's
throat went dry, but April laughed.

"You's too slow, you pided devil! Summer's gone!
I kin kill you easy as Breeze kills a chicken! Lawd! you
is old! You' rattles looks like a cow's horn. Come on!"

He batted the snake's head to one side with a deft blow, and, putting the stick's fork over its neck, held it fast to the ground, until he could seize it below the throat in a steady powerful grip. As he lifted it up off the ground, the thick body wound wildly around his arm in a terrible struggle to wrench loose, the flat eyes glared, the wide mouth yawned. April stood firm as a tree.

"Fight, boy, fight! Stretch you' mouth wide as you kin! Dat ain' wide enough yet! I want to spit clean down in your belly! Show you' fangs! Dey ain' nuttin! I got blue gums too! You may as well stand still and pray! You' time is out! You gwine meet you' Gawd to-day!"

With a whoop April threw his head back, then he spat straight into the yawning mouth.

"Dat shot got you!" he cried, and spat again. "You can' harm me, son! You is a-weakenin'! I see it! My spit is pizen as you' own!"

"Come, Breeze! Looka dis scoundrel! Lawd, e sho' is a whopper!"

The snake's muzzle was covered with plates, its scaly brown body marked with yellowish square shapes; its eyes, full of hate, stared out from the front of its heart-shaped head. Breeze's own blood had frozen in his veins, and his legs were almost too numb to carry him.

"You got blue gums, Breeze. Come spit in dis mouth so you'll know how to do it next time!"

"Don' make me do dat, Cun April."

"You ain' no gal-baby, is you?"

"No, suh."

"Den come on. Git you' mouth full. Now, aim straight fo' de fork in his tongue."

Breeze's lips twitched so that he missed the snake

[135]

completely the first time, but the next effort was a success.

"Dat's good. You got mo' grit dan Sherry. Sherry never would try dis. But den, Sherry ain' got blue gums like me an' you."

The snake's plunging and twisting grew less violent. The huge body writhed sluggishly. Had April really poisoned the creature by spitting into its tongue? Or had he choked it to death? Its life was going out, that was certain.

Suppose April's fingers took cramp. What would happen then? April turned his face toward home.

"Le's go, Breeze. It's too late to git a turkey. I'll take dis snake to Uncle Isaac. He axed me to git him one to make some tea for his rheumatism. Po' ol' man. Rheumatism'll make a Christian out o' em yet!"

Full daybreak shed its light everywhere. Night and stars were gone out of the sky. The sun would soon be up. But at Uncle Isaac's cabin, the doors and windows were shut tight.

The snake couldn't die altogether until sun-down, but April dropped it on the ground and used his forked stick to beat hard on the sides of the house.

"Hey, Uncle! Hey! Wake up!" He shouted until the old man opened the door. "I got a present fo' you! A rattlesnake! Me an' him had a tight time dis mawnin'! Lawd! Yes! I sho' love to fight wid a snake!"

Uncle Isaac hopped around, exclaiming over the snake's size. He was glad to get him. He'd fix some snake tea to-day.

As they walked home down the avenue, April talked cheerfully. He said Uncle Isaac had taken so much snake cut that snakes got weak if they crossed his path. If one came near him it got stiff as a stick, and helpless.

Next time Breeze saw the old man he must look at his ankles where they'd been cut and cut for snake poison to be rubbed into them. His feet were full of scars too, but Uncle Isaac had worn shoes ever since he chopped off a big toe.

April had walked up on snakes that were stricken by getting too close to Uncle Isaac. They'd be blind and numb, unable to move a step. God gave Uncle Isaac a strong sweat too. If he had never taken snake cut, he could send any snake into a trance by wetting his hands at his armpits and waving them in the snake's face. They'd faint right off, and stay dead a long time.

Breeze ought to learn Uncle Isaac's magic. He'd been born with a second-sight. Learning magic would be better for him than learning books. Black magic, as well as white magic; Uncle Isaac knew both. Uncle Bill too. But Uncle Bill gave magic up for religion. A poor swap. A deacon or a preacher is not much more than a woman. Not much more!

April's down-heartedness had completely passed. Loitering along, he chatted pleasantly. Although the sun had risen he was in no hurry.

XII

DUCK-HUNTING

SHERRY promised Big Sue plenty of wild ducks for her quilting dinner if she'd persuade Uncle Bill to row him.

"Lemme go, too, Sherry. Please, Sherry," Breeze begged.

"If you'll kill some ducks, you could go."

"I ain' got no gun."

"Plenty o' guns is yonder in de Big House. Cun April is got de key."

"I'll git you a gun, Breeze," Big Sue offered, and before the day was out Breeze went into the Big House with April, through the same side door out of which April and Big Sue came that first morning.

The side passage led into a wide front hall and a queer feeling of intrusion seized Breeze as he went past rooms where pictures of white people looked at him from the walls. Brass andirons and fenders gleamed out from big fireplaces. Unlit candles left the high ceilinged rooms in a dim uncertain light. Dark shadows hid under the heavy furniture, until April pressed a button and a chandelier hung from the ceiling became hundreds of dazzling icicles, dripping with light.

April took Breeze to a room where a rack held guns of all sizes and shapes, each one polished, well oiled, ready for work. April handed Breeze one after the other to try, making him put them up to his shoulder as if he aimed at something. When one was found to fit, April cautioned him, "When you shoot, fo'git you' gun. Fasten you' eyes on de t'ing you want to hit, den pull de trigger. Try em now, son! Don' squint up you' eyes! Keep all two wide open. Shootin' ain' hard work! It's for pleasure! You can' hit nothin' if you frown."

Breeze was glad to get out of the silent house with its book-lined walls and rug hidden floors. He took the gun home, but he could scarcely go to sleep for happy excitement over the prospect of going hunting.

Uncle Bill sat waiting in the stern of a small narrow boat, but he got to his feet when he saw Big Sue. While he held the boat steady for Breeze and Sherry to get in, he kept an eye on Big Sue as he warned her please not to touch Breeze, and he kept saying to Breeze:

"Mind, son. Don' put you' hand on Miss Big Sue. When a man is gwine a-huntin', it'll ruin his luck to let a lady touch him. Be careful!"

He wanted Breeze to sit alone in the bow of the boat, but Sherry considered and then said, no, Breeze must sit beside him on the narrow board seat in the boat's middle. Uncle Bill shook his head and muttered in disapproval, but Sherry wouldn't give in.

"No, Uncle Bill, Breeze wouldn't be safe settin' in front o' me dis morning. My gun feels too ready to shoot. I can' trust em. It's so quick on de trigger it might miss and aim at his head or his back instead o' at a duck."

"Wha' dat is got you so nervish, Sherry?"

"When my mind runs on some people, I wants to shoot right den!"

"Dat is sinful, son. Awful sinful! I hates to hear you talk so!"

To Breeze, the boat seemed very narrow and the seat

scarcely able to hold two. He knew he couldn't swim if he fell out, but he said nothing, and soon Uncle Bill swung them out into the middle of the deep clear stream.

Instead of being brown-black like the river, this arm of that stream was filled with the blue of the sky. But its dark depths looked bottomless and dangerous, and Breeze sat mute, with his eyes staring down in it until Sherry nudged him and made him look up. "You got to learn how to swim, son, den you won' be scared o' water! You get dis straight in you' head now too; when a man starts out huntin', e mustn't never let no 'oman put her hand on him. If e do, his luck is gone. Uncle Bill is even scared for my right hand to touch you, for you ain' no more'n a li'l' gal. But I'll risk it. My luck kin stand a lot. It don' fail me."

Breeze listened and answered, "Yes-suh," but he did not altogether understand, and Sherry's eyes glanced over the water's surface.

"Lawd! Looka de creek, how blue e is dis mornin'! Winter or summer, e stays blue. Dat is what gives de plantation de name, Blue Brook. Cun Big Sue ain' told you dat yet?"

Behind them Uncle Bill hissed, "Sh-sh," and Sherry leaned to whisper, "We mustn' talk. De ducks'll hear an' we won't git a shot. Is you know how to load you' gun?"

In his excitement Breeze had forgotten, but Sherry took it and showed him again how to slip two neat yellow, brass-trimmed shells into place in the clean steel barrels, how to make the gun "safe" and "ready." Then he took up his own gun and with quick slidings and clickings slipped half a dozen shells into its snug chamber. Breeze noticed that Sherry had purple shells and wondered what the different colors meant, but before he could ask, a sharp "sh-sh" from Uncle Bill hissed behind them again.

"Go easy," Sherry's big mouth buzzed back in a whisper. To Breeze he mumbled, "Git you' gun ready, son."

The tide must have been going with them for they flowed along without a sound. Breeze saw no ducks until suddenly dark wings flashed everywhere in front of them. The gun in Sherry's hands fired, again and again. It was all quickly over. Echoes banged back and forth at one another, then died, and everything was still. On the water in front of them three limp bundles of feathers were floating, not caring at all where they went.

Uncle Bill's laughter cackled out. "Sherry, you can' be beated! Son, you's a shot-man, fo' true! Yes, Jedus! You don' never miss!"

He shot the boat forward and Sherry leaned far out to pick up the lifeless bodies of the ducks he had killed. How strong he was! And as much at home in this cramped-up boat as on the ground.

"Poor creeters!" he pitied, holding the gay-colored bill of one of them between his fingers. "Ain' e a beauty!"

"I hope you ain' gettin' chicken-hearted," Uncle Bill twitted, and Sherry grinned back.

"Maybe I is, Uncle." Sherry's big fingers gently ruffled the feathers on the duck's breast to show them to Breeze. They were beautiful, indeed. The trim head had a high crest of purple and green and black feathers. White lines were above and below the poor death-dulled eyes. The throat and warm breast, colored soft tan like a chinquapin, and spotted with white, were bloodstained across the fine black markings. The bill was bright pink; the feet and legs, bright orange. Sherry said they were safe to be loud-colored, for they were hidden under water most of the time.

[141]

The drake's mates were less gay. The brown and gray and white feathers on their trim bodies were quiet as shadows on the water.

All three of them were quite dead, and Sherry tossed them back to Uncle Bill who put them far back under the seat, saying as he did so:

"We better hide 'em fo' true. Dey's all summer ducks. It's five hundred dollars to kill one! Five hundred!"

"Shucks!" Sherry answered, reloading his gun. "Dem white folks way off yonder to Columbia sho' do make some fool laws!"

"If de game warden was to slip up on you right now you'd wish you had kept 'em, dough. Where'd you git de money to pay?"

"Oh, I know I'd go straight to de gang as a martin to his gourd," Sherry answered cheerfully. "But I trust to my luck to don' git caught."

All three of them laughed, and Uncle Bill thrust the boat silently on. Once Sherry pointed to a hollow high up on the body of a leaning cypress. The tree's feathery top rose far above the mesh of interlaced vines and branches on the bank of the stream. As likely as not a summer duck made her nest in that hollow. They choose knot-holes or hollows, sometimes forty feet high, sometimes near the water. Queer fowls. Hard to fool.

As they rounded a bend on the stream a faint splash sounded in front. Sherry listened with pent breath. "Ducks, enty, Uncle?" he whispered.

"Great Gawd, Sherry! Wha' dat ail you' years?"

Almost at once they swung into sight of April in a boat much like their own. He had a load of sacks and packages and its back was piled high with oysters in the shell. His trousers were inside his laced-up boots and a silver watch-chain dangled from a side pocket.

[142]

Uncle Bill hailed him, "Good mawnin', son! How come you so dressed up? I don' like dem boots. You's a good swimmer fo' true, but boots kin drown a fish. A watch kin fool you too. I wouldn't trust to no watch. Not me!"

"I rather drown dan let oyster shells cut my feets all up. Plain shoes don' hinder 'em. But how you like dese fish?" He held up a string of long, smooth, snaky-looking creatures. They could have passed for short fat snakes.

"Great Gawd, de eels! You sho' had luck wid you dis mawnin'."

"Luck stay wid me!" April bragged, but Sherry laughed.

"You must be mean Bad Luck, enty? If I'd catch a' eel, I'd call it Bad Luck!"

"How come so?"

"I can' stand to look at a' eel, much less eat one. Not me!"

"When did you git so pa'ticular, Sherry? You must be kissed you' elbow an' turned to a lady, enty?" April sneered coolly.

"No matter how long you cook a' eel, it'll turn raw soon's it gits cold."

"Who'd let a eel git cold? Not me, I know," April returned hotly. "Eels ain' nothin' but he catfish. How come you love catfish so good an' scorns eels?"

"Sho' dey is!" Uncle Bill affirmed promptly. "Dey's de men catfish. Sho'! Anybody'll tell you dat." April shoved his boat forward.

"Well, I'm glad you don' want 'em, Sherry! It would be too bad if you did. But I tell you, when Big Sue gits dem seasoned up right in a pot dey would make you pure bite you' fingers just to smell 'em."

Sherry said no more, and April's boat glided on. A
[143]

bend in the stream closed its gate behind it, shutting him and his boatload of food out of sight.

Uncle Bill took a chew of tobacco. "April's de luckiest man I ever seen," he ventured, but Sherry said nothing at all.

Through breaks in the trees Breeze caught glimpses of drab, level, water-covered spaces. Old rice-fields. Deserted. Marsh-grown. They lacked the color and the look of life that filled the thick-tangled growth of trees and thorny-looking vines and bushes encircling them.

"Sherry," Uncle Bill rested his paddle, "you don' hold nothin' against April, does you?"

Sherry's answer was slow coming, "Not nothin' much, suh."

Uncle Bill began paddling again, and Sherry put down his gun and stretched, then said that since April and his boat had scared all the ducks out of this creek, they'd better go across the river into some of the creeks around Silver Island where lots of ducks raise and there'd be a chance to get some good shooting.

Sherry's good humor was gone. He sat dumb, his forehead all knotted up in a frown. The eels or April or something had crossed him. Breeze was glad to hear him ask, "Who named Silver Island, Uncle? You reckon any money's buried on it?"

Uncle Bill didn't know. It was named long ago, when each bit of land here was given a name. These marshes were all fields in the old days. Rice was planted everywhere then. He pointed to old rotting pieces of wood that held the tide back until it gurgled as it strained to get over them.

"See de old flood-gates? De old trunks? Dey used to let de water in and out. Dey used to know dere business to!" He sighed. "But dey time is out. De old days is gone. De tide does like it pleases now."

On an old piece of wood, brown with rot and soaked by the flood-tide, yet standing guard beside an opening on the bank, several small black tortoises sprawled out flat, sunning themselves. As the boat got nearer they all slid into the water for safety.

It amused Uncle Bill mightily. He chuckled and called out that they needn't hide from him.

"You like cooters, Uncle?" Sherry asked him with a laugh.

"No, suh!" the old man said shortly, "Not to-day, anyhow. De sky's too clear." He cast his black beady eyes up and scanned the blue overhead. "I don' see no sign of thunder nowhere, an' if a cooter bites you e won't never let go till it thunders."

Sherry laughed. "You know, don't you, Uncle?" Then he told how once when Uncle Bill was a boy a cooter caught his toe and held on to it for a whole day and night.

"Fo' days, son!" Uncle Bill corrected.

"Was it four, fo' true, Uncle?" Sherry asked doubtfully.

"Yes, suh! An e'd 'a' been holdin' on till now if it didn't thunder," Uncle Bill spoke solemnly.

"What did you do all dem four days, Uncle?" Sherry asked.

"I watched de clouds an' prayed for de thunder to roll, son."

When Breeze hoped one would never bite him, Uncle Bill grunted. "You right to hope so, son. I hope so too. A cooter is a contrary creeter."

"De people used to say Uncle Isaac was crippled by a cooter. E makes like e's plagued wid rheumatism, but I have hear tell e ain' got no big toe on one foot. Did you know dat, Sherry?"

"How come so?" Breeze inquired.

"Well, now, I tell you, dis might not be so. But I used to hear de people say it was. Old man Isaac is a heap older'n me an' all dis happened before I was born. But my mammy used to laugh 'bout em. Plenty o' times when e'd come hoppin' up to de house a-talkin' 'bout how it must be gwine rain soon by de misery in his knee was so bad, my mammy use to say his big toe wasn't buried straight an' dat was what hurt Uncle Isaac. T'ings have to be buried right or dey can' rest at all."

"Whe' was de cooter?" Breeze asked.

"De cooter was in de corn-field, son."

"An' whe' was Uncle Isaac?"

"E was in de corn-field too, choppin' grass."

"Did de cooter bite his toe off?"

"No, you wait now an' le' me tell em my way."

"When Uncle Isaac was young e used to run round a lot at night instead o' being' home 'sleep, like he had business to be. E used to catch a nap in de day time whilst he was hoein'. Plenty o' people can stand straight up in de field an' lean on dey hoe an' sleep good. I never could, but a lot o' people can. Well, Uncle Isaac was gwine long hoein' a spell, den dozin' a spell. One time when e opened his eyes to look e thought e seen a cooter's head right side his foot. E chopped down hard to cut em off. But it wasn't no cooter head dat time. It been his own big toe! Dat's how come e's hoppin' to dis day. An' a-lyin' 'bout em too."

"Po' ol' man!" Sherry laughed along with his pitying. "I don' blame em fo' lyin' 'bout dat. I'd be shame' to tell de truth. Dey say if you tell a lie an' stick to it, dat's good as de truth anyhow."

"I dunno," Uncle Bill answered doubtfully, "I reckon sin is easier to stand dan shame."

A blue dragon-fly flitted along close to the water.

"Does you know his business?" Sherry asked Breeze. But the fly was catching gnats and mosquitoes right then and anybody could see what its business was. Breeze laughed at Sherry's question.

"You's wrong," Sherry laughed back. "You's talkin' 'bout his victuals, not his business. Dat's a snake doctor. A sick snake is around here somewhere now. You watch out. We'll see him. Den we'll kill him and hang him up on a limb to make it rain. It's powerful dry dis fall."

"If you hang a dead snake on a limb, dat couldn' make it rain?"

Sherry's laugh was so merry that Breeze grinned at his own ignorance.

"Great Gawd, boy! You didn't know dat! Sho', it will! In less 'n three days too. Won't it, Uncle?"

"Sho'!" Uncle Bill answered stoutly, but he added there was no use to bother with the snake, for it was going to rain in less than three days, anyhow. "The new moon hung in a ring last night and only one star was inside it. That means it will rain after one day. If they'd find the snake and kill him he couldn't die until the sun went down. Neither can a frog nor a cooter, nor a wasp. Lots of things can't die if the sun shines."

Breeze felt he was learning a lot, and he listened so attentively that Uncle Bill went on talking.

"Most people have to wait until night to die, and even when night comes, dey can't die until de tide turns."

"How can dey tell if dey's sick in the bed?" Breeze asked, and Uncle Bill explained that the people themselves didn't know. The life that stays inside them, that knows.

"It knows mighty nigh everything," the old man declared, "and when de time comes for it to go, it goes,

[147]

an' leaves a man dead as a wedge.'' This statement left
Breeze wondering, but Uncle Bill went on telling how
the rice-fields were full of all kinds of snakes, some of
them poisonous, and some not. But the snake he feared
most, more than even a rattlesnake or a moccasin, was a
coach-whip.

''If a coach-whip catches you, he will wrap his body
round you an' tie you to a tree an' whip you to death
wid his tail. Lawd, boy, when a coach-whip blows dat
whistle in de end of his tail, put you' foot in you' hand
an' run!''

''Yes, suh!'' Sherry agreed, ''I too 'fraid of coach-
whips myself. I never did see one do it, but a coach-
whip can outrun a man any day. If you get to out-
runnin' him, e will grab his tail in his mouth and roll
after you like a hoop to catch you. An' tie you to a
tree an' whip you. Enty, Uncle?''

''Sho'?'' Uncle Bill was astonished at his asking.
''Sho it's so! I've seen a coach-whip do it plenty o'
times.''

He spat far out into the stream when he had said it,
then held one oar still in the water to wheel the boat
to one side, as he asked:

''Did you ever catch one of dose pretty little garter
snakes an' see him break hisself all up into little joints?
Dey go back all togedder again when dey gits ready.''

Sherry never had.

''Well did you ever burn a blacksnake an' make him
show you his feet. You must be have done dat,
Sherry?''

''No, suh,'' Sherry answered solemnly. ''I ain'
done em not yet, but I've seen plenty o' people what
has done em.'' And after a thoughtful silence he added:

''Deys one t'ing I do know, Uncle. If a snake bites
you and you don't die, all you' hair will drop out every

time dat snake sheds its skin. Dat's so, 'cause my own done it about ten years until Uncle Isaac told me to put a boxwood poultice on my hand ebery night las' spring. An' dat cured me.''

''Sho'!'' Uncle Bill agreed. ''Boxwood's good for most eberyt'ing what ails you.''

''Poultices made out of boxwood will make you' hair grow and cure tooth-ache or either rheumatism. Boxwood tea'll cure de itch or de spring fever, too.''

''I heard so,'' Sherry approved. ''Boxwood roots is good for foot troubles too.''

''Yes, suh. It's a good medicine. Sho'! De white people knowed it and dats how come dey fetched it across de water wid em. All de flowers gardens on dis whole Neck is full o' boxwood. Some's grows high an' some low. Some ain' no taller dan my finger, an' it's old as de Big House, too.''

''Lawd, how times is changed! Changed before yunnuh was born. Looks like all de good old days is done gone.''

''We done well enough till de boll-evils come, enty, Uncle?''

''But de boll-evils is come. Dey ruint de whole crop year befo' last.''

''De crop was good last year after we pizened 'em.''

''But I tell you, I sho' don' believe in pizenin' 'em. No, suh! Gawd sent dem here an' we better leave dem lone. If I was you, I wouldn't run no pizen machine. At night too, when de cotton is wet wid dew, a pizen dust'll stick to you' feets. When I look out o' my door at night and see dat pizen dust a-floatin' over de cotton fields in dem big white cluds, an' dat machine a-singin' like a locust, a-creepin' up and down de rows, th'owin' out pizen I git too scared to look. No wonder de mens hates to take part in it. Dem pizened blossoms is done killed all de bees on de place, an' a lot o' de turkeys and de guineas died from eatin' de pizened evils. Better let weeds grow in de fields, I say. We kin do widout money till we git some crop to take de place o' cotton. Cotton's time is out. I 'member when dey had to give up plantin' indigo, and people said we was ruined. But cotton done just as good. Now cotton is failed, and we ought to wait till we git some kind o' crop to take its place.'' Uncle Bill heaved a mighty sigh as he said it. ''April is too brazen. E would buck Gawd A'mighty. Don't you try to be like em, Sherry. No. If April keeps on, e will land in Hell, sho' as e was born.''

''You t'ink de place'll ever be sold, Uncle?'' Sherry asked him presently.

''No, son. Not long as de li'l' young Cap'n is livin'! E was born wid two li'l' teeth, and when dem two li'l' teeth got ripe an' fell out, my Katy took 'em an' went to de graveyard an' buried 'em in a clear place right longside his gran'pa.

''No matter whe' da li'l' boy goes or how long e stays gone from here, dis place'll hold to him. Dem li'l' two teeth'll make him come back to die an' be buried right here. You'll see. It's so. Just like I'm tellin' you. It'll be dat way. Katy was a wise-minded 'oman.''

The boat moved steadily forward all the time, for Uncle Bill's arms didn't slacken the oar's paddling once.

As Breeze listened thoughtfully to all that was said, his eyes wandered unseeing over the beauty that lay thick around him, for he was trying to understand some of the things he had heard.

The rice-fields blurred by yellow sunshine were tinged with ripeness and flecked with brilliant color. Purple shadows were cast by crimson branches, scarlet berries sparkled on slender vines and adorning gray thorny branches. The bright water, gay with reflections, ran sober edges under blue cypress.

The tide of the year, more deliberate but as constant as the tide from the sea, was almost full, almost at its height. It would soon pause, mature and complete, its striving over, for a little rest; and start ebbing.

A great owl, roused by the boat's passing, spread out wide wings and flew from the shadowy darkness of a dense moss-hung tree. Marsh hens, that couldn't be seen, cackled out shrill strident notes from the marsh-grown, water-covered mud flats. Solemn blue-and-white herons stood motionless at the water's edge, gravely watching the boat. High overhead, thin lines of ducks sliced across the sky with swift slashing wings. When the boat rounded a bend where the creek met the river, Uncle Bill began a careful, precise paddling with his one long oar, and with settled, even strokes thrust the boat forward into the wide dark stream.

"For Gawd's sake, be careful, Uncle! Don' go too fast against dis current. I'd sho' hate to be turned over dis morning. Dat water looks mighty cold."

Sherry gave a shiver and laugh as he said it, but Uncle Bill's reply was full of reproach. Why would Sherry think of such a thing as turning over? He was inviting trouble.

The boat had run silently for some little time, close to the river's bank, when Uncle Bill broke into a sputter of words. Breeze turned to look at him. His eyes, two bright black berries in the dull black surface of his skin, were fixed on something away ahead. Breeze tried to see it too. He searched the distance ahead. But nothing showed except miles of wide river swelled out beyond its banks into the flat old rice-fields. Palmetto trees showed now and then among the willows and cypresses. Low-lying marshy islands, fringed with vine-covered scrubby bushes, were cut into patterns by narrow creeks.

Sherry was watching the distance too. "Wha' kind is dey, Uncle?" he murmured.

"Bull-neck, son," Uncle Bill answered promptly.

"I wish my eyes was trained to see good like your'n. I wonder why dey ain'!"

"I dunno, son. I dunno. I reckon dey ain' had to look hard as mine," and he chuckled with pleasure at the compliment Sherry paid him.

Uncle's calm black face filled with a warm friendly smile. Uncle's bright eyes, keen and cold, flitted swiftly from Sherry's face to Breeze's, then beyond them to the ducks he saw in the distance. Breeze began to see more in Uncle Bill's black features than he did at first. They were more than wrinkled flesh that time had creased and withered, for not only shrewdness, but wisdom and pity shone in the clear-seeing eyes; and the old mouth, where so many teeth were missing, tightened its lips in a way that meant more than caution and prudence.

Breeze gazed at every bit of the surface ahead, starting with the water where sunshine dazzled close beside the boat and ending where the hazy sky dropped down to join the earth, but he couldn't see any ducks.

"Looka right yonder!" Uncle Bill pointed to direct his eyes and he made out two tiny black specks side by side on the water.

"You must shoot dose two," Sherry said. "It ain't against de law to kill bull-necks, and maybe dey'll stay on de water until we get in gunshot."

"You better shoot 'em, Cun Sherry. I can't hit 'em." Breeze hesitated although his heart was beating fit to burst with excitement at the thought of shooting a gun.

"No, dem's you' ducks. You must kill 'em," Sherry insisted. "If you do like I tell you, you can' miss em. I don' mind breakin' de law, so I'll hit de summer ducks and you kill de lawful ones."

"I'm scared I'll miss 'em." Breeze's voice quivered so shakily Sherry laughed.

"No you won't. I'll tell you how to do," he said gently.

Uncle Bill headed the boat straight for the two small dots which were swimming toward it, and soon Breeze could see the gray of their feathers and the bright orange color of their bills. They seemed not to know their danger even when Uncle Bill stopped paddling and Sherry whispered to Breeze.

"Cock your gun now and hold em close up to you' shoulder. Look straight at de duck you want to kill and pull de front trigger."

Breeze did just as Sherry told him, but the drake he aimed at sat quite motionless on the water, as if he had not even heard the gun's explosion.

"Fine, son!" Sherry exclaimed. "He didn' know wha' hit him. Now, shoot de hen duck. Hold you' gun up close to you' shoulder, den look straight at em an' pull de back trigger."

Breeze's fingers were trembling but he shot again, and the hen duck made wild splutterings on the water.

"Po' creeter! You hit em, but you got to shoot em again. Put us up a li'l' closer, Uncle. Load you' gun, Breeze."

Breeze's tense fingers shook as he unbreached his gun and replaced the two empty, smoking shells with heavy new ones. As the boat swung near to the wounded duck that swam round and round its dead mate, Sherry spoke to him sharply.

"Hurry up! Shoot em again!"

How could he do it? The poor wounded fowl was fluttering in agony now.

"Quit you' triflin', boy!" Sherry ordered sternly. "Put em out o' dat misery."

Breeze's fingers tightened on the trigger and the gray-feathered body quivered into bloody shreds as the swift lead from his gun tore through it. Breeze felt wretched. Killing that duck gave him no pleasure.

Uncle Bill paddled up close to the two dead bodies and Sherry picked them up out of the water.

"Dey's plump!" he commented as his fingers examined the breasts to see.

"We has all de ducks we can eat now, but dis boy ought to shoot one flyin' befo' we go home."

"Den we'll go on," Uncle agreed.

They crossed the river and entered a creek much like the first one. It branched right and left, becoming narrower all the time. Uncle Bill began a stealthy creeping around the wooded bends. Sometimes ducks were there, sometimes not. Breeze shot wildly each time one rose. Sherry declared he killed two of those that fell. He may have, he didn't know. Sherry may have just said so to encourage him.

This was a strange world to Breeze. Gray water, unfamiliar trees, long stretches of ripening marsh grass where odd-looking birds made outlandish cries as they passed.

Uncle Bill paddled steadily on with a measured stroke. Past islands lined with ranges of sand-hills where tall pines above the willows stood against the sky. Through channels choked with weeds where white cranes fed. Long streets of water, curving, dustless, houseless, settled only by light and shade and the images of trees and clouds and sun they faithfully reflected.

At a sudden "S-st" from Uncle Bill, Breeze looked at the low wooded hillside and glimpsed a doe, followed by her fawn. They had come down to the water's edge to drink. Sheer terror held them rigid for a brief instant and then both were gone.

"Jedus, Sherry," Uncle Bill chided. "You could 'a' got all two if you had 'a' tried!"

"I didn' want dem," Sherry answered. "We's done killed enough for one day. My mammy says if you kill too much o' t'ings at a time you'll git so you smell like death. I don' want to. I kills a while and den I stops."

Uncle Bill laughed, and the silence was so deep that his voice echoed and reechoed.

Breeze was glad the killing was over, for he'd rather hear the two men talk than to see Sherry kill.

The boat flowed evenly, almost silently, over the water's smooth surface. Uncle Bill kept it close to the bank to avoid the full sweep of the current in the middle of the stream.

Great dark birds, startled by its passing so close to their homes, flew up out of the water with a loud flopping of wings, but there was little talk for the rest of the way.

The water slipped swiftly past them. The small whirling circles made by Uncle Bill's paddle widened until they reached the bank's willowy edges where vines and bushes wound tight together, choking and strangling one another as they wrestled for a narrow foothold.

When Uncle Bill paused and cleared his throat Breeze knew he was going to ask Sherry a question.

"How come you don' like April, here lately?"

"Who say I don' like em?" Sherry answered.

"I say so."

Sherry's white grin was cold. Hard. His answer slow in coming.

"April's legs is most too long fo' de foreman of a big plantation like Blue Brook."

"Wha' you mean, son?"

"Dey kin tote him too far f'om home sometimes."

"You mean April kin walk too far atter dark?"

"Yes, suh," Uncle Bill sighed.

"Gawd is de one made 'em long. April ain' had nothin' to do wid dat. Gawd made you' own not so short, Sherry. Don' fo'git dat."

Sherry said no more and Uncle Bill worked faster with his paddling.

The afternoon sun was a great red ball floating among thin smoky clouds. A light haze was creeping out from underneath the trees on the banks of the creeks. The shrill call of a cicada rose, swelled into quick breathless notes, faded away, then was taken up, answered by a mate. Yellow sunshine fell between lacy blue shadows cast by cypress trees. Dark green thickets crouched wet-footed, beside narrow winding paths of tide water.

The marshes were buried. All the sticky miry mud exposed by the morning was hidden. Through old flood-gates the rising water gurgled and bubbled into forsaken rice-fields. Grass, vines, trees, bushes rank, thorny and fetid, crowded and trampled one another, trying to gain a deeper, stronger foothold down in the broken dikes. Breeze gazed around him with long looks. As far as his eyes could see the earth was flooded. Wasted. Unsown. Abandoned.

Uncle Bill sighed. It made him sad to think how the tide had destroyed the work of years. At first it crept timidly in, hardly enough for its shallow trickling to show. But it grew bolder and stronger as it took back the rich land, acre by acre, until it owned them all. All!

The first white men who came here found the whole face of the earth covered with a thick forest growth of cypress and gum and ash, matted, tangled with powerful vines, and held by the tides that rose and fell as they do now, twice every day. Those men bought slaves, Breeze's and Sherry's and his own great-grand-fathers and mothers, African people fresh from the Guinea Coast. The slaves diked and banked up the land so the forest growth could be removed, then they canaled and ditched and banked it into smaller well-drained tracts which were planted with rice. And rice made the plantation owners rich.

For years the lands were held by children and grandchildren of those first settlers, but nearly every old plantation home has been burned or sold or abandoned. The rich rice-fields are deserted. The old dikes and flood-gates that stood as guardians are broken and rotted. The tide rolls over all as it did before the land was ever cleared. It has taken back its own.

A whistle not far away gave a shrill ugly shriek. "Lawd, de boat is lated to-day! Wha' time it is, Uncle Bill?"

Uncle cast a quick glance up at the sun. "A li'l' after four, son."

Sherry considered. "De boat ain' but two hours lated. Pretty good, for dat old slow coach, enty?"

"Kin you tell de time, Breeze?"

"I kin tell if it ain' cloudy, neither rainin', in de daytime."

Sherry said there were many other ways to tell; the tide runs true, rain or shine, morning-glories and lots of other flowers open and close by the time. Big Sue's yard was full of four-o'clocks. They'd be wide open now. Birds change their songs with the turn of the afternoon. "Listen! You can hear a red-bird

[157]

whistlin' right now. Dis morning he went so——"
Sherry pursed his lips and mimicked a bar of bird song.

"Now e says to dis ——" And he whistled a few
notes that the bird himself echoed. "Dat bird knows it's
past four. A red-bird knows de time every bit as good
as Uncle. Grass blades moves wid de day too. Dey
leans dis way an' dat to get de light. A lot o' t'ings is
got mo' sense dan people, enty, Uncle?"

"Sho'!" Uncle Bill declared. "If you watch t'ings
close, you'll git wise. Wise! Take Uncle Isaac; e can'
read readin' or either writin' but he knows more'n any
school-teacher or either preacher dat ever came to Blue
Brook."

"Wha' de name o' de church Uncle Isaac b'longs
to?"

Uncle Bill smiled gently. "Po' Uncle! E j'ined de
white folks ch'uch yonder at de gate, long time ago.
Dat's named 'Piscopalian. Den e went to town on de
boat an' seen a white folks' chu'ch named de Presbe-
teerin. Uncle mixed de two togedder. E calls hese'f a
'Piscoteerin'. Po' Uncle! If e don' mind, e's gwine
die in sin yet. You boys mustn' wait too long to pray.
Pray soon. Git religion young. It's a heap easier den.
I waited so long I mighty nigh missed gittin' it myse'f.
But I ruther have religion dan to have all Uncle Isaac's
knowledge. E kin put a 'hand' on anybody long as dey's
in dis world. E kin take a 'spell' off anybody long as
dey's dis side o' de grave. But dat ain' so much after
all. Dis life is short. It's de other side o' Jordan we
got to fix for. Dem sweet fields in Eden, yonder in
Canaan's land. Dat's de country I'm aimin' to reach.
You boys must try to reach em too."

"Uncle, you believe any white folks is in Heaben?"

"Gawd knows, son. White folks is mighty smart
people. Dey knows a lot o' tricks we don' know."

XIII

THE QUILTING

BEFORE day was clean Big Sue got up out of bed and went to the front door to look at the weather. The cool air was soft and still, trees and birds were asleep. The earth itself was resting quietly, for the sun tarried late in his bed. The stars had not yet faded from the clear open sky, but Big Sue was full of excitement. Only a few hours more and she must have everything ready at Maum Hannah's for the quilting to commence.

Her own big room was almost large enough for a quilting, but it was better to go to Maum Hannah's. The meeting benches could be brought in from under the house where they stayed, to make seats enough for the company, and Maum Hannah's quilting poles stood always in the corner waiting for work to do. Plenty of pots sat on her hearth and two big ones out in the yard besides. Most of the plantation quiltings were held at Maum Hannah's house, the same as the night prayer-meetings.

The raw rations were all ready to cook. Plenty of rice and corn-meal. White flour and coffee and sugar from the store. She'd pot-roast the ducks, and fry the fish, and make the turtle into a stew. She'd roast the potatoes in the ashes. The corn-pone would bake brown and nice in the big oven on the hearth. With some nice fat white-flour biscuit to eat last with the coffee, she would have enough to fill everybody full.

Breeze must get up and hustle! She called him and

he tried to raise up his drowsy head, but sleep had it too heavy for his strength to lift. If she'd only let him take one more little nap! But she shook him soundly by the shoulder. To-day was the day for the quilting. He must get up and dress, and get some fat kindling wood to start a fire under both the big pots in Maum Hannah's yard. He'd have to fetch water for those pots too, and tote all the quilts there, and the sack of newly ginned cotton April had given her for lining the quilts, besides all the rations that had to be cooked for the quilters to eat at dinner-time.

With a sleepy groan Breeze rose and pulled on his shirt and breeches, then his sluggish feet shambled toward the water-shelf where the tin washbasin sat beside the water-bucket. Big Sue made him wash his face, no matter how soon or cold the morning was. He might as well do it, and get it over with.

As he reached a heavy hand up for the gourd that hung on a nail beside the water-bucket, his arm lengthened into a lazy stretch, the other arm joined in, and his mouth opened into a wide yawn. Then his fingers dropped wearily on to his head where they began a slow tired scratching.

Big Sue stopped short in her tracks, and the sparkle in her beady black eyes cut him clear through to the quick.

"Looka here, boy! Is you paralyze'? I ain' got time to stop an' lick you, now. But if you don' stir you' stumps, you' hide won' hold out to-night when I git back home. Dat strap yonder is eetchin' to git on you' rind right now! Or would you ruther chaw a pod o' red pepper?"

The long thin strip of leather, hanging limp and black against the white-washed wall not far from the mantel-shelf, looked dumb and harmless enough, but

Breeze gave a shiver and jumped wide awake as his eyes followed Big Sue's fat forefinger. That strap could whistle and hiss through the air like a black snake when Big Sue laid its licks home. Its stinging lash could bite deep into tender naked meat. But the string of red pepper pods hanging outside by the front door were pure fire.

He wanted to cry but fear crushed back the misery that seized him, and gulping down a sob he hurried about his tasks. First he hastily·swallowed a bite of breakfast, then he took a big armful of folded quilt tops, and holding them tight hurried to Maum Hannah's house with them.

The sun was up, and the morning tide rolled high and shiny in the river. The air was cool, and the wind murmuring on the tree-tops strewed the path with falling leaves. Some of them whirled over as they left the swaying boughs, then lay still wherever they touched the ground, while others flew sidewise, and skipped nimbly over the ground on their stiff brown points.

The sunlight smelled warm, but the day's breath was flavored with things nipped by the frost. The sweet potato leaves were black, the squash vines full of slimy green rags. The light frost on the cabin steps sparkled with tinted radiance as the cool wind, that had all the leaves trembling in a shiver, began to blow a bit warmer and melt it back into dew.

This was the second frost of the fall. One more would bring rain. The day knew it, for in spite of the sun's brave shining, the shadows fell heavy and green under the trees. Those cast by the old cedar stretched across the yard's white sand much blacker and more doleful than the sun-spotted shade cast by the live-oaks.

Maum Hannah's house was very old, and its foundations had weakened, so the solid weight of its short square body leaned to one side. The ridge-pole was warped, the mossy roof sagged down in the middle, and feathery clumps of fern throve along the frazzled edge of the rotted eaves.

Two big black iron washpots in Maum Hannah's yard sat close enough to the house to be handy, but far enough away to kill any spark that might fly from their fires toward the house, trying to set fire to the old shack, tottering with age and all but ready to fall.

Inside Maum Hannah, dressed up in her Sunday clothes, with a fresh white headkerchief binding her head, a wide white apron almost hiding the long full skirt of her black and white checked homespun dress, awaited the guests. She was bending over the fire whose reddish light glowed on her cheerful smile, making it brighter than ever.

"Come in, son. You's a early bird dis mawnin'. You's a strong bird too, to tote sich a heavy load. Put de quilts on de bed in de shed-room, den come eat some breakfast wid me. I can' enjoy eatin' by myse'f, and Emma went last night to Zeda's house, so e wouldn't be in my way to-day."

The bacon broiling on a bed of live coals, and fresh peeled sweet potatoes just drawn out from the ashes where they had roasted, made a temptation that caused Breeze's mouth to water. But he hesitated. Cousin Big Sue was waiting for him, and he knew better than to cross her this morning.

"If you can' set down, take a tater in you' hand an' eat em long de way home. A tater's good for you. It'll stick to you' ribs."

Breeze took the hot bit from her hand and started to hurry away, but she stopped him, "No, son! Don' grab victuals an' run! Put you' hands in front o' you, so. Pull you' foot an' bow, an' say 'T'ank Gawd!' Dat's

[162]

de way. You must do so ev'y day if you want Jedus to bless you. All you got comes from Gawd. You mustn' forgit to tell Him you's t'ankful.''

Most of the cabin doors were closed, but the smoke curling up out of every chimney circled in wreaths overhead. Little clouds of mist floated low over the marsh, where the marsh-hens kept up a noisy cackling. Roosters crowed late. Ant-hills were piled high over the ground. All sure signs of rain, even though no clouds showed in the pale blue sky.

As soon as Breeze's work was done, Big Sue had promised he could go to Zeda's house or to April's, and spend the rest of the day playing with their children, and now there were only a few more lightwood splinters to split. The prospect of such fun ahead must have made him reckless, or else the ax, newly sharpened on the big round grind-stone, had got mean and tricky. Anyway, as Breeze brought it down hard and heavy on the last fat chunk to be split, its keen edge glanced to one side and with as straight an aim as if it had two good eyes, jumped between two of his toes. How it stung! The blood poured out. But Breeze's chief thought was of how Big Sue would scold him. Hopping on a heel across the yard to the door-step he called piti-fully for Maum Hannah.

''Great Gawd!'' she yelled out when she saw the bloody tracks on the white sand. ''What is you done, Breeze? Don' come in dis house an' track up dis floor! Wha' dat ail you' foot?''

She made him lie flat on the ground and hold his foot up high, then taking a healing leaf from a low bush, growing right beside her door, she pressed it over the cut and held it until it stuck, then tied it in place. That was all he needed, but he'd have to keep still to-day. Maybe two or three days.

[163]

By ten o'clock Big Sue was outside the yard where Zeda stirred the boiling washpots. Onion-flavored eel-stew scented the air. The stout meeting benches had been brought in from under the house, two for each quilt. The quilting poles leaned in a corner waiting to be used. The older, more settled women came first. Each with her needle, ready to sew. The younger ones straggled in later, with babies, or tiny children, who kept their hands busy. They were all kin, and when they first assembled the room rang with, "How you do, cousin?" "Howdy, Auntie!" "How is you, sister?"

Leah, April's wife, had on somewhat finer clothes than the other women. The bottom of her white apron was edged with a band of wide lace, and she wore a velvet hat with a feather in it over her plaid head-kerchief. But something ailed her speech. The words broke off in her mouth. Her well-greased face looked troubled. Her round eyes sad.

"How you do, daughter?" Maum Hannah asked her kindly. "You look so nice to-day. You got such a pretty hat on! Lawd! Is dem teeth you got in you' mouth? April ought to be proud o' you."

But instead of smiling Leah's face looked ready to cry. "I ain' well, Auntie. My head feels too full all de time. Dese teeth is got me fretted half to death. Dey's got my gums all sore, an' dey rattles when I tries to walk like dey is gwine to jump down my throat. I can' eat wid 'em on to save life. De bottom ones is meaner dan de top ones. I like to missed and swallowed 'em yestiddy."

"How come you wears 'em if dey pesters you so bad?"

"April likes 'em. E say dey becomes me. E paid a lot o' money fo' dem, too. E took me all de way to town on de boat to git 'em. But dey ain' no sati'-

faction." She sighed deep. "An' de blood keeps all de time rushin' to my head ever since I was salivate."

Maum Hannah listened and sympathized with a doleful, "Oh-oh!" while Leah complained that the worst part was she couldn't enjoy her victuals any more. She'd just as soon have a cup and saucer in her mouth as those teeth. It made no difference what she ate, now, everything tasted all the same.

"Fo' Gawd's sake take 'em off an' rest you' mouth to-day!" Maum Hannah exhorted her. "You may as well pleasure you'self now and den. April ain' gwine see you. Not to-day!"

"Somebody'd tell him an' dat would vex him," Leah bemoaned.

But Maum Hannah took her by the arm and looked straight in her eyes. "Honey," she coaxed, "Gawd ain' gwine bless you if you let April suffer you dis way. You an' April all both is too prideful. Take dem teeth off an' rest you' mouth till dis quiltin' is over. It would fret me if you don't."

Screening her mouth with both hands Leah did rid her gums of the offending teeth, but instead of putting them in her apron pocket she laid them carefully in a safe place on the high mantel-shelf.

The room buzzed with chatter. How would such a great noisy gathering ever get straightened out to work? They were as much alike as guinea fowls in a flock, every head tied up turban-fashion, every skirt covered by an apron.

Big Sue welcomed every one with friendliest greetings, and although her breath was short from excitement, she talked gaily and laughed often.

A sudden hush followed a loud clapping of her hands. The closest attention was paid while she appointed Leah and Zeda captains of the first quilts to be laid out. Zeda stepped forward, with a jaunty toss of her head, and, shrugging a lean shoulder, laughed lightly.

"Big Sue is puttin' sinner 'gainst Christian dis mawnin'!"

Leah tried to laugh, her tubby body, bulky as Big Sue's, shook nervously, as her giggling rippled out of her mouth, but her eyes showed no mirth at all.

"You choose first, Leah. You's de foreman's wife."

Leah chose Big Sue.

"Lawd," Zeda threw her head back with a laugh, "Yunnuh two is so big nobody else wouldn' have room to set on a bench 'side you."

The crowd tittered, but Big Sue looked stern.

"Do, Zeda! You has gall enough to talk about bigness? T'ank Gawd, I'm big all de way round like I is." She cast a wry look toward Zeda, then turned her head and winked at the crowd. But Zeda sucked her teeth brazenly. She was satisfied with her shape. She might not look so nice now, but her bigness would soon be shed. Just give her a month or two longer.

"You ought to be shame, wid grown chillen in you' house, an' a grown gal off yonder to college."

"When I git old as you, Big Sue, den I'll stay slim all de time. Don't you fret." Zeda laughed, and chose Gussie, a skinny, undersized, deaf and dumb woman, whose keen eyes plainly did double duty. When Zeda looked toward her and spoke her name, Gussie pushed through the crowd, smiling and making wordless gurgles of pleasure for the compliment Zeda had paid her by choosing her first of all.

"I take Bina next!" Leah called out.

"Bina's a good one for you' quilt. E's a extra fine Christian."

"You better be prayin' you'se'f, Zeda," Bina came back.

"Who? Me? Lawd, gal, I does pray." Zeda said it seriously, and her look roved around the room. "Sinners is mighty sca'ce at dis quiltin'. Who kin I choose next?" She searched the group.

"Don' take so long, Zeda," Big Sue chided. "Hurry up an' choose. De day is passin'. You an' Gussie is de only two sinners. You' 'bliged to pick a Christian, now."

"Den I'll take Nookie. E's got swift-movin' fingers."

The choosing went on until eight women were picked for each quilt, four to a side. Then the race began.

The two quilt linings, made out of unbleached homespun, were spread on the clean bare floor, and covered over with a smooth layer of cotton.

"How come you got such nice clean cotton to put in you' quilt?" Zeda inquired with an innocent look across at Big Sue.

When Big Sue paid her no heed, she added brazenly, "De cotton April gi' me fo' my quilt was so trashy and dark I had to whip em wid pine-tops half a day to get de dirt out clean enough to use."

Still Big Sue said nothing.

"You must be stand well wid April." Zeda looked at Big Sue with a smile.

Big Sue raised her shoulders up from doubling over, and in a tart tone blurted out, "You talks too much, Zeda. Shut you' mouth and work."

"Who? Me?" Zeda came back pleasantly. "Great Gawd! I was praisin' de whiteness of de cotton, dat was all."

Two of the patch-work covers that Big Sue had fashioned with such pains, stitch by stitch, square by square, were opened out wide and examined and admired.

[167]

"Which one you want, Zeda? You take de first pick."

"Lawd, all two is so nice it's hard to say."

Gussie pointed to the "Snake-fence" design, and Zeda took it, leaving the "Star of Bethlehem" for Leah. Both were placed over a cotton-covered lining on the floor, corner to corner, edge to edge, and basted into place. Next, two quilting poles were laid lengthwise beside each quilt, and tacked on with stout ball thread. The quilts were carefully rolled on the poles, and the pole-ends fastened with strong cords to the side-walls. All was ready for the quilting.

Leah's crew beat fixing the quilt on the poles, but the sewing was the tedious part. The stitches must be small, and in smooth rows that ran side by side. They must also be deep enough to hold the cotton fast between the top and the lining.

Little talking was done at first. Minds, as well as eyes, had to watch the needles. Those not quilting in this race stood around the hearth puffing at their pipes, talking, joking, now and then squealing out with merriment.

"Yunnuh watch dem pots," Big Sue cautioned them. "Make Breeze keep wood on de fire. Mind now."

The quilts were rolled up until the quilting poles met, so the sewing started right in the middle, and as the needles left neat stitches, the poles were rolled farther apart, until both quilts were done to the edges. These were carefully turned in and whipped down, with needles running at full racing speed. Zeda's crew finished a full yard ahead. The sinners won. And how they did crow over the others! Deaf and dumb Gussie did her best to boast, but her words were stifled in dreadful choked noises that were hard to bear.

Big Sue put the wild ducks on to roast. They were

fat and tender, and already stuffed full of oyster dressing, the same dressing she fixed for the white folks. She said the oysters came from near the beach where the fresh salt tide made them large and juicy.

What a dinner she had! Big Sue was an openhanded woman, for truth.

Some of the farm-hands stopped by on their way home for the noon hour. Coming inside they stood around the fireplace, grinning, joking and smoking the cigarettes they rolled with deft fingers.

Everybody was given a pan and spoon. Zeda and Bina helped Big Sue pass around great dishpans of smoking food, and cups of water sweetened with molasses. For a time nothing was said except the exclamations that praised the dinner. Indeed it might have been a wedding feast but for the lack of cake and wine.

The wild ducks, cooked just to a turn, were served last. Their red blood was barely curdled with heat, yet their outsides were rich and brown. Lips smacked. Spoons clattered. Mouths too full dropped crumbs as they munched.

A grand dinner.

"Take you' time, an' chaw," Big Sue bade the guests kindly. "You got plenty o' time to finish de rest o' de quilts befo' night."

As soon as the edge was taken off their appetites they fell to talking. Big Sue did not sit down to eat at all, so busy was she passing around the pans of hot food, and urging the others to fill themselves full.

As more men came by and stopped, the noise waxed louder, until the uproar of shouting and laughter and light-hearted talk seethed thick. When all were filled with Big Sue's good cheer, they got up and went out into the yard to smoke, to catch a little fresh air, and to wash the grease off their fingers. The pans and spoons and tin-cups were stacked up on the water-shelf out of the way where they'd wait to be washed until night.

The quilting was the work in hand now, and when the room was in order again, and the women rested and refreshed, Big Sue called them in to begin on the next set of quilts.

April went riding by on the sorrel colt, on his way back to the field, and Big Sue called him to come in and eat the duck and hot rice she had put aside specially for him. But he eyed her coolly, rode on and left her frowning.

Zeda laughed, and asked Big Sue if April was a boy to hop around at her heels? Didn't she know April had work to do? Important work. The white people made him plantation foreman because they knew they could trust him to look after their interests. He not only worked himself, but he kept the other hands working too.

Leah sat silent, making short weak puffs at her pipe.

Maum Hannah's deep sigh broke into the stillness.

"I ever did love boy-chillen, but dey causes a lot o' sorrow. My mammy used to say ev'y boy-child ought to be killed soon as it's born."

"How'd de world go on if people done dat?" Bina asked.

"I dunno. Gawd kin do a lot o' strange t'ings."

This made them all stop and think again.

The kettle sang as steam rushed out of its spout. The flames made a sputtering sound. The benches creaked as the women bent over and rose with their needles. Bina sat up straight, then stretched.

"If all de mens was dead, you could stay in de chu'ch, enty, Zeda?" Bina slurred the words softly.

Zeda came back, "Don' you fret 'bout me, gal. Jake ain' no more to me dan a dead man."

"Yunnuh stop right now! Dat's no-manners talk. Jake's a fine man, if e is my gran. I know, by I raise em. When his mammy died an' left em, Jake an' Bully and April was all three de same as twins in my house." Maum Hannah spoke very gravely. Presently she got up and went into the shed-room. She came back smiling, with a folded quilt on her arm. "Le's look at de old Bible quilt, chillen. It'll do yunnuh good."

She held up one corner and motioned to deaf and dumb Gussie to hold up the other so all the squares could be seen. There were twenty, every one a picture out of the Bible. The first one, next to Gussie's hand, was Adam and Eve and the serpent. Adam's shirt was blue, his pants brown, and his head a small patch of yellow. Eve had on a red headkerchief, a purple wide-skirted dress; and a tall black serpent stood straight up on the end of its tail.

The next square had two men, one standing up, the other fallen down—Cain and Abel. The red patch under Abel was his blood, spilled on the ground by Cain's sin. Maum Hannah pointed out Noah and the Ark; Moses with the tables of stone; the three Hebrew children; David and Goliath; Joseph and Mary and the little baby Jesus; and last of all, Jesus standing alone by the cross. As Maum Hannah took them one by one, all twenty, she told each marvelous story.

The quilters listened with rapt attention. Breeze almost held his breath for fear of missing a word. Sometimes his blood ran hot with wonder, then cold with fear. Many eyes in the room glistened with tears.

The names of God and Jesus were known to Breeze, but he had never understood before that they were real people who could walk and talk. Maum Hannah told about God's strength and power and wisdom, how He knew right then what she was doing and saying. He could see each stitch that was taken in the quilts, whether it was small and deep and honest, or shallow and careless. He wrote everything down in a great book where He kept account of good and evil. Breeze had never dreamed that such things went on around him all the time.

Yet the quilt was made out of pictures of the very things Maum Hannah told. Nobody could doubt that all she said was the truth. In the charmed silence, her words fell clear and earnest. The present was shut out. Breeze's mind went a-roaming with her, back into the days when the world was new and God walked and talked with the children He had so lately made. As she spoke Breeze shivered over those days that were to come when everybody here would be either in Hell or Heaven. It had to be one or the other. There was no place to stop or to hide when death came and knocked at your door. She pointed to Breeze. That same little boy, there in the chimney corner, with his foot tied up, would have to account for all he did! As well as Breeze could understand, Heaven was in the blue sky straight up above the plantation. God sat there on His throne among the stars, while angels, with harps of gold in their hands, sang His praises all day long. Hell was straight down. Underneath. Deep under the earth. Satan lived there with his great fires for ever and ever a-burning on the bodies of sinners piled high up so they could never crumble.

Maum Hannah herself became so moved by the thought of the sufferings of the poor pitiful sinners in Hell, that her voice broke and tears dimmed her eyes, and she plead with them all:

"Pray! Chillen! Pray!

"Do try fo' 'scape Hell if you kin!

"Hell is a heat!

"One awful heat!

"We fire ain' got no time wid em!

"Pray! Chillen! Pray! For Gawd's sake, pray!

"When de wind duh whip you

"An' de sun-hot duh burn you

"An' de rain duh wet you,

"All dem say, Pray! Do try fo' 'scape Hell if you kin!"

On the way home through the dusk Breeze stopped short in his tracks more than once, for terror seized him at the bare rustle of a bird's wing against a dry leaf. When the gray shadow of a rabbit darted across the path and the sight of a glowworm's eye gleamed up from the ground, Big Sue stopped too. And breathing fast with anxiety, cried out:

"Do, Jedus! Lawd! Dat rabbit went leftward. A bad luck t'ing! Put dem t'ings down! Chunk two sticks behind em. Is you see anyt'ing strange, Breeze?" She sidled up close to him and whispered the question.

Breeze stared hard into the deepening twilight. The black shadows were full of dark dreadful things that pressed close to the ground, creeping slowly, terribly. The tree branches rocked, the leaves whispered sharply, the long gray moss streamed toward them.

"Le's run, Cun Big Sue." Breeze leaped with a quick hop ahead, but her powerful hand clutched his shoulder. "Looka here, boy! I'll kill you to-night if you leave me. No tellin' what kind o' sperits is walkin'. I kin run when I's empty-handed, but loaded down wid all dese t'ings a snail could ketch me! You git behind me on de path."

The black smoke rising out of the chimney made a great serpent that stood on the end of its tail. For a minute Breeze was unable to speak. His heart throbbed with heavy blows, for not only did that smoke serpent

[173]

lean and bend and reach threateningly, but something high and black and shapeless stood in front of Big Sue's cabin, whose whitewashed walls behind it made it look well-nigh as tall as a pine tree. It might be the Devil! Or Death! Or God! He gave a scream and clung to Big Sue as the figure took a step toward them.

"Yunnuh is late!" April's voice boomed out.

"Lawd!" Big Sue fairly shouted. "I was sho' you was a plat-eye. You scared me half to death! Man! I couldn' see no head on you no matter how hard I look. How come you went inside my house with me not home?"

April grunted. "You better be glad! I had a hard time drivin' a bat out o' you' house."

"A bat!" Big Sue shrieked with terror. "How come a bat in my house? A bat is de child of de devil."

April declared the bat had squeaked and grinned and chattered in his face until he mighty nigh got scared himself.

"Lawd! Wha's gwine happen now? A bat inside my house! An' look how de fire's smokin'!"

She hurried Breeze off to bed in the shed-room whose darkness was streaked with wavering firelight that fell through the cracks in the wall. Fear kept him awake until he put his head under the covers and shut out all sight and sound and thought.

He was roused by a knock on the front door. Big Sue made no answer, and another knock made by the knuckles of a strong hand was followed by a loud crying, "Open dis door, I tell you! I know April's right in dere!" This was followed by the thud of a kick, but no answer came from inside. Breeze could not have spoken to save his life, for sheer terror held him crouched under the quilts and his tongue was too weak and dry to move.

Where in God's world was Big Sue? The first of

those knocks should have waked her. Sleep never did fasten her eyelids down very tight, yet with all this deafening racket, she stayed dumb. Had she gone off and left Breeze by himself? The voice calling at the door sounded like a woman's voice at first, but now it deepened with hoarse fury and snarled and growled and threatened, calling Big Sue filthy names. Breeze knew then for certain it was some evil thing. His flesh crept loose from his bones. His blood ran cold and weak. He realized Big Sue was not at home. Maybe she was dead, in her bed! The thought was so terrible that in desperation he lifted up his head and yelled:

"Who dat?"

At once the dreadful answer came.

"Who dat say 'who dat'?" Then a silence, for Breeze could utter no other word.

Outside the wind caught at the trees and thrashed their leaves, then came inside to rustle the papers on the cabin's walls, and whisper weird terrible things through the cracks. The thing that had knocked on the door was walking away. Its harsh breathing was hushed into sobs and soft moans that made Breeze's heart sink still deeper with horror.

For a minute every noise in the world lulled. Nothing stirred except the ghastly tremor that shook Breeze's body from his covered-up head to the heels doubled up under his cold hips.

A sudden fearful battering in company with despairing howls, crashed at the door! It would soon break down! There was no time to waste putting on clothes! Hopping up into the cold darkness, Breeze eased the back door open and slipped into the night.

The horrible door-splitting blows went right on. Thank God, somebody was coming. Running, with a torch. Breeze forgot that snakes were walking, and

[175]

leaped through the bushes over ground that felt un-steady to his flying feet. His heart swelled with joy and relief, for the man hurrying toward the cabin lighting his way with a fat lightwood torch was Uncle Bill. Twice Breeze opened his mouth to call out, but the only sound he could make was a whispered—"Uncle Bill—Uncle Bill!"

Following the torch's light he could see a black woman cutting the door down with an ax. Who in God's name would dare do such a thing? Uncle Bill walked right up to her and shook her soundly by the shoulder.

"What is you a-doin', Leah? Is you gone plumb crazy? Gi' me dat ax!" He jerked the ax from her hands and she began shrieking afresh, and trying to push him back. But she couldn't budge him one inch. Holding her off, with his free hand he made a proper, polite knock, although the door was split and the dim firelight shone through its new-made cracks.

"Dis is me, Bill, Miss Big Sue," he called out, a stern note deepening his voice.

Leah shrilled out harshly. "You better open dis door! You low-down black buzzard hussy! You wait till I gits my hands on you' throat! You won' fool wid my husband no mo' in dis world!"

Fully dressed and quite calm Big Sue appeared. She answered with mild astonishment:

"Why, Leah! How come you makin' all dis fuss? You must want to wake up de whole plantation? You ought to be shamed. I never see such a no-manners 'oman!"

"Whe's April?" Leah howled. "Whe's April, I tell you? Don' you cut no crazy wid me to-night! I'll kill you sho' as you do!"

"Fo' Gawd's sake, Leah! Shut you' mouth! I

dunno nuttin' 'bout April. You is too sickenin'! Always runnin' round to somebody's house a-lookin' fo' April!'

"Yes, I look fo' em. You had em here too! See his hat yonder on de floor right now! You fat black devil!" Seizing Big Sue's kerchiefed head with both hands Leah tried to choke her, but Big Sue wrenched herself loose and with a wicked laugh raised one fat leg and gave Leah a kick in the middle of her body that sent her backward with a slam against the wall.

"You'd choke me, would you? I'll tear de meat off you' bones!" Big Sue screamed, but Leah crumpled sidewise and fell flat on the floor, her eyes lifeless, her face stiffened.

Big Sue had roused into fury. She staggered forward and bent over and rained blows with both fists on Leah's silent mouth, until Uncle Bill grappled her around her huge waist and dragged her to the other side of the room.

Big Sue bellowed. "You'd choke me, enty? You blue-gummed pizen-jawed snake! Gawd done right to salivate you an' make you' teeth drop out."

For all the signs of life she gave, Leah may as well have been dead. She lay there on the floor, limp and dumb, even after Uncle Bill took the bucketful of water from the shelf and doused her with it. She didn't even catch her breath. Uncertain what to do, Uncle Bill knelt over her and called her name.

"Leah! Leah! Don't you die here on dis floor. Leah! Open you' eyes. I know good and well you's playin' 'possum."

Except for the fire's crackling and the low chirping of one lone cricket, the stillness of death was in the room.

"Put on you' shirt and pants, Breeze. Run tell

April Leah is done faint off. E must come here quick as e kin.''

The darkness of the night was terrible as Breeze ran through it toward the Quarters. A cedar limb creaked mournfully as the wind wrung it back and forth. Its crying was like sorrowful calls for aid. Breeze tried to hurry, to make his legs run faster, but they were ready to give way and fall. His feet stumbled, his throat choked until he could scarcely breathe. His brain wheeled and rattled inside his skull. How horrible Death is!

A few stars twinkled bright away up in the sky, but the waving tree-tops made a thick black smoke that covered the yellow moon. High-tide glistened in the darkness, all but ready to turn by now. Leah's soul would go out with it if something wasn't done to help her.

Lord how awful her eyeballs were, rolled back so far in her head! Jesus, have mercy! The thought of them made Breeze senseless with terror. Tears gushed from his own eyes and blinded him.

April was not at home, and Breeze raced back, but already Leah was coming to. She lay on the floor, her fat face, black as tar against the whiteness of the pillow under it now, was set and furrowed. Her tooth-less jaws moved with mute words, as if she talked with some one the others could not see. She kept fumbling with the red charm-string tied around her neck, as her dull eyes rolled slowly from one face to the other.

Breeze longed to fling himself on the bed and cover up his head, but Big Sue sat storming and panting with fury. Leah ought to be ashamed of herself, running over the country at night trying to bring disgracement on her.

''Whyn't you answer Leah when e knocked?'' Uncle Bill asked her.

Big Sue jumped at him angrily. "How'd I know Leah wasn' some robber come to cut my throat? Just 'cause Leah is married to de foreman an' livin' in a bigger house dan my own, an' wearin' finer clothes, dat don' gi' em no right to break down my door wid a' ax! No. Leah ain' no white 'oman even if e do buy medicine out de sto'. No wonder e got salivate. Gawd done right to make dat medicine loosen all Leah's teeth an' prize 'em out so e ain' got none to be a-bitin' people up wid. T'ank Gawd! Bought ones can' bite. I wish all e finger-nails would drop off! E toe-nails too! Leah's a dangerous 'oman. E ain' safe to be loose in dis country. No. Leah'd kill you quick as look at you!"

XIV

CHURCH

SUNDAY morning rose with a pale clear sky, and a sun that glittered bright and hot as it mounted.

Big Sue was already up when Breeze waked. She was fussing around, cooking dinner to take to church, fixing a basket, and China dishes to hold it. Her best clothes, and Breeze's, were laid out on chairs to be put on. They must be ready when Uncle Bill came for them in his new buggy. He had to go ahead of time, for he had charge of the communion as well as of the Bury League which would be organized when the service was over and the dinner eaten. The head man of the Bury League had come to preach and to form a Society to Bury. Big Sue baked rising bread yesterday in the Big House kitchen stove. The brown loaves, uncovered, sat in a row on the shelf, waiting to be wrapped up. They'd turn to Jesus' own body when the preacher prayed over them, and blessed them. Blackberry wine, in the two big demijohns in the corner of the shed-room, would turn into Jesus' blood. Breeze couldn't make it out in his head exactly, but Big Sue said it was so. Breeze had picked the blackberries that made the wine, and he'd bought the white flour for the bread from the store. How could they turn to Jesus? But Big Sue said prayer can do anything. Anything! When a fine preacher like the Bury League leader prays. Not everybody knows how to pray right, but he did. Yes, Lord, he did!

Before taking time to swallow down a mouthful of

[180]

bread for breakfast, Breeze and Big Sue put the demijohns on the front porch, ready to go to church. They
packed up all the fine dinner in one box, and the communion bread in another, so when she was dressed in her
Sunday clothes, she'd have nothing to do but sit still
and wait and rest.

How different she looked with her body pulled in
tight with a great corset full of steel bands! Like a
cotton bale pressed too small. The frills of her petticoat
were lace-trimmed. Over them, hiding them carefully,
was her new purple sateen dress.

She sat down on the porch with a pan of breakfast
in her lap and began to eat. Breeze was back in the
shed-room dressing when he heard her laugh and
scramble to her feet to say in her company manners
voice:

"How you do dis mawnin', Reverend?"

Breeze peeped through the open door in time to see
her draw a foot adroitly behind her in a low curtsey
to a strange man who answered in a familiar voice:

"Quite well, thank you, Mrs. Good-wine. How you
do this morning?"

"Not so good," she said sweetly. "Bad luck's been
a-hangin' round de plantation lately."

"Bad luck ought not to pester a lady who can fix
frog legs like the ones you sent us last night for supper.
They were elegant."

Breeze stood still and listened. He knew that voice,
sure as the world. The Bury League preacher was his
own stepfather. Hurrying into his clothes he tipped
across the room to the window to see better, but Big
Sue's antics held his eyes. She was down on her knees,
shaking all over in the drollest way, with laughter that
took her breath. Her company manners were gone.
Between gasps and shouts she gurgled, "Great Gawd!

[181]

You ought o' seen dem frogs dis mawnin'. Dat fool Breeze didn' kill em! He cut off dey hind legs an' turned dem loose in de back yard! I liken to a broke my foot jumpin' when I missed an' stepped slam on one!''

"Who did you say done it?" The Reverend was disturbed. The greenish cast of his long-tailed coat and derby hat spread over his swarthy face, and he sat down so suddenly on the steps that Big Sue's roars hushed and her company manners came back. Scrambling to her feet and casting a fierce look toward the window where Breeze stood, she sympathized:

"I'm too sorry. No wonder you's sick! Eatin' de legs of a livin' frog! But dey's dead now. I made Breeze knock 'em in de head a while ago. Breeze is a crazy boy. When I git home to-night, I'm gwine gi' em de heaviest lickin' ever was. I ain' gwine leave a whole piece o' hide on em. No, suh! I'm gwine bust his crust, sure as you' bawn.''

"Whe'd you git dat boy? Is he you' own?" The Reverend's voice was weakly.

"No, Lawd. My son, Lijah, is got plenty o' sense. Breeze is a li'l' boy I got f'om Sandy Island to stay wid me, by I was so lonesome in de night by myself.''

The Reverend took a handkerchief out of the pocket in the tail of his long coat and wiped the sweat off his face, then he leaned his head on his hand. Big Sue was anxious.

"Would you like a li'l' sweetened water, suh?"

He shook his head.

"How 'bout a li'l' cookin' soda? Dat might settle you." He didn't need a thing. He must go now. He and Miss Leah were to talk over the hymns so she could lead the choir. He was subject to spells of swimming in the head, but they didn't last long.

His mention of Leah's name changed Big Sue's tone altogether. She laughed out.

"Lawdy, I bet Leah'll strut to-day. April took em to town an' bought em some teeth. Dey don' fit good like you' own, dough. Leah wouldn' trust to chaw wid 'em, not fo' nothin'. I don' blame em, dough. I'd hate to broke 'em if dey was mine. Leah is sho' tryin' to look young dese days. E natural hair is white as cotton, but e polishes em wid soot an' lark.''

Except for Big Sue's displeasure about the frogs, Breeze would have told her that the Reverend was his mother's husband who disappeared the day his grandfather cut the big pine, but the boy's one wish was to have her forget him, and maybe she'd forget the licking she promised to lay on his hide.

When Uncle Bill drove up to the door with one of the biggest pertest mules from the barnyard hitched to a one-horse wagon, Big Sue, instead of praising the beast's fresh-clipped mane and tail, looked doubtfully at the cloth strings tying the harness in many places.

"If de mule gits to kickin' or either runnin', how you gwine rule em?" she asked anxiously, but Uncle Bill laughed at her fears and helped her to the seat in front, putting the basket of dinner and the communion bread and wine back where Breeze sat on the floor.

At first the mule could not be moved out of a slow walk, but when the wagon crossed over a root in the road and the wheels made a creak and a bump, the mule jumped so that one demijohn turned over, its stopper flew out and some of the wine spilled. Big Sue scolded Breeze for letting it happen and told him to steady the jugs the rest of the way. She couldn't. She couldn't even bend with her corset on. It cut her wind and had her so heated she had to take off her big sailor hat and fan herself to catch air.

The wagon wheels ground slowly along in the deep sandy ruts. White clouds of dust rose above the slow-moving hoofs of mules and oxen that toiled along, pulling buggies and wagons and carts crowded with black people going to Heaven's Gate Church. Other church-goers were walking, many of the women in their stocking feet, carrying their shoes in their hands along with their dinner baskets. Well-greased faces shone, everybody saluted everybody else, some with simple bows, others with bows beneath upraised arms.

Heaven's Gate Church stretched its whitewashed length from the road clear back to the picnic tables made of clean new boards nailed together and fastened to wide-spreading trees whose shade made the grounds cool and darkened. The sweep of the open well was kept busy drawing water. The churchyard swarmed with people hurrying about like a nest of ants before summer rain. Women crowded behind the church, putting on shoes, fixing hair, smoothing crumpled dresses and aprons. Big Sue sucked her teeth at the sight of Leah who was strutting, sure enough. Big Sue grumbled bitterly because Leah was not only the choir leader to-day, but chairman of the lemonade committee. Leah had no judgment. The last time she fixed the lemonade, she had it sour enough to cut your very heart-strings. Leah pushed herself. She gave nobody else a chance. No wonder she got salivated.

The chain of wagons and buggies and carts that had stretched along the road crowding out people on foot, now filled the churchyard completely. Every low tree limb, every bush, held a tethered beast. Oxen chewed cuds. Mules dozed, roused to switch off gnats and stinging flies with close-clipped tails, then dozed again.

Every bench inside the long low whitewashed church was finally packed with people, waiting respectfully until the time came for the Reverend to get up in the pulpit and preach God's word. He was very different from Reverend Salty, the kind old preacher who had lately died and left the congregation of Heaven's Gate Church like sheep without a shepherd.

Reverend Salty was fat and easy to laugh, but this Reverend was slim and tall and solemn. He was so educated that he could read scripture right out of the Book. No word could trip his nimble tongue, but he said he had to wear glasses because he had strained his eyes searching the scriptures day and night to find out how to lead the people.

As he adjusted his glasses, carefully placing the curve of the gold frames behind his small ears, Maum Hannah, who sat next to Breeze on the front bench of the Amen corner, boomed right out with an earnest, "T'ank Gawd for life, son! T'ank Gawd! Praise be to His blessed name! I too glad I could git here to hear you read Gawd's book dis day!"

The Reverend cleared his throat and stared sternly at her, but when his eyes slipped a glance at Breeze, they turned quickly to another direction. Big Sue in the choir on the other side of the pulpit shook her head, but Maum Hannah was wiping her joyful tears on an apron string, and she saw nothing until Uncle Bill's old Louder trotted in and lay down near her feet, then she smiled and welcomed him with a gentle, "I glad you come to pray, Louder."

The first scripture lesson told how Moses led the Children of Israel over Jordan on their journey toward Canaan, the promised land. The Reverend stopped, and took off his fine glasses with fingers that trembled, and it seemed to Breeze the preacher looked more at him than at Maum Hannah. Getting a white fresh-ironed pocket handkerchief out of his pants pocket, he un-

[185]

folded it and made little delicate wipes at the corners of
both his eyes. He polished each spectacle glass, cleared
his throat and coughed until his voice was clear, then
he read the second lesson. April, who had come in late,
listened intently. Lord, how the man could read.
He used to read at meeting on Sandy Island sometimes. He read now, about charity, which he said
meant love, and as the familiar words fell clear on Maum
Hannah's ears, the beauty of them stirred her heart.
Her eyes closed, her body rocked from side to side. She
murmured low praise to God, then louder words of encouragement to the preacher. "Tell de people, son!
Don' hold back! You's a stranger in a strange land.
but you's a child of Gawd! Read em, son, read em!"
she crooned. "Read de word of Gawd. Let de people
hear all wha' Jedus say! We got to love ev'ybody!
Sinners an' all! Love de sinners! Hate de sin!"

Old Reverend Salty had never objected to Maum
Hannah's taking a part in the service, but this preacher
was new. He didn't understand that Maum Hannah's
heart was so moved that she had to speak out. He got
more and more nervous and fretted. Every now and
then he turned his head to one side and cast a dis-
approving frown toward her, but she was too happy to
notice that anything was wrong.

When he began lining out the hymn:

> "Come ye that love the Lord
> And let your joy be known,"

Uncle Bill leaned close and whispered in the old
woman's ear, "You mustn' talk out loud, Auntie. Dis
preacher is used to town ways."

Leah raised the tune, and her strong voice, swelled
by the congregation, made it hard to hear what Uncle

Bill said. Maum Hannah gave him a puzzled questioning look, and her old lips haltingly inquired:

"Enty?"

Whole stanzas were sung before she joined in with the great volume of harmony. Did Uncle Bill say she mustn't talk out loud because the preacher was used to town ways? Breeze nodded. That was exactly what Uncle Bill said. Maum Hannah sighed, and mumbled. She didn't mean any disrespect. His beautiful reading had moved the spirit in her and stirred her heart so deep, her tongue could not lie dumb in her mouth. She'd try not to talk out loud again.

When the hymn was done Reverend stepped to the side of the pulpit to say he would add something new to the service. The Ten Commandments. People must understand what the laws of God are before they can keep them rightly. He would read them, one at a time, and at the end of each the congregation must pray.

"Do, Lord, help us to keep this law."

"Does everybody understand?"

A roar of answers came back, "Yes suh, we understan' good, suh!" but Maum Hannah shook her head and objected in clear distinct words, "No, son, dat's how de white folks pray! Gawd ain' used to we prayin' dat way!"

April smiled, but Uncle Bill was worried. "Hush, Auntie! You'll git de preacher all tangled up."

She gave up. Her eyes fell. Her hands caught at each other and held fast. The thin-veined, blue-nailed fingers, knotted at every joint, twisted into a tight uneasy grip, then sank into a fold of her white apron. Tears ran out from under her shut eyelids.

The preacher opened the Bible, and turned the leaves over for the right place. When it lay under his eyes he began a solemn,

[187]

" 'Thou shalt have no other gods before me'!"

When he raised his eyes to the congregation Uncle Bill led a ragged wave of voices into a loud, "Do, Lawd, help us to keep dis law!"

The preacher smiled and nodded approval, then bent over the Book to read the next commandment. It was a long one. The people didn't know exactly when it ended, but he started them off, and they responded with an eager rush, "Do, Lawd, help us to keep dis law!"

The Reverend lost his place, his long forefinger had to help his eyes find it, but presently he began with a loud, " 'Remember the Sabbath day'!" He read on and on. The congregation listened breathlessly for the end, and when his voice fell, every soul broke into the crashing prayer, "Do Lawd, help us to keep dis law!" April frowned.

Maum Hannah's head dropped, her chin was on her breast, her eyes were shut tight, her lips moving in whispers. Breeze could tell she was praying alone, quite apart from the preacher and the congregation which had strangely become two beings: one, a lone, black, shiny-skinned, shiny-eyed man in the pulpit, repeating God's commandments, in the high singsong, and clapping his hands for the people to respond; and the congregation, now knitted into a many-mouthed, many-handed, many-eyed mass, that swayed and rocked like one body from side to side, crying to God in an agonized, "Do, Lawd, help us to keep dis law!" A shrill voice screamed out of the rumbling body, "Halle-lujah! I feel de sperit!" A chill crept over Breeze. He felt something strange himself. He couldn't hear his own voice in the flood of shouted praying, but he knew he was one with the rest. The preacher's tall form swayed this way and that, his long slew-feet patted the floor. He was like a tree rocked by a strong wind.

"Honour thy father and thy mother," he chanted. His upheld hands opened and clenched into straining fists, but the congregation was too full to wait for the rest. Their fierce, full-throated cry rang out, "Do, Lawd, help us to keep dis law!"

"Thou shalt kill!" His voice swelled and thickened with hoarseness, his arms swung about.

"Do, Lawd, help us to keep dis law!"

The preacher's tongue was twisted by his fervor, the ears of the congregation deafened by their own shouting.

"Thou shalt commit adultery!" he yelled.

"Do, Lawd, help us to keep dis law!" they yelled back.

Breeze's blood seethed hot, his heart beat wildly, the whole church full of people boiled with commotion. Shouts of praise to God broke into the din and tumult of prayer.

"Thou shalt steal!" came like wind on a flame and the congregation's answer sprang hot from the heart, "Do, Lawd, help us to keep dis law!"

Maum Hannah jerked up her head and listened. Her hands wavered apart, then reached out toward the preacher. She got to her feet and waved her arms, "You got em wrong, son! Wrong! Great Lawd, don' say em dat way!"

Nobody paid her any attention but Uncle Bill, and he pulled her by the arm and made her sit down, "Wait, Auntie! It ain' time to shout yet. Set down till after de sermon." Then he joined in with the others, whose words lost in feeling, surged back and forth, throbbing, thundering, until the old church trembled and shook.

"Thou shalt bear false witness against thy neighbor!"

The preacher's flashing eyes blazed with fire, as they

gazed at the people, his shortened breath panted his words, and the congregation burst into prayer, "Do, Lawd, help us to keep dis law!"

From his seat in the Amen corner Breeze could see every face. Standing out by itself, April's bold daring countenance was lit with a cool sneering smile.

The Ten Commandments were all said, but the preacher knew others.

"Thou shalt be a father to the fatherless!"

"Do, Lawd, help us to keep dis law!" The holy spirit filled the close-packed swaying crowd.

"Thou shalt be a husband to the widow!"

The ever-rising tide of prayer rolled into a flood that swallowed every soul but April. He sat upright. Unmoved. Passionless. When the preacher's ranting halted to give out a hymn, April got up and walked down the aisle, and on out of the door. A no-mannered brazen thing for anybody to do. Every eye gazed at him, the preacher stared, but Uncle Bill hurriedly raised the hymn.

The congregation sang it as the preacher lined it out two lines at a time. When it was finished, then he opened the Bible and took his text. "Hold fast and repent!" He read it twice and closed the Book, then shut his eyes and prayed in silence before he asked the question:

"Does all o' you members fast?" Throughout the church a solemn silence fell, then a great cry answered:

"Sho'! Sho'! Yes, suh."

"You can not pray rightly without fasting."

"No, suh! It's de Gawd's truth."

"The longer you fast, the better you can repent!"

"Yes, brother! You right!"

"The longer you fast, the quicker your sins will be forgiven!"

"Praise His name! Hallelujah!" Leah led the women of the choir into a low humming tune.

"Jesus fasted forty days and forty nights!"

"Yes, Gawd!" The choir's humming swelled and spread to the women of the congregation.

"He got stronger and stronger as He fasted."

"Yes, suh!" Bodies rocked and swayed to the mournful tune.

"He got strong as the devil!" The preacher's eyes flashed bright behind his glasses, but Maum Hannah jumped forward at such reckless words.

"He beat the devil at his own game!" The Reverend shouted as he shook his clenched fists.

"Glory! Hallelujah!" The congregation cried loud above the women's solemn wordless chanting.

"Yunnuh hold fast! Get strong like Jesus!" The preacher stamped on the floor.

"Yes, Gawd! Praise His name!" The women were getting to their feet and patting time.

"God'll feed you on the bread of life!"

"Do, Master!" Maum Hannah cried out so clear, that he looked at her and caught Breeze's eye. The holy spirit left him all of a sudden. Maybe he thought of the frog legs, maybe of old Breeze, but he stopped short and cleared his throat and fumbled with the leaves of the book. He presently said the time had come for making their offerings. They must sing an old hymn, and the people must come forward and lay their gifts on God's holy altar, which was a small pine table in front of the pulpit. They crushed into the aisle, an array of gaudy dresses, weaving in and out among the dark men. Both aisles were choked with singing people. Waves of hot breath smote Breeze in the face. Sunday shoes squeaked. Outside in the churchyard a mule brayed long and loud. Coins rolled and clinked against one another on the table. One rolled on the floor and fell through a crack, lost, as Uncle Bill gave Breeze a brownie to carry up.

[191]

The hymn was all sung, and the preacher went behind the pulpit again. In a high voice he declared that the stay of Jesus on earth was divided into four parts: the birth, the life, the death and the resurrection. "Which was the biggest part? Which, brethren? Speak out!" he urged them, for the congregation was hushed with interest.

"De resurrection!" Uncle Bill shouted.

"De life!" somebody else chimed.

"No, son!" Maum Hannah stood up. "No! De birthin' was. If his mammy didn' birth em Jedus couldn' live or either die. No, suh! De birthin' was de biggest part."

But the preacher wasn't listening. He blared out his answer to his own question:

"The resurrection of Jesus took the sting out of death! Brethren! Sisters! The resurrection brought angels to the tomb! The resurrection showed Heaven in the sky!"

Breeze's head ached as the sermon went on. His neck hurt. His feet went to sleep.

When it was at last ended, sinners were invited to come up to the mourner's bench and kneel for prayer, the preacher plead with them not to wait and be damned, but to come up and promise God they'd seek forgiveness for their sins until He gave them some sign by which they'd know they were saved. A multitude thronged forward and fell on their knees, sobbing and calling on Jesus for mercy.

The preacher begged God to look down. To come near and bring His holy spirit to save these souls. Breeze's heart beat hammer strokes against his breast. He wanted to be saved too. He wanted to go kneel with the rest of the sinners. The fear of Hell, and timidity, combined, shook his knees, and broke him out in a cold

[192]

sweat. All his blood felt frozen, leaking through his skin as he staggered forward and knelt down, and shut his eyes, and tried his best to pray.

A rough hand gripped his shoulder. and Big Sue whispered harshly in his ear, "Is you gone plum crazy, Breeze? Git up an' go on back an' set down. Don't you jerk 'way from me! You ain' got no business seekin'! If you miss an' find peace an' git religion you couldn' bat ball on Sunday wid li'l' young Cap'n when he come! Not if you's a Christian! Git up! You don' know nothin' 'bout prayin!"

Breeze got up sheepishly and went to his seat, but he thought bitterly; Big Sue didn't care if he burned in Hell. Many a time she had told him how those wicked, hell-bent buckras spent Sundays in sin. Riding horses. Singing reels. Dancing and frolicking on God's day. Young Cap'n played ball, baseball, under the trees, on the holy Sabbath, just as if it were the middle of the week. Big Sue said God didn't like people to even pick a flower on Sunday. And now she wanted him to have sin right along with those brazen white people. She didn't care how much he burned in Hell. It wasn't right. It wasn't fair. When he got bigger he was going to pray, no matter what Big Sue said.

The prayer for the sinners was done, and the sinners went to their seats. The deacons passed the Lord's Supper; small squares of bread piled up on a plate, and water glasses full of blackberry wine. Each member took a crumb and a sip, no more.

Maum Hannah's fingers shook and fumbled over the bread and a tiny crumb fell off the plate in her lap. A bit of Jesus' own body. Broken for the sins of men. As soon as Maum Hannah stood up, it would fall on the floor and be trampled under foot. Why not get it and eat it? Nobody'd know.

Breeze watched it. Once it seemed to move toward him, to creep nearer to his fingers. The congregation was singing. Their voices rose, some high, some low, Maum Hannah's and Uncle Bill's with the rest.

Nobody was looking. Why not take that crumb and taste it?

Breeze's unsteady, frightened fingers stole sidewise, following the apron's folds until they got in reach of the bit of bread. They closed over it and eased back to safety, then they slowly, slyly thrust it into Breeze's mouth.

It fell on his tongue which kept still, trying to get its flavor. But it was small. Too small. It melted quickly and slipped down his throat before Breeze could stop it. A bit of Jesus' own precious body. The preacher said it was that. Poor Jesus. Sold by His friend to bad people who killed Him, hung Him on a cross. He let them do it. He wanted to show God how sorry He was to see poor sinners going down to Hell. Hopping. Burning. Weeping. Gnashing their teeth for ever and ever. Jesus was a good man to do that. Breeze's heart was rapt with pity. His body quivered. Tears ran down his cheeks in floods. God must have a a hard heart to let Jesus suffer so bad.

> "Nee-ro my Gawd, to thee—
> Nee-ro to thee——"

the congregation sang. Old Louder raised up his head and bayed, like his heart ached too. Nobody noticed him but Maum Hannah who leaned and patted his head. "Hush, Louder. Keep quiet. Pray easy, son. Easy."

The service was finally over, the benediction said, people crowded the aisles, poured out through the wide-open doors, slowly, quietly, until the church was empty and its yard full.

An empty hogshead, got from the store, was half filled with water from the spring at the picnic grounds. Lemons were cut and squeezed and added. A great cloth bag full of sugar was poured in. A great block of ice was stripped out of its sack and washed clean of sawdust, and dumped into the barrel with the lemons and sugar and water.

Maum Hannah disapproved again, and some of the old people sided with her. She said ice wasn't a healthy thing. But the fine stylish town preacher said she was mistaken. Once, a long time ago, people used to think ice was not healthy, but everybody knows better now. In town people never drink lemonade without ice. Never.

Uncle Bill was worried because the ice's coldness seemed to soak up the sugar. The lemonade didn't taste at all right. There was no more sugar to put in unless they sent all the way to the store, and this was Sunday. It would be a sin to buy sugar on Sunday.

The men on the lemonade committee were arguing about what to do, when the Reverend, who had been walking around through the crowd shaking hands with the people and patting the children's heads, came up with Leah, who was smiling and talking and putting on many fine airs. The preacher said he was sure, Leah, Mrs. Locust, knew all about lemonade. She could tell exactly if they'd have to send for more sugar or not. Just give her a taste. She'd decide for them.

Zeda laughed out. Big Sue muttered something, but both stood aside to make room for Leah, who giggled happily, and stepped up to the barrel.

The Reverend took up the long clean hickory paddle Uncle Bill had used to mix it, and leaning over, gave it a vigorous stirring. He must have stirred too hard, for the cold air rose up out of the barrel into Leah's nose, and before she had time even to turn her head, she gave one loud sneeze and all her white teeth flew out of her mouth right into the barrel of lemonade.

It was a bad time. Leah said she'd have to have her teeth back right now. But they were mixed up with all those hundreds of lemon skins and that big block of ice. Every man on the committee took a hand at stirring for them, but the teeth rose up and grinned, then hid deep in the bottom of the lemonade before anybody could snatch them out. The preacher said pour the whole hogshead of lemonade out on the ground! The idea! Breeze felt relieved when the committee was firm. Leah would have to wait. The lemonade would soon be low in the barrel. The people were thirsty. They'd drink it up in a hurry. Leah didn't argue but went off one side and began sniffling and crying with her mouth hidden behind her pocket handkerchief. Big Sue chuckled out loud. Uncle Bill stepped forward with a long handled dipper and filling it brimming full handed it to the Reverend, with a low bow, "Have de first drink, Reverend. I know you' throat's dry after all de preachin' an' prayin' you done to-day! Gawd bless you, suh!"

The Reverend fell back a step, and shook his head and coughed behind his hand.

"If you'll excuse me——" He stammered it, then coughed again, and walked over to where Big Sue stood with a broad smile on her face.

But April suddenly appeared.

"What's all dis?" he asked, looking straight at the Reverend, with a glitter in his eyes.

"Your wife—ah—Mistress Locust—has—ah—met with a little accident——"

"Didn' Uncle Bill hand you a dipper o' lemonade?"

[196]

"Why, yes, Brother Locust."

"How come you didn' drink em? Don' you be
brotherin' me, either."

"Why—ah, I'm really not thirsty, Mr. Locust."

"You ain' thirsty, eh?"

"Why, ah, no."

April's Sunday clothes made him look even taller
than usual. His hair was newly cut, and his face
shaved clean, except for a small mustache. He made a
fine-looking, powerful figure to Breeze's wide-stretched
eyes.

His mouth smiled as he spoke to the preacher, but
his words snarled. It was plain that he was furiously
angry. Breeze felt as if he'd choke with excitement.
The breath was squeezed out of his body as the crowd
pushed closer, and his bare feet were trod on until
he felt his toes were mashed too flat ever to walk again.

The stillness was broken only by Leah's sniveling,
and April's hurried breathing.

Uncle Bill put up a warning hand when April slowly
took off his hat. "Keep you' hat on, April. Don't you
dare to butt dis servant of Gawd! You'll git struck
dead, sho' as you do!"

April smiled knowingly, then pulled his hat down
tight on his head.

"I doubt if Gawd would knock me 'bout dat, but I
don' b'lieve I want to dirty my skull on such a jackass,
not no mo'. I butt him good de last time we met. E
ain' fo'got."

"Great Gawd! April, shut you' mouth!"

"Did you cuss me for a jackass?" the preacher
shrieked and darted furiously at April.

Women screamed out. Children wailed. Men mumbled protests. But before anybody suspected his inten-
tion April leaped forward and seized the preacher's

head with two powerful hands, held it like a vise, and bit a neat round mouthful out of the cheek next to him.

Making a horribly ugly face he spat out the morsel of flesh. Old Louder, Uncle Bill's faithful hound, caught it and swallowed it down.

A fearful outcry arose. Men groaned. Women shrieked and yelled. Some went off into trances. The wounded preacher toppled, fell over, limp as a rag, his high white collar reddening as it swallowed the blood that streamed out of the hole in his face. Poor man. His face would rot off now. Poison would swell it up, bloat it, then peel it off.

Uncle Bill scolded Louder terribly and frailed him with a stick until the poor dog cried out pitifully. Breeze felt sick and faint enough to die. His hair stood on end. His flesh shook cold on his bones. God would strike April sure as the world.

The people rushed forward, some calling for water, some threatening April. Everybody shouted until the noise and confusion waxed loud and frightful.

Leah and Big Sue vied with each other in stormy torrents of words and weeping.

April's fury spent itself with the bite. His strained muscles unbraced, unbuckled, he cleared his throat and spat. "Dat meat taste too sickenin'," he grumbled. Then squaring his shoulders he walked away. Cool. Master of himself. Alone.

XV

FIELD WORK

ALL the cotton had been picked except scraps in the tip-top of the stalks. When these were gathered, the last chance for the women to make a little money would be over until early next spring when the stables were cleaned out and the black manure put in piles for them to scatter over the fields.

The sultry day was saturated with heat. The swollen sun shone white through a fog that brought the sky low over the cotton field. The cotton pickers swarmed thick, sweat poured off faces and hands and feet. Slowly, steadily they moved, up and down the long rows of tall rank stalks, carefully picking every wisp of staple out of the wide-open brown burrs.

Everybody was barefooted, most of the boys and men wearing only shirts and overalls, and the women had their skirts tied up almost to their knees.

Not the smallest gust of wind stirred the steamy air. Sweat blackened sleeves and shirts and dresses, yet the talk stayed bright and chatty.

Breeze had picked all morning except for one little while when he stopped to eat a piece of cold corn-pone and drink a few swallows out of his bottle of sweetened water. He wanted to pick a good weight, but the cotton was light and sparse. April was paying a whole cent a pound instead of the half a cent he paid when the cotton was green and heavy.

If Big Sue would pick faster instead of talking so much, together they ought to get a hundred pounds. Maybe even a hundred and twenty-five.

Side by side they trudged along, but too often Big Sue stopped and straightened up her bent shoulders and stretched her arms for a rest. Leaning over so long had her all but in a cramp. Yet when Breeze stopped to eat she scolded him. This was no time for lingering. Every pound picked meant a cent.

"Wha' de news f'om Joy?" Leah called across the rows.

"Joy wa'n't so well when I heared last."

"Wa'n't Joy kinder sickly all last summer?"

Big Sue admitted it grumly.

"I hear say Joy have changed e boardin' place since e went back to school."

Big Sue took her time to answer. After picking several stalks clean she said Joy had changed, fo' true. She was staying right on the campus now. Right with the teachers and the professors and all the high-up people.

Leah spat on the ground. "Lawd, Joy must be know ev'yt'ing by now, long as e's been off at school. How much years? Five or six?"

"Joy do know a lot, but 'e ain' been off but four years. You know it too, Leah."

"Joy's a stylish gal, Big Sue. Even if e is puny." Zeda was plainly siding against Leah.

"Joy ought to look stylish, much money as I spent on em. When e went back to school dis fall, Joy's trunk looked fine as a white lady's trunk. Not a outin' gown in em! Not a outin' petticoat! Even to de shimmys, Joy had ev'yt'ing made out o' pink and blue and yellow crêpe. Joy is a fine seamster, if I do say it myse'f. Joy's clothes is fine as any store-bought clothes."

"Wha's Joy gwine do when e finish college?" Leah asked presently.

Big Sue was uncertain. Joy was working to get a depluma. When she got that she could be anything she liked. Joy was sickly last summer because she had so much learning stirring around in her head. Leah laughed—innocently. There was no need to worry, as long as a girl was sickly from things stirring in her head.

"Wha you mean by dat, Leah?" Big Sue stopped short and her narrowed eyes gazed fixedly at Leah who went on picking.

"I ain' say nothin' to vex you, Big Sue! You's too touchous! Joy ain' gold neither silver."

"You keep Joy's name out you' mouth, Leah!" Big Sue snapped the words out in a stinging tone that cut through the heat.

Zeda stood still and gave a wide-mouthed yawn and a lazy laugh. "Do hush you' wranglin'. When it's hot like dis, I can' stan' to hear nobody tryin' to start a brawl. You womens ain' chillen! Joy's a nice gal. Fo' Gawd's sake, le' em 'lone!"

She looked up at the sun hanging low in a whitish glow, then down at the short shadows and the heat wilted leaves. Not a bird chirped. Not a locust or grasshopper spoke.

"I bet Joy'll marry some o' dem fine professors or either preachers," Bina drawled.

"Joy might, fo' true," Big Sue bragged.

Zeda said nothing, but her eyes darted a sharp look at Big Sue, then turned toward the rice-fields where the river crept up without a murmur or a shimmer of light on its surface.

Breeze picked on and on long after his back was tired and his fingers sore from the sharp points of the stiff burrs. The crocus sheets spread out along the road at the side of the field were piled higher and higher with cotton which was heaped up, packed down, running over. The last picking yielded more than anybody expected.

Thank God, the sun was setting at last. Wagons were rattling in the distance, coming to haul the cotton to the big gin-house! This year's crop was done.

XVI

PLOWING

Breeze was to do his first plowing, but instead of being up and dressed and ready to go to the fields when dawn first streaked the sky he lay sobbing underneath the clean bright quilts, which were all rumpled up over his bed, the big, high, soft feather-bed in the shed-room where Big Sue's Lijah used to sleep.

He was wretched and lonely and sore from head to heels. The feather-bed hurt wherever it pressed its fat cushiony sides against his naked body, although that feather-bed was made out of the finest down of wild ducks and geese. Big Sue liked to tell how she took years to save so many, for she wanted her Lijah to have the finest feather-bed on the whole plantation. Whenever the hunters brought wild fowls to the kitchen for her to roast in the big oven there, she carefully picked the softest pinless feathers off the breasts, and put them in a bag and kept them until she finally had enough for Lijah's bed. Lijah liked a soft bed. He was like her.

Joy was different. A feather-bed made Joy hot and unrestful, and she liked to sleep on a mattress filled with cotton tacked tight to keep it firm and hard and in place. Joy and Lijah were different altogether. But Lijah left his feather-bed soon after it was made, and went away to a far country. Big Sue was not sure whether the country was named "Fluridy" or "Kintucky." Sometimes she called it "Kintucky-Fluridy."

[203]

The fine softness of Lijah's bed meant little to Breeze, for he was homesick and unhappy. He'd a lot rather go back to his mother's cabin, on Sandy Island, and sleep on a pallet made out of a ragged quilt spread on the splintery hard floor, than to stay here with Big Sue and sleep in this nest of down feathers that had once warmed and comforted other children with bill and wings and webbed feet.

He turned and twisted and heaved with mute sobs. He felt all alone in the world. He had learned not to cry out loud. Big Sue had taught him that people with manners cry low and easy. Manly boys never cry at all. If Big Sue would only take time to beat him right away when he did wrong, he could somehow bear the pain better, but to be waked up before daylight, and stripped naked, and made to stand still under the cuts of a strap, or a switch, that's hard.

When she waddled home at night, after the day's work and pleasure were done, she was too weary to do anything but drop down in a chair and rest. Breeze had to undo the wide-strung-up shoes and take them off her fat feet, and fill up her pipe and light it. She'd smoke a little while and go to bed, worn-out, too tired to whip Breeze, no matter how much he needed a licking. She always waited until next morning, when she woke up fresh and strong, ready to raise Breeze and teach him manners. Her usual morning greeting was, "Git up, Breeze. Git up and strip. I want to git down to you' rind," his rind meaning his naked skin.

She declared that licking Breeze hurt her as much as it hurt him. She hated to have to do it, but Breeze was a poor, ignorant, no-manners boy. She had to beat him to do her duty by him.

A long, thin, black leather strap stayed up on the mantel-shelf, ready to give lickings. It had a blacksnake's hiss, and a crack as sharp as a pistol-shot. But this morning Big Sue couldn't lay her hands on it, so she broke a switch off the plum tree growing beside the cabin's front door. There were all kinds of switches outside. Big Sue could easily have got a smoother, better one, but she was in a hurry and the plum switch was in easy reach of her hand.

In the weak morning light she didn't see that thorns stayed on it when she pulled off its limbs. Those thorns had sharp teeth, and Big Sue drove them deep into Breeze's back and thighs. Now as he stroked his hurts with both hands he felt blood warm and wet on them.

Breeze's mother had never talked to him about manners. Big Sue said she didn't know them. At Blue Brook plantation, manners are the most important things in the world, but they stand between you and everything you want to do. Nobody ever eats the first sweet black walnuts that fall on the ground, for eating green walnuts makes lice in your head, and it is bad-mannered to be lousy.

To play with the funny hop-toadies, whose little black hands look just like a tiny baby's thumbs and all, makes warts come on your hands, and it's bad-mannered to have warts.

If you drink goat's milk, although it is sweeter than cow's milk, you'll hate water, just like goats hate it. You won't want to wash. And it's bad-mannered not to like soap and water.

If your feet get cold as ice and you can't get them warm any other way, you must not put them on the warm black pots on the hearth, because the soot on the pots will stick to your feet, and it's bad-mannered to have sooty feet.

To put a finger in your mouth is bad-mannered. Everything is bad-mannered!

Breeze's reflections and sobs were checked by a call from Big Sue to get up! To make haste too! He hopped up and pulled on his clothes, and taking a piece of cold bread in his hand, hurried to the barnyard. Daylight had already spread through the sky, and was creeping over the earth. The fall day smelled like spring. One old apple tree in the orchard had been fooled into blooming by the drowsy warmth. Poor silly thing!

The creek babbled low as the tide swelled it high up near the bank, and a cow, followed by her new-born calf, ventured in knee-deep, and sucked up the water noisily. As she lifted her head to look at Breeze, drops falling from her mouth were suddenly shot through with a streak of light. The sun was up! He was late! Lord, he must run! Every flower had its face turned eastward to meet the day. They knew it had come.

Cocks began a fresh crowing. Jay-birds chahn-chahned. Partridges whistled. A mocking-bird trilled. Tiny brown birds fluttered through the thickets like dead leaves come back to life. Wagon wheels rumbled on a road out of sight, the pop of a whip cracked out. Everything was astir, ready for the day's work.

In the barnyard a lively confusion of men and beasts made a thick din that filled Breeze's heart with excitement. To-day he would begin doing a man's work. On Saturday he'd get his pay, like Sherry and all the other farm-hands.

He could hear the men hailing one another. The mules neighed. Trace-chains tinkled between shouts of "Whoa" and "Gee" and "Haw" and "Git-up." On the near side of the barnyard fence a long-legged funny mule colt went staggering behind old Sally, Uncle Bill's old bay mare. When he lagged she whinnied to him to come on.

PLOWING

A litter of pigs huddled around a lean black sow wallowing comfortably in a filthy mud-hole. They squealed to her to lie still and let them feed, but she grunted lazily, and rolled still deeper in the mire. Near by an old dominecker hen clucked sharply to her biddies and scratched eagerly for worms in the rich black earth. She'd better mind. That old sow would eat her up, feathers and all, and swallow the biddies down like raw oysters.

The fine fall day felt like spring. Men and mules stepped briskly, glad to go to work.

For the first time since the boll-weevils came and pestered the cotton, the crop had been abundant, and now the field must be cleared of old stalks for the winter.

The summer's dry weather had been a big help. No rain came to wash the poison off. Sherry ran the poison machine over the fields at night when the cotton was wet with dew and the thirsty weevils drank poisoned dew and died. It was a scary thing to see these great white clouds of poison dust rising and settling to kill. The people scarcely dared to look.

Now, every lock of cotton was picked, and the plows were to turn the stalks under so deep in the earth the boll-weevils would not have as much as one lone cotton leaf to eat during the winter. April was planning already to make such a big crop next year, the gins would have to run day and night when fall came, to get the cotton packed into bales by Christmas! Money would be plentiful one more time!

A score of men were plowing, most of them tall strong fellows, straight and slender as tree-trunks. Their ease and skill made Breeze almost despair, for plowing was a hard job to him. But Sherry was chaffing them, calling them scary ladies who stayed at home and

[207]

slept with the women and children while he and April fought boll-weevils all night long.

He wouldn't hold it against them if they'd work well in the daytime and plow the crop fast and keep the ground-crust broken and the grass killed. He and April could attend to the weevils next summer, all by themselves. With that big poison machine and three mules, he could poison forty acres a night. Instead of resenting what Sherry said, the men laughed good-naturedly and declared they were satisfied to leave the boll-weevils to Sherry and April. Let the devils fight the devils.

Leah's Brudge was there, right in among the men. He plowed last year and showed he felt important. At first he scarcely noticed Breeze who struggled and strove to hold his unruly plow steady and straight like Sherry's.

Each man had his own mule, taught to his ways. Sherry's mule, Clara, was a beauty. Sleek and trim and spry, she understood every word Sherry spoke. Brudge had Cleveland, an old brown mule with sprung fore-knees, but with a steady gait and a nice coat of hair. Breeze had old Cæsar, a shaggy, logy beast, mouse-colored, except where bald spots marked his hide black. One blind eye was like a hard-boiled egg and the other had an uncertain peep, but Sherry said Cæsar had sense like a man. All Breeze needed to do was hold the lines and the plow handles together and walk straight behind. Cæsar would do the rest. Breeze wished he might have had a handsomer beast, but even old Cæsar made his heart thrill.

The earth had been dried out by the warm autumn sunshine and it sent up clouds of dust as the sharp steel of the plows cut it deep, and long rows of rank stalks were uprooted and turned under and carefully covered with dark smooth soil.

April stood alone, watching the men and mules walking sturdily across the field, then back. When they neared him, their talking hushed except for words spoken to the mules.

Overhead a blue sky looked down; the breath of the stirred earth, scented strong with life, rose and brimmed up, filling the air.

When the plowmen reached the far side of the field again, turning slowly they moved along, side by side, talking and laughing. Their gay racket hushed in a hurry when April's voice floated to them from where he stood, a tall speck by the trees in the distance. Clear and sharp his words fell through the sunshine.

"Hey dere! Yunnuh quit so much talkin' and laughin'. I want all dem cotton stalks covered up deep!"

Every man of them stepped a little slower, every plowstock was gripped with a tighter hold after the correction. Merry chatter changed to stern shouts that chided the patient mules. "Hey, mule!", "Watch you doin's!", "Gee!", "Haw!", "Come up!" The mules pulled harder and the crunching of the earth as the plows cut deeper took the place of laughter and gay bantering words.

The day moved on, warm and drowsy, with yellow sunshine still hot enough to cast black shadows, and draw sweat out of both men and beasts. April stood watching, hour after hour, while the swarm of mules and men trudged back and forth from the water's edge to the woods and then back again, never stopping for even a breathing spell. The sun rode high in the sky. Shadows shortened. Breeze longed for the noon hour, time to stop and eat and drink and rest.

Once or twice as Brudge passed Breeze and Cæsar, he looked at the old mule and giggled. Then he called

[209]

out, "Breeze is plowin' a spring puppy!" When he had gone a little way past he looked back and said something that made the plow-hands laugh out. But Sherry stopped Clara short in her tracks.

"You better shut you' mouth, Brudge!" he warned. "You gits too big for your breeches sometimes. Breeze can' lick you, but I kin an' I will."

Breeze couldn't hear Brudge's answer, but he caught up in time to hear the end of Brudge's outburst of abuse of Sherry. The other men went on plowing, except one of the older ones, who stopped to shame Brudge for the vile words he had used.

"What de matter ail yunnuh?" April called.

Nobody answered, so he started walking leisurely toward them.

Sherry stuck his plow's point deep in the earth, dropped his plow lines on the ground, then undid the trace-chains and hung them up on Clara's collar.

Brudge stood looking at him, then back at April. "I ain' botherin' you, Sherry. You better left me 'lone," he whined.

If Sherry heard him he gave no sign, but stepped lightly over the furrows toward Brudge, who gave an outcry and started to run. Sherry's long arm reached out and caught him, drew him up close, held him fast, while Sherry's words fell fast and hard as fire-heated rocks.

"I ain' gwine butt you fo' what you called me. No. I'm gwine crack you' skull for dat what you call my mammy." Sherry tilted his head back, and Brudge gave a shrill yell.

"Don' butt me, Sherry!" The words were scarcely out when Sherry's slender powerful body swayed lightly forward from the hips, and his forehead crashed down right on Brudge's skull.

For a second or two after the terrible blow fell home, Brudge made no sound. Sherry turned him loose, and he staggered a few paces and fell, screaming at the top of his lungs. Sherry had killed him! His head was broken to pieces. Prone on the soft plowed ground Brudge twisted and writhed, like a fish out of water.

Sherry paid no attention to him at all, but went back to Clara, hitched the trace-chains, took up the rope lines, and clicked his tongue. "Git up, Clara!" he said quietly, and the mule stepped off.

To Breeze, April was the very greatest man on earth, but all of a sudden Sherry seemed to grow. His limbs became taller, straighter, his shoulders broader, his supple waist slenderer. His eyes were terrible when they flashed at Brudge, ashine with furious light, and his strong white teeth ground together as if they could bite Brudge's body in two.

April was coming toward them. A little faster now. What would he say when he got there? The plow-hands stopped and waited. One shamed Brudge for his lack of manners, then turned his head away and spat on the ground with disgust.

April's long legs strode leisurely across the soft new furrows, his stout hickory stick stepping lightly beside him. When his eyes looked at Brudge there on the ground, holding his head in both hands, rolling up his body and rocking it back and forth, then falling on the ground again, howling with pain and shame and anger, April's lips curled up from his big yellow teeth in a scornful smile.

"What kind o' plow-hand is you, Brudge? Is dat de way you does a man's work?"

"Sherry butt me!—E broke my skull!—I got a bad headache!"

"Do shut you' mouth, an' git up off de ground! Unhitch you' mule an' go on home to Leah. Baby!"

Brudge got up slowly, and moaning low but steadily did what he was told. With April, he was very humble. His trembling fingers fumbled at the lines and trace-chains, but he kept up a furious sobbing all the time he worked at knots and links.

"Help him, Breeze!" April's order cracked out like the snap of a whip.

Breeze hurried forward obediently, not that April had ever mistreated him, or even scolded him, but because he knew that April ruled everybody and everything on the plantation with a heavy hand. People, beasts, even plants and insects, had to bend to his stubborn will, or suffer.

"Hey, Sherry!" April called. "Come dis way! Left Clara whe' e is! Git a move on you, too!"

April was rarely unjust, and sometimes he was almost gentle, but now his voice stung the air. Sherry had better not vex him further, or there'd be trouble.

Although Sherry walked without hurry, he was out of breath when he reached April. His hands shook a little as men do when a chill is about to seize them.

"How come you butt Brudge?" April asked him coldly.

"You ought to be glad I butt em. Brudge is a no-manners scoundrel."

"If he done wrong, whyn' you tell me?"

"I ain' no news carrier."

April's eyes glittered as he shifted his hickory stick from one hand to the other.

"You ain' Brudge's daddy, you know?"

"No." And Sherry smiled. "I ain' nobody's daddy, not yet."

"Wha' you mean by dat?" April's voice rose, and

in a sudden burst of anger he seized Sherry by the shoulder. "You can' sass me, Sherry! You know it too! If you wanted to butt somebody, whyn' you come try my head, instead o' mashin' up a li'l' half-grown boy like Brudge? I got a mind to make mush out o' you' brains right now. You ever was a' impudent black devil!"

Sherry's eyes gleamed, his fists clenched, and he drew closer to April. "I didn' had no cause to butt you, dat's why! But I just as soon butt you as anybody else."

April smiled. "I hate to kill you, Sherry. You's a good plow-hand, an' I need you."

Sherry's answer didn't lag one iota, and he met April's eyes with a steadfast look. "Come try me! Just stick you' neck out! One time! Just one time! You t'ink you's de onliest man got a skull on dis whole plantation. I got a bone in my head, too. Come try em! I'll butt you' brains out same as if you wasn' my daddy!" Sherry's eyes glared, his head crouched between his shoulders, he came forward with a rush. But April jerked him clear up off his feet, and his big head came down on Sherry's forehead with a butt that brought the blood streaming from both men's nostrils.

Sherry staggered back a step, then leaped forward, but April's powerful outstretched arms hurled him toward the plow-hands, who caught him and held him fast, for April warned them.

"Yunnuh hold dat boy. If e comes back at me I'll kill em. An' we ain' got time to be diggin' a grave, not till de cotton's all plowed under."

"You mens lemme go, I tell you! I ain' scared o' April. Lemme go!"

"Yunnuh ain' to fight! Great Gawd! Yunnuh'd kill one anudder. You can' git loose, Sherry. No, suh!"

[213]

Sherry struggled fruitlessly. Then he stood still. April wiped his nose on his shirt-sleeve, picked his ragged hat up off the ground, set it straight on his head, then quietly buttoned up the neck of his shirt, for a sudden gust of wind came up cool from the rice-fields.

Casting his eyes up at the sky where a flock of small ragged clouds hung high and white, he said calmly, "Yunnuh better git back to plowin'. It's gwine rain in a few days an' we must git dis big field finished befo' den."

He tried to speak coolly. Quietly. To hold up his head triumphantly. But his shoulders had a dejected droop, as he turned his back and went toward the woods.

After a few steps, he turned around, "Sherry, you an' me can' live on de same place. Not no mo'. I'll kill you sho' as we try it. For a little I'd kill you now. You git on off. I don' care whe' you go, just so I don' see you, not no mo'! Git outen de field! Right now, too."

Breeze felt hot, then cold. The blood rose in his throat and choked him. If he could only help Sherry kill April! But he stood shaking, shivering, with lips twitching, until April asked, "What is you cryin' about?" And Breeze stammered weakly, in a thin reedy voice, "I ain' cryin', suh." The glare April gave him made him dizzy like a blow between his eyes.

"Den git at you' work! Don' be wastin' good time on a mawnin' like dis!"

Sherry held up his head and fastened his look on April, but the tears that ran down his cheeks belied his hard reckless smile. In a voice broken by hate and fury he cried out:

"You stinkin' ugly devil—— Quit scarin' dat li'l' boy! You's got a coward-heart even if you' head is too

[214]

tough fo' Hell! I hope Gawd'll rot all two o' you feets off! I hope E will——'' Sherry stretched out a fist and shook it helplessly, then broke into sobs.

"Hush, Sherry! You better left April alone now. You done said enough,'' warned one of the men, but April strode away. If he heard Sherry's cursing he made no sign of it. And Sherry walked across the field to Clara, who stood, still hitched to the plow, waiting for him to come back. He patted her nose. "Good ol' Clara. I'm gwine. Breeze'll take you to de barnyard, won't you, Breeze?''

Breeze tried to answer a loud "Yes, Sherry!'' but a dumb sob shook his words.

"Good-by, mens!''

"Good-by, Sherry!''

That was all. Sherry walked away toward the Quarters. As Breeze watched him go the sunshiny noon grew dim. The plows went on cutting down stalks, burying them, but the men were silent as death. Birds kept singing in the forest trees, but their notes had a doleful sorrowful sound. The day had paled. The rice-fields meeting the sky yonder, so far away, were hazy and sad. The wind itself wept through the trees. A flock of crows passed overhead, croaking out lonesome words to one another.

The field lay dark. Dismal. Its rich earth changed to dry barren land. The men who plowed it walked in a distressful silence.

Sherry was gone. Zeda's Sherry. The most promising young man on the whole plantation. April's big-doings bullying had run him off. April would pay for it. He'd poison cotton by himself next summer. He could make the men do almost anything else, but he'd never get them to poison boll-weevils. They knew better than to fight Providence. April wasn't God. No.

From the Quarters a scream rose and swelled until its long, weird, melancholy note went into a death-cry! Zeda's grieving! Breeze had to clench his teeth to keep from bursting out crying himself. Suppose April got mad with him some time, and butted him? What would he do? He couldn't do anything but stand still and take it and die.

He went on plowing, side by side with the rest in the painful silence that hung on stubbornly. The soft flat-footed pattering of the men's bare feet, the dead flat thudding of mule steps, the sullen waving of the branches in the wind, the low murmuring of the water, all fell together into a dull batch of doleful sound.

Flocks of field-larks rose up and cried out plaintively as their feeding-ground was turned under. Old Louder chased them in a slow trot, sniffed at them, then at some smell in the earth. Coming up to Breeze, he rubbed against his legs and whined. Breeze gave him nothing in return, only a low word or two, and a furtive pat on the head, so he trotted off to one side, and sat on his haunches, watching the plowmen with sorrowful eyes. He missed Sherry too.

When the bell rang for noon, Breeze was near the rice-fields side. His mule stopped short and seized a mouthful of grass, as he gazed toward Sandy Island. It was far away to-day. The haze had every sign of it hidden. A broad sheet of water sparkled and glittered, as bright reflections of white clouds floated softly, silently on its shining surface. All the channels were buried. What was his mother doing now? And Sis? He swallowed a sob and turned the mule's head toward home, and saw Big Sue waddling across the field. She didn't follow any path, but came on straight toward him, over the soft plowed earth. Why was she coming to the field at noon? He had his breakfast long ago, and he always went home for dinner. Maybe she wanted to talk about Sherry. She stopped and said a few words to April but she came on to Breeze.

She gave Breeze a hand-wave as she got nearer, but her face was solemn, without any show of a smile. "April says you kin come straight on home, Breeze. Somebody else'll take de mules to de lot."

Giving his shoulder a gentle pat, she drew Breeze up to her with a little hug. She didn't say a word, and her eyes looked wet.

April was waiting at the path, and he walked on home beside them. Tall, solid as a tree, rugged, tough-sinewed, double-jointed, yet the cruel look in his deep-sunk eyes that blazed out when they looked at Sherry, had given way to something else. They glowed bright as he turned back and looked across the rice-fields toward Sandy Island, and said gently:

"Sandy Island is way back behind de clouds to-day." His anger with Sherry had passed.

His voice sounded unsteady, his features were haggard and ashy.

Big Sue looked at him, then at Breeze. "You break de news to Breeze, April. I ain' got de heart."

April shook his head. "Me neither."

Big Sue's small eyes blinked. "Son," she hesitated strangely, and laid a hot fat hand gently on his shoulder, "you t'ink you got a mammy, enty?"

Of course Breeze thought so. He was so sure of it. What on earth was Big Sue aiming at?

"No, son." She shook her head slowly. "You ain' got none. You' mammy went out on de tide befo' day dis mawnin'."

What did Big Sue mean? Breeze felt confused. Where had his mother gone on that before-day-tide? He didn't understand what Big Sue was talking about.

Marsh-hens cackled gaily out in the rice-fields. A crane croaked. A fish-hawk circled high, then halted to poise himself for a swoop.

Taking Breeze by the hand Big Sue led him on through the greenish shade cast by the live-oaks over the road and the cabin's yard. Her bright cold eyes peeped out sidewise at him now and then. She was trying to be kind. Once she said, "I'se gwine to be you' mammy now, since you' own mammy's dead and gone."

Breeze felt as if he was in a dream, walking in his sleep. His legs were numb and heavy.

"Hurry up, son! You must walk faster. We got to dress an' go to de buryin', cross de river in a boat. April'll let Sherry take we across de river in de boat, enty, April?"

"No, not Sherry. Somebody else'll take you. Sherry's done gone off. To stay."

"Wha' dat you say, April? Sherry's gone?"

"I run em off de place a while ago."

"Great Gawd! What is dis! April, don't you know Zeda's gwine kill you? Man! I'm glad I ain't you. You might be strong, but you ain' strong as dat conjure Zeda's gwine put on you."

Louder had followed them from the field, and now sat on his hind quarters, listening, watching, snapping at a fly now and then. As a squirrel ran down the trunk of a tree and across the yard, he jumped up and ran a few paces, then came back and sat down again, as as though he had done his duty.

"Come on in de house an' dress, Breeze. I don' believe you got it straight in you' head yet. You' ma is dead, son! Dead! De people is gwine put em in a grave soon as dis same sun goes down."

Breeze looked up at each of the grown people. He

[218]

felt hurt, as if his mother had abandoned him just when
he wanted to see her most, to go back home to her.
Sherry was gone away. She was dead. Nobody was
left, but Uncle Bill. Leaning toward Big Sue he hid
his face in the folds of her skirt and wept.

"Don' cry, son," she soothed him. "Come on an'
eat some dinner. You got to go wid me to de buryin'.
Enty, April?"

She led him inside and made him sit in a chair
beside April, while she fried links of sausage to eat with
the bread and cups full of sweetened water. The sausage had a savory smell, and Breeze bit into it and
chewed it a long time, but he could scarcely swallow it
for the choking lump in his throat. His mother was
dead. She was no longer yonder at Sandy Island with
Sis and the other children. She had flown up into the
sky, where Heaven was, and Jesus and all the angels.
April washed his food down with great swallows of
water. How dumb he was.

"Lawd!" Big Sue grunted as she came out of the
shed-room with her Sunday dress on her arm. "Ain' it
awful to die in sin? It pure scares me half to death
when I think on Breeze's mammy a hoppin' in Hell
right now! Great Gawd! Wid fire a scorchin' em!"

"How you know?" April thundered out.

"How I know? I know e was a' awful sinner. You
know so too. E got dis same Breeze right here at Blue
Brook whilst a revival meetin' was gwine on. You don'
call dat sin?"

April didn't so much as crack his teeth, and she
looked at him with narrowed eyes.

"You an' her all two better had got religion dat
summer."

"You better keep you' mouth shut, now, Big Sue.
You's a-talkin' out o' turn. Better help Breeze dress.

E's a settin' yonder on de floor wid jaws hangin' open! Boy, you's gwine swallow a fly if you don' mind.''

Breeze was trying to think. His mother, his dear, kind, good mother, was hopping in Hell. Burning in a fire nine times hotter than the fire on earth!

"April!" Big Sue called out, "you ought to buy Breeze a nice pair o' shoes an' stockin's to wear to de buryin'.''

"Brudge is got a pair Breeze kin borrow an' wear. I ain' got time to go to de sto' now.''

"Please go git 'em fo' me.''

April got up stiffly and walked away. In a little while Brudge came bringing a pair of Leah's shoes. He had lost one of his own, but Leah sent her slippers instead. April said they would do. They were low-cut and shiny, with high heels and a strap across the instep. Breeze made such a poor out at walking in them, Big Sue couldn't help laughing, although she declared she was not making sport of him.

"Take 'em off, son. Tote 'em in you' hand till we git to Sandy Island,'' she suggested, and Breeze did.

Uncle Bill rowed the boat that took them to Sandy Island, and although he pulled hard with his oars, the sun was almost down when they reached the cabin up on the hill above the river.

Mules and oxen hitched to carts filled the yard, and the house was crowded with people.

Big Sue made Breeze sit down on the ground and put on Brudge's stockings and Leah's shoes. They made his feet stumble about miserably, but Big Sue said that made no difference, since they looked nice.

He was terribly excited, but as he walked hand in hand with Big Sue up the steep path into the yard he could hear people say:

"Lawd, Breeze is grow fo' true. Looka e fine clothes!''

Seeing his old home made him forget to be polite.

Big Sue whispered, "When de ladies an' gentlemens speaks to you, bow an' pull you' foot an' say, 'Good evening.' Don' grin at 'em like a chessy-cat! Be mannersable!"

When Sis came to the door Breeze broke away from Big Sue's hand and ran, half falling up the steps. Sis grabbed him and held him tight. He put his arms around her and squeezed her, and they laughed and cried together. Poor Sis! Her body felt like a pack of bones! Where was the baby? Where were all the other children? Sis whispered they'd been sent off to a neighbor's house until after the burying was over. She didn't have time to feed them and look after everything else.

Big Sue interrupted the tight hug Breeze was giving Sis: "Come on in, boy, an' look at you' ma. Dey's ready to put em in de box."

The cabin was full of a queer smell. Breeze hated to go inside, but Big Sue held him fast by the arm and drew him toward the shed-room door. The room was dim, for the one wooden shutter was closed so that very little light could filter through. Breeze saw only a few solemn-looking black women standing around the bed. He couldn't bear to go any farther. But Big Sue's firm hand urged him on, its strong jerks making it useless to draw back.

"Don't you cut no crazy capers wid me, Breeze. You got to come look at you' ma. I want de people to see I raised you to have respect fo' you' parents. Open de window, Sis!"

The small room looked even smaller on account of the low ceiling, and the bed, the only piece of furniture, was pushed out from the wall leaving a narrow way all around it.

Sis undid the window latch and flung the shutter back. The sun flooded the white bed with blood-red light, and marked a long slim thing under a sheet. One of the black women turned the sheet slowly down and exposed a pinched face. A chin bound with a white cloth. Two bony black hands crossed on a sunken breast. Two feet whose black skin showed through thin white stockings. The feet were still, not hopping.

That strange stiffness could not be his mother! Breeze shut his eyes tight to keep from seeing it.

"Open you' eyes, Breeze. Stand 'side you' ma an' look at em good fo' de last time. You ain' never gwine see em no mo'."

"No! No! Cun Big Sue! Don' make me look at em! Please, Cun Big Sue!"

Breeze began screaming in spite of himself. He wanted to be good. To please Big Sue. To have manners. But that thing on the bed was too fearful.

He felt himself lifted in Big Sue's strong arms. Her hot breath puffed on him as she bore him close to the bed. The terrible scent filling the house rose in his nostrils. Screams split his throat. He couldn't hold them in to save his life. Although his eyelids squeezed tighter shut, tears poured through them.

Big Sue's determined fingers tugged at them, pulling them apart, until his eyes, naked, except for tears, were held over his mother's face. Her two dead eyes peeped out from half-closed lids, her black lips cracked open over a grin of cold white teeth. He strove wildly to get away, but Big Sue held him until a soft darkness swallowed everything.

When Breeze came to himself he was flat on the ground, so near the cape jessamine bush that a cool clean blossom touched his cheek.

Where were Big Sue and Sis?

He raised up, and saw men with white gloves on their hands bringing a long new pine box through the door. They came down the steps and went toward a wagon. As they passed an old mule, the beast tried to break his tether and run. A man yelled at him, another jerked him by the bit, a third got a stick and frailed him, but Uncle Bill called out, "Don' lick em, son. Dat mule smell death and it fret em. Pat em. Talk easy to em. Death kin scare people, much less a mule."

Everybody was leaving the house. They had forgotten Breeze. He couldn't stay here by himself, with nothing to keep him company but that strange smell that followed the box out of the shed-room and settled right in the cape jessamine bush. It drowned the scent of the blossoms.

Hopping to his feet he ran humbly to Big Sue, and slipped a hand in hers, "Lemme go wid you, Cun Big Sue. I ain' gwine holler no mo'."

Big Sue gave his hand a painful squeeze, "I'm dat provoke' wid you, Breeze, I can' talk. But you wait till I git you home. You's de kickin'est nigger I ever did see. But you wait till I git you home. I bu'sted one sleeve clean out o' my new dress a-tryin' to hold you."

With his heart tingling Breeze tottered on. His eyes blurred. His legs scarcely could carry him down the sandy road toward the graveyard under the tall trees.

The afterglow fell clear from the sky on an open grave with dark earth piled high on each side of it. It was outlined by flaming smoking torches held in the hands of the mourners, who marched slowly around it, singing a funeral dirge. One man, dressed in a long white robe, stood at the head of the grave, his deep voice chanting the solemn burial service. Breeze's mother belonged to the Bury League, and all the members carried a white lily. When the leader gave the sign they held the flowers, arm high, and yelled, "Christ is Risen!" but the leader was a strange man, not his stepfather.

A hymn, or spiritual, was raised, and the whole crowd joined in with great questioning waves of sound, sometimes harmony, sometimes dissonance. Breeze's heart ached. He wanted to cry out too, to the great Creator of Life. He felt bewildered when Sis gave a piercing shrill wail, that rose high and sharp above the somber death chant. Her cry had scarcely died away before an answer came echoing from the opposite side of the grave. Big Sue looked at Uncle Bill with a mischievous grin that shocked Breeze. How could anybody laugh here? The very woods reechoed the unearthly death cries!

The mournful singing gradually changed into a confused din, a whirlwind of grief. Men and women shrieked and shouted. They shook and shimmied their shoulders, and jerked their arms and gyrated about in a frenzy of grief and excitement. Some of the women went wild. They beat their breasts and cried above the roaring hubbub. But all the time Sis' shrill, piercing, falsetto wailing kept steadily calling across the grave. Her screams rose high and then melted into the life of the air.

The tall brown trunks of pine trees around them loomed up until their plumy tops touched the sky. They waved gently, mysteriously, above the confused group of people. Red sweaters and blue overalls, green and purple and yellow dresses, wide white aprons and turban-bound heads, black hands and faces, were all tinged with a rosy glow dropped over them by the sky as night began creeping out of the forest.

The strong damp odor of the woods freshened, and mosquitoes stung Breeze's face and hands and ankles.

He was unhappy. Wretched. When Big Sue said, "De mosquitoes is too bad. Dey got me in a fever! Le's go," he felt a relief to get away from it all.

Not even Sis paid them any attention as they turned around, facing homeward. She was too absorbed in grief, in the terrible thought of Death, that strange mystery which had just stricken Breeze's mother.

Breeze hurried along the road, fearing snakes less than the sound of that inferno of mourning which followed behind him.

Sandy Island was quiet; the cabin on the hill empty; the dusk on the river so deep that the boat was scarcely outlined against the water; but Breeze could see the old dead pine down on the white sand. It's head had fallen. Its whole length rested on the ground.

His brain whirled in his skull. Cold tremors ran through his body. His mother had buried all her money at the foot of that tree. So had old man Breeze. But nothing less than strong iron chains could have dragged the boy one step nearer it.

Uncle Bill helped Big Sue to her seat in the boat's stern, where she sat solemn and stiff and ruffled like a sitting hen.

They went in silence. The water whispered in bubbles, but the wind had died out of the trees.

In the cabin, a big fire blazed up the chimney, and a delicious scent of food came to meet them.

"Who dat in my house?" Big Sue cried out, when April came to the door.

"You got company."

"Who? You?"

"No. You guess again."

"I dunno, an' I'm too weak to walk, much less talk."

"It's Joy. E come on de boat dis evenin'."

[225]

Big Sue stopped short in her tracks, dumb-struck. "Great Gawd! You don' mean it! Whe' is Joy?"

Instead of hurrying forward she gazed at the cabin with black dismay as if she turned some terrible thought over and over in her mind, but a warm laugh gurgled out, and a low voice called:

"What did you tell Ma for, Cun April? I been want to fool em!"

A girl in a bright red dress and with red-stockinged legs came bounding across the yard to meet them.

"How you do, Ma? I bet you is surprised to see me!" She held her mouth up to meet Big Sue's, their kiss made a loud smack, then Uncle Bill hurried to shake her hand.

"Lawd, Joy! Just de sight o' you would cure de sore eyes! Honey, you looks sweet enough to eat!" Breeze stared at her. Deep down in his heart he felt Uncle Bill spoke the truth. He had never seen any one like Joy before.

She leaned to pull up one red stocking tighter over a knee, but she grinned up into Uncle Bill's face. "Do listen at Uncle Bill! A-sweet-talkin' me right here befo' ev'ybody!" Her eyes beamed, her low soft drawl was full of friendliness, and she turned to Breeze with a blithe greeting:

"How you do, son? I'm sho' glad to see you here wid Ma!" A small bold hand shot out to meet his, but Breeze cast his eyes down, bashful and afraid. The hand gave his shoulder a light pat, took one of his and led him toward the house.

"You ain' scared o' me, is you, son? Come on in by de fire. I want to see you good."

Breeze couldn't say a word, but as they walked in April threw a fat pine knot on the fire to make a better light. The fire blazed up, crackling merrily, making the room hot and bright, but shyness kept Breeze's face turned away from Joy, until with a quick laugh she wheeled him around and lifted his chin.

"How come you won' look at me, son?" Her face was so close Breeze could feel her breath when she laughed again, but his eyes were riveted on her twinkling shoe-buckles.

"Left de boy 'lone, Joy. E don' feel like playin'. His ma was just buried dis evenin'. Come unstring my shoes, son. I ain' gwine let Joy plague you."

As he knelt to unlace the shoes Joy appealed to him: "I ain' plaguin' you, is I, Breeze? Me an' you is gwine be buddies, enty?" Breeze looked up and met her slanting eyes, and the smile that lit them seemed to him so lovely, so gentle, he fairly tingled all over. He had never seen anybody like Joy before. Her slight body in its scant, red satin dress was not tall, but it had the straight, swift, upward thrust of a pine sapling. Her slim black arms, bare from the elbows, and held akimbo, came out from shoulders lean as his own. Her short skirt gave a flirt and Breeze's glance darted to the skinniness of her red-stockinged legs. But her smile had thrilled the fear out of him, and given him confidence enough to feast his eyes on her gay overripe little figure, from the bright buckles on her shiny black slippers to the short coarse straightened hair on her small head.

"Set down, honey. Talk to Uncle Bill an' you' Cun April whilst me an' Breeze fixes supper." Big Sue's bare feet pattered back and forth from the hearth to the four-legged safe against the wall, mixing bread, and smoothing it on a hot griddle, slicing meat and dropping it on a hot spider, once in a while scolding Breeze for dawdling, or asking Joy a question about the town or the school. April smiled and joined pleasantly in the talk Joy led. A necklace of blue glass beads clinked against the smooth black skin of her neck, gold bracelets glittered on her slim wrists. Breeze was bewildered, rapt with the glamour of her. Her sparkling eyes strayed from one face to another until they met April's, bold and staring. Joy's flickered and fell and her laughter chilled. Like everybody else, she feared him, and his shining gaze, fixed on her alone, withered all the fun out of her and put something sober in its place.

Except for the fire's crackling a hush filled the room. Big Sue suddenly straightened up from bending over the pots and, looking over her shoulder, said, "Git de plates out o' de safe, Breeze. How come yunnuh is so quiet? Dis ain' church!"

April laughed and shifted in his chair and his eyes turned from Joy to her mother. "De victuals smells so good, I'm gone got speechless!"

"Me too," Joy chimed, but Uncle Bill got up to go. He had already stayed longer than he intended. He must go see if everything at the barnyard was in order.

April stood up to say good night, tall, straight-limbed, broad-shouldered, hawk-eyed.

"Stay an' eat wid us, Cun April, you too, Uncle Bill! What's you' hurry?"

Uncle Bill had to go. He had left Jake to see about feeding the stock, and Jake was mighty forgetful and careless. Nobody could depend on him.

In spite of the fineness of her red satin dress, Joy took the plates from Breeze and piling two of them with the collards dripping with pot-liquor, and chunks of fat meat and pieces of the newly baked corn-bread, she gave Big Sue and April each one.

"Yunnuh must eat all dis I put on you' plates," Joy bade them gaily, but silence had fallen over them. Both their faces wore a troubled look. April's eyes held both darkness and light, and a kind of sadness Breeze had seen sometimes in Sis' eyes.

"How was de buryin'?" April asked when the edge of his appetite was dulled.

"Fine! Fine! All but dat fool boy Breeze. E made me pure shame." Big Sue's words were smothered by food in her mouth, but Breeze felt the sharp sting of their bitter contempt. He longed to get up and go back into the dark shed-room and hide, but shame chained his feet to the floor and made his neck so limp his head drooped lower and lower.

"Wha' dat Breeze done so bad?"

April leaned his head against the mantel-shelf, and listened without a word to Big Sue's story. Most of the time he looked into the fire, deep in thought, forgetting to eat his supper.

When Big Sue's tale was done, Breeze listened for April's abuse, but instead of scolding him, April spoke kindly, gently.

"Don' be too hard on de boy, Big Sue. Death kin scare bigger people dan Breeze. I don' like to look on em myself. Gawd made people so. Mules too. When Dukkin put pizen in de spring last summer and killed Uncle Isaac's old mule, Lula, I had a time gittin' em dragged off to de woods. Sherry said he could hitch Clara to em, but Clara was so scared, e reared up and kicked an' tried to run away. Sherry had to blindfold Clara wid a cloth over both eyes befo' she'd go anywhere nigh old dead Lula. It's de Gawd's truth. An' Clara is a mighty sensible mule."

"Po' li'l' Breeze," Joy pitied softly, and Breeze's heart warmed, for April and Joy both took his part. Big Sue wouldn't lick him to-night. She never did lick him when April was there.

"You-all stop talkin' 'bout death. You scare me so

I wouldn't sleep a wink to-night! Whe's Sherry?"
Joy asked suddenly.

Big Sue looked at April instead of answering. April
stirred in his chair, his big feet shuffled on the floor, his
slow answer was a growl.

"Sherry's left de plantation, Joy. I run em off."
His black brows knit into an angry line.

"Why—why—how come you done dat, Cun April?"
Joy's teeth looked white and sharp, her red satin dress
shimmered in the firelight, her words were husky, half
whispered.

"I had to, Joy. Sherry is a impudent rascal. I'd 'a'
killed em if e had 'a' stayed here."

April scratched his head and his eyes turned uneasily
toward the door, but before he spoke, tears welled up in
Joy's eyes, a deep sob burst from her bosom, and she
got up and ran back into the shed-room where she lay
on the bed and wept, in spite of Big Sue's reproaches.

"Why, Joy! You ought not to take on so! Why,
Honey, Sherry'll be back befo' long."

XVII

HOG-KILLING

Now that Joy had come home for good, Big Sue planned to fix up the cabin. April sent Brudge to help Breeze whitewash the outside with oyster-shell lime, burned and crushed right on the beach. Fresh clean newspapers were brought from the store with eggs and each wide sheet spread with white flour paste and stuck fast to the inside walls over the old soiled worn-out papers that were cracked and broken by last year's wind and weather. When this was done, the cabin was snug and tight. With the window blinds pulled in and the doors closed, not a bit of cold air could get in except through the cracks in the floor.

But Joy's blood must have got thin, for she wore her long black cape constantly, and had spells of shivering in spite of its warmth.

The weather was scarcely cold enough for hog-killing, but Big Sue said Joy needed some rich food to thicken and hotten her blood. The girl took little interest in anything. She'd stand and gaze vacantly out of the window as if her soul were gone far away and her eyes tried to follow its flight.

Jeems, the shoat in the pen, must be killed. Joy's appetite must be tempted somehow before her blood turned to pure water. She ate scarcely enough to keep a bird alive.

Somebody must have conjured her. Those long half-drowsy spells were not natural, and sometimes she sobbed

[231]

in the night, hag-ridden with evil dreams. Jeems must be killed for Joy to eat.

Big Sue waked Breeze early. She gave him no chance to dawdle, for much had to be done in preparation. Joy offered to help, but Big Sue made her stay in bed and rest. Breeze washed the sleep out of his eyes, then tipped to Joy's bedside for a word from her, but the dawn showed her eyes closed, and her quiet regular breathing told him she was sleeping. He turned his eyes away quickly to keep them from waking her.

Before the sun was up he had the big washpot in the yard, brimming full of water and a fire built under it. Uncle Bill brought a sound barrel and laid it slantwise and steady in a dug out place in the ground. He'd scald Jeems in that.

He took out his great pocket knife and opening its longest blade told Breeze to look how its sharp point was flashing! That knife was trained. It had sense like people. It was pure itching to stick in Jeems' throat and slice his neck in two. When he had to kill a hog, he just pointed that knife blade toward the beast and gave it a push. It would fairly leap to the right spot. It never missed the big vein. His eyes twinkled with affection for his faithful tool as he ran a thick thumb lightly over its keen edge and felt its shining point.

"You hold em, Breeze, till I get de ax. De ax has to do a li'l' work ahead o' de knife."

As he walked toward the wood-pile, Big Sue hurried out. "Do don' knock Jeems, Uncle Bill!" She panted anxiously.

"I'm 'bliged to stun em, honey!"

"You'll ruin all de brains."

"I can' help dat, Miss Big Sue. I couldn' stick Jeems whilst he was in his right mind. No, ma'am."

"Knockin' a hog on de head makes de head cheese

all bloody. Please don' do dat! Go on an' stick em. Don' knock em!''

Uncle Bill stopped and scratched his head.

''I'd do mighty nigh anything to please you, Miss Big Sue, but I can' suffer a hog any more'n I have to. I got to knock Jeems senseless, or I couldn' kill em at all. Me an' Jeems is been friends too long.''

''For Gawd's sake don' be so chicken-hearted.''

''I ain' chicken-hearted, but I couldn' stan' to suffer Jeems whilst he was a dyin'. No. Come on, Breeze. Le's get dis killin' over wid!''

Jeems' black snout showed through a crack, and his short impatient grunts meant he was hungry, for Breeze had not fed him since yesterday noon. Breeze's heart ached for his friend. How could Uncle Bill bear to knock Jeems in the head with that ax, while the poor beast's eyes gazed up with such trustful friendliness!

''Jeems, old man! You' time is out, son. Git ready to meet you' Gawd!'' Uncle Bill's voice was sad.

Jeems held his fat face up, straining to see them better, for his eyes, almost closed with fat, were hampered by ears flapping over them. Poor Jeems!

Uncle Bill had his coat off, and his rolled-up shirt-sleeves showed the play of his powerful sinews under the skin. The ax rose high in the air, then leaped out and tightened, as Uncle Bill brought it down with a thud on Jeems' forehead. The squeal in the hog's throat changed to a strangled gurgle. The short forelegs staggered and gave way. The great heavy body fell sidewise to the ground. But Uncle Bill was already astride it with his knife's bare blade ready.

A quick sharp stick in the neck brought a spurt of blood which a deeper thrust turned to a stream. Red, warm with life, its steam rising like smoke in the cool sunshiny air, Jeems' blood poured out and wasted in the filth of his pen, until Big Sue's cries brought Breeze to his senses.

"Great Gawd, Breeze! Ketch dat blood! You standin' like a fool lettin' em waste! I good mind to kill you! Blood puddin' is de best o' de hog-killin'!"

Breeze scrambled over the boards of the pen, and slipped a pan under Jeems' unconscious head, and held it in place in spite of the kicking death-struggling legs, saving the bubbling red stream for a pudding. The smell of it made him sick, and he couldn't meet the look of those half-closed staring eyes.

Poor Jeems! His time was out. His kicks were getting weaker. His eyelids were wilting down over his dull sightless eyes. His soul would soon be gone home to God. Breeze looked up at the sky, but Big Sue called out to give her the pan before he turned it over. It had caught enough for a small pudding.

The hog was hurried into the barrel and scalded before the life cooled out of him, and his skin scraped clean of hair. As Uncle Bill worked he told Breeze he must always be careful to see that the moon is right before he killed a hog. A wrong moon will set the hair in a hog's skin so no knife on earth could move it. Meat killed on a waning moon will dry up to nothing, no matter how you cook it. A certain quarter of the moon will make the meat tough and strong, another will rot it, no matter how much salt you pack around it. If Breeze would learn all the moon signs he'd be spared a lot of trouble long as he lived. White people leave money to their children, but black people teach theirs signs, which is far better. Money can be taken from you, but knowledge can't.

When Jeems was scalded and scraped and washed and cleaned, he was hung up by a hickory stick run through the white sinews in his hind legs. The carcass must cool before it was cut up, for meat, like bread, is spoiled if cut while it's warm.

Bina had come to help Big Sue, and the two women bent over a wooden washtub, sorting out the liver and lights and chitterlings, putting the small entrails aside for sausage casings. The hog's fine condition made Big Sue cheerful. She declared she'd make a lot more lard than she'd expected, for all of Jeems' insides were coated with fat.

The higher the sun rose the faster they worked, even when the neighbors dropped by for a little neighborly talk and to see how the hog-killing went on.

At noon they stopped for a breathing spell and bite to eat. Hot brown corn-bread and bits of fried liver were washed down with sweetened water. The grown people smoked one pipeful apiece, then set to work again, for Jeems had cooled enough to be quartered.

The back door slipped off its hinges made a table large enough to hold him. Uncle Bill's big knife cut off the huge head, and separated the hams and shoulders and sides from the long backbone. He trimmed them neatly, throwing the scraps of lean meat into one tub for sausage meat, and bits of firm white fat into another for to-morrow's lard making.

He wanted to give Breeze the pig-tail to roast on the coals right then, but Big Sue said Breeze had no time to be playing with pig-tails now. If he'd work hard Uncle Bill might find the hog's bladder for him, and to-night he and Brudge could pleasure themselves blowing it up like a balloon.

A number of the plantation dogs had gathered, and they had to be watched, specially the hounds and cur-dogs. The bird dogs were better-mannered. Big Sue wanted to scald the lot of them for the pesky way they nosed around, but Uncle Bill wouldn't let her. God made dogs so they hankered after hog meat. It was sinful to be short-patienced with them.

One pot simmered and stewed with liver and lights and haslets and rice liver pudding. Another pot slowly, carefully sputtered and spat as the blood, mixed with seasonings, thickened into pudding. The brains were taken out of the skull, which was put on for headcheese.

Breeze felt neither sadness nor squeamishness now. His mouth watered as his nose sniffed at all the appetizing smells.

The sun began throwing long shadows and Big Sue kept him hurrying. Every single hog hair had to be picked up and saved to plant in the potato patch next spring. Every hair would make a potato.

The waste had to be thrown in the creek. Breeze cast it in, a bucketful at a time. Horrid filthy stuff. It made him shiver, but the water swallowed it down with scarcely a splash, then flowed on smooth and clear, reflecting the bright clouds in the sky, shimmering in the last sunbeams, rising with the incoming tide to water its banks, which were yellow with marsh daisies. The willows were almost bare of leaves, and the slim naked trunks and branches bent over, looking away down into the Blue Brook's quiet depths.

Sunset gilded the earth and cabins and trees, and streaked the white sandy yard with golden light. Uncle Bill hoped that such stillness would not bring rain soon, for the hay was in shocks in the field yet, and the corn not all broken in. He looked up at the sky as he spoke, and at once a light breeze sprang up to tell him tomorrow would be fair. He laughed with relief, and the big trees bowed gently, saying that they knew the little breeze had told the truth. Even the frost-faded grasses nodded and waved!

To stay fair the weather must turn cooler, and that

would be good for Big Sue's fresh killed meat. It would
have a good chance to take the salt well. Such big hams
needed careful curing.

Breeze must clean up the pen to-morrow and scatter
ashes all over it, so Uncle Bill could bring Big Sue one
of Melia's red pigs to grow and fatten into a fine shoat
by late spring.

Each piece of pork was rubbed well with salt and
stored in Uncle Bill's small log barn. There, they'd be
safe until the morning, when they'd be rubbed again
with salt mixed with sugar, and packed into a barrel to
cure.

Old Louder sat on his thin haunches, patient and
polite. He knew better than to beg, but his long ears
failed to hide the pleading, wistful look in his eyes.
Breeze tossed him a morsel of meat now and then and
before one could touch the ground Louder caught and
swallowed it with a deft snap of his jaws. Big Sue fairly
screamed out:

"Feedin' a dog wid my good meat, enty? I seen you.
I'll learn you better'n dat to-morrow mawnin'."

As a rule Breeze said nothing, but the falling dusk
looked so mournful, his body felt tired, his legs sore, his
back and arms achy with so much work. This was the
time of day he gave Jeems his supper, after the chickens
and guineas were gone to bed. Now the pen was empty.
Jeems was dead.

Pity for Jeems and himself made a sob heave up into
his throat. Big Sue must have heard it, for her big
moist salty hand closed over his mouth, "Shut up dat
cryin'. You ain' nuttin' but a gal-baby! A-cryin' here
an' me fretted half to death 'bout Joy! Drop you'
pants. I's gwine lick you."

Next morning, not a streak of daylight was showing

through the house cracks when Breeze heard Big Sue up, stumbling around, dressing. She fumbled with the door bar, taking it down, then went outside. She wanted to see how her meat was. Breeze turned over, but his dozing was broken up by a long terrible shriek. Without putting on even his breeches, he hopped out of bed and ran out to see what was wrong. Somebody's house must be afire. Joy followed him, her teeth chattering, although she had a quilt wrapped around her.

Never in his whole life had Breeze heard such screams as Big Sue was making. Everybody in the Quarter came hurrying, nobody fully dressed. At first all stood dumb, panic-stricken with amazement, while Big Sue wailed out, between body-wrenching sobs, Jeems was gone! Stolen! Not a hair nor hide was left! The iron hasps holding the chain and lock in the door were pulled clear out of the door-frame. Outraged shouts broke from the crowd. Who here was mean enough to do such a thing? They eyed one another suspiciously. Even fists were clenched, for no such thing was ever heard of. If a ham or a side or a shoulder had been taken, that would have been bad enough, but a whole hog! It was too terrible to think about.

They tried to find some trace, maybe some tracks on the ground around the barn, but nothing was there plainer than Big Sue's own flat barefooted ones.

She shrieked and beat her breast by fits and starts, weeping bitterly all in between.

Jeems was the finest hog ever butchered! She had never seen one lined thicker with fat! His meat would have lasted until next summer! And now it was gone! Stolen!

Her grief could have been no greater if Joy herself had been stolen. Howling with rage she beat her head against the side of the barn until the blows of her skull had it fairly quivering. The neighbors' efforts to console her failed. Not even Joy could make any impression on her raving. Breeze was at his wits' end. The sunny day itself got somber. The birds chirped low and sorrowfully.

Leah was the last person to come. Fat, wabbly, she strolled up, smoking her pipe, one arm akimbo, and beneath her red headkerchief, her eyes gleamed strangely.

"Wha' dat ail Big Sue? E's gwine on like e got in a hornet's nest!"

They told her the news, but instead of grieving Leah sucked her teeth. Big Sue was just trying to make fools of them. Who'd take a whole hog? How could anybody do such a thing? Just as likely as not Big Sue had the hog right yonder in her shed-room.

They all looked in that direction, then back at Big Sue, who had paused in her wailing.

"Wha' dat you say, Leah?" She was panting with rage, and only a narrow piece of ground lay between them, but Leah gave a taunting wicked laugh. "You hear me good enough. It ain' no use to say all dat over."

"You low liar! You varmint!" Big Sue's voice was heavy. Her reddened eyelids, puffed with fat and tears, squeezed as tight as her clenched fist.

"Yunnuh hear Big Sue cuss me, enty?" Leah cried.

"Hush, Leah! You come on home wid me!" April stepped up and would have led her away by the arm, but with the fury of a cyclone, she shook him off and with a savage yell rushed up to Big Sue and spat in her face.

Like a flash they closed. Arms, fists, heads, bodies, whirled, staggered, fell, rose. All efforts to pull them apart were useless. Leah was the first to waver. After an awful blow in the face her arms dropped. She stood still, then tilted back on her heels trying not to fall. As she struggled for breath her mouth stretched wide open, gasping as fish gasp out of water.

April ran up and caught her and eased her gently down on the ground. Horrible fear rose in Breeze's heart, for the glazed look in Leah's eyes was the same that filled Jeems' yesterday, when death struck him.

People crowded around her. Somebody ran for a bucket of water and poured it all over her head and face.

Breeze could hardly see for the mist in his eyes, but he knew Leah was dying for one of her girls gave a long piercing death-cry.

"You is sho' ruint now, Big Sue!" Bina said distinctly.

"You spit in my face an' I'll kill you de same way!"

"Hush, Ma. Fo' Gawd's sake, hush!" Joy plead.

"Leah's de one stole my hog," Big Sue bawled, "Leah's de very one!"

"Hush, Ma! Fo' Gawd's sake, hush! Uncle Bill, do come make Ma go home."

Next morning Big Sue was too ill to get out of bed. Joy kept cool green collard leaves tied on her forehead, and rubbed the palms of her hands and the soles of her feet with tallow, but she groaned and complained with every breath.

Joy sent Breeze with some sweetened bread for Leah's children to eat with their dinner, but he took a long time to get there. Dread made his feet lag. He slunk along the path, scared by every moving shadow. Ready to jump out of his skin at the crackle of a twig.

He felt relieved when he saw Uncle Bill in April's yard helping make Leah's coffin out of clean pine boards lately sawed at the saw-mill. As the sharp plane smoothed the wood, yellow curls fell on the ground. One string exactly Leah's length and another her breadth, showed how to fit the box to her size.

Breeze finally had to go inside the house to deliver the bread and Joy's message that Big Sue would not be well enough to attend Leah's burying. He gave both to Bina, who had a wilted mock-orange bough in her hand, fanning flies away from the bed where Leah lay covered over with a sheet.

"Big Sue's right to stay sick. You tell em I say so, too," Bina said tartly. But in a more kindly tone she asked Breeze if he wanted to see Leah. When he shook his head, Bina said Leah looked mighty nice. Just as peaceful as if she was sleep.

That day was as long as a week. The sun hung still for hours at a time. There was scarcely a breath of wind. Breeze was afraid to stay alone, and both Joy and Big Sue kept to their beds. Once he whispered, "Joy, is you sleepin'?" and she answered gently:

"No, son, I'm wake. Come lay down on de bed 'side me. I know you is lonesome. I is myself."

Reaching her hand out to meet him, she drew his burning face down against her own soft cheek which was cold and wet with tears. He raised up and met her eyes, and the look in them was so sad, so sorrowful, it cut him clean through to the heart.

At last the sun dropped westward, setting in Leah's grave. Curiosity made Breeze want to see what went on, but fear of death kept him in calling distance of Joy. He went up the road far enough to see the dust raised by the funeral procession, but the wailing death-cries ran him home.

Joy stood by the open window listening. When one lone cry rose high above all the rest, her full lips twitched, her sad eyes stared more gloomily and **farther** away, big bitter tears rolled down her cheeks.

Big Sue stayed in bed in the darkened shed-room, drinking root teas that smelled strong and rank.

At last night fell. Bedtime came. Breeze knelt down and tried to whisper his prayers. "O Lawd," he began, but he got no further for Uncle Bill's old hound, Louder, who had been resting and scratching fleas on the porch, suddenly lifted up his voice in a long mournful howl, and Breeze jumped into bed and covered his head.

Early next morning Bina came, pretending to ask about Big Sue's health, but her eyes were round and her breathing quick with excitement. Had they heard the news? No? Everybody on the plantation was talking about it!

Somebody had put an awful conjure on April! Leah's death-sheet had been folded and laid across the foot of April's bed. When he woke this morning, there it was, tucked in at each side so it couldn't slip off on the floor. Nobody knew who did it.

April wanted to throw it in the fire, but Maum Hannah stopped him. Burning a conjure bag, or a death-sheet, is the worst thing you can do. They have to be drowned. Maum Hannah sent for Uncle Isaac, and they both tried to make April drown the sheet in the Blue Brook, but he was too stubborn and hardheaded to mind them. Before they could stop him he dashed it on the red-hot coals. Uncle Isaac grabbed it out, but it was all blackened and scorched and burned.

Uncle Isaac took what was left of it and tied a rock up in it to make it sink. When he threw it in the Blue Brook the water splashed and bubbled and made a mournful groan, then turned green as grass! That sheet must have been loaded with conjure poison. Uncle

Isaac stood just so and counted to ten like the old people used to do. Bina got up to show them. Holding out the fingers of her left hand she counted them over twice with the forefinger of her right, singing as she did it.

> Dis-sem-be! Jack-walla!
> Mulla-long! Mullinga!
> Gulla-possum! Gullinga!
> Sing-sang! Tuffee!
> Killa-walla! Kawa! Ten!

"Uncle Isaac done it just so."

Big Sue was glad. Anybody could see that. She got up and started putting on her clothes. She seemed to shed her worries. To get almost cheerful. Once in a while she sighed. "I'm sho' sorry for April. Too sorry. E ought not to 'a' scorched dat sheet."

The day turned off rainy, dreary, the whole world was wet and blurred. Big Sue said rain always falls after a burying to settle the dust on the grave.

Joy's head ached, and she went to bed. Big Sue dampened a cloth with vinegar and tied it on Joy's forehead, then she went slushing toward the Quarters.

She had hardly got out of sight when Joy jumped up and began a hurried dressing. She put on a dark dress, and tied a white towel over her head.

Breeze cried out in astonishment. Where was she going?

"Nowhere!" answered Joy. "If Ma comes and asks where I is, you don' know nothin' at all. Nothin'!"

"Tell me whe' you's gwine, Joy." Breeze begged.

With a sad little smile she leaned over and hugged him.

"I's comin' back, Breeze. I'm gwine be you' mammy after to-day. Ma can' lick you no more. But don't you tell nobody. I'm gwine to see if de boat brings me a letter from Sherry.''

"Lemme go, Joy."

"No, you stay home till Ma comes."

He let her go, out in the rain. He couldn't help himself. For a while he pottered about the room, for there was no use to go out into the mud and rain. Then he crawled back into bed, and went sound asleep. Once he roused, and heard the boat puffing on the river. It blew for the landing and stopped, then went pounding on into the distance.

Big Sue came in at noon, vexed about something or other. She began abusing Breeze for letting the fire die, soon as she entered the cabin.

"Whe's Joy?"

"I dunno, ma'am.''

"How come you dunno?"

"I dunno how come."

"You ain' got no sense, dat's how come! Blow up dis fire befo' I lick you to death!''

Fear put strength into Breeze's blowing, and the fire soon blazed up, cheerful and bright, but Big Sue was bursting with gall which she vented on Breeze.

He ran about trying to please her, his mouth dumb-stricken with misery. But her bitter abuse stung him to the very quick and overcame him completely. He burst out crying, just as the soft mud outside sucked loud at somebody's footsteps.

Uncle Bill called in through the door, "Is anybody home?''

Big Sue's voice shifted into a pleasanter key as she invited Uncle Bill to come in, then upbraided Breeze for crying like a baby about nothing.

Uncle Bill took Breeze's part, and with a big red pocket handkerchief wiped Breeze's face and eyes with gentlest care, and stroked his hands and tried to comfort him.

"Don' cry, son. You' eyes is like scraps o' red flannel. Joy'll think you's a baby fo' true. She wouldn' b'lieve you kin shoot a gun an' plow an' ride a mule good as a man."

Uncle Bill slipped off his wet shoes to dry them, and sat in his bare feet. "Whe's Joy?"

"I dunno an' Breeze wouldn' tell me whe' Joy went. I reckon e's yonder to Zeda's house a-listenin' at Zeda's brazen talk."

"Zeda's talk ain' brazen since Sherry's gone," mused Uncle Bill. "No, Zeda's down-hearted as kin be."

His shoes and feet steamed in the heat, and he drew both back to a safe distance. Then he showed Breeze how his ankles were marked with tiny scars. "See my snake-cuts? Uncle Isaac fixed me when I wa'n't no bigger'n you. You ought git him to fix you next spring."

He explained how the short gashes were made near a vein, and poison from a rattlesnake and a moccasin rubbed in. This was repeated until the dose no longer caused sickness. No snake could ever harm him again. They knew it. They kept out of his way. Yet snakes had him out in the rain now, taking a bucket of milk to April's children. Snakes had been worse than usual this fall. They were not satisfied with eating all the eggs out of the hen nests, but they sucked the cows dry too. April's cow might as well be dry so far as giving milk for the family to drink.

"April's got a lot o' hogs. Hogs'll suck cows same like a calf," Big Sue reminded him.

Uncle Bill was sure the hogs were innocent. And besides, April's cow came from a fine breed. She wouldn't let a hog suck her. But snakes are tricky.

While the cow was dozing, in the night, they'd slip up and wrap themselves around her leg and suck her dry as a bone and never wake her. Hogs were too awkward to get all the milk. And a fine nice cow like April's wouldn't stand any foolishness from a hog.

"Maybe de cow is lost her cud. Dat'll dry up de milk," Big Sue suggested again.

Uncle Bill dismissed that with a shake of the head. Cows did lose their cuds. One of his own cows lost hers every time the hags rode her, and that was mighty near every young moon. Giving her an old greasy dish-rag to chew on helped her get it back for a while, but she got so bad off, even that failed. Finally he had to go to Uncle Isaac and get him to take the conjure off her. She was conjured, no doubt about that.

"Who you reckon done it?" Big Sue's ears had pricked up with the word "conjure," but Uncle Bill wouldn't say. It was better not to talk too much about such things. When they come, rid yourself of them the best you can, but don't talk about them after they go. The less they get into your mind, the better off you are.

"Cows suck dey own se'f, sometimes," Big Sue went back to the old subject. "April's cow might be a-doin' dat."

Uncle Bill was certain that wasn't so. Somebody would have seen her. Cows did it, he knew. He once owned a fine one that did it and her mother before her did it. Every daughter she had did it too. They had to wear pens around their necks, but nothing could ever break them from the ugly habit. It was born in their blood, just as some dogs are born gun-shy. It's in the breed. People and dogs and cows are born to be what they are. They may cover it up for a long time, but it will come out sooner or later.

Big Sue nodded, agreeing, "Dat's how come I went

clean over de river to Sandy Island when I wanted a
boy to raise. I knowed Breeze come f'om good seed.
E's good stock.''

"You's right. Sho'! If you want to raise corn,
plant corn seed, not cotton seed.''

"April ever was a mighty rash man, Uncle Bill.''
Big Sue hinted at something dark, and Uncle Bill slipped
a look at her, then turned his eyes to look out in the
rain, where a mocking-bird was whistling exactly like a
young turkey. Big Sue got her sewing and sat down to
talk.

"April wouldn' rest not till e pizened dem boll-
evils. I couldn' hardly sleep in de night all las'
summer fo' dem machines a-zoonin'. Everybody was
scared to look out de door whilst April an' Sherry was
gwine round de fields. De pizen dust was same as a fog.
Lawd! I slept wid my head under a quilt ev'y night.
April better had left dem boll-evils right whe' Gawd put
'em. I don' kill no kinder bugs exceptin' spiders. Not
me! Fightin' Gawd's business'll git you in trouble.
April's got off light so far, but e better quit tryin' to
do all de crazy t'ings de white people says do. E sho'
better! Bad luck's been hangin' round ever since dat
radio-machine at de Big House started hollerin' an'
cryin' an' singin' year befo' last. People ain' got no
business tryin' to be Gawd. Not black people anyways.
Let de white people go on. Dey is gwine to hell anyhow!''

She took a fresh thread and moistening the tip of a
finger in her mouth made a fat knot in its end. But
before she stuck it into the cloth, she looked at Uncle
Bill with bright points of light in his eyes. Her words
troubled him.

"You is talkin' mighty fast now, daughter. I been
workin' wid white people all my life an' I ain' got no

complaint to make of dem. No. Ol' Cap'n raise' me
to have respect fo' everybody.''

"Whe' you reckon Ol' Cap'n is to-day, Uncle Bill?''
The old man pressed his lips tight together until they
puckered, and shook his head.

Big Sue laughed, "You don' want to say, enty? I
don' blame you. But between you an' me I spec' e is
whe' I hope e ain't; a hoppin' in Hell dis minute!''

"Shut you' mouth, gal! Gawd'll strike you dead
first t'ing you know!'' Uncle Bill gave her a hard look.
"Ol' Cap'n had his faults, but e was a man! Yes,
Gawd! A man!''

Uncle Bill wasn't listening. He had gone back to the
past, "Lawd, I kin see Ol' Cap'n now. High an'
straight. Slim till de day e died. His eyes could go
black as soot an' flash wid pure fire when e got vexed,
but dey could shine soft as gal-chillen's eyes too.''
Uncle Bill's own eyes brightened as he talked.

"Dat man could ride horses dat would 'a' killed anybody else,'' he boasted. "An' Uncle Isaac, yonder, used
to be a man too! E drove de carriage wid a pair o' coal
black horses. When dey'd pass you in de big road dem
horses' breath was hot as pure steam. Dey nostrils was
red as any blood! De gold an' silver on de harness
would blind you' eyes same as a flash o' lightnin'!
You'd have to stop an' stand still an' cover up you' face.
Dem was de days! You young people don' know
nothin'! Not nothin'!''

A merry laugh crinkled up his eyelids, and filled the
hollows in his thin old cheeks. It tickled him when he
thought about the case Ol' Cap'n was. He was a case.
A heavy case! Sometimes his company would get drunk
and reckless with pistols. Cap'n would always caution
them to be careful not to shoot any of his servants. He'd
always brag that he had the best stock of niggers and

dogs and horses in the state, and he didn't want any of them hurt.

"I 'member. E was powerful big-doin's. But when death come for him, he had to go same as anybody else. Whe's e now, Uncle Bill?"

Uncle Bill made a wry face at Big Sue, "I dunno. An' you dunno. But Gawd knows Ol' Cap'n had a big heart. A good heart. E wan' no po' buckra, or either white trash." A sly smile lightened his solemn face.

"Dat new preacher preaches dat de Great I-Am is a nigger! Don' let em fool you, gal. Gawd is white. You'll see it too when Judgment Day comes. An' E ain' gwine be noways hard on a fine man like Ol' Cap'n. He knows gentlemens. Sho'! An' if Ol' Cap'n couldn' exactly make Heaven, I bet Gawd is got him a comfortable place in Hell, wid plenty o' people to wait on him. An' dat's all e wants, anyhow. E had plenty o' milk an' honey an' gold an' silber down here, an' e didn' count none o' dem much, nohow."

The stillness was so intense that when the clock on Big Sue's mantel banged out an hour, Uncle Bill jumped with a start at its call back to the present. He must be going on to April's house with the bucket of milk. Time was moving. He had a lot of work to do before the white folks came. Some of the fences needed patching. Blinds had to be fixed in the rice-fields for the duck-hunters and the old trunks had to be mended in places so the ducks could be baited. There were many things waiting for him to do them.

"Did you hear f'om de buckra lately?" Big Sue's little eyes got smaller as she asked it.

"Not so lately," Uncle Bill admitted, "but I don' fret. No news is good news wid dem. I sho' will be glad to see li'l' young Cap'n, dough. It's hard to believe dat one li'l' boy is de onliest seed de ol' Cap'n is got left in dis world. E's de last o' de name. De last o' de race. It make me sad to think on dat!''

"Dat same boy is a chip off de ol' block! Lawd, e's a case!"

Uncle Bill started up. "You sound like you got somet'ing against de boy? Dat ain' right. No. When e mammy died, all o' we promised we'd help raise dat baby to know right f'om wrong. You promised de same way like I promised."

Big Sue did not answer and Uncle Bill went on, "Ol' Cap'n, neither young Miss, wouldn' rest still in dey graves if we didn' do right by dat li'l' boy. I too sorry his stepma keeps em yonder up-North most all de time. It ain' good. It's a wonder Ol' Cap'n don' rise out de grave an' haunt em."

Uncle Bill took up his bucket of milk. He must go. Big Sue asked him to tarry longer. Dinner was well-nigh done. He refused politely.

He got as far as the door, when he stopped still, "Miss Big Sue, I gwine tell you something. Ol' Cap'n was a lily of de valley. E was a bright an' mawnin' star. When Death took him, it took de Jedus of dis plantation. Blue Brook ain' never been de same since den. No."

A soft drizzle of rain sifted through the trees, the wind moaned drearily.

Big Sue shook her head. "Gawd made Heaven fo' de humble, Uncle Bill. Hell's de place where de proudful goes. When a man, white or black, gits to trustin' to his own strength, 'stead o' Gawd's, e is done-for, sho' as you' born."

After Leah's death April seemed lonelier than ever. He passed Big Sue's house almost every day, but he never looked in nor spoke. He didn't even turn his head, but walked by, stern, unseeing. Big Sue always stopped

what she was doing to go to the door and watch him.
She'd nod her head and wink and shrug. Everywhere
on the plantation, the talk was thick with prophecies
that April would walk himself to death. Day and night
he walked, never sitting down anywhere. A bad way
for a man to do. That death-sheet had his feet conjured.
They'd never rest again in this world, or in the other,
unless April made a change in his ways.

Joy took to walking too. Not like April, day and
night; but in the evenings, just after sunset, she'd wrap
her long cape close around her and go away down the
path. Big Sue paid little attention to Joy for her own
troubles filled her mind. Occasionally she sent Breeze
to see where Joy went, then got in a rage when Breeze
reported invariably he couldn't find her.

Sometimes Joy walked fast, sometimes slow. Nearly
always toward sunset. Sometimes when she sat down
on a tree root to rest, she'd talk to herself. At last
Breeze felt sure she was trailing April, for when she
glimpsed him through the trees she'd stop still, with
her eyes fastened on him.

Breeze wondered if Joy was going crazy. Had somebody cast a spell on her too! As the days dragged on
toward Christmas, she grew more and more silent. She
spent much of the time in bed, but whenever the boat-
whistle screeched out it had reached the landing, she
either got up and went for the mail herself or sent
Breeze to ask if any letter had come for her.

She took less and less notice of people and things,
but stood by the open window for long stretches, looking
out at the trees or the rice-fields beyond them.

Once when she started out alone in the dusk, Breeze
offered to go with her. She smiled kindly and told him
to come on, but Breeze felt hurt by her steady silence
for it told him plainly that she cared no more for his

company than for the wind, although his one thought was to please her.

The first time they met April, face to face, he would have passed without speaking but Joy stopped him. "Cun April——"

April turned his haggard face toward her and looked down with eyes that were deep sunken and reproachful instead of bold. "Is you called me, Joy?"

She stood dumb, motionless, a second, then spoke softly, distressfully.

"Cun April, I want to tell you, Ma ain' been well, not since Cun Leah died. Ma frets all de time. Day an' night. I can' sleep fo' de way she moans an' goes on. All night long. It's so pitiful. Please, suh, come talk to her sometimes. Ma never meant to do such a harm dat day. I wish you wouldn' hold such hard feelin's."

April had aged a great deal. His shoulders stooped. His feet inclined to drag. His voice was low and husky. But he answered Joy kindly.

"I don' hold nothin' against you' ma, Joy. Leah was in de wrong too. Leah had no business to throw Big Sue's whole hog in de Blue Brook. No. Leah done wrong, I know dat."

Joy stared at him. What he said made her speechless with astonishment at first, but she controlled herself enough to say.

"Stop by an' see me an' Ma, sometimes. Please, Cun April. We gits so awful lonesome after dark."

April promised he would. Promised in words that were very gentle. Then he stalked on, a tall lonely shadow, moving under the trees.

April came to see Big Sue that very night, dropping by so unexpectedly that the sight of him made her dumb for a while. She tried to be natural, to hide her agitation, but her breath caught fast in her throat every time she opened her mouth to talk, and her words were un-certain and stammering.

But April paid little heed to her. He seemed scarcely to know she was there, for his eyes spent much of the time looking at Joy. Breeze thought he saw them flash once or twice, but it may have been the firelight in them.

April declared he had eaten supper and cared for nothing either to eat or drink, but Joy fixed him a cup of water, sweetened with wild honey, flavored with bruised mint leaves, from the mint-bed by the back door. When he tasted it he smiled, and the dull fire in the chimney blazed up, and everything seemed brighter, more joyful than in many a long day.

When April got up to go Joy followed him to the door. She made him shake hands with her and promise to come back very soon.

After that when Joy walked out in the dusk she al-ways let Breeze know she'd rather go by herself. Not that she ever hurt his feelings, but she made some sort of flimsy excuse to be rid of him. He hadn't shut up the coop where the hen and youngest biddies slept, or he hadn't cut up enough fat kindling wood, or couldn't he go fetch a fresh bucket of water from the spring?

Then Breeze discovered that April walked with Joy. He had forgotten Big Sue altogether.

Once Breeze saw them walking shoulder to shoulder, arm touching arm. They talked so softly their words were drowned by the rustle of the leaves under their feet. When April stopped and bent his face so close to Joy's that she drew back a little, Breeze's heart almost quit beating. He let them go on unwatched, hidden by the deepening twilight.

When Joy came home Big Sue grumbled as she handed her a panful of supper and a spoon.

"How come you so love to walk out in de night? It ain' good. You'll ketch a fever or somet'ing worse. You ain' been home to eat supper wid me since last Sat'day night was a week."

But Joy sat mute, looking into the fire, with eyes that gleamed back at the flames.

After that, Joy was always gentle, but except for her evening walk she went nowhere, not even for the mail. For days at a time she scarcely uttered a word. Lying on the bed, or sitting by the fire, she did nothing but think, all the time. When visitors came she said she wasn't well, and went to lie down in the shed-room. Even Big Sue's constant scolding got few words out of the girl.

Late one afternoon Big Sue went to see Maum Hannah, whose crippled knee was being troublesome. In the cabin a bright fire blazed merrily, and Breeze and Joy shelled parched pindars to make some molasses candy before time to cook supper. Breeze ran to Zeda's house to borrow a pinch of cooking soda to make the candy foam up light. When he came back he found April talking to Joy in a strangled husky voice. Both were standing up by the fire, the shelled nuts were scattered on the floor; the smell of the molasses boiling over and burning, made a bitter stench in the room.

"Wha' you say, Joy?" April asked it very low.

Joy stood dumb, motionless, then she lifted her eyes to his face. "Is you want me fo' true, Cun April?"

His eyes were on her, so bold, so full of admiration, that she shrank back in confusion, although her white teeth were flashing with excitement.

April leaned closer and whispered, and her beaming eyes darted up sidewise to see by his face if he meant all he was saying. She reflected in silence, with a down-cast look. But when she answered him softly, she looked straight up again into his eyes.

[254]

His breath came quick. His eyes glinted fiercely. Joy drew back, but she was nodding yes all the time. April caught her and squeezed her to him and kissed her. She started struggling to free herself, but Big Sue's steps sounded outside and April hurried away out of the door. Joy's eyes followed him until the darkness had swallowed him, and only the tramp of his feet could reach her ears. She pulled a chair up to the fire and sat down, with her eyes fixed on the flames. She sat there a long time. Once she smiled to herself, then she frowned, but her eyes stayed glittering like a high spring tide under a full noon sun.

"Joy," Big Sue called her name sternly, "I b'lieve you's conjured. I know April is. Dat death-sheet is had him walkin' his feet off ever since Leah was buried. You's a fool to let dat man talk wid you. I wish to Gawd e'd stay way f'om my house."

When the boat blew for the landing early next morning on its way to town, Breeze and Big Sue had gone in Uncle Isaac's cart to the lime mill near the sea-shore to get lime enough to whitewash the front of her house fresh for Christmas. Every cabin on the whole plantation was being scoured and scrubbed and dressed up with papers. Big Sue wanted hers to be the finest of all. Breeze had wrung next year's supply of straw brooms out of the old unplanted fields and had swept the yard clean with a new dogwood brush-broom.

Joy had helped some, but in a half-hearted way. She wouldn't even ride out with them to get the lime. Her excuse was that Julia looked wild. Breeze knew she didn't mean it, for no mule ever moved more sluggishly. Breeze had to get a stick and frail Julia to make her trot at all.

Noon had passed when they got back home with their load.

Big Sue called Joy to see what nice white fresh-burned lime it was. Like flour. Not a lump in it. But Joy was not at home and Big Sue grumbled.

"Gone to Zeda's again. Joy keeps hankerin' to hear news from Sherry. E may as well quit dat. Sherry's gone! Fo' good! E ain' got Joy to study 'bout! Not no mo'! No!"

When the sun went down, a great red ball, floods of brilliant light gushed up around it, foretelling a cold night and a windy day to-morrow. Water birds flew over the rice-fields, crying out in dread. The trees were full of sighs. The open window blinds creaked dismally. A puff of smoke came down the chimney. Winter was coming.

Dusk fell and the night closed in dark. Joy's supper waited on the hearth. Where could she be so late?

Breeze went to ask Zeda, but she wasn't at home. Maum Hannah's house was dark, so he stopped at Bina's to ask if any one there had seen Joy lately.

Bina looked at him with searching eyes, "You is tryin' to be smart, enty? A-actin' fool to ketch sense!" She sucked her teeth scornfully, but Breeze didn't understand what she meant.

"Don' stan' up an' lie to me, boy! You know Joy an' April went off on de boat dis mawnin'."

Breeze could scarcely believe his ears heard Bina right.

Joy and April gone? Together? Where had they gone?

Why hadn't Joy told somebody?

He flew to tell Big Sue.

Instead of meeting the news with an outburst of grief, Big Sue chuckled, "Who'd 'a' thought my Joy could catch April! An' Leah not yet cold in her grave! Lawd! April's old enough to be Joy's daddy! Well,

all I got to say is dis! April was born fo' luck. E ever
did git de best o' ev'yt'ing on dis plantation.''

The boat was due to return three days hence. When
the time came the whole plantation was at the landing
to meet it.

As the old battered hulk hove in sight, around
the bend, a hush fell on the crowd, and every eye was
fixed on the lower deck where April and Joy stood, side
by side, smiling happily. April took off his hat and
waved it. Joy fluttered a hankerchief to greet them.

They were both dressed fit to kill. Joy, gay as a pea-
cock, in a dress striped with yellow bands, and a hat with
green ribbons and red flowers. April looked youthful
in a brand-new suit that showed off his broad shoulders
and slim waist well. He held Joy's hand and led her
carefully over the unsteady gangplank, and she fell into
Big Sue's arms while April looked on smiling and rub-
bing his hands awkwardly.

The crowd crushed around them, wishing them
happiness, hoping they'd live like Isaac and Rebecca,
wishing them joy and a gal and a boy. Breeze pressed
forward too until he could touch Joy's hand, and she
bent down and gave him a smacking kiss, then a hug.

''Looka li'l' Breeze, Cun April,'' she said, and April
reached out and shook his hand, and Joy added; ''I done
told you I was gwine be you' mammy, Breeze, and Cun
April's you' daddy, now.''

The people crammed too close around them. Breeze
could scarcely breathe. He got out quickly as he could,
and went to the store steps to wait with old Louder, who
sat wagging his tail, and making short whines of
pleasure. Breeze and Big Sue, and most of the neighbors, went with them to April's cabin, where a huge fire
was built, and the whole room made light as day.

Big Sue and Bina bustled around cooking supper, and April's children and Breeze all helped. Sweetened bread and fried bacon and coffee with plenty of cream and sugar, were passed around. The cabin was filled with the fragrance of the food. But Joy couldn't eat. Big Sue pressed her to take something, but she said she couldn't swallow a bite to save her life.

April had eyes only for Joy. He leaned over and whispered softly, "Is anyt'ing ail you, honey?"

But she shook her head. She was only weary, too weary to eat.

Some of the young folks suggested a dance, but April said they must come back another night; Joy was weary. The boat trip was long, and the chill of the river wind had her trembling yet.

When everybody had something to eat and drink, they said good night, and tramped out into the night, Breeze and Big Sue last of all.

The dark roads and paths swarmed with merry people, the air rang with songs and laughter.

"April sho' is a fool over Joy!" Big Sue grunted as they turned into the path toward home. "A pure fool. A ol' fool is de worst fool too."

Joy and April took supper with Big Sue Christmas Eve, and they helped fill Breeze's stocking. He knew, for soon after supper he was sent to bed. They were in a hurry to get to Maum Hannah's house where an all-night meeting was to be held.

Breeze wanted to go too. He wanted to stay up for all the singing and shouting, and see the cows kneel down and pray at midnight, and the sun rise shouting in the east in the morning. But Big Sue said he was too sleepy-headed for her to fool with him, and if he didn't go to bed like a good boy old Santy Claw would leave his stocking empty.

They all said good night and went out of the door and Breeze thought they had gone for good. He was about to hop up and look at his stocking when Joy ran back in, and, falling on the bed where he was, burst out crying.

What on earth! Big Sue and April hurried in, and did all they could to quiet her. Was she sick? Had somebody hurt her feelings? April petted her and called her tender names, but she cried on even when her tears were spent and broken sobs shook her of their own free will.

Big Sue called April into the other room and whispered to him. He came back and asked Joy if she wouldn't rather stay quietly with Breeze and rest? He'd stay too if she liked, or go to meeting with Big Sue. Whatever she wanted was the thing he wanted too. She got up and wiped her eyes. She'd go home and go to bed. He could do whatever he liked. Her words sounded cold, almost bitter.

But soon the next morning she came to show Big Sue the Christmas presents April had given her. A watch to wear on her wrist, and a diamond ring! The two must have cost twenty-five dollars, if not more.

The winter days passed slowly, many of them dull, gray, with an overcast sky, where low clouds sailed and cast their murky color over the ground. The first March day came in bright and warm, with a wind that roared over the land, whipping the trees, snapping off their rotten limbs, lifting old shingles off of roofs, sweeping yards and woods clean, thrashing fields until clouds of dust and sand rose and floated in the sky. But everybody rejoiced that winter was over and gone. And besides, a windy March is lucky. Every pint of March dust brings a peck of September corn, and a pound of October cotton. Let it blow!

Such a high wind could never last. A March that comes in like a lion will go out as quiet as a new-born lamb. Let it blow! But watch the fires! One little spark can easily be fanned into a flame.

New leaves quivered and glittered on the restless boughs. Old leaves, dead for months on the ground, hopped out from their resting-places and skipped and flew, making brown leaf whirlwinds that spun around dizzily, then settled in new sheltered places.

The wind lulled a little at sunset, and the night fell black and cloudless. A multitude of stars crowded the sky, foretelling rain close at hand. The rain was waiting for the blustery gale to hold still so the clouds could gather and agree. In the night the wind rose and beat against the cabin's sides. It shook the walls, and whistled and whined through the cracks. The front door banged wide open, as the nail that held the bar frame was jerked out by its force. Finally Big Sue made Breeze get up and get a hatchet and a long nail out of the tool-box Santy Claw had given him, and she held the door while he nailed it up.

Big Sue was frightened. She kept talking to Breeze, trying to keep him awake with her, but he was too sleepy-headed to listen. When he woke at dawn a flood of rain was pouring down, and thunder roared louder than the rain or wind.

As a fearful crash shook the earth, Big Sue opened the back door and peeped out and quavered, "Git up, Breeze! Lightnin' is struck dat big pine yonder, close to April's house! It's afire! Dat bolt shooken de whole earth. I bet April'll find it. Lawd! E's been diggin' at de roots o' struck trees to git a bolt a long time! An' now one mighty nigh hit him!"

"What's a bolt, Cun Big Sue?"

The wind howled as she answered, "Why, son, a

thunder bolt is a' iron rod. If you finds one, you'll have de power to rule life an' death!''

The cabin was closed tight, yet so fierce was the lightning it blazed through cracks right into the room. Blood-red streaks of light took turns with others that were blue. Breeze shut his eyes and put the pillow over his head. He finally dozed off, and slept until the morning had come, clear of rain and wind, and filled with the warm breath of the earth.

He was alone. Big Sue had gone to see April's struck pine, so he dressed and ran to see it too.

A crowd of people were around the burning tree, and others were coming. All were talking excitedly. God must have His eye on April to aim a thunderbolt so close to his house. He had a narrow escape. His house might catch fire yet, for pieces of burning limbs were falling, and water could not put out fire started with lightning. Nothing could, but new milk from a cow with her first calf. Where would April get enough of that to do any good?

April was brazenly unafraid. He laughed at the notion of getting a heifer's milk. He said he'd make water outen this fire, or any other fire, that bothered his cabin. They'd see.

April sat in front of the fire on his hearth, and when Big Sue fixed his breakfast in a pan and handed it to him, he called to the neighbors, standing outside, ''Yunnuh come an' eat some breakfast wid me. We's got a plenty fo' ev'ybody.'' At first all of them answered, ''No, thank you,'' but when April insisted, a half-dozen or more went in and took a piece of bread, or a mouthful of sweetened water.

''How's Joy?'' Bina asked Big Sue politely.

''Joy's awful nervish since dat tree got struck. I made em stay in bed dis mawnin'.''

"Joy ain' been well in a good while," Bina commented.

Big Sue's eyes snapped. "Joy ever was a delicate child, Bina. You know dat good as me."

The thick high trees, lapping their branches overhead, sheltered the cabins from a sun that burned down, fierce and bright, drawing a strong steamy stench up from the heated mud-flats left naked by the outgone tide.

The fields were all too wet for plowing, and the blacksmith shop was the center for the day's work. Plowshares needed to be filed and sharpened. Plow-stocks mended. Mules' feet trimmed. Manes and tails clipped short. A few of the older, thinner beasts had got lousy. The hair must be cut off them and their hides wet with tea made out of china-berry leaves.

The men laughed and talked and chewed tobacco and smoked, as they worked leisurely at their different tasks. A difference of opinion rose as to the best place to twitch a mule to make him stand still for his hair to be cut off. A twine-string could be twisted around an ear, or tied to the upper lip. Uncle Bill preferred the lip. He said mules have pockets inside their ears and a string twisted tight enough to hold the beast quiet, will tear that pocket in two. April objected to the twitch on the lip, for it often caused a painful swelling.

The question was still unsettled when Brudge came running hard as he could, crying out that Joy had been taken with a death-sickness. She was lying on the bed in a trance. She couldn't speak a word. Brudge almost popped out his eyeballs showing how her eyes were rolled away back in her head. Her hands and feet were cold as clabber. Big Sue said April must hurry or Joy would be gone before he got there!

April did not wait to hear the end of Brudge's talk, but flew home ahead of them all with Breeze close at his heels. Lamentations and outcries met them as they got nearer. Big Sue's above all the rest. Joy was dying. Nothing but a death-sickness could strike a young woman down so hard.

Breeze was almost petrified with terror, but he dragged himself on to the cabin, which was already filled with the neighbors. Joy lay on the bed covered over with a quilt, up to her very neck. Her eyes were shut. Her head moved from side to side. Her lips whispered things nobody could hear at all.

Big Sue sat near the bed in a low chair, her fat body rocking. Big tears rolled down her cheks as she chanted over and over.

"Do, Jedus! Don' let Joy dead!

"Oh, my Gawd! Help my chile! Help em!

"Oh, Lawd! Oh, my Gawd!

"Don' let Joy dead dis mawnin'!"

April broke through the crowd surrounding the bed, and taking one of Joy's hands from under the cover felt her pulse, then leaned over to hear what she was saying. "No. No, honey," he crooned, "you wouldn' dead an' leave me. No. No. I couldn' do widout you nohow. I wouldn' 'a' left you last night in dat storm, but I was 'fraid de stables would blow down an' kill all de mules an' horses. De storm is gone. De lightnin' didn' hurt nobody. Death is gone away off now. E can' take you. No!"

Breeze pricked up his ears. Was death about to take Joy?

As her life fluttered uncertainly, Big Sue's wailing and misery were less hard to bear than April's fierce resolute manner.

Joy had to get well. No matter what ailed her. If she was conjured, Uncle Isaac had to take off the spell. If the storm had scared her until her heart-string was strained, she must keep still and rest until it went back into place. Nobody must come in the room to worry her with talking. Send for Maum Hannah. No matter if she was at the end of the earth instead of the end of the "Neck," go fetch her! Hurry! Don't tarry and waste any more time! Fetch Maum Hannah! Joy had a death-sickness!

Uncle Bill hitched up the fastest horse in the barn-yard to the lightest cart, and went flying down the road for Maum Hannah, who had gone to a sick woman some miles away. When he got back, several hours later, the horse was lathered with sweat, and all but broken winded, but Joy was still alive.

The room was chock-full, the door choked with people, both windows were dark with heads. Big Sue's mourning that had fallen into a low mumbling prayer to Jesus now changed and livened to:

"Do, Maum Hannah! Help my Joy!

"Do, Maum Hannah! Don' let Joy dead!

"Do, Maum Hannah!"

Maum Hannah hurried up the steps as fast as her crippled knee would let her. She was all out of breath, but instead of pitying Big Sue, she stopped still and eyed her with an impatient grunt. "Do shut you' mouth, Big Sue! You ought to be shame' to cut all dis crazy! You can' fool dese people. No! Everybody knows wha' ails Joy, 'ceptin' April. An' e ought to take you out an' duck you good in de creek fo' makin' such a fool out o' him! Dat fine horse is most dead! Bill made em run so fas', de wind likened to 'a' cut my breath off. You people go home. Gi' Joy a chance to turn dat chile loose. Joy done well to hold em dis long but e can' hold em no longer. Yunnuh go on! Go on, Breeze! Yunnuh clear de room!"

Big Sue stopped grieving and stared, but Maum

Hannah's talk stung April to the quick. He stepped up to her angrily, but she stopped taking off her cloak long enough to pat his arm, "Don' be vexed wid me, son. I'm tellin' yunnuh what Gawd loves, de truth! Joy's done well to hold dat chile dis long. You married in de Christmas, enty? Well, Joy can' hold em six more months. I know dat. Dat gal's got to turn em loose, no matter if it do hurt you' feelin's!"

Joy trembled like a leaf in a storm. Her dazed eyes turned from Maum Hannah to April, who was silent, except for one word. "Bitch," he snarled, and his eyes blazed like lightning flashes, as he turned and left the room.

Breeze left too, but he scarcely knew where he was, or where he was going. April had cursed Joy and she a-dying!

He dragged himself home and fell across Joy's own bed, for Big Sue was not there to stop him. He wept until his tears failed him. He tried his best to pray, "O Gawd, don' let Joy die—" but he went fast asleep. He slept heavily until a harsh hoarse voice waked him. He came instantly to his senses, and tried to stammer out some excuse, but Big Sue's grim swollen face made his words falter, and the slap her hand laid on his jaw brought shining stars in front of his eyes.

"Git up and go borrow a piece o' fire f'om somebody! Hurry, too, befo' I kill you!"

He ran to April's house, but stopped at the step for a tiny baby was crying inside. He ran all the way to Zeda's and borrowed a piece of fire, then flew home. As he made up the fire for Big Sue, she walked around the room unsteadily, mumbling between her teeth. If April mistreated her Joy now, she herself would put a "hand" on him; one so strong that it would wither his hands! And his feet! She couldn't keep still or stop talking.

Her tongue lashed April and Joy too, and each word was a poison sting. Who was he to blame Joy? He had children scattered from one end of this "Neck" to the other. Now he cursed Joy as if she were lowest of the low. It was a shame! A heavy shame! Joy must leave him at once!

The wind had risen and whistled through the trees, tossing the branches, making them moan. Big Sue talked on and on. Breeze was glad when she went back to April's cabin, although she left him without a bite to eat. He'd go somewhere and get supper. Maybe Uncle Bill was at home. He'd go see.

To his surprise April was there too, sitting by the fire, miserably dejected, while Uncle Bill talked to him, trying to cheer him.

Breeze had hardly got inside when Zeda arrived and, brushing past Uncle Bill, walked up to April and put a hand on his shoulder. Look at me, April. I got somet'ing to say to you." Bitter spite hurried her words.

But April, instead of looking up as she bade him, leaned forward and spat in the fire.

"Wha' ails you, now, Zeda?" he asked curtly.

"I kin easy say what ails me; dat new-born child yonder 'side Joy is my gran'! But e's you' gran', too! Joy had dat chile for Sherry, an' you ain' gwine put no dis-grace-ment on em. No. If nobody else can' hinder you, I kin. I already got you' feet so dey can' rest. Wid Leah's death-sheet."

April heard her, and although he didn't answer, his jaw set his teeth hard enough to bite a ten-penny nail in two. Zeda smiled.

"You may as well give in, April," she persisted. "Sherry's you own, an' who is Breeze, but you' own? Ev'body knows dat. It's a wonder somebody ain' cut you' throat long time ago. If you wa'n't so lucky you'd 'a' been in hell wid some o' dem women you sent dere."

"How come you meddlin' in my business so raven?" April suddenly flashed out.

"Dat li'l' chile is my business. Joy had em fo' Sherry, a li'l' boy-chile, too. You go on home an' tell Joy to hurry up an' git well. 'Tain' no use to hold hard feelin's 'gainst em. No! Joy's had you a gran'son."

When he did not stir, she blazed out: "You' neck is stiff, enty! So's my own! An' I hope a misery'll gnaw you' heart in two. I hope you'll die of thirst an' hunger. I hope ev'y lawful yard-chile you had by Leah'll perish. I hope you' feet'll rot——"

"You shut you' mouth, Zeda. If you cuss me again I'll choke you' tongue down you' throat." April got up and fled from her bitter words.

XVIII

For days after Joy's child was born, Big Sue kept to her cabin. Joy had disgraced her, made her ashamed to show her face in company. She'd never forgive Joy as long as she lived. Never. Joy saw Leah drop dead in her face, yet she went straight on and married Leah's husband. A shame! Joy would sup sorrow yet. She might bewitch April and make a plumb fool out of him, but she'd pay for bringing disgrace on her mother who had worked her knuckles to the bone to keep Joy in school!

If Joy had behaved herself, she might have married anybody instead of a man old as her daddy, and conjured to boot. That death-sheet had put a spell on April. Sure as preaching. He'd never be the same man again. He'd have run Joy out of his house if he had been in his right mind.

She talked so fast and loud one morning she didn't see Uncle Bill until he was at the door-step. "How come you tiptoes around so easy dis mornin'!" she asked tartly.

"Gawd knows how I'm a-walkin', I'm so fretted."

"Wha' dat ail you now?"

"Joy sent me to tell you."

"How come Joy don' fetch e own answer?"

"Joy's too troub-led."

Big Sue shot a look at him and sucked her teeth.

"Joy's mighty late gittin' troub-led," and a hard, wicked smile touched her mouth.

"Joy's troub-led about April. April ain' well, Miss Big Sue."

Big Sue sniffed and said April was due to have something wrong with him, wicked as he had lived, hard as he had been with everybody that crossed him. What kind of sickness did April have?

"Somet'ing ails his feets."

"Dat ain' surprisin'. April slept wid a death-sheet on 'em a whole night."

"Uncle Isaac took dat spell off em."

"Well, who put dis spell on em, den?"

Uncle Bill sat down on the step. He was so troub-led in his mind, it was difficult for him to say what ailed April. At first it favored chilblains; then ground-itch, for April went out barefooted in the dew every morning God sent, and any little scratch that lets dew get inside your skin may give you ground-itch. But none of the chilblain or ground-itch cures helped him at all. His appetite was clean gone. He had eaten nothing but spoon-victuals for a week. He was thin as a fence rail.

Big Sue made an ugly mouth. What did she care? Why hadn't April married a settled woman who could cook decent rations instead of a scatter-brained girl like Joy who didn't know the name of one pot from another? He needn't be sending word here about victuals. Let April eat what Joy fixed for him. Love would season up lumpy hominy and make doughy bread taste good.

Uncle Bill sat frowning, chewing his tobacco wearily, studying. Joy had said she hated to worry Big Sue. She was sorry for all that had happened. Joy was a good girl. She had slipped up once, and made a bad mistake, but any young inexperienced girl is likely to miss and do that. April did right to excuse her.

[269]

Big Sue sneered. Joy had worked one sharp trick. Leah herself couldn't have fooled April any slicker. Joy ever was tricky, though. Just like Silas for the world. Likely as not, Joy had April conjured right now.

Uncle Bill pursed up his lips so tight, they looked as if they'd never open and speak again, and his eyes were full of worry.

"Whyn' you go see Uncle Isaac? E might could help April?" Big Sue asked presently.

"I done seen em. When de bear-grass poultices and de violet-leaves tea failed, I went an' got Uncle Isaac. Joy sent me. I don' like charms. I don' trust 'em. I know a Christian man ain' got no business foolin' wid 'em. But Joy was so fretted, I done it to please her. I kept a-studyin' over it; one mind said do it; another mind said, no, I better ask all de Christian people to hold a prayer-meetin' an' ask Gawd to help April; I listened at dem two minds arguin' one whole night befo' I give in to Joy. An' now I wish to Gawd I didn' heed em."

"How come so? April wouldn' wear em, I bet you!" Big Sue was listening with interest now, anxious to know what happened, but Uncle Bill took his time.

April did everything Joy said. Wilful and unruly as he was with every one else, he tried to please Joy. And yet when Joy brought that charm to him and began coaxing him to let her tie it around his neck, he balked. Joy had to outtalk him.

For a whole day and night April wore it, a little cloth bag, tied with a white horse hair; but because it didn't cure his feet right away, he jerked it off and threw it in the fire. Such a pity. Even strong charms take time to start working. April ever was a short-patienced man. He made trouble for himself by hastiness. A man can be hot-blooded and pettish with people but not with charms or magic.

Joy snatched the bag out of the flames, but it was scorched and a hole burned in one side. A speck of the mixture inside it spilled out on the coals and smoked such a strong smoke, April sneezed three times!

Right then, the gristles in April's feet got hard. Hard as a rock! God only knew if they'd ever go back to their rightful softness.

Uncle Isaac made Joy take the bag off to the woods and bury it at the foot of a locust tree, but April got worse and worse. His feet were numb and hard and dry. Joy wanted to send for a white doctor. They might get one to come on the boat from town, and with the crop so promising they'd have money to pay him next fall. But April wouldn't have it. He said Maum Hannah knew more than any white doctor.

Big Sue kept shaking her head and grunting shamelessly until Uncle Bill got up painfully to go. Something in his sad face must have moved her, for all of a sudden she scrambled to her feet, letting her scraps fall on the floor. "I made some nice little sweetened breads dis mawnin'. Take some to April. I sho' am sorry 'bout his feets. You tell em so. I'm gwine broil em a fat pullet, too."

"Ev'y man has to manage his own dueness, but how 'bout gwine along wid me, to see April, Miss Big Sue? You done chastise Joy long enough. De gal's in trouble."

"I can' go, not so well, right now, Uncle Bill, but Breeze kin go if e'll thread me two or three needles first." She started to say more, but she changed her mind and kept silent, her eyes cast down on her sewing. When she did speak it was to say Joy had been mighty shut-mouthed about April. Joy had funny ways.

Breeze and Uncle Bill found April with a quilt around him, sitting alone by the fire, looking at his feet. Looking and looking. His heavy black brows overshadowed his sad eyes as they lifted and hovered over Breeze, then Uncle Bill. But as soon as he shook hands and said "thank you" for the food, they fell, and settled on his feet, which were bare and on the hearth very close to the fire.

The weather had turned off cool in the night, but there was no reason for April to keep his feet so close to the fire. Uncle Bill told him he'd scorch them, but April shook his head and said they felt no heat at all. Not a bit. They had gone to sleep or something. They felt like blocks of wood. And he moved them stiffly, as if they were.

He complained that he had no appetite. He was tired too. Sitting still was the hardest work he had ever done in his life. If he could read, or if he had somebody to talk to, if he had something pleasant to think about, it would help pass the time. But he couldn't read, and he didn't want anybody to stay at home out of the field. Cotton needs fast hoeing during these warm wet days. He wished he could stop off thinking. Stop short off. He'd like to go to sleep and never wake up any more. He'd go crazy if he had to stay still and look at his feet much longer. What in God's name ailed them! Nobody seemed to know!

Uncle Bill tried to tell him the plantation news, but April's eyes stayed on his feet. Uncle Bill offered to teach him to read if he wanted to learn. Now would be a good time for April to learn how to write. He ought to learn to write his name if no more. Every man ought to know how to write his name. But April said he never had much faith in books and reading. Black people were better off without it. It takes their mind off their work. It makes them think about things they can't have. They're better off without knowing how. Uncle Bill didn't argue.

All of a sudden a coal popped out of the hearth with a sharp explosion. It fell right between April's feet, as if it could see and did it on purpose. It lay there, red, bright, like a dare. April opened his tired eyes wide, and leaned forward and looked at it, for instead of dying out it burned freer. April carefully raised one long black bony foot and placed its heel on the coal. He waited a moment; then he lifted it up and stared at Uncle Bill. His scared eyes told what had happened. Breeze knew too.

April had felt no heat. His foot was dead. It couldn't feel fire! April grabbed the fire shovel, and scraped up a batch of live coals from under the fire and dropped them on the hearth. He'd see if fire had stopped being hot. Uncle Bill didn't raise a finger to stop him when he lifted his other foot and pressed its heel down on the coals and mashed hard on them.

The bitter smell of his burned flesh stung the air. April's eyes glared, and he laughed a harsh discordant laugh. But a sob quickly caught him by the throat and choked him. He leaned over and picked up a live coal in his fingers, then dropped it quickly, for his fingers were alive. They could feel. The coal burned them. But his feet were dead. They couldn't feel even fire!

"Oh, Gawd!" he moaned, and his long fingers knotted and clenched, his strong tobacco-yellowed teeth ground together.

Joy came in from the field to feed her little baby. Nobody heard her bare footsteps, until she spoke to Uncle Bill and Breeze. She went up to April and put a hand on his arm, and asked how his feet were. She leaned over and looked at them, but he drew them under-

neath his chair. He didn't want her to see. He reached
for the quilt on the floor beside him and covered them
over.

"My feets is all right," he told her gruffly.

But Joy sniffed the air once or twice, she searched
the fire with her eyes, then she swept the hearth clean of
the coals. She patted April's shoulder, and said gentle
things to him. He must have patience. She'd make
some fresh violet-leaves tea and soak his feet. She was
sure that would help them.

Bright tears ran out of April's eyes, down his thin
hard cheeks, and fell on the bony clasped hands that
held tight to each other in his lap. Breeze could hardly
bear to see those tears. Uncle Bill got up and tried to
say something, but his voice broke, and he began punch-
ing the fire. For April was crying out loud. Saying he
had given out! He couldn't go on any longer!

Joy put her arms around him and held his head on
her bosom, and patted his face and tried to hush him.
She wiped his tears away with her homespun apron, and
smoothed his eyelids softly. Her fingers were trembling,
but April became quieter. She stroked his head and
begged him to go back to bed and lie down and rest.

He was hard and sullen, and frowned as if she
had insulted him. He'd stay right where he was. Bed
and chair were the same to him now. Joy stood with
her eyes on the red embers, never answering back a
single time, even when anger made the words strangle
in his throat. It was hard for him to bend his neck
under such a galling, hellish yoke.

Until now he had never asked a favor of anybody in
his whole life. He had always worked, and made others
work. His women and children too. And now his feet,
the feet that had carried him faithfully through all
these years, the only ones he could ever have, had failed

[274]

him. They made game of him. And it was more than he could bear. He bellowed out recklessly, but Joy got a pan and spoon and dipped some hot soup from a pot on the hearth and urged him to taste it. He shook his head. He didn't want soup. He didn't want anything to eat. He'd rather starve to death than be helpless. Joy began some pleasant talk. How fast the cotton was growing. The fields were green. Last night's shower was the very thing spring oats needed. He leaned back in his chair, humbled, crushed with misery. Uncle Bill said he would come back a little later and bring April some medicine. Some strong medicine from the Big House medicine chest. It would help those feet.

April reached out and took his friend's hand. He put it up to his cheek, but dropped it, for the back log burned in two and broke and a shower of sparks spun threads of fire that reached out and threatened to catch the quilt!

"I'll stay wid em," Joy said gently. "I'll warm up de nice chicken an' rice you brought an' feed em wid a spoon."

When Breeze got home Big Sue asked him lots of questions about April. How his feet looked? Did April seem down-hearted over them? Was Joy with him? How did she take his trouble? Breeze told her all he remembered, and she shook her head. She was sorry for April.

It was past mid-afternoon when Uncle Bill came back, and asked Big Sue to lend him a quart cup and a teaspoon. He wanted to measure some water and medicine for April's feet. He was going to soak them in water flavored with a medicine the white folks used. She offered to lend him her new tin washtub, but Uncle Bill said Joy had plenty of tubs.

"Dey might not be new an' clean as my own," **Big**

[275]

Sue insisted. "Joy ever was careless. A new tub is better anyhow."

Uncle Bill consented, and Breeze went along to carry it. They found Joy sitting by the fire patching, and April holding a pan of food in his lap.

Joy asked them to come in and sit down and talk to April and coax him to eat his dinner. His appetite was slow. She did her best to talk cheerfully.

But April's face was glum, and his voice lagged wearily as he said, "I don' wan' to eat." With a bony hand he held out the pan, still full of food. "Take em. I got 'nough."

Joy took it and moved away without speaking. As she walked toward the shelf she almost stumbled into a small boy, who hopped nimbly into the room, laughing and out of breath. She put her hand on his shoulder and shook him, and he got sober. Soon the other children came trooping in, little and big, and all in-between size, one with Joy's baby in his arms.

"Mind. Keep quiet," Joy warned. "Pa don' like no fuss."

Then they tipped around quietly, and whispered to Breeze to come with them while they cut some wood and brought it in, and went to the spring for water. The older ones said, "How you feelin', Pa?" That was all, for April did not turn his head or answer.

Every child glanced at his feet. April saw it. And he saw how they all looked away quickly, except one little boy who giggled out loud.

Joy shook her head vexedly, and motioned to the child to go on out, for anger crazed April. His own child had laughed at him! He sat up and blazed out, "Dat's de way! Let a man git down an' e's de butt o' his own flesh an' blood! Dat's de way! Chillen don' hab respect fo' nobody! Not dese days!"

Breeze felt afraid. He didn't want to play. He'd rather stay close by Uncle Bill. When things got quieter again, Uncle Bill suggested kindly:

"April, son, I tell you wha' le's do. Lemme hotten some water an' gi' you' feet a good soakin'. You would feel better when dey's had a dose o' dis medicine f'om de Big House." He held up the small bottle. It had a skull and cross-bones label. The white liquid in it trembled, with a glitter.

April did not answer, and Joy filled the big black kettle on the hearth with water, and pushed it up nearer the red coals.

As soon as it sang out that the water was hot, Uncle Bill poured it quart by quart into the tub. Then he carefully measured quarts of water from a bucket on the shelf to cool it. He felt it with his hand, and Joy felt it too, so it would be neither too cold nor too hot.

"It's 'bout right," she said, and Uncle Bill put in the medicine. One spoonful to every quart of water. How it smelt! Joy pushed the tub closer to April, then lifted the helpless feet, one at a time, and put them into the water.

"It's 'bout right, enty?" she asked him.

"I dunno," April gloomed. "I can' feel em."

And she turned away with a sigh.

The clothes to be patched were on the floor in a pile. Joy mended the fire, then moved nearer its light to sew. Uncle Bill sat and talked pleasantly while April's feet soaked. The crops were promising. Cotton and corn, and peas and potatoes, and rice all were up and growing. Everybody ought to be thankful with so many blessings. The fire kept up a spiteful popping, aiming bits of live coal at each of them. Some fell into the water and died; others hit Joy's pile of clothes.

April moved restlessly. "I'm ready fo' lay down,"

he said dully. "Uncle Bill, you help Joy git me to bed."

Joy got up, letting her lapful of things scatter over the floor. "Wait. Lemme git something soft fo' wipe you' feet on." She hurried to an old trunk in the corner and got out a piece of soft worn cloth. Then she came back and knelt down by the tub.

April and Uncle Bill both jumped when she gave a sharp outcry and sat back flat on the floor. She stared. Then she leaned over with squinting eyes, as if the light hurt her eyes. She gasped like her wind-pipe was cracked, "Great Gawd, what has you done, Uncle Bill!" Her body was trembling and her eyes had a foolish roll as they lifted to April's face. She was shivering all over. She was having a chill, or some kind of a stroke!

April told Breeze to call some of the children to come to Joy. He put out his hand to help steady her. But she sat back on her feet and put a hand to her head. Maybe she ate too much dinner. Breeze felt giddy himself, and tired and unhappy. His head swam when he moved. He wanted to go home, but he couldn't leave Uncle Bill to bring Big Sue's tub.

"Set down, Joy. Set down!" April scolded fretfully. "Don' try fo' stan' up. You might fall. None o' we ain' able to ketch you if you do. You haffer take care o' you'se'f now. I ain' able fo' look atter you."

He spoke quickly for his patience was short.

"You must 'a' strained you' eye on de sewin'. Lay flat on de floor till you feel better. I kin wait." April moved stiffly, with a deep sigh.

But Joy's wide-opened eyes stared at the tub. She was gone plumb fool! Plumb daffy!

"Uncle Bill——" her lips shook so they could hardly make his name. "Looka! Fo' Gawd's sake!" she whispered. "De medicine must 'a' been too strong!"

Breeze could scarcely tell what she said, for she ran her words all together and she shook with a chill. Fever makes people so sometimes.

"Do talk hard, Joy. I can' hear no whisperin'! Who you scared gwine hear you? A sperit?" April scolded.

Breeze's eyes followed Joy's to the tub. He stared too. He saw what made her teeth click together——
April's toes.

They had come loose from his feet, and floated around in the tub. In the clear warm water, sharp-flavored with the strong white medicine. Breeze felt dazed. His head was queer. The room, the walls began to move around and wave up and down.

When April saw the toes he began to laugh. An ugly croaking, high-pitched laugh that chilled Breeze's blood, and made the water swish in the tub.

The toes, all loose, free from the feet, swam around swiftly and circled and danced. One big toe slid next to a little one and stopped!

April half-rose to his feet and shouted:

"Look! My Gawd! Is you ever see sich a t'ing in you' life? My toes is come off. Dey runs by deyse'f! Fo' Gawd's sake!"

His reddened eyes shone. He tried to step. Then he sat down clumsily. Heavily. He leaned forward, spellbound, whispering horrified words. Breeze shook with terror, for April's words were as strange as the toes jumbled together. He glared at Breeze, then at Uncle Bill. "Yunnuh hurry up! Hurry up!" he yelled fiercely, getting up on his feet again. "Do somet'ing! Quick! My toes is off!"

He tottered, for the bottom of the tub was slippery footing for his broken feet, and with a crumple he fell forward on the floor.

Joy cried out sharply, and begged Breeze to go call the children. Then she ran to the open door, and stretching her body to its utmost height, tilted back her head and sent out long throat-splitting calls that cut into Breeze's ears! She stopped to tell Uncle Bill to go fetch Maum Hannah, who had gone way down the country, catching children.

She wrung her hands and wailed. That medicine must have been too strong! Too strong! Uncle Bill said maybe that charm did it! April wore it a whole day around his neck! Did that old hoodoo doctor over the river have aught against April? That charm was too strong. Maybe Joy had buried it wrong! Maybe it ought not to have been buried at all—maybe—maybe—Leah's death-sheet was to blame.

Breeze tried to help Joy and Uncle Bill get April to bed, then Joy slipped out of the door. She'd go try to find that charm. But if she found it, what could she do? April's toes were off. No charm could put them on again. That was certain.

Uncle Bill was sure he measured the medicine. Over and over, he said it; a teaspoonful to the quart of water. That was all he put. It couldn't hurt a tender baby's feet. He had seen the white people use it, and they have weak skins. But April's toes were off! And there was no way to put them back on. That scorched charm must be to blame, unless poisoning boll-weevils last summer poisoned his feet too. Uncle Isaac had drowned the death-sheet, and killed its spell—in spite of Zeda.

April didn't seem to realize what had happened. He kept saying, over and over, "How'm I gonna walk widout toes?" He was too stiff in his joints to bend over far enough to look at his feet. Uncle Bill got the mirror that hung by the open window. A small square wavy looking-glass that made foolish-looking images. The old man tried to hold it so April could see the feet in the mirror, but his hands shook so that Breeze had to take it and hold it. The horror in April's face made Breeze's own blood freeze. April's lips and tongue went stiff. They could scarcely say, "How'm I gonna walk widout toes."

He asked to see the bottle of white medicine Uncle Bill used in the water. He took out the stopper and smelled it, touched it to his tongue. It was too strong! Yes! Too strong! It cut his tongue!

Two days later when the boat came Uncle Bill and Brudge took April to the town in the river's mouth, so some white doctor might see him and cure him. But when they came home Uncle Bill said the white doctor had taken April to a hospital and cut both his legs off, at his hips! The doctor said blood clots in the veins of April's legs had cut off the blood flow to his feet. That was why they died. The doctor called it gangrene. He said no charm could cause it, not even a death-sheet. April would get well after a month or two, and he could wear wooden legs with steel joints. They'd walk and carry him as well as his old legs had done, when he learned how to rule them and make them step. But it would take time. April would have to have patience now. Long patience.

The white doctor was kind, polite. He would write Joy exactly how April mended. She mustn't worry. Everything would come right. April was no common weak man to give up. Never in this world. The plantation people must all pray for April to keep in good heart, and not get scared about himself. And Joy must have faith that April would get safely through this great trial.

Uncle Bill went to see the preacher April had bitten. His cheek had not rotted off at all. The white doctor had fixed it. But it looked queer, for it was drawn up tight like the mouth of a tobacco sack pulled together with draw-strings.

From that day Joy showed no sign of weakness. She shirked nothing, yielded nothing to Leah's children who gave up being impudent to her face and did their grumbling about her behind her back.

When the stables were cleaned out and the black manure piled out in the corn-field, Joy went out at dawn with the other women, barefooted, scantily dressed, a rough crocus sack made into an apron to hold the stuff, and scattered it all day long, up and down the corn rows, leading the women as they marched abreast, singing, ''Follow me—'' to their chorus, ''We's a-followin' on,'' and ending, ''I'll lead you gentel-eee home!''

When the cotton was up to a thick stand and ready to be thinned, she tied her skirt up high out of the dew and took her hoe and chopped row for row with the best hoe hands, leaving the stalks one hoe's width apart and cutting out every grass blade. She hung up eggshells to make the hens lay well, fed them sour dough to make them set, patched the garden fence and filled the rich plot of earth with seed.

She set hens and took them off with broods of biddies and dusted them with ashes to kill the lice. For one so frail-looking, Joy did wonders.

Everybody praised her but Leah's children, who had naught against her except she had married April, and Big Sue, who kept her distance, pretending that Joy had disgraced her. But Zeda said Big Sue was jealous of Joy's getting April.

Joy visited few of her neighbors except Maum Hannah and Zeda, and she took no part in the plantation quarrels and disagreements, or in the arguments about what had caused April's trouble. People asked her a thousand questions, but she was a close-mouthed woman. She didn't know anything about anything, to hear her tell it, and she listened, mute, dumb, when they came to her, wondering if the death-sheet or the scorched charm or the white folks' medicine had ruined April? Joy agreed with them that charms were dangerous. But store-bought medicine is not to be trusted either. Leah got herself salivated by taking one lone teaspoonful of a scentless, tasteless white powder. It looked weak as flour, yet it loosened every tooth in her mouth and made them all drop out, whole. If April hadn't been a mighty faithful man he'd have left Leah altogether right then. Where's another man would stick? Leah was a fool to prank with things she didn't understand. April did well ever to look at her again, for no man could be raven about a salivated woman, yet he even took her to town and bought her new teeth. No man could have done more than that. They cost more than a bale of cotton. Leah was ever contrary. Jealous. Maybe it was Leah that had tricked him now. Who could tell? She died too hard to rest easy in her grave. And she never took her eyes off of April while she lived. No doubt her spirit was after him still.

The weather was exactly right for the cotton; mornings wet with dew, noons fever hot; nights still and steamy and stifling. Except for the accursed boll-weevils the crop was most promising. The tender leaves multiplied and widened, and from morning until night they lifted their faces to get every bit of sunshine they could hold. The three-cornerd squares clustered on the limbs, but not a blossom showed, for swarms of boll-weevils punctured these buds and made them drop off before a creamy petal could form. Well-nigh every fallen square held a grub. A few days more and they'd be weevils, ready to lay more eggs in new squares, and hatch more weevils. Unless something was done to stop them, the crop might as well be thrown away.

Uncle Bill and Uncle Isaac were upset. What were they to do? They sent every man and woman and child on the plantation to the field to pick the squares and try to catch the weevils, but the squares fell off behind them as fast as they picked those in front, and the pesky weevil fell off the stalks on the ground, too, as soon as anybody came near them. They played dead like 'possums, and they were colored so near like the dirt, the sharpest eyes couldn't find them.

Uncle Bill walked up and down the rows watching, and frowning darkly. At last he stopped beside Zeda, and asked her where Sherry was. He'd have to come home and poison the cotton or the whole crop was done for. Not enough money would be made on the whole place to buy a pair of rope lines. Sherry would come back if he knew how bad things were. He wouldn't hold hard feelings against April if he could see him. God had punished April enough to wipe out every sin he had ever done in his life. Sherry must forgive him too, and come back and help fight the weevils. Zeda listened coldly. She looked at Uncle Bill, then at the others.

"Uncle Bill is talkin' out a new side o' his mouth to-day, enty?" She tried to laugh indifferently, but everybody knew Sherry's going had cut her to the quick and she'd be glad enough to get him back.

"You's right, Zeda. I is talkin' a new talk. But de ox is in de ditch. An' de ditch is deep. De plantation is in distress, an' nobody can' save em but Sherry."

All the people stood still heeding every word, now and again making low remarks to one another.

"You's right, Uncle. I know I don' relish plowin' f'om sun to sun not lessen I'm doin' some good. De more we plow, de more de cotton grows an' de more it

[284]

puts on squares to feed de boll-evils. April pizened
'em last year. Sherry helped em den. Le's send at
Sherry to come home. Git a letter wrote to em an' tell
em if he would come home we mens'll make em foreman.
How 'bout dat?'' asked Jake, Bina's husband.

The men looked at him, searched one another's faces,
growled among themselves. The women fell into groups,
the loudest talkers laying out opinions, some for, some
against, Sherry's being made foreman. True enough,
they needed a foreman. No plantation as large as Blue
Brook could half-way run without a man to head the
hands and be their leader. Sherry was young. Wild.
Head-strong. He wasn't even married and settled.

Zeda called out impatiently:

''Talk it over good! Make up you' minds! Sherry's
comin' or not comin' is one to me! E's got a fine job,
yonder up-North. E's makin' money hand over fist.
His wages fo' one day is more dollars dan e would see
in a month here at Blue Brook.''

Her words struck home. After a few silent moments,
the people began saying:

''Write em to come, Zeda!''

''Tell em we want em fo' foreman!''

''Tell em de crop'll be ruint widout em!''

''We sho' do need em!''

Casting a side-glance toward Joy, alone at one side,
saying nothing, yet keeping track of every glance that
passed between the others, Zeda stood a little straighter,
and cleared her throat that her words might be plain.

''One more t'ing; I ain' told nobody before. Not
yet. But Sherry is married to a gal yonder up-North.
She might not be willin' to come to Blue Brook.''

Joy's body stiffened, her eyes widened, her arms fell
to her sides, but the others laughed and joked over the
news until their voices ran into an excited chorus.

"Write Sherry to bring dat gal on home!"

"Lawd, dat news sho' do surprise me!"

"T'ink o' Sherry takin' a wife in dat strange country!"

"Lawd, dat boy done fast work! Jedus!"

"Who's gwine help Sherry pizen de cotton if he do come?" Zeda was in earnest.

"All o' we!"

"All de mens!"

"Sho'! Ev'ybody'll help em!"

Zeda bowed. That settled it. She'd get Joy to write a letter to send off by the next mail.

The crowd felt such relief, they broke into gay laughter. Merry jokes were cracked. The boll-weevils were left in the field. Sherry would fix them.

The people all turned home. In groups of three or four they talked and laughed boisterously, boasting what a good crop would be made this year. The cotton plants were strong. Able. The grass well-nigh killed out. Poisoning would do the rest.

Every trace of down-heartedness was gone. Discouragement forgotten. Sherry would come back and kill all the boll-weevils. Blue Brook would roll in money next fall.

Joy plodded home, stopping at times as if she didn't see the path clearly. Once or twice she stumbled. The whole way, she stayed mute. At April's house she stopped, but instead of going in, said to Breeze:

"I'm gwine an' ax Ma to let you come stay wid me. I want you to mind my baby. Brudge an' dem other chillen is so awful careless wid em. You'll come, if Ma says so, enty?"

Breeze opened his mouth twice to answer before he got to speak out loud enough for her to hear.

"Sho', I'll come, Joy."

[286]

XIX

AT APRIL'S HOUSE

THE first night Breeze spent in April's cabin was a
bad one, although he slept in the same room with Joy
and her baby.

Joy wrote to Sherry for Zeda that same afternoon,
and when she mailed the letter she bought some sweet
animal crackers from the store for supper. She had
a good supper. She pressed them all to eat a-plenty, and
when they were done, she bustled about briskly, washing
dishes, straightening things; but she had nothing to say
to a soul. What was she thinking about, to stay so
silent?

She and Breeze and Leah's children sat by the fire
for a while. It burned low and dim, for the night was
too hot to keep it bright. Nobody talked. Now and
then one of the flies sleeping on the newspapered wall
roused and buzzed. The leaves on the trees outside
made a timorous noise. Brudge darted glances at
Breeze and cleared his throat again and again, but
everybody was polite.

One by one they went off to bed until only Joy and
Breeze were left. She got up.

"Come on, Breeze. Le's go to bed. Me an' you an'
de baby, we stays in here."

Breeze slept on a cot in the corner of the room and
Joy in the bed where Leah's dead body had been.
Where was Leah now? Breeze gazed at the dark. He
could hear things moving about in the yard. Something

[287]

fumbled at the door. The latch rattled. The steps creaked. Somewhere in the distance a dog howled. Joy's little baby cried out, but she patted it and sang softly:

> "Bye, baby buntin'
> Daddy's gone to de cow-pen
> To git some milk fo' de baby.
> Go to sleep."

Breeze lay open-eyed. Restless. The cabin was stifling hot. Fear had him sweating.

When the long night, baked with heat, passed into a warm, dewy morning, the baby woke and Breeze took him to see the men pass with the mules and plows on their way to the corn-field, then to watch Leah's children and Joy stick sweet-potato cuttings into the ground. Time went slowly. If one morning could be long as this, when would those cuttings ever make a crop? The baby's weight burdened his arms. His shoulders ached. He'd go sit on the step and sing it to sleep, then he'd rest. "Bye an' bye, when de mawnin' comes!" Breeze sang, and the baby's eyelids drooped. "Bye an' bye, when we's gathered home!" The eyelids closed down tight. "We'll t-e-l-l de story! H-o-w we over-come," Breeze sang it softly, the baby was ready to ease down on the bed. His tired arms could rest a while. He might take a nap himself.

The day was so quiet when he sat on the step again and leaned his head back against the door-facing that the old tree, bending its head across the yard toward the cabin, whispered every time a breath of air stirred it. A wood-pecker's tapping made a tumult of sound. The twitterings of a pair of wrens with a nest in a knot

[288]

hole under the eaves made a distinct clamor. Drowsiness glazed Breeze's eyes, stopped up his ears. The morning flowed on by.

When the noon bell rang he jumped, awake, with the bare shadow of a gasp. Then he remembered he was living with Joy, not Big Sue, and he stretched his mouth in a lazy yawn.

The Quarters soon bustled with people coming in from the fields. The women, first, with hoes on their shoulders, then the men. Hens cackled, telling of eggs they'd just laid. Ducks quacked. Pigeons wheeled in low circles.

Joy arrived ahead of the children, her arms drooping, her steps lax and careless, her eyes noting naught around her, not even Breeze, who got up to let her pass. Then something on his head made her heed. "Wha' dat on you' head, Breeze? Who put em dere? Great Gawd, Breeze whe' you been?"

Breeze put up a scared hand and felt all over his head. There was nothing so far as he could tell. "Wha' e is, Joy? I ain' feel nothin'."

"Looka!" Joy lifted a white horse hair and held it in front of his eyes. "Take em an' drown em, Breeze. Drown em quick. I bet Brudge done dis. De scoundrel! Brudge is tryin' to scare you. Dat's all. He can' do you nothin'. No. Brudge don' know how to cunjure nobody. But you go chunk dis in de Blue Brook anyhow. Tie em on a rock an' chunk em far in as you kin. But don' le' Brudge know you done it."

Breeze writhed with cold fear. That short white horse hair was a burden to his shaking fingers. He shifted it from one hand to the other, until he reached the Blue Brook's bank. When a lizard scurried under a log to hide, its light rustling made Breeze almost drop his load. But he found a pebble, twined the hair around it, and after looking all around to be sure nobody saw, he cast it into the water.

As it fell with a light plop a giggle broke in the stillness. Breeze's blood turned hot with fury. If Brudge had dared to follow him, watch him, laugh at him, he'd get a stick, a rock, something that could kill, and kill the scoundrel.

His eyes searched the surroundings, but nothing was at hand. Festoons of trailing moss floated from the limbs of the enormous live-oaks, making a weird canopy over his head; a cicada chanted shrilly in a clump of vine-tangled shrubbery; huge coiling, writhing roots spread around great rough trunks, then dropped out of sight, burying themselves in the earth. No weapon for him to use was anywhere in sight. He'd hunt until he found one. A narrow bit of a short blue skirt flickered from behind a tree-trunk and disappeared. Emma's! Maybe it was she who had tricked him, not Brudge! He stopped short with a sharp indrawn breath. He'd slip up on her, catch her, hold her—maybe push her in the water!

Tipping stealthily forward, he went toward the tree, holding his breath for fear Emma might hear him and get away. He'd make her pay for teasing him, scaring him, making him believe somebody had put a conjure spell on him with that white horse hair.

When Emma peeped out to see where he was, he grabbed her by the arm so suddenly she gave a little frightened cry.

"I got you! Now I'm gwine drown you!" he growled, but instead of pulling away, trying his strength, her eyes filled, her mouth quivered.

"I was jus' playin' wid you, Breeze—you oughtn' to be mad wid me—a-jerkin' me——"

The moss waved softly overhead, the grass heads

leaned sidewise in the gentle wind, two round drops of water dreaned out of Emma's eyes and ran down her cheeks. They cut clean to Breeze's heart, startling, paining him. The small arm inside his fingers was soft as Joy's baby's. He wouldn't hurt it for the world.

"I ain' mad. I'm a-playin' wid you, too," he explained.

"Enty?" Emma's smile was so sudden, so merry, Breeze felt confused, troubled.

The Blue Brook trickled on with a soothing purl, its surface shimmering as the wind stirred it into rolling ripples. Roses and honeysuckles added fragrance to the stench of decaying leaves and wood. A deep stillness began spinning a web over them all.

"Oh—Breeze!" Joy was calling.

"Ee—oo! I'm a-comin'!" He answered, and Emma was gone.

Joy sent him to the post-office, and when he came back with a letter, she snatched it out of his hand, but it was from the hospital and said April was improving. He'd soon come home, and he sent messages to all his friends. He craved to see them.

Dewberries were ripe, wild plums reddening, may-pop vines had the roadsides purple with bloom. The day drowsed with heat, the rice-fields smelled sweaty, the sun, half-way between noon and sunset, drew out perfume from the grass and flowers.

Breeze was in the pasture picking berries for supper when the boat whistle made a long extra blow for the landing. He stood up and held his breath to listen, for he knew something unusual had happened. It wasn't long before Brudge came in sight, waving his arms and shouting, "Sherry's come! De boat fetched em just now!"

Breeze sprang up in such haste, he spilled every berry in the bucket and had to stop and pick them up.

"How do e look, Brudge?"

Brudge made a face. "E look ugly as ever to me."

"I got a good mind to choke you," Breeze threatened.

"Come on an' choke! I'll mash you' goosle flat! Wid one hand! Ha! Ha!"

Burning with hate for Brudge and joy over Sherry's coming, Breeze flew home by a short-cut. Joy sat on the steps, feeding her baby, but it was plain she knew Sherry had come, for her words halted so she could hardly speak, and her eyes were wide and bright.

"Sherry's come!" Breeze panted, all out of breath. "I'm gwine to see em." She stroked her baby's fat little legs, then clasped both small feet together.

"Tell em—tell em—— No, don' tell em nothin'. I'll go tell em myself."

She laid the baby face down across her lap and began unfastening him in the back. "Go git me some clean clothes fo' em befo' you go."

She leaned quickly and kissed the back of the tiny neck where the head joined the plump body, leaving a hollow shaped just right for her mouth.

She slipped his one garment off his soft rolly body, slipped the clean one on over his head, laughing at the way his head wabbled, then suddenly cuddled him close in her arms. She held him so tight, his restless arms and legs squirmed to get loose.

Breeze hurried to Zeda's cabin so fast he had no wind left to tell Sherry how glad he was to see him. Sherry gave him a hand-shake, then a mighty hug that squeezed Breeze into a happy laugh.

"Lawd, boy, you is growed! How's Clara? Did e kick you yet?"

Breeze could do nothing but grin. How much bigger Sherry looked! How much finer! He was a town man now, with shoes and cravat and a white straw hat, and presents for everybody. Breeze was so happy blowing his new mouth-organ he didn't see Joy until she asked, "You don' know me, Sherry? Is I changed dat much?" Her words shook, her smile trembled.

"No, Joy, you ain' so changed. No—— But I didn' know you had a baby——"

"Sho' I is. Look at em. Ain' e de fines' t'ing you ever see? E kin 'most talk, enty, Breeze?"

Breeze could hardly take his eyes off Sherry long enough to answer her, but the baby cooed and his wabbly head bobbed back and forth against Joy's arm. His toes stretched out in the hot sunshine, and both tiny balled-up fists tried to thrust themselves into his small drippy mouth. He gnawed at them, then let them go, and a disappointed wail suddenly wrinkled up his small face and made it so funny-looking, even Sherry had to laugh.

"Wha' e name, Joy?"

"E name Try-em-an-see, but I calls him Tramsee fo' short."

"Whe' you git dat name?"

"Maum Hannah helped me to make em up. It's a lucky one, too." Joy turned away suddenly, and her full short gingham skirt twirled about her thin legs. They were bare and matched her small wiry body well, and her face had been greased until its black skin shone hard with glints of blue in the sun. Her ripe breasts strutted full under her tight-fitting dress. Her bare head had its wool wrapped into tight cords with white ball thread. She looked very different from the stylish town-dressed Joy who came home just before Christmas. No wonder Sherry stared at her.

All her town airs were gone. She was as countrified

as Zeda. Sherry gazed at her so hard, Joy dropped her eyes. Her lips twitched and the hollows at the corners of her full mouth deepened.

"I'm sho' glad you come home, Sherry. Whyn' you bring you' wife?"

The slim fingers of one hand plucked at a button on the back of the baby's dress. Her voice, raised and strengthened, sounded clear and hard.

"E wouldn' come South, Joy. But I thought you had mo' sense dan to go take Leah's husband. You'd sleep in dat house fo' Leah to hant you? You kin rest dere?"

Joy's eyes flickered and shifted in a side-glance toward him, then beyond him, where trees fringing the rice-fields shimmered blue like trees in a dream.

"Sho', I kin rest dere. April's a fine man, Sherry. E treat me white too. I wish to Gawd e didn' got sick. De crop has been a-needin' him bad."

"Whe' e is now?" Sherry's eyes were cloudy, his voice dull.

"To de horspital."

The china-berry tree full of purple blossoms cast a pool of hot shade at Joy's feet. Reddish scions, sprung up around the root of the crêpe myrtle, gave out a sickly scent as Sherry's restless feet trampled and bruised them. The yellow afternoon glare stressed a stern look in his eyes and marked a swift-beating pulse that throbbed with tiny strokes in a vein of his thick strong neck.

It was a relief to hear Joy say coolly, "April'll be glad you's come. De boll-evil is swarmin' in de cotton."

And Sherry answered, "I'm glad to git back, Joy. Yonder up-North ain' like home."

"Stay an' eat supper wid us, Joy. You an' Breeze all two," Zeda invited cordially.

Breeze looked at Joy and waited for her answer. "You stay, Breeze," she said. "But don' stay late." And she walked on home to April's cabin.

Sherry slept a good part of each day, but at night the big poison machine hummed over the cotton-fields, puffing out clouds of white poison dust until every stalk was covered, every leaf silvery. The dry weather was a help. No rain came to wash the poison off. Plows kept the middles of the rows stirred and the fallen squares buried. After a week's rest the poison machine ran all night again. The cotton throve. The stifling nights were perfumed with the honey of cotton blooms. Already bolls were showing, some as large as hickory nuts! April himself could have managed no better than Sherry.

Joy bustled about working hard all day, but she sang at her work and night found her unwearied. Brudge got more and more sullen and surly. He was often impudent to Joy, but she paid him no attention. One night when the supper things were washed and put away she slipped out of the door and walked off in the darkness alone. When the others had gone to bed Brudge barred all the doors so she couldn't get in. As if she were not April's wife and the mistress of the house. But even then she laughed and treated it as a joke.

The next day her baby lay on the bed sleeping. Brudge walked up and looked at it and called it an ugly name. Joy heard and before Brudge had time to catch his breath, she grabbed him and gave him such a beating he yelled for mercy.

After that Brudge spied on her all the time, even jumping out of bed to see if anybody came home with her at night. And Joy drove him to his work every day as if he were a lazy mule. They quarreled constantly.

[295]

The cabin became a wretched place to Breeze, except those times when Joy sat on the steps in the dusk and talked to him and told him how much she thought of him and of the help he had been to her.

With her face wreathed in smiles and her eyes bright with gladness, she'd look up at the stars shining through the tree-tops and Breeze would hold his breath and listen at her voice and sigh with love of her, and forget that life was ever painful or burdensome.

One night Sherry walked home from meeting with Joy, but when they reached April's house she didn't ask him in. He stood by the step and rolled a cigarette, lit it and walked away. Brudge watched him with eyes full of cunning and when he was out of hearing laughed: "Sherry t'inks he's somebody. My Gawd!"

"Sherry is somebody," Breeze defended. "Sherry is de foreman now."

"You wait till Pa gits home. You'll see who de foreman is den. Me an' Uncle Bill is gwine to town to git Pa befo' long. I bet a lot o' t'ings'll change den. You'll see it too."

The moon glittered thin and sharp in the sky. Crickets chirruped. Katydids droned long shrill cries. A whip-poor-will called and called. Breeze was so fretted that he forgot Joy sat on the step beside him. He jumped when she spoke, although she spoke quietly: "Sherry an' Uncle Bill is gwine to town on de boat to fetch Cun April home. You is not gwine, Brudge."

Joy's voice was husky, perhaps from the dew or from singing so long at meeting. Brudge made no answer, but in a little while he got up and slunk off to bed without even saying good night.

The people met the boat to welcome April home just as they met it when he brought Joy, a bride. All except Joy herself. She stayed to have everything ready for him at the house. She knew he'd be hungry and the soup must be kept hot, the chicken nice and tender but not too done. Unwatched rice is easy to scorch. And besides, the chicken's raw heart had already mysteriously disappeared! Out of the pan! After she had washed it and salted it! She told Breeze this in a whisper.

Sherry picked April up in his arms and brought him ashore. April was not much longer than Joy's baby, now, and tears poured down his cheeks, but he seemed not to care at all who saw them. Lord, he was so glad to get home! There was no place like Blue Brook!

The close-packed crowd listened, motionless and hushed, for April's voice was low and broken and his words like somebody else speaking. Lord, how the man was changed! His lean body with its broad bony shoulders and long thin arms was a shocking sight. No matter what wrongs he had done, he had been punished enough. More than enough! Uneasy and curious, but filled with respect, they pressed around him. They fed their eyes on his terrible plight. April was no longer a man. Poor soul! God's hand had fallen hard, heavy, upon him.

A grave silence held most of them, but April, so full of joy at getting home again, called out cordial greetings to every one of them by name. He was so glad to hear the crops were good, so glad Sherry was back, so glad for the dry weather.

When he paused to take breath, their sorrowful pitying words fell: "Do, Jedus!" "I too sorry fo' em!" "My Gawd!" "I ain' never see sich a t'ing!"

Breeze's heart shrank smaller until it felt no larger than the heart of a mouse in his breast. Old Louder gave a long sad howl. The birds sang no more. The sun in the west hid under a dark drab cloud.

April was the only cheerful person in the whole crowd.

"How yunnuh likes Sherry fo' de foreman?" he asked brightly.

No answer came at first, then Jake cleared his throat and spoke out:

"Sherry does de best e kin, but e ain' got no time wi'l you, April. No."

Then many other answers chimed in, "Shucks, nobody livin' could make de foreman you was!"

"Dat's de Gawd's truth!" Sherry's voice praising April as loud as any.

Uncle Isaac had Julia hitched to Uncle Bill's buggy to take April home, and when the old mule became terrified at the boat's whistle, April laughed at the beast's lack of sense. Poor Julia! So old and so foolish!

Breeze had never realized how much April loved everybody. "How all o' yunnuh do?" he asked affectionately. "How's all home?" He had to choke back a sob as he looked into their serious faces.

Sherry put him on the buggy seat beside Uncle Isaac, who held the reins, but April couldn't keep his balance, and Uncle Bill had to get in and hold him steady.

April excused himself by saying he was weak and nervish from lying flat down on his back so long. A bed draws a man's strength in a hurry. Even a chair will do it.

Over and over he said how good everything looked. He breathed deep of the smell of the woods full of bay-blossoms. The splash of Julia's feet in the shallow branch made the water come into his eyes. Everybody who walked alongside the buggy could see it.

When they got in sight of the barnyard, Julia broke

into a trot. It was her supper time and she was in a hurry to eat. April laughed at her sudden willingness to go. "No, Julia. You can' stop at de barnyard, not dis time. You got to pull me home. You don' know I can' walk, enty?" But his voice broke, and Uncle Bill began telling about the crop, how fine it was, how loaded with fruit. When he got stronger, April must take Julia and the buggy and ride everywhere. Sherry did very well, but he was young and needed advice about a lot of things.

Joy and Leah's little children stood waiting out in front of the cabin to meet him. A quiet awed group. April was the only one who felt at ease.

"How you do, honey?" he said gently to Joy, who came forward first, but she looked uncertain what to do or say. "I reckon I is look strange to yunnuh. But I'm thankful to git home widout comin' nailed up in a box."

The children huddled together watching April as if he were a perfect stranger.

"Come speak to you Pa, chillen," Joy bade them, and they came forward slowly, shyly. Brudge snuffled and sobbed right out loud, so moved was he, but one of the littlest boys looked at his father's shortened body and giggled. Joy grabbed his shoulder and shook him soundly and sent him behind the house, just as she did when he laughed at April months ago.

"E don' mean nothin', April. E ain' got so much sense. E'd laugh if e was a-dyin' himself. His mammy must 'a' marked him so."

Joy spoke kindly, but April's face changed. His mouth quivered; a strange weary look wrung all the life out of his eyes. His own child had made sport of him. Laughed at his shame. The last time it happened he had reared and pitched, but this time his bosom heaved and he wiped his eyes with his sleeve.

Joy helped Sherry to take him inside the cabin and lay him on a bed in the shed-room. It did look inviting. The feather mattress was puffed up high and covered with a clean white spread. April sighed deeply as he sank in its soft depths, and he closed his eyes in enjoyment.

His head was too low to see well, and he asked Joy to get him another pillow. She looked at the long empty trousers that twisted about foolishly over the white counterpane. April whispered to her that she'd have to cut them off shorter for him, or pin them back. Joy didn't answer, but she got a quilt from another bed. When April saw what she was going to do, he protested that it was too hot to lie under a quilt. But something he saw in Joy's eyes made him change his mind, and he let her cover him up.

Big Sue came to see if there was anything she could do for April's comfort. She spoke kindly to Joy and told Breeze he looked well and grew fast. April hardly heard Big Sue's offer, for his friends had crowded into the room and called to him from the open windows. They meant to be kind, still no one of them could conceal astonishment and horror that April had no feet, no legs, at all. There were gentle murmurs of:

"God bless you, son, how's you gwine do widout legs?"

"I'm sho' glad you lived to git home, but what's you gwine to do?"

April's pleasure at being home was somehow chilled. He kept saying he thought two or three times he'd never see them again and he had to pull hard to do it, but his cheerful tone had faded into gloominess.

Uncle Bill suggested that the people had better leave. April had had a long trip. He was tired. He had been very weak. He wasn't strong enough to stand much excitement. They were all good-mannered about it. They passed out of the door with little to say, and their tones were subdued when they spoke.

When the last one had gone, April burst out crying. He held Uncle Bill's hands and blubbered out he was nothing but a baby! He had no manhood left at all! He couldn't even stand kindness! Everything made him cry! Everything!

Joy came back into the room and stood by the bed and looked down at him and he reached up a long arm and took her hand uncertainly and called her by name. No eyes were ever more appealing, no voice in the whole world ever plead for tenderness as April's did then.

"Joy, you don' mind me bein' dis way, enty? I'm gwine git wood legs befo' long."

Joy stood silent, a shudder ran through her, her fingers lay limp in April's. April groaned and let her hand go.

Then Joy tried to smile bravely and say she didn't mind. She had fretted herself half to death about him and now she was happy because he had come. But it was too late. She couldn't fool April. He had seen how she felt; and he drew away from her as from a stranger.

She turned and went briskly out of the room, and April turned his face to the wall. His thin breast lifted, while one deep bitter sob after another shook him. He had fought a long hard fight with Death, and now he was sorry he had won! If he had known how things would be, how Joy would feel, he would have given up, but it was the thought of Joy that made him try to live.

April stayed on the bed in the shed-room day after day, looking out over the rice-fields where the tides rose and fell. Breeze's work was changed from minding

Joy's baby to staying with April, keeping the flies off him, handing him water to drink.

Few plantation sounds could reach this shed-room at the back of the cabin and when staying by April became unbearable, Breeze would go outside and walk as far as the water's edge, or stand by the window watching cranes and kingfishers. One old bald eagle spent much of his time on a branch of an old dead tree and when a fishhawk dived and got a fish the eagle took it from him.

April complained little. Once when the night was damp and the sound of the poison machine louder than usual he got very restless. He said it was hard to lie helpless. Without legs. Flat on his back. Most of the time alone. While another man took his place. But except for sighs and a few moans, that was all.

At first the people on the place came often to see him. They brought him things to eat. A chicken, a few eggs tied up in a cloth, a bottle of molasses, whatever they had that they thought he might enjoy. Occasionally some friend put a piece of money in his hand. But his persistent low-spiritedness and down-heartedness did not encourage them to come back. Soon they stopped only long enough by his window to say, "How you do to-day, April?" or "How you feelin'?" as they passed by, with troubled glances.

Uncle Bill was the exception. He came very often and he'd sit and listen as long as April wanted to talk about his weariness or his misery.

April never grew tired of telling over and over his experiences at the hospital. About the nurses and doctors, their kindness to him and interest in him. How he had fought through the long dark nights with pain. At first it was a steady fight, then after a while the pain came in showers. But he had thought out many things.

He'd learned that every man has to bear his suffering alone. He realized that the doctors could not help him. Neither could his children, nor any friend. He had to go the whole way through by himself—to the very end.

When April first came home, Joy stayed with him every night, then she began going to parties and birth-night suppers once in a while, and finally, every night as soon as the supper was over and the dishes washed and put away, she'd tip quietly down the steps and go. Without a word.

April said little about it. Nothing to Joy herself. What was the use? What was he? Just half a man, that was all. He had no right to expect Joy to stay always at home with him. Breeze was always there to mind the flies or give him a drink of water, or tie a collard leaf on his aching head.

Joy shirked no household duty. She had learned to cook almost as well as her mother. He had no cause to complain of the food she gave him. It was well seasoned enough for those who had appetites to eat. Joy was young. She had to pleasure herself. He hadn't the heart to forbid it. And nobody could say she was a gad-about. She kept the house clean, the clothes washed and patched, and she did her full share of the field work too.

April talked fairly enough to Maum Hannah and Uncle Bill and Zeda, even to Big Sue, who came to see him once in a while. But all of them could see that jealousy was disturbing him, making him fretful and suspicious.

Hour after hour he stared doggedly out of the window, moaning, sighing, wishing he could go to sleep and never wake up. His gloom filled the whole cabin. Breeze could hardly bear to stay with him, and Uncle Bill came in as often as he could spare the time.

One night Uncle Bill begged April to pray. It was the only way to find peace, to be satisfied. If he would do like Jacob, and give God no rest day or night until he had some sign his prayers were heard, his whole heart would be changed and filled with rejoicing.

April answered that he had lost faith in God's fairness. What had he ever done to make God deal with him so? Would any decent man on the plantation treat a dog any worse than God had treated him? Or suffer a worm as much?

Uncle Bill admitted God had laid a heavy hand on April. Had smitten him hard, but if April's suffering would make him pray, and save his soul from everlasting torment, then all suffering would be gain. Pure gain.

Joy had a Bible and Uncle Bill could read well enough to teach April to spell out a few verses. At first he learned a few of them by heart, then he strove to learn how to find the right place in the Bible and to read them there. "The Lord is my Shepherd" was the first one he located. It was the easiest of all to find and learn. Next he learned "In my Father's house are many mansions."

Sometimes Uncle Bill read a whole chapter to him, but it was a hard task for them both, labored work for Uncle Bill to read and for April to understand.

The one April liked best was "Behold, He that keepeth Israel shall neither slumber nor sleep."

Breeze wondered who Israel was and who kept him, but he durst not ask.

One day Uncle Bill stumbled on this verse: "As a man chasteneth his son, so the Lord thy God chasteneth thee." The words were scarcely spoken before April put up a hand.

"Don' read dat one, Uncle. E's done me too bad.

E ain' treat me fair. Looks like E ought to let up on me. E done suffer me so long——"

April turned his face toward the window to hide the tears that poured out of his eyes, and there was Sherry in full view, riding the sorrel colt and holding Joy's baby in his arms!

April's face went a ghastly gray, his moist features shriveled. Tremors shook the muscles in his jaws, but he said nothing.

Uncle Bill stroked out the fingers of one long, blue-nailed hand, but they curled back into the palm as soon as they were released.

"You must be gittin' a chill, April." Uncle Bill's eyes were full of fear. "How 'bout a mustard plaster on you' back?"

"Nemmine, Uncle. Nemmine," April chattered.

As the dusk fell Zeda came to inquire about April, but she found him shaking as with ague. He said he was cold through and through and his insides felt wrung and twisted. The very heart in his breast ached sorely.

Zeda said if April had a chill Joy had better give him some red-pepper tea. She'd go home and make some tea out of her own red pepper. Her pepper was strong, hot, she had gathered it at noon on a sunshiny day.

The jangle of a cow bell broke through the still night. On and on it rang, saying it was meeting night. Uncle Bill had promised to lead, and when he got up to go, Joy suggested that Breeze go along with him. Not that Breeze cared especially for the singing and praying, but anything for a change would do him good.

Maum Hannah's house was crammed. Half the people had to stand outside, and heads crowded the windows so not a breath of air could come in or go out. The night was stifling hot and sweat trickled down Uncle Bill's forehead as he read the Bible by the dim smelly flame of the smoky lamp. He read about a man named Jonah who sinned, and a great whale in the sea swallowed him whole! God sent the whale to get him!

Uncle Bill closed the book when the chapter was ended and talked slowly, sorrowfully, about the sin that prevailed on the plantation. The people bickered with one another instead of living in love and charity. Instead of praying for each other, they spent good money for charms to conjure one another. They danced and sang reels instead of shouting and singing spirituals and hymns. Unless they changed, no telling what would happen! God is patient. Long-suffering. He gives men every chance to get saved. But they had overlooked every warning. They had forgotten that the jaws of Hell were stretched wide that very minute, craving to swallow every soul in that room just as the whale swallowed Jonah. Jonah got out of the whale after three days, but no man ever gets out of Hell. Sinners spend eternity burning in fire and brimstone.

Why not give up sin? Why not trust in Jesus instead of putting fresh stripes on His bleeding wounds? Every sin cut Him to the quick! Not only the sins of grown men and women, but the sins of little children. Jesus was crucified over and over again by the sins of people right on Blue Brook Plantation. And yet He had died on the cross to save them from that awful place where there was nothing but weeping and wailing and gnashing of teeth!

The members moaned and groaned until Maum Hannah lead the spiritual, "God sent Jonah to Nineveh Land, Jonah disobeyed his Lord's command."

The congregation sang answers in a solemn refrain.

Verse by verse the whole story of Jonah's awful punishment was told.

Breeze had never heard it before and he shuddered

[306]

from head to foot with horror and pity for poor Jonah.
God seemed as cruel and awful as the Devil. Between
the two, there was small chance for any safety. Poor
Jonah! Poor April! Poor Breeze!

On the way home through the night he held to Uncle
Bill's hand so tight that Uncle Bill asked what was the
matter. Breeze admitted he was afraid. Afraid of the
dark, of God, of the Devil, of everything, especially
while it was night.

"De spirit is strivin' in you' heart, son. Strivin' to
convict you of sin. You start prayin' to-night. Soon
as you git home. Rassle wid God. To-morrow, you
go off by you'self in de woods. Wallow on de
ground an' pray. Don' rest, not till you done found
peace, so you won' never be 'fraid no mo'. I'll
come stay wid April to-morrow whilst you seek salva-
tion. Start to-night, son. Pray hard as you kin. Ax
Gawd to le' you be born again. You is a human chile
now, subject to sin an' death an' hell. When you's
born again, you'll be Gawd's chile. Free! Nobody
can' touch you or either harm you. Nobody!"

The cabin was dark and silent. Joy opened the door
and whispered that April was asleep. Uncle Bill
whispered back he'd come next day and stay with April.
Breeze was going to start seeking.

"Brudge come in just now an' said he was gwine
seek too."

"Well, I declare! Dat is de best news I heared
lately! De sperit is workin' fast to-night."

Joy put the door-bar in place and Breeze went to
bed. As soon as he crawled under the covers he tried
to begin his praying for the dread of Hell racked him
as bitterly as the fear of God. A round spot of moon-
light fallen through a hole in the roof made an eye on the
floor. A round, shining eye, that stared at him, winkless.

XX

It was early dawn when Joy woke him. He must get up and fetch plenty of water, and cut some wood. By that time Uncle Bill would be here to stay with April and he could go to the woods and seek.

Breeze sat up and rubbed his eyes and tried to listen, but it was all he could do to keep from sinking back deep under the covers and pulling them over his head. He didn't want to seek, he'd a thousand times rather sleep. But April spoke:

"Git up, Breeze! You don' hear Joy talkin' to you!" And Breeze opened his heavy eyes and sprang to his feet. He dressed, then put his bed in order, and went at his work. By the time it was done, Uncle Bill had come, and he was set free to pray.

Cocks were crowing, birds chirping, crows cawing. Uncle Bill said they were saying their morning prayers. Breeze must listen how earnestly they did it, and learn how to pray just as hard.

Everything out-of-doors was silvery with dew, and the early sun gave the earth a mysterious radiance that dazzled Breeze's drowsy eyes as he dragged himself slowly along. The woods looked far away. In the distance their hazy darkness blent into the sky. The path to the corn-field was shorter, and it led toward the sunshine, whose warm yellow light drew every flower face toward it.

He reached the corn-field before the morning dew

[308]

was dry. The black furrows between the tall green rippling blades felt cool and damp. As a light breeze blew, the corn rustled and waved and the silks added their perfume to the fruity blossomy fragrance in the air.

Breeze sat down on the ground and looked up at the sky overhead, pondering. He couldn't remember his sins. He hated Brudge, but that couldn't be sinful, mean as Brudge was. Anybody who knew Brudge would hate him.

"Oh, Lawd," he began, then halted. If he knew how to pray it would be easier. Where was Jesus? How could he make Jesus hear him? The blue sky where Heaven was looked high and far and empty.

Getting on his knees Breeze closed his eyes and repeated the words of Uncle Bill's prayer as nearly as he could remember. Over and over he said them, until in spite of all his striving to keep awake, the stillness overcame him and he fell into a gentle doze. Something tickled his nose, then crawled across his lips. He jumped, hit at the pest, a straw. The sun's midday light was a hard hot glare; the black shadows short. Emma stood over him, her white teeth shining in a broad grin that vexed him bitterly, a wisp of dry grass in her fingers.

"How you duh sleep! You ain' gwine pray?" Emma giggled as she asked it.

Breeze rubbed his eyes and looked all around. He hated being caught, and Emma had no business tickling his face while he slept. Stung to the quick with shame and vexation, he snapped out angrily:

"How come you duh grin like a chessy-cat? Who you duh laugh at so frightenin'?"

His ill humor sobered her and she made haste to explain, "I ain' laughin' at you. I'm a-laughin' at

Brudge. Brudge is done found peace in dem woods back o' we house. Lawd, e hollered so loud, I thought sho' e had got in a yellow-jacket's nest! Jedus, you ought to heared em!'' Emma's laugh rippled out and shook her slim shoulders so that the beads Joy had given her chinked merrily against the hot black skin of her little black neck. Her three-cornered face glowed with fun, her slanting eyes sparkled as they met Breeze's, but he shrugged disdainfully. "I know dat ain' so. Brudge didn' start seekin', not till dis mawnin'. E couldn' find peace, not dat quick. You can' fool me. Shucks!''

"I ain' tryin' to fool you. Gramma made me go see wha dat was ail Brudge, made em squall an' holler so loud." Emma's face had got serious, her teasing eyes grave.

In spite of the too-big, ugly dress she wore and the long awkward sleeves that hung over her small hands, the child had a half-wild grace and lightness, and as she knelt down in the soft dusty furrow and one hand crept out from the folds of her dress toward Breeze, he grabbed it and held it before it could draw back.

"Breeze——" her husky little voice made his name a new thing. He could feel a smile twitch at his mouth. "Breeze—if you'd find peace, you wouldn' be scared to git baptized?''

Breeze knelt beside her and he glowed, all on fire with courage now. "Who? Me? Lawd, I ain' scared o' nothin'. Not nothin'!''

Emma's eyes widened with wonder and respect for his boasting. "You ain' scared o' nothin' in de world?''

Breeze turned his head and spat far away like a grown-up man. "Not nothin' in de world.''

Breaths of hot air drove the clouds along over their heads. A grasshopper played shrill faint music, a dove mourned softly, the corn blades rustled gently.

Breeze dropped her hand and grasped her thin shoulders, but she tore herself from his hold with a breathless laugh. Then he caught her arm, but she was stronger than he thought. The muscles in her small arm tightened under his fingers and, wriggling herself loose, Emma went flying down the corn row, calling back mockingly, daringly:

"Better go on an' pray. A witch might git you!"

And Breeze answered boldly, his fear of God and the Devil all forgotten,

"I ain' gwine pray. No! Wait on me, Emma! Don' run so fast! You t'ink you kin outrun me! Good Lawd, you can' do dat! I'll show you so right now!"

At the cabin a crowd of people gathered. Breeze could hear them babbling together, then keeping silent while one voice rose high. There was no making out what it said, and Breeze went as fast as he could, eager to know what was the matter. He found Brudge telling his experience. The boy had told it over and over until his voice was hoarse and trembly, yet he kept on, excitedly, as the people, mostly women, urged him to tell them again what God had done for him. Brudge said he was away off in the woods praying. Down on his knees with his eyes wide open, looking up through the trees at the heavens, begging God to hear him, to give him some sign, to let him know his sins were forgiven, just as Uncle Bill said he must do. He had been there for an hour or two, calling on Jesus with every breath, when all of a sudden the light cut off, just like the lights in the Big House at night when the white folks go to bed. Everything was pitch black dark. There was not one sound anywhere. He thought he had died and it scared him so he raised up and hollered loud as he could; the light came back quick as a flash, with such a brightness he was mighty nigh blinded. All the trees over his head began waving their arms and shouting. All the clouds up the elements broke in half, and in the middle of them he could see people, crowds of people waving their arms and shouting. He jumped up and shouted with them! He felt light as any feather! The wind fair blew him along as he ran home to tell the people what he had seen this morning!

"Great Gawd, what a vision dat boy did have!"

"Dat's de first time anybody on dis place ever did see right spang into Heaven!"

"Son, Gawd is sho' blessed you to-day!"

"It makes me pure scared to hear de boy talk!"

"It sounds to me like Brudge is called to preach!"

"De Holy Sperit sho' did knock em on de head. Listen how de boy talks!"

"Now ain' it so? Brudge must l'arn how to read an' write."

"Sho'! A preacher has to read readin' an' writin' too."

"Don' you know Leah is happy in Glory to-day!"

The mention of Leah's name brought pitying groans.

"Po' Leah. Gawd took em home too soon. Leah ought to be here to-day."

Brudge's ranting became louder, more breathless, as he declared God had made him so strong he could lift up a mule by himself. He would pray for April's legs to grow back. God would answer his prayer. The people would soon see. April would be well.

April lay on the bed by the window, his short body covered over with a quilt. When Breeze peeped in at him, he threw out his long arms with an impatient gesture that made the flies rise with a buzz.

"Tell Uncle Bill I say come here!" he ordered, then he groaned and put his clasped hands under his head.

Breeze felt vaguely uneasy. He whispered to Uncle Bill to hurry, and the old man's feet stumbled up the steps, for Brudge's unexpected conversion had him shaken and bewildered. But he steadied when April burst out furiously, "Whyn' you make Brudge hush dat fool talk? Brudge's mind ain' never been solid, an' now yunnuh's gwine run em clean crazy! Tell dem people to go on home! Brudge went to sleep in dem woods. E ain' seen nothin' but a dream! No!"

Uncle Bill patted his shoulder and tried to cool his heat. "Brudge is just happy, son. Dat's all. I know ezactly how de boy feels. I felt de same way when I found peace. You ain' never been saved. Dat's how come you don' un'erstand. Brudge is called to preach, April. Sho' as you' born. You ought to be so t'ankful!"

"Great Gawd!" April fairly bellowed. "You is fool as Brudge! Whe's Joy? Tell Joy to make Brudge hush dat fuss! I can' stand so much racket! No!"

April's eyes glowed fever bright and his forehead held drops of sweat. Nobody but Uncle Bill would have dared to cross him, and even Uncle Bill was upset.

"You mustn' fret dis way, April. You'll git you' liver all hottened up. I'll make Brudge stop talkin', but you mustn' holler like a baby. People'll t'ink you' mind ain' solid. Anybody else but you would be rejoicin'!"

The yard was soon empty, the cabin still. Only Joy and Uncle Bill sat outside on the steps, talking in whispers.

That night Joy went out in a blustery wind and rain, and did not come home until late. The heavy steps that always left stealthily came inside along with hers. Doors creaked sharply. There were little hissing sounds like whispers. Maybe it was the wind.

[313]

April raised up on an elbow. Listened. Leaned toward Joy's room and listened. Crawling out of bed on his long thin arms, he crept across the floor and strained his ear against the wall between his room and the room where Joy slept.

He crouched and listened but he made no sound. It was not the wind that he heard.

Suddenly, something inside him seemed to break. Something in his head or his breast. With a yell he beat on the door, and tried to break it down. Then he lost his balance and fell back on the floor where he lay and raved and cursed himself and Joy and God.

During the days that followed, April's darkened room was filled with his wild delirium. Joy sat by him for hours at a time, brushing the flies away, wiping off his face with a cool wet cloth, trying to hush him, to lower his fever with the root teas Uncle Isaac brewed for him. Outside in the heat, the trees slept, the moss on them hung limp, the tree ferns were brown and lifeless.

Whenever Joy flung herself down on Breeze's straw mattress in the corner to rest, Uncle Bill took her place, watching, waiting for some change to come. His big rough hands, blue at the nails and knuckles, squeezed each other distressfully, or stroked April's restless fingers trying to stop their plucking, plucking, at the cover. Coaxing them to stand still. His old ears constantly listened at the window for the marsh birds to tell him if the tide came in or went out and his eyes were dim with pity and sorrow and love for April, who tossed on the bed, mumbling, raving.

Sometimes April thought the mules were loose in the fields and trampling the cotton, and cried out to stop them! Once he thought he had swallowed Joy's fine diamond ring and it was cutting his chest to pieces. He babbled of boll-weevils and poison and ginning the cotton.

Uncle Bill tried to hold the weak nerveless hands, to steady them and keep them quiet. Over and over he prayed to God to have mercy on April, to give him back his right senses, not to let him die out of his mind, and at last his prayer was heard.

The night was sultry, the cabin parching hot. Joy had broken down, panic-stricken, and she knelt on the floor with her head on Uncle Bill's knee. She burst into a storm of weeping that drowned out April's raving, but Uncle Bill put his arms around her and took her into another room and made her go to bed. She must sleep. He'd wake her if he needed anything. Breeze would sleep with one eye open and jump up the minute Uncle Bill called him. Zeda and Jake were both coming at the first turn of the night after midnight. Joy must not fret and wear herself out. She'd poison her breast milk and make her baby sick.

Midnight must have passed but dawn had not come when April called Uncle Bill so distinctly Breeze woke up, leaped to his feet, but Uncle Bill was at April's bed.

"Uncle," April called again weakly, "you's wake, enty?"

"Yes, son, I'm right 'side you." Uncle Bill took both April's hands and held them close, while he leaned low to hear every word the sick man spoke.

"My time's come, Uncle. I ain' got much longer——" April's voice climbed up, then dropped.

Uncle Bill looked up at the rafters. "Do, Jedus, look down. Do have mercy!"

"Don' stop to pray! De time's too short now!" April's short patience had come back, but his shortened breath held it in sudden check.

"Uncle—my feets is cold—I feels death up to my knees——"

"Son, you ain' got no feets; neither knees! Is you forgot?"

"No, I ain' forgot. But I feels 'em—dey's cold—— Listen, Uncle——"

April's sense had come back. He was in his right mind, even if he did feel the feet and legs that had been gone for months. His low husky words were earnest.

"I ain' scared to go. I'd sooner go dan stay. My time's out. I'm done for. I know it. I got one t'ing to ask you. Not but one. You'll do it, enty? I couldn' rest in my grave—if you fail me——"

His breath cut off his words and he closed his eyes as it came with a rattle through his teeth. Uncle Bill called Breeze to open the window.

"Open em easy, son. Don' wake up Joy, not yet," he cautioned.

"Not yet," April's whisper echoed.

Outside, the black trees sounded restless. An uneasy pattering and rustling ran through the dry lips of the leaves. Flying insects buzzed into the room and beat against the walls with noisy humming wings. Moths flew wildly about the glass lamp on the floor at the foot of the bed. They were crazed by its smoky yellow bitter-smelling light.

"Uncle——" April's breath stifled, his eyes widened with the strain, but he forced his lips to twist out the words he wanted to say.

"Bury me in a man-size box—— You un'erstan'?— A man—size—box—— I—been—six—feet—fo'—Uncle—— Six feet—fo'!"

The blaze in his eyes fell back, cold, dim. A long shudder swept over him. The tide had turned.

THE END